LONGEYE

SHARON LEE & STEVE MILLER

LONGEYE

Copyright © 2009 by Sharon Lee & Steve Miller

A Baen Books Original

Baen Publishing Enterprises
P.O. Box 1403
Riverdale, NY 10471
www.baen.com

ISBN: 978-1-4391-3429-0

Cover art by Tom Kidd

First Baen paperback printing, March 2011

Library of Congress Control Number: 2008049713

Distributed by Simon & Schuster
1230 Avenue of the Americas
New York, NY 10020

Pages by Joy Freeman (www.pagesbyjoy.com)
Printed in the United States of America

Prologue

THE DOOR HAD VANISHED, LOST WITH THE WALLS in a swirling malignancy of mist.

He stopped, striving to hold himself utterly still, ignoring the beguiling movement of the mist, waiting for the path to show itself.

There was always a path. One needed only to recognize it.

About him, the mist grew thicker, peppered with flares of unattached *kest*. Very like the *keleigh*.

In fact, extremely like the *keleigh*.

He laughed, softly. The trap had a certain amusing audacity to it. Who would dare to use the artifact against the artificer? And she had surprised him, had Zaldore, his erstwhile co-conspirator in the downfall of the Bookkeeper Queen. He had expected treachery... eventually. That she acted now, and with such boldness, argued that she considered her potential gain to outweigh any cost that might fall due, should her stratagem fail.

As he had quite decided to take her life for this little pleasantry—which she certainly must have supposed he would do—that made for a fascinating contemplation of the stakes.

Perhaps he would question her, before he drained her of power and watched her die.

First, however—there was the matter of the trap.

It was, he allowed, a clever trick; derivative, of course, but clever.

Zaldore could not continue to expend *kest* at this rate for many days, so plainly, she expected him to succumb—to *fail*—quickly. In that much, at least, he would certainly disappoint her. Learning the trick and turning it—as he no doubt would—that might consume some time. It was possible that Zaldore's *kest* would fail before he had fairly won free—though he hoped not. He had always disliked a win by default.

Had the mist thickened? Surely not. The path had yet to appear, which was worrisome, or not. If the trap were constructed like unto the *keleigh*, then time, along with all other natural forces, would be subverted. He might equally have stood here debating with himself for nine thousand nights or a single heartbeat.

No matter.

"I am Altimere," he said conversationally to the mist, "of the Elder Fey." It was well that he recalled his name; and well that the mist—so very like the substance that formed the *keleigh*—should hear it.

He focused his attention, teasing out a careful strand of mist. Why should Zaldore not see to the comfort of a guest, he thought whimsically, as he worked the substance into the shape he desired. And if this use of her power discommoded her, then she

was not the philosopher her trap would have him
believe her to be.

The texture of the mist was...not entirely pleasant. Sticky, and...warm, it initially resisted his will,
then surrendered, as of course it must. He applied
the smallest touch of *kest*, and the mist-woven shape
solidified into a chair.

Altimere smiled. He leaned back comfortably, and
crossed his legs. A chair worthy of a guest, to be sure.

He closed his eyes against the swirling uncertainty
about him, and released his will to probe the boundar-
ies of the trap, so to discover its weaknesses.

Chapter One

THEY MEAN YOU NO HARM, RANGER, THE TREE SAID, perhaps intending it for comfort.

Across the green, the house—built of wood, dead, dry, and without virtue—the house *vibrated* with power, *kest* rippling off of it in waves, like heat; slashed with brilliant bars of color.

Meri stopped beneath the wide branches of the elder elitch, and closed his eye—a useless protest; the assault upon his other senses continued, like an aurora, he thought, danced with knives.

"I cannot go into that," he said, his voice flat with fear.

Ranger, they mean you no harm, the voice of the elitch insisted softly inside his head, like a grandsire soothing a fractious sprout.

"A branch shaken loose by the wind wounds what it strikes, regardless of the tree's intent."

You are supple enough to bend, and strong enough to stand.

Trees, Meri reminded himself, like any grandsire, had a store of proverbs from which to choose during arguments with wrongheaded younglings. He winced as a particularly brilliant blade of power smote him. His meager *kest* responded, rising like spring sap, blindly seeking to meld.

Meri gagged, and gasped, drinking down green-scented air. Slowly, counting as if he were in fact the merest sprout, he brought his base instincts under control, shivering as his *kest* retreated to pool at the base of his spine. A roaring sounded in his ears, not unlike the voice of the ocean, and it seemed that the colors of the Newmen auras dimmed somewhat, as if seen through spray. When he licked his lips, he tasted salt.

What, he thought, not for the trees, but for himself. *What in the name of root and branch am I doing here?*

That at least was easily answered. He had not... quite...gone mad, coming unprotected and alone into this place. No, no. He was here because his cousin Sian, whom he supposed to care for his interests because there was no one else to do so, had bid him go, to care for the trees. He was Wood Wise, and a Ranger; and he could no more refuse a charge to care for the trees than he could refuse to breathe. So here he stood, perhaps a little mad, after all, alone among Newmen, the very same beings who had tortured him, and who had brought Faldana to her death.

Not the very same beings, Ranger, the voice of the elitch sounded in the depths of his mind. *Merely the same sort.*

"Well enough," he muttered gracelessly. "The same sort."

He sighed, opening his eye as the door in the

power-full house swung wide. A Newoman stepped into the twilight, her auburn hair blazing in the sun's last rays. She stood a moment just outside the door, a stocky, capable figure outlined in a blare of glory, her head tipped to one side, as if listening.

"Master Vanglelauf?" Her voice was calm, perfectly audible over the roar of the ocean in his ears.

Meri took a deep breath and stepped forward, out of the comforting shadow of tree branch, into the open green.

Seen closer, the woman's face was square, her eyes a soft blue. The resemblance to Sam Moore, who had at Sian's word guided him to this place, was striking. Despite the brilliance of her aura, she exuded a nearly treelike tranquility.

Halfway between the trees and the house, safely out of easy reach of the Newoman's hand, Meri stopped and bowed.

"I am Meripen Vanglelauf, sent by the Engenium's word, in aid of the trees."

She smiled and returned his bow.

"I am Elizabeth Moore. Be welcome among us, Meripen Vanglelauf," she said, gravely, and gave him a sideways smile. "My son admires you already, and gives us to understand that our kind hosts, the trees, do the same."

"Jamie Moore is a likely sprout," he said, which had the double advantage of being both politic and true. "The nest he built for my comfort is everything that I could want."

"It pleases me to hear you say so," Elizabeth Moore murmured, and looked about her as one just discovering her environment.

"What a very pleasant evening!" She turned back to him with a broad smile. "I wonder, Ranger, if you would indulge me by speaking with a few of us out here under the sky. It is *far* too fine to huddle within walls."

Meri blinked, and bowed again, to cover what must surely have been his too-obvious relief.

"I would be pleased indeed to speak with persons of merit, and share the evening breeze with them."

Elizabeth Moore laughed. "Very courtly," she said, and gave him a roguish wink. "Make yourself comfortable on yon bench and I'll just fetch the others out."

She turned, light as a flutterwisp, and was gone, leaving Meri to return beneath branch. He sank onto the bench with a heartfelt sigh of relief. His hands were shaking; he pressed palms against thighs to steady them.

They mean you no harm, Ranger, the tree commented, which was the third time. Meri shivered and bowed his head.

"So it would seem," he murmured.

Becca came awake with the feeling that someone had spoken her name. The room was filled with green shadows, as if her couch were tucked inside a tree's lush canopy. The shadows moved about her, rustling, admitting a long spear of butter-yellow light, giving her a glimpse of a tapestry ocean, a low table a-glitter with glass, a rug done in leaf brown, gold, and crimson.

It was not a room she knew.

She reclined half-seated against sloping pillows. When she tried to move, she found her limbs dead weights; the light blanket binding her to the couch as effectively as any rope.

Memory followed her tardily into wakefulness, the weight of a collar in her hand, the realization that there was but one way to make certain of her freedom; the stretch for the knife—

Then nothing.

"Rebecca Beauvelley," a clear voice murmured, "do you wake?"

"You know that I must," she said into the shadows, and spoke the name that came to her tongue, "Sian."

"Must I?" The green dimness beyond the low table parted like curtains for the Engenium in her sharkskin leggings and wide-sleeved shirt. "Now how would that be?"

"Did you not put the sleep on me?" Becca asked bitterly. "Of course it is you who calls me out."

"She does," another voice said, this one high as birdsong, "have you there, Cousin."

"One point only, though I believe she may think I hold the game." Sian came to the edge of the couch where Rebecca lay bound and dropped to one knee beside it.

"You have broken the geas that bound you, and stand a free woman."

"Stand?" Rebecca asked. Hidden yet inside the green shadows, the bird-voiced woman trilled a laugh.

"You are not," Sian said over her shoulder, "helping."

"Nay, nay! What aid might I lend to one so disadvantaged?"

Sian bent her attention to Becca. "Give me your word that you will not attempt to harm yourself and I will release the bonds upon you."

Her word, Becca thought, and moved her head from side to side against the pillows. Trapped, bound, and in thrall to a Fey. If only she had been quicker with the knife, or taken one leaf more of the kindly duainfey... Becca swallowed, and moved her head again. She had learned something from her bondage to Altimere: She would not participate in her own entrapment. Not this time. Let them expend their precious *kest* to bind her. They would get no aid from her.

"What," she asked, "do you want?"

The shadows lightened, melting away as a Fey woman in a hyacinth-colored robe stepped to the Engenium's side. Her hair was long, rippling in broad bands of gold, crimson, brown, and black, braided with stones, shells, leaves, and flowers. A dozen rings adorned the long white fingers that rested on Sian's shoulder.

"I am Diathen the Queen," she said in her high, musical voice. "I would learn what you know of Altimere's plans and designs regarding myself and the Vaitura, if you will tell me." She sank gracefully onto a stool that hadn't been there a moment before and smoothed her robe over her knees.

"Sian," she said. "Please release Miss Beauvelley to her own will."

The Engenium doubted the wisdom of that; Becca saw her hesitate, then felt a slight sparkle of energy along her limbs. Freed, she pushed the coverlet away one-handed, and slipped her legs over the side of the couch, sitting up to face Diathen the Queen, whom Altimere had called "upstart," bookkeeper, and worse.

"Altimere wishes to depose you," Becca said baldly,

which was perhaps not how one ought to address a Queen, and *certainly* not how one ought to address a High Fey. "He wants to lower the *keleigh* and bring... my people... under Fey dominion. As is," she finished bitterly, "your right and privilege."

"Acquit me," the Queen murmured. "I dominate but indifferently, as Altimere and his allies have doubtless taught you. And to throw down the *keleigh* is not something that I, in my bookkeeper's soul, can find equitable."

"And yet," Sian murmured, "we cannot continue as we are."

"So I hear from the philosophers on my right hand, while those on my left urge me to increase the forces already in play and seal us in, safe as a child in a closet."

"The *keleigh* consumes *kest*," Becca said, remembering Altimere's demonstration. "But throwing down the *keleigh* will—release *kest* in unexpected ways."

"Aptly put," the Queen murmured. "Was Altimere teaching you?"

"No," Becca said, bitterly. "He only needed me to harvest power."

Silence. Sian and the Queen exchanged a glance before Diathen brought her attention back to Becca.

"I feel that we have now reached my subject, Rebecca Beauvelley. I would count it a favor, if you would allow me to know just how such harvesting was done and where this harvested power has gone."

Becca took a breath, tasting cinnamon and apple, watching the play of the silvered green nimbus that limned the lady's slender form.

"My philosophers are studying the necklace and the

geas woven into it," the Queen said after a moment. "I fear but little remains of the original working. Altimere is, after all, an artificer of some skill and subtlety; old in his craft. I would hazard that it was the means of harvesting, but—"

"No," Becca said, and it seemed that the flavorful air in the green-shadowed room was too thin, very nearly too hot to breathe. "No, *I* gathered the *kest*; the necklace was to—to control me and bind me to...his will."

The Queen tipped her head. "Forgive me. It seems extraordinary that Altimere would require so much to tie you to him. Your name alone—"

"I kept my name!" Becca snapped. "If I had known what it meant, I would have gladly given it away!"

Sian's hand rose, long fingers shaping a sign. It flared, briefly turquoise, and faded as a breeze flowed in amongst the shadows, damp and tasting of salt.

"So," she said, her voice soft as a thought. "You harvested *kest* at Altimere's will, holding your name the while. And yet I do not see that you hold so *very* much power..."

Becca hung her head. "I gave it to him," she said miserably. "To Altimere. I—I gave him my power and my future..."

"Perhaps your power," Diathen the Queen said, her high voice sharp as broken shell. "*That* can be done. But a *future* cannot be given away, Rebecca Beauvelley."

Becca shook her head. "What is one, out of so many?" she whispered, rocking back and forth now, her maimed arm cradled on her lap.

Diathen shared a worried glance with Sian.

"You must forgive me," the Queen said to Becca, "for having broken your sleep. I can only plead a need to know what Altimere intends. I will leave you now to continue healing—"

"No!" Becca thrust to her feet, and would have fallen except for Sian's hand beneath her elbow. Diathen rose to face her, purple eyes hard.

"I will not have my will overridden again!" Becca cried, feeling a flow of molten gold flowing up her spine. "I am my own person; I hold my own name; I am not a *play*thing!" Sparks lit the gloom: green and gold and crimson. She took a breath. "I *demand*—" she began—

And crumpled into Diathen's arms, asleep before her knees gave out.

❦

They were gentle, and most courteous, Meri admitted, and careful not to overwhelm his senses. Not merely with the arranging of the meeting out-of-doors, where he might feel unconfined, but also in the numbers that they chose to field: himself, Elizabeth Moore, a white-haired elder called Jack Wood, and the sprout Jamie.

The trees would have it that the sprout was fruit of a melding of the Newoman Elizabeth and a Wood Wise named Palin, which strained credulity. Yet, the trees *had* said so, and certainly the shy greens of the boy's aura were more Fey than the hectic and gaudy displays of his elders.

Jamie the sprout carried a chair out of the house and placed it for the elder. Elizabeth Moore settled herself comfortably on the grass between chair and bench; at a sign from her, Jamie settled next to Meri, his cool aura showing yellow sparkles of curiosity.

"Sam sends apologies," Elizabeth murmured. "He's with our mother, in case she should wake."

"I grieve for the elder's illness," Meri answered politely. "May her *kest* soon rise."

"Thank you. We all hope for her recovery."

"No more'n I do," the elder Jack Wood said in a voice like the wind blowing through reeds. "Just her an' me left o' those who walked the hellroad. Stubbornest woman I ever known, that side er this, and I don't think we woulda won through, if not for the tongue in her head, and the wit that drove it."

Meri turned to him. The elder Newman's aura was a complex weave of silvers and blues, as vivid and as dangerous as glass.

"You crossed the *keleigh*?"

The old one laughed, his aura shimmering, and shook his head. "Some long seasons ago, that was! Eliza there was a babe in arms—slept through the whole passage, for all the sound she ever made. Sam, now, he was born this side, same as Gracie an' Thomas an'—"

"And me!" Jamie piped up from Meri's side.

"You!" Another laugh, warm and welcome as new bread. "Ain't no doubt regarding *you*, Sprout."

"No doubt at all," Elizabeth said, with a calmness at odds with the brilliance of her aura. "But the Ranger hasn't come to hear our lineage. His concern is to hear what ails our good friends, the trees."

"Aye, aye!" Jack Wood raised a hand gnarled and spotted like an old branch. "Mind you, now, it was Lucy give the trees our parole back when we first found this spot. And 'twas the trees sent young Palin along to have a look at us. I put myself forward as caretaker, for I'd been a woodsman, back there, and fancied I knew something of trees." He chuckled. "They soon learned me different, and Palin, too, after he brung Lucy back from swearing us to the good lady of Sea Fort."

"So," Meri said carefully, into the silence that followed this declaration. "You have been caring for the trees. The Engenium—the good lady of Sea Fort— had given me to understand that your folk were... not tree-wise."

"Nor are we," Jack Wood told him. "I'm no Ranger, young master—far from it! Oh, I'm canny enough to take off a sick limb, and to keep the burrowers away from new roots. But there's a need in the forest of late that I'm not understanding, a—" He moved his hand again, as if fingering the word from the passing breeze. "A—*mistiness*. My lore tells me the stand's old; and in the natural way of things some o' the elders'll be fallin', the same as with Lucy, and—soon enough— myself. This though—I'm thinking this is something different, something... not of root nor branch." He sighed and shook his head, sending Meri a rueful grin.

"You'll see why we asked our good lady for a Ranger, eh? It goes far beyond me, and this one—" He jerked his head at Jamie.

"The trees talk to me!" the boy said hotly and the old man chuckled.

"Who said they didn't, eh? But are they speakin' of their affliction?"

There was a pause. Jamie sighed, visibly wilting on the bench, and shook his tumbled head.

"No."

"Nor would they," Meri said briskly, "burden a sprout. We are all as children to the elder trees, and in truth there are those whose thought is strange, even to we who are Rangers." He looked again to Jack Wood. "Surely, though, the trees would speak to their own."

The old man blinked. "Eh?"

"The Ranger means Palin, I think," Elizabeth Moore said from her comfortable recline on the grass, and gave Meri another of her smiles. "Palin wanders," she said softly. "He does errands, for the trees, for the Engenium at Sea Hold, for us, for other Wood Wise— for the Hobs, too, when they ask him. He belongs to the trees, certain enough, Master Vanglelauf, but less to *these trees* than we do." She moved her shoulders in an easy shrug. "We had thought perhaps someone who was tied to the Engenium's lands, as we are . . ."

"Which I am not," Meri said softly.

"But the trees like you!" Jamie said exuberantly. "They're pleased you've come!"

"And so I am pleased to have come," Meri said firmly. He looked, first to Elizabeth Moore, then to Jack Wood.

"I will undertake to identify the problem," he said slowly. "You understand that this will mean that my time will be spent—"

"Can't you use your longeye?" the sprout interrupted. "Sam says you saw our village from leagues away!"

"Seeing is not the same as *going among*," Meri said, patiently, for it was the duty of those elder to teach the young. "In addition, the longeye is a gift of the sea, and is less use than you might think, among the trees."

"I—" began the sprout, and pressed his lips suddenly together as his mother raised a hand.

"You," she said, "have been quite rude enough for one evening, Jamie Moore." She turned her head and gave Meri a smile. "We understand that you are here to aid the trees, Master Vanglelauf. It is what we asked of Lady Sian. Had we wished for a jester, that is what we would have asked her to send."

"And right daft she would have thought us, too," Jack added, with a grin.

Elizabeth nodded, and seemed about to say something else when there arose an outcry from the house across the green, the accumulated power flaring into new and terrifying patterns.

"Gran!" Jamie cried, flinging to his feet, running heedlessly back toward the house, with his mother not two paces behind.

The Newman elder rose more slowly, and turned, staring at the house without moving. Meri gained his feet also—courtesy, he reminded himself, though he trembled at this new display of raw, potent power.

"May I escort you, sir?" he asked, desperately hoping that this proper and polite suggestion would be rejected.

Jack shook himself—"Eh?"—and looked over his shoulder. Meri could see that cheeks were wet.

"Nay, then," he said softly. "That's a gentle offer and I'm obliged, but—I can walk on my own." He shook his head, seeming not to notice the tears that ran into his beard.

"Never thought she'd go first," he said, "and leave me at the last."

Chapter Two

WAKING WAS A LONG, LANGUOROUS BUSINESS.

Becca stretched, luxuriating in the smooth slide of sheets along her limbs and the flex of muscle and flesh. She slipped back into a drowse, becoming by degrees aware of the warmth of sunlight upon her face, and a ruddy glow beyond her eyelids. A sweet, riotous scent tickled her nose—roses, lavender, teyepia and gradials—beneath it the prickle of pine and the clean, woody odor of elitch, a touch of turned earth.

She smiled and nestled her cheek into the cool pillow, a little closer to awake now, lazily following the frenzy of birdsong until she smiled and stretched once more.

"You may wish to bear in mind, in the interest of your future well-being," a clear voice said dryly from near at hand, "that one does not *demand* of a Queen. Even so mild-natured a Queen as Diathen."

"Yet it was not the Queen," Becca answered languidly, "who struck me down."

A short silence and then a sigh that sounded more

irritated than comfortable was her answer as she drifted inevitably toward the shores of true wakefulness.

"A Queen," Sian said at last, "depends upon those who owe her loyalty to protect her. Does it become necessary for her to raise a hand in her own defense, she cannot afford to be seen as . . . less than strong. Are you awake, Rebecca Beauvelley?"

"For the moment, it seems that I am." Becca opened her eyes and met Sian's sea-green gaze firmly. "Until you decide otherwise."

"This conversation has a familiar odor to it," Sian observed, perhaps to herself. She sat a-slouch at some remove from the daybed, one boot planted firmly on the glass-topped table, the chair tipped precariously back on two legs. She moved her arm in a meaningless sweep. "I grant it may seem mere whimsy on my part, but you must own that twice I've acted to preserve your life."

"A boon," Becca snapped, fully awake now—and fully irritated, "I neither requested nor desired!" She sat up and thrust the covers aside, faintly surprised that these things were allowed her.

Sian raised a thin golden brow. "Come now, would you rather be dead?"

"In fact," Becca answered, swinging her legs over the edge of the bed. "I *would*! What do you think I was doing when you interfered with me in Altimere's garden?"

"Seeking clear thought," Sian said, and brought her hand before her face, fingers spread wide, as if in defense. "Do not glare at me, madam! I only repeat what you yourself told me."

Becca snapped to her feet, and flung out her good arm to catch her balance. "I do not—"

"You saw the collar for what it truly was, did you not?" Sian continued. "Certainly, with all the artifice woven into it—forged signature and will-to-fail among the lesser evils that Diathen's philosophers have found!—certainly, you were correct to seek clear thought before attempting to deal with such a thing for the third time. That you triumphed—"

"Had to do with—" Becca bit her lip, while inside her head a deep, amused voice told her, *Good morning, Gardener.*

Sian tipped her head. "Had to do with?" she inquired politely, and crossed her arms over her breast, waiting.

Well, and what does it matter, now? Becca thought angrily. *Surely, I might be excused for having run mad.*

"Had to do with the trees!" she snapped. "They came to my aid at the last."

Sian closed her eyes. "A very familiar odor, indeed," she murmured. She raised her boot from the table, the chair crashed down onto four legs, and she was on her feet.

She made, Becca admitted privately, a brave figure, with her hands on her slim waist, her sleeves billowing and bright in the fresh breeze, her legs shapely in their tight trousers, and the cool blue flames outlining her against the air.

For herself, she felt . . . somewhat grubby, her dress draggled with having been slept in, and her hair knotted and none too clean—and the weight, not entirely unfamiliar, of dread anticipation pressing down upon her shoulders.

"Why," she demanded, "have you wakened me, this time? Has Altimere returned?"

Sian lifted both eyebrows. "In fact, he has not, nor
has Councilor Zaldore, and the Queen's Constant has
gone into recess for the lack of them. I am therefore
redundant, and my kinswoman, gentle Diathen, the
Queen, has deemed you to be my problem."

"The Queen," Becca said, snappishly, "is in error."

"That's as may be," Sian returned mildly. "But she
is the Queen."

Becca raised her chin. "I am a—a free woman in
possession of my own name," she stated, in a hot,
small voice that did not seem quite like her own. "I
refuse to be dominated."

Silence. Sian turned her head to stare out the
window. "Oh," she said. "Do you."

"Surely that is my right?" Becca challenged her.

"Surely, it is your right to resist domination, should
it be offered, to the fullest extent of your power,"
Sian murmured, her attention still seemingly engaged
by the scene outside the window. "To *state* that you
refuse . . ." She shrugged, and at last glanced back to
Becca. "Of course, you must say so. Anyone would.
However!" She raised her hand imperiously. "It is
not domination, but care that is offered, since you
apparently lack the wit to perceive it. Think, Rebecca
Beauvelley! Your situation is perilous at best and dire
at worst! Might a friend—or even two—be beneficial?"

"Perhaps so. Do you put yourself forth as my
friend, Engenium? I warn you—terrible things happen to my friends."

Sian shrugged. "Terrible things have happened to
my friends, as well. And neither of us wishes to dwell
long upon the fates which have overtaken Diathen's
friends, now and again." She sighed.

"Put your wits to work, girl! Altimere the master artificer has vanished, and with him she who would be queen in Diathen's place! Does that frighten you? Certainly, it casts *my* nerves into disorder—and you may make of *that* what you will!"

Becca swallowed, her right hand curling into a fist at her side. "The thought that I might meet Altimere again . . . terrifies me, if you will have it," she said, her voice low, but steady. "And, since you bid me apply my wits, allow me to say that I know the Queen wishes to keep me in her pocket until my testimony may be used against him. Nonetheless, I must insist that I be allowed to go free."

Sian blinked. "Free," she repeated, as if the word were some strange artifact that had only now been put into her hand. "And where will you go, free?"

"I would go across the *keleigh*." The words had scarce left her lips when her stomach heaved. Becca clamped her teeth against sickness, took a breath—

Peace, Gardener, murmured the voice of the trees. A cool wash of green flowed through her, cooling her tumultuous blood, uncramping her stomach.

She took another breath, tasting the distinctive sweetness of duainfey in the air. Duainfey, which gave the gift of clear sight; and surcease from pain. A healer's friend, duainfey, the death it gifted as sweet as the taste of its leaves.

She had eaten two duainfey leaves—enough to achieve clarity of vision. The third leaf had been taken from her before she could complete her resolve.

"You would cross the *keleigh*." Sian sounded openly skeptical.

"I've crossed the *keleigh* once," Becca said, lifting

her chin with an effort. "It holds far fewer horrors for me than the possibility of meeting Altimere again."

The Fey woman nodded. "You do have wits, then. Still, the *keleigh*, though less horrifying than Altimere, is no small obstacle. And, as you say, the Queen has her own reasons to keep you close. Best you come with me, to a more protected location, and await her command."

"I—" Becca stopped, looking down at her draggled garments. What, after all, awaited her at home? She was ruined—even if she managed to keep the details of her life under Altimere's ... protection ... a secret. After all, she had been wanton enough to elope with the man! She had been ruined before the first night was through. All else—*everything* else she had accepted or had forced upon her—merely confirmed her in shame. Women like her were remanded to Wanderer's Villages, or hanged by the Board of Governors, as an example for obedience and chastity.

And yet—to remain in the Vaitura, where she was prey and worse? A *kest*-less being to be dominated and used by those who held more power—which would, she thought dismally, be anyone, including a child not yet out of nursery.

You are not so unprotected as that, Gardener, nor so friendless.

The thought warmed her, even as she recalled that the trees had been unable to preserve Elyd's life.

"Forgive me, Rebecca Beauvelley," Sian said, breaking into these thoughts. "You were about to say?"

"A moment," Becca said curtly. She closed her eyes, forcing herself to *reason*.

The first thing to do, she told herself carefully, was

to remove herself from Altimere's orbit. He might, after all, return home at any time. Therefore, to accept the Queen's dictate—for now!—and accompany Sian was, in its way, wisdom. Later, when she had had time to plan, and to proceed from a position of safety—or at least such safety as was available to her here—later, she would see what else she might contrive.

She sighed, and raised her head to meet Sian's eyes.

"I will not leave my horse here," she said, firmly, "nor my lore books."

Sian's mouth twisted into an ironical smile. "These books—they are in Altimere's house?"

"Yes, and my horse is in his stable," Becca answered tartly. "Is that so wonderful?"

"Scarcely wonderful at all," Sian said, and made Becca a sudden, extravagant bow.

"Lead on, by your kindness! I shall, of course, accompany you."

It was, Becca thought, shameful that she should feel quite so much relief at hearing these words.

Sian is not an ill friend, Gardener, the tree told her confidentially, which, for all she knew, was so.

And, in any wise, she really had no choice.

Head high, she walked past Sian, across the room. The hallway door opened to let her through.

Meri had returned to the nest and curled down 'mong the sweet grasses, thinking to make an early start on the morrow. Sleep, however, eluded him, held away, no doubt, by the sounds of wailing on the air, and the flares and flashes of the Newmen's auras, terrible and seductive in grief.

At last, he removed to some small distance from the nest, sank to the ground, and put his back companionably against a dozing culdoon tree. Night had come on, and the early stars were preening. Meri pulled out his knife and began to tend it, less for necessity and more for the comfort involved in performing so commonplace and usual a task.

"If sleep is denied me, I might as well begin my task in the wood this night," he murmured, his voice hardly louder than the purr of whetstone down blade.

It may be that your task here is not yet done, the deep voice of the elitch answered, and Meri sighed, without needing to ask what was meant.

"Tell me of this Palin Nicklauf," he said then. "He wanders, so I'm told, and serves the needs of trees and Engenium alike. Has he no wood of his own to tend?"

Lightning flashed—but no. It was merely the Newmen's grief, blaring for a moment, then falling. Surely, Meri thought, the Elder had sublimated by now.

Palin Nicklauf is his own wood. The elitch spoke slowly, its thought forming with a degree of uncertainty marked in a tree—and said no more.

His *own* wood? Meri wondered. And how did that come about?

There was no immediate answer from the tree, which was not, on reflection, entirely surprising.

Ranger, the elitch spoke again. *Shallow roots bear the fruit of fear.*

"So I have heard, and so was I taught," Meri said politely, his attention more than half on the knife.

My roots are deep and I shelter many. Allow me to give a gift.

The whetstone stopped its steady stroke. Meri closed

his eyes, hearing Faldana's broken whisper, pleading with him as he held her shattered body. "Beloved, allow me to give the gift. You may live. I...cannot."

"I..." He cleared his throat. "Elder, I am honored by your regard, but—I am so weak, and you are so mighty...I fear that your fires would overwhelm mine. Let me...grow in the usual way. A slow settling is surest," he added, which the trees in Vanglewood had been particularly fond of quoting at a sprout.

Silence, as if the tree pondered, then—

You are the best judge of your own health, Ranger. The gift is yours, should you need it. Only ask.

"Thank you," Meri whispered, his throat tight with emotion.

It is the trees who thank you, Meripen Vanglelauf.

Bemused, Meri tested the edge of his blade with his thumb. Satisfied, he slid it away, stowed the whetstone, and considered what other comfortable, needful task he might be about to while the night—

There was a sound, to his left and ahead, as if a foot had been set unwarily among the leaves and grasses.

Meri tipped his head, listening as the steps, soft, but perfectly audible, moved toward his nest. Whoever approached must assume him asleep, so carefully did they move, saving that one misstep only. Their breathing, however—that was noisy, and irregular, as if they labored under strong emotion.

"Jamie Moore," Meri said, pitching his voice no louder than the whisper of the breeze through the trees.

The footsteps hesitated, then sounded again, moving toward Meri's position at the base of the culdoon.

The boy was disheveled, his brown face pale, and

sticky with recent tears, his quiet aura stitched with crimson. His task, Meri thought with a private sigh, as the trees had foretold.

"Sit," Meri invited, patting the grass beside him. "And say what is in your heart."

It was more collapse, but however it was done, the lad was facing him, properly cross-legged, his hands flat on his thighs.

"Why did the trees let Gran die?"

The boy's voice was unsteady, as well it might be, bearing the burden of such a heart-question—indeed, *the* question. Wood Wise, even Rangers, tended to believe that the trees were all-powerful. It seemed inconceivable that beings so old and so wise could be limited in any way, and yet—

"Even trees die," Meri said softly.

Jamie sniffled. "But trees, they share themselves with the whole forest," he said. "Their *thought* doesn't die."

Root and branch. Who expected such insights from a sprout?

"It is true that their wisdom endures," Meri agreed; "but the voice—that one, distinctive and unique viewpoint—it is gone forever. The forests may learn and treasure, but the forests have learned from, and treasure, many." He paused, considering the boy's bowed head, and the tender curve of his exposed neck. Young he might be for these questions, yet he had asked and so deserved an answer, in fullness.

"It is the best we may do, Wood Wise, Newman, or tree, to pass on our knowledge and our dreams to the ones who come after, so that those things we have learned are not lost, and our good deeds stretch beyond us, while our ill deeds are not repeated." He paused again. The boy did not lift his head, but there was a certain set to his shoulders that said to Meri that he was listening—and thinking.

"Your gran, then," Meri continued slowly. "She was old and very wise, was she not?"

Jamie sniffled again, and nodded without raising his head. "She was our herbalist, and our doctor, and our historian." He raised his head at last and met Meri's eye. "She came over the hellroad—you heard Jack tell it. She said—she said her hair was as red as Violet's when she walked in, and the color of salt when they came to settle, like she'd walked down thirty years in that one crossing. Martin Kinderman, his hair went from grey to black, and the lines melted out of his face, though there were still old thoughts in that young head of his..." The boy's voice had taken on a cadence unlike his own, as if he were retelling a story he had listened to many times before, in the storyteller's own voice. "He died soon after they settled, like the youth was an illusion, and Gran, she kept on, not changing at all past the change that she'd already borne, caring for us. She asked the trees if we could stay and she gave the Engenium at Sea Hold our whole-oath, that we would serve her and her lands. And here we've been ever since."

"You were born to this land, Jack Wood said," Meri murmured, when a moment or two had passed and the boy had not taken up the threads of his tale.

"There's six of us second-borns," Jamie said slowly. "The Engenium at Sea Hold...Gran swore to her that we wouldn't outgrow our land, and— Father says the land holds us to our oath."

Of course the land holds them to their oath, Meri thought. And it also explained why Sian was so certain

of her secret band of Newmen. She held the oath of
the Old Woman, which was potent, indeed. But—the
Old Woman was gone, passed beyond oaths and the
Engenium, alike. Meri took a breath.

"Did Sam renew the oath when he came to be
headman?" he asked, carefully.

Jamie nodded, and Meri felt a flutter of relief. "Sam
picked up the oath and Mother renewed our kinship to
the trees," he said solemnly—repeating, Meri suspected,
a lesson learned but perhaps imperfectly understood.
No matter. The Newmen were bound, to the Vaitura
no less than to the trees themselves. Mischief could
always be done, of course, but such ties were potent.

"It seems that you are well-situated here," he
began—

Brilliance shattered the night, confusing Meri's
senses, so that he flung an arm up to shield his eye.
Came the sound of running feet, sobs, a shout—and
he was up, his back against the culdoon, his hand
on his knife. He fingered the hilt, but did not draw.
Beside him, likewise braced against the tree, was
Jamie Moore, his breathing quieter now.

"Violet!" The shout came again, and now Meri
recognized the voice of Sam Moore, though he had
never heard it carry such a depth of pain.

"No!" A girl's voice, clearly distraught, the girl
herself the merest suggestion of shadow behind the
blare of her aura. "Sam, leave me alone!"

"Violet, I know you're upset, but you can't just
refuse—at least think about it!"

"I *have* thought about it!" the girl cried, spinning
around to face her pursuer. "The fact is that I'm not
a healer! I don't know enough!"

"You know more than you think, right now." Sam's voice was calm, with an edge that suggested to Meri that it was hard-won. "Mother told me you were learning your lore well and that she was certain that you would be her equal or better."

"Gran *died*!" Violet shouted, and suddenly, she was bent sideways, like a bird protecting a broken wing. Her voice wavered, blurry with tears even as her aura sharpened painfully with the force of her grief. "She died because I didn't know enough to save her!"

"She died because it was time," Sam countered, which was, Meri thought, only common sense. The Newman stepped forward and gathered the girl into his arms, their combined auras thundering against Meri's senses.

"Violet," Sam murmured. "I know. We all expected Gran to be with us forever. I know that you haven't had your complete training. You've been flung from 'prentice to master all of a sudden. But I know you can do it; *Gran* knew you could do it."

The girl continued to sob. Meri saw their silhouettes through the blare of their auras: the girl with her head against Sam's shoulder as he gently stroked her hair, offering comfort and, perhaps, common sense.

Hidden from the two Newmen by the kindness of the tree, Jamie Moore moved—and stilled, which Meri considered well done. Their presence would only increase the girl's grief and Meri, for one, had no wish to approach that hectic aura.

"Listen," Sam murmured. "What if I ask the Engenium to send us a Fey Healer for a little time? Just until you find your feet and get over the—"

"No . . ." the girl moaned. "Fey heal by—even Father—he knows the plants, but he draws on their *kest*. The process of making a poultice, or brewing a restorative tea—it's not what they do . . ."

Delicately, Meri queried the trees, receiving a bewildering series of images: a white-haired woman working over a table, drying leaves, grinding roots, making pastes and liqueurs . . .

The healing arts, the elitch added, *take many forms.*

So it would seem, Meri replied, bemused.

"Let us send for another healer," Violet sobbed against Sam's shoulder. "Before I kill someone else in my ignorance."

"Send?" Sam sounded honestly baffled, as Meri, his fingers clutching knife hilt, went cold all over. "Where would we send, child? As far as I—and Lady Sian—know, we are the only folk of our kind on this side of the hellroad."

"Then send to the other side!" Violet cried.

There was a moment of charged silence before Sam answered, his voice chilly. "You are overwrought. Come, let me take you inside. You should have a cordial and go to sleep. Rest is what you need."

"Sam—"

"No," he said firmly. "We will talk again *after* you have rested. In fact," his voice grew a little louder. "It is time for Jamie to seek his bed, as well."

He turned, then, guiding the bent and still weeping girl back toward the house. Jamie sighed and shifted away from the tree.

"Sam's got good eyes," he said. "Even Father says so." He sighed again. "I'd better go." He danced back a step—then darted forward, touching Meri on the shoulder as if they were comrades of the branch. "Thank you, Master Vanglelauf."

"You are welcome, Jamie Moore," Meri murmured. "I think that Sam is correct; rest if you can, and survey your thoughts when you are calmer."

The boy nodded. "That's exactly what Gran used to say," he murmured, his voice husky. "Root and branch, Master."

"Root and branch, Sprout," Meri answered, and watched the child slip away through the shadows.

Chapter Three

BECCA PAUSED, HER HAND ON THE VINE-WRAPPED gate, staring. Unlike the overpruned, stringently controlled grounds around Altimere's country house, the garden here in Xandurana had been—well, scarcely a garden at all. An exuberance of green life, the plants had clambered over each other, mixed willy-nilly, grudgingly ceding a few handspans to the thin walkway. It had hardly been possible to move in the garden without stepping on leaves, bending stems, or endangering flowers. She recalled her efforts to prune and thin the overfull beds, not to impose order or artifice, but to give the plants room—and she recalled how they filled in again, almost before she had cleared the clippings away.

She remembered that last day, sitting on the bench beneath the elitch tree, duainfey leaves in her lap, green life rioting all about her, and the tree-or-trees sharing her thoughts.

"What has happened?" she breathed.

You spoke to us of seasons, of an orderly march from seed to seeding, each plant according to its nature, all according to their kind. The memory was buried deep, but the trees recall.

It was true, Becca saw. All of what she knew to be summer plants were sere, as if kissed by autumn. The breeze, however, was not autumnal, but spring-like, precisely as always, nor had the height of the sun in the sky shifted by so much as a finger's width. Across the gate, the thin walkway lay uncontested all the way to the back door of Altimere's house.

"Trees," she said.

Yes, Gardener?

"Is Altimere at home?"

"He is not," Sian said from just beyond her left shoulder. "If he were, we should be hearing the bells, summoning all of the Queen's Constant to their places at the table."

"He might have no wish to—to bruit his return about," Becca said. "And trees might notice what others do not."

"Depend upon it, the trees of this city notice much, and forget little. But they do not notice *all*, and things may be hidden from them. Also..."

Becca looked over her shoulder and up, into a pair of ironical sea-colored eyes. "Also?" she repeated.

"It is well to recall that trees—wise as they are and amiable—are... naïve with regard to certain matters. I rejoice in a cousin who is Wood Wise—as unpredictable and as willful as anyone might wish. Leaving aside what his kin might make of him, he is much beloved of the trees, and even he owns that their thought is sometimes beyond him."

Altimere, the voice was loud inside her head, *has passed beyond our ken, Gardener.*

Becca's heart lurched. Was he dead, then? Was she free of him at last, and truly? Her eyes filled, the tears making the garden into a wonder-weave of greens and silvers. She blinked, clearing her eyes, her hand gripping the gate so tightly her knuckles ached.

Sian reached past her to work the latch. The gate swung open, and Becca staggered, unbalanced, into Altimere's garden.

"Forgive my hastiness," the Engenium said, dryly. "I have been long absent from my own country and yearn to be on the road to home." She slid a steadying hand beneath Becca's elbow. "Gather your belongings quickly, Rebecca Beauvelley."

As simple as that. And yet, Becca thought, as she walked up the pathway, each step a compromise between fear and necessity, how could it be otherwise? Sian was High Fey. Exalted, and full of power. *She* could have no fear of meeting Altimere, of having her will overridden and her good name destroyed, all in the service of another's ambition.

Becca's feet slowed on the path. Mindful of Sian at her back, she forced herself to move on, knees trembling. There was the place where they had taken her, one with his manhood in her mouth, the other buried in her anus, while Altimere—her *protector!*, who had named her a treasure of his house, whom she had trusted, once, and found fair—while Altimere had looked on, his protection withheld, even the false wantonness stripped from her so that her abusers might fully *savor* her anguish...

"Rebecca Beauvelley?" Sian's voice was low, tinged

with an emotion Becca in her agitation could not name. Perhaps it was concern. Or perhaps it was only boredom.

Becca bit her lip, drawing blood, trembling where she stood, unable to go on, the events of that night before her eyes, overlaying even the bank of sweet-carpet where she and Benidik...

"Rebecca Beauvelley?" Sian's voice was sharper, now.

Becca cleared her throat. Benidik, she thought. Benidik had promised. She did not believe that the Fey woman cared—she would not believe so much of any Fey again. But Benidik... might be careless. She had been in Zaldore's train, which meant she was no friend to Diathen the Queen. It might be that Benidik would see advantage to herself, in letting the evidence to Altimere's crimes slip away.

"I ask," she gasped, her voice odd and breathless, her eyes on the sweep of purple flowers, recalling promises made in the throes of passion. "I ask that I be placed in the care of the High Fey Benidik. Until such time as the Queen has need of me."

Behind her, Sian laughed. "You do not circumvent the will of a Queen so easily, Rebecca Beauvelley! My problem Diathen has declared you to be and my problem you shall, I fear, remain, until such time as she declares elsewhere. Gather your things, now, and quickly."

It had, Becca told herself, been worth the asking, though she might have known Sian would refuse her. She forced her feet to move again on the path, and raised her hand to wipe at her cheek, unsurprised to find that it was wet.

Sian is not an ill friend, Gardener, the tree or trees

said for the second time. *She is canny, and strong, and sometimes wise*.

"*Sometimes* wise?" Becca muttered, forcing her feet to move again on the path.

She is yet young.

Her feet faltered again as Becca approached the season wheel she had planted in an attempt to demonstrate a proper cycle to what she had then thought of as the intelligence of the place. Like the rest of the garden, the summer plants showed sere and brown. The plants of the other three seasons, however, showed as hale and hardy as if they were in the peak of their growth.

"There is a *process*," she said, speaking to the trees as if they were a peculiarly backward 'prentice. "Seedlings begin; they grow, leaf, blossom, give fruit if that is their nature, fade, and fail. They do not spring forth and stand tall in all the strength of their youth until they are struck down."

"What would you teach them?" Sian asked, stopping beside her and considering the wheel in her turn.

"The orderly progression of the seasons," Becca said with a sigh and a shake of her head. "To have all and everything bloom at its own discretion is— unnatural!—and in the end, dangerous. For plant and Fey alike," she added, for the trees' benefit. She turned her head slightly, considering the side of Sian's face. Comely, as the High Fey were, and if her skin was somewhat tanned, it was smooth and unlined. Surely, Becca thought, she was too young—but so had Altimere seemed youthful.

"Were you in the war, Engenium?"

Sian laughed. "Wind and wave! The war was done and the *keleigh* in place long before I had accumulated *kest* enough to braid my hair, much less fight!" She sobered, met Becca's eyes and shook her head. "Not many of the Elders remain. Donaden, Altimere, Sanalda—"

Becca cringed, the smell of blood suddenly overpowering the sweet scent of growing things.

"Art well, Rebecca Beauvelley?"

She shook her head, swallowing hard. Compelled or not, she was surely not about to confess the murder of one of the few remaining Elders.

"I am frightened," she said, instead, which was only the truth. "What if the Gossamers try to hold me?"

"Now, I knew there was a reason that I asked to accompany you," Sian said, her voice sharper than humor might call for. "And soon we shall know. It appears that you are expected."

The door into the kitchen was open. Becca's steps faltered, even as the voice of the tree spoke inside her head.

The lightless ones approach, Gardener.

Indeed, they did, and she saw them as never she had before—clearly. Not as ghostly gloves, but as pale, bloated shadows from which velvet-tipped tentacles waved softly.

A scream rose in her throat; she gritted her teeth, but not before a soft whimper escaped. The Gossamers paused, their aspect suddenly tentative, as if they were as wary of her as she of them. Becca forced herself to take a breath—another, and another. She forced herself to recall the many kindnesses she had received from the Gossamers: They had bathed her, fed her, watched over her—even assisted her in the garden! While they were certainly Altimere's creatures, yet she had never felt that they wished her harm—and had often felt that they had cared for her beyond the scope of whatever orders they had received from their master.

"Good day," she said, her voice not as strong as she would have liked. "I require a bath."

Before her, the misshapen shadows roiled. A pair of Gossamers detached themselves from the confusion, and faded, leaving a pair yet to confront Becca and Sian, tentacles waving inquisitively.

Her stomach roiled uneasily. Becca swallowed, and motioned unsteadily. "The Engenium is my guest. Pray—" *Pray, what?* she thought wildly. *Treat her as you would myself?*

"Pray treat her with all respect due the cousin of the Queen."

There was a small sound from behind her right shoulder, as if Sian had sneezed. Becca waited, but the Fey woman made no other sound.

"Very well," Becca said. She moved forward one deliberate step, then another. The Gossamers drifted back from her approach, escorting them properly into the house. They passed through the tidy, cold kitchen, past the hall to the dining room, where a single place was set at the gleaming wooden table, to the entrance hall.

There the Gossamers halted, transparent nightmares barely visible against the textured woods.

Becca turned toward Sian, who had followed, silent.

"Can you see the Gossamers?" she asked politely, and gained an ironic lift of a neat brow for her courtesy.

"Surely. Can you not see them?"

"I see them...somewhat changed from what they were," Becca answered, with emphasis.

Both of Sian's brows rose. "Do you indeed? They seem precisely as they have always seemed to me."

Good sun, Becca thought weakly. What other horrors had she been blind to in this house?

"Would you care to wait in Altimere's library?" she asked Sian politely. "They will guide you."

"In fact," Sian said, with a sudden broad smile. "I would very much like to see Altimere's library. Pray send for me when you have done with your toilette, and are ready to ride. There is no need to hurry on my account; I have nothing other to do than wait upon you."

Becca glared, but Sian had already turned and was following the Gossamers across the foyer. With a sigh, and telling herself that the Fey woman would be perfectly safe, she turned and mounted the ramp.

Her room was unchanged; the bed covered in yellow damask, turned down to reveal a dozen achingly white pillows and linens as fresh as the season's first snow. Sunlight parted the living vine curtains, and gleamed along the glazed green tiles at the top of the wall. Her combs and brushes were laid out on the vanity, and her reflection ghosted in the depths of the mirror as she passed by.

She paused, staring, not at the ruined dress or her hair like a mare's nest, though certainly both were worth at least a stare. No, what caught her eye and held it was the blare and blossom of color swirling about her shape. This was nothing like the silvery nimbus that surrounded Diathen the Queen, or the wash of turquoise that played about Sian's slim form—no, *this* was color in every shade and hue, so that she seemed to be a woman afire.

Involuntarily, Becca looked down at her hands, only to find them brown and cool, with a spiderweb of white scars across the fingertips of her right hand, where the duainfey had blistered her skin.

She looked back at the woman burning in the glass, down-tilted brown eyes beneath winging brows, and a thin, unlined brown face. Frowning, she gazed directly into her own eyes, but could see nothing different in their regard. Was this yet duainfey's virtue at work? Clarity—perhaps clarity was not always to be desired, she thought painfully. Surely, it was no boon, to see the Gossamers' true shape. And this fiery halo—had she always sported such a thing, and simply been blind to its existence? Was *this* what the Fey saw, who had looked upon and desired her?

Something moved beyond in the mirror, resolving into gently waving tentacles. She glanced to once side, and saw the door to the bath room move suggestively.

"Of course," she said aloud. "I will bathe now, thank you." She walked toward the doorway. "Please send for Nancy," she said, coolly, as one spoke to servants. "I'll want her to dress me when I'm through."

She paused at the edge of the deep tub, and closed her eyes. The Gossamers disrobed her with their accustomed gentle efficiency, then took her by the arm—she forcefully snatched her imagination away from the thought of tentacles surrounding her wrist—and led her into the water.

Elizabeth Moore had filled his pack with all manner of savory things to eat, as if she expected him to be gone on walkabout, or thought him unable to feed himself adequately from the land. After a brief struggle, and only a little prompting from the elitch, he recognized her gift as kindness. He thanked her for her care before turning toward his work, steps measured deliberately, so as not to overtire the elder Newman Jack Wood.

"I won't slow ye long," the Newman said. "Just want to point ye out the way."

"Your care is appreciated." Meri repeated the same courtesy that had won him a sideways smile from Elizabeth Moore. From Jack Wood, he gained an edged chuckle and a shake of the venerable head.

"My intrusion into bidness you know better'n any is being tolerated with patience, is what you mean to say." He raised his stick and pointed to the right. "That'll be it, right there."

"There" was a stand of larch, slender trunks showing swatches of vermilion, which was a sign of great age among those trees.

Good growing, Elders, Meri sent politely, as he and Newman Wood approached.

The larches did not answer; indeed the whole area seemed unnaturally quiet. No birds sang from their graceful limbs, no tree-mice scampered among the leaves. And about the larches themselves, there was—a silvery nimbus, more like ice than proper *kest*, with no such flickers as might even attend a tree's aura.

Meri frowned slightly, and glanced at the Newman.

"Caught it, have ye?" The elder nodded his hoary head. "Took me a month or more o' passin' 'em by before I twigged there was something off. Can't say what it is, though. Just . . . off."

"Recall," Meri murmured, straining to make sense

of what he was seeing, "that my life has been devoted to trees. Any...oddity will be immediately apparent."

What, he asked the trees silently, *do I find here? Is the entire wood afflicted, or only this stand?*

Jack Wood laughed. "That's exactly what I said to Lucy when I first spotted it. 'Whatever's going on with them trees,' I says to her, 'it ain't natural. An' if it *is* natural, it ain't nothing I'm able or willing to take on.'"

Ahead, the larches remained silent and solitary. Meri sighed and looked away, to a neighboring pine, whose venerable branches were hosting a boisterous game of tree-mouse tag, to the tree's sleepy amusement.

"You were," he said to Jack Wood, "wise to send for a Ranger."

"Well, that's a comfort," the old man said dryly, and jerked his head at the lightsome, unnatural trees. "What *is* off? If you don't mind saying."

The trees were silent, as if they, too, awaited his answer. Meri sighed.

"I don't know," he said, and turned to look into Jack Wood's old and canny eyes. "I've never seen anything like it."

❧⟩⟩⟩⟨⟨⟨❧

Nancy was waiting when she emerged from her bath, dried with soft towels wielded by deft tentacles, and swathed in a robe of sunshine yellow brocade. It was a relief to see her as she had always seemed—an absurdly tiny creature, wings folded like a garnet and green cloak along her thin back, as she perched on the mirror's frame.

She leapt into the air as Becca took her place on

the bench, snatched the comb up in quick fingers, and began to gently work it through the damp knots.

"Thank you, Nancy," Becca murmured. The sight of her flame-limned reflection upset her stomach. She closed her eyes and concentrated on the sensation of her hair being combed.

Eventually, the tugging came to an end. Carefully, Becca opened her eyes, and saw Nancy hovering just behind her fiery left shoulder, apparently at a loss as to what she should do next.

"A single braid, please," Becca said, her voice hoarse. She cleared her throat and continued. "Pin it up securely so that it will go under a hat. I will be riding out immediately." There was a movement at the corner of her eye. She turned her head to look at the Gossamers hovering there.

"Please saddle Rosamunde and have her brought 'round," she said, wondering if this order would be obeyed as thoroughly as the others. If she had to force the Gossamers—well, how *could* she force such creatures? They were not her servants. They were Altimere's... *creatures*, bound to him in ways she she really did not wish to think about. Say, indeed, that they were her jailers, whatever they might desire in their private hearts.

If they had hearts, private or otherwise.

It seemed to her overwrought nerves that the Gossamers did hesitate, tentacles meditatively stroking the busy air. Just as Becca despaired of being obeyed, Nancy spun in a flash of wings, one hand at her hip, the other shaking the comb fiercely. Very nearly Becca could hear her scolding—"You have your orders, then! Be off with you!"

As if they, too, had heard Nancy's mute scold, the Gossamers were gone, fading into the sunlight. Nancy gave a satisfied nod, hefted the comb to part Becca's hair, and began to braid it.

The path had failed to reveal itself. Which was, Altimere owned . . . disturbing.

He expected complications and misdirection from Zaldore, not subtlety. Perhaps she had learnt more from her grandmother than he had supposed. Now, *there* had been a philosopher both subtle and wily. Lost in the war, of course, like everyone he had known, once.

The mist swirled 'round him, and it seemed for a moment that he saw the curve of a cheek, heard the firm tone of her voice—and *that*, he told himself, shaking the illusion away, was no more subtle than a bludgeon. Tanalore the White had fallen before despair and extremity had pushed those few of the Elders who were left into madness. *She* was no mist-wraith.

The mist, though. The mist. There was an odd texture to it, a coarseness, and a will to adhere that he did not associate with the similar mists of the *keleigh*. Perhaps confinement altered its substance. Though, if it were confined, he had yet to discover the walls that bound it.

Perhaps, he thought, it was *not* after all the same mist the *keleigh* manifested, but some other, created to mimic those terrible forces. He could not fathom the purpose of doing such a thing. Nor could he fathom Zaldore's reasons for turning upon him *now*. He had expected her to use him, and the *kest* he had collected, in her cause to depose the Bookkeeper Queen.

After—that was when he had looked for treachery. Well. Soon enough to learn the answer to this mystery when he had won free.

Perhaps, he thought, he had not been quite wise to accept Zaldore's invitation armored with only a tithe of the *kest* his pretty child had gathered for him. But, there. His own *kest* and wits had always been quite enough protection; and the gleanings were intended for another use.

It was warm in this place, wherever it was. Altimere shook a handkerchief from the mist and daubed the sweat from his forehead. He wondered—he did most seriously wonder, if he dared leave his chair and attempt to forge his own path through the mist. That would be a bold move. And risky; very, *very* risky.

If he meant to survive such boldness, he would need to move while his *kest* was resolute and his faculties intact. Too much of this—he dropped the handkerchief and watched it unmake itself, back into mist—too much of this would strain the reasoning even of an Elder.

Could it be, he asked himself, the thought skewering him like a bolt—that Zaldore's purpose was to strip him, not of *kest*, but of sanity?

Altimere sighed and settled back into his chair. Now *that*, he owned, was a disturbing thought, indeed.

Chapter Four

"NO," BECCA SAID, STANDING IN SHIFT AND PANTALOONS at the foot of her bed. "A *riding dress*, Nancy. *That* is a party dress."

It was a very pretty party dress—a confection of pale blues and pinks, cut low over the bosom, the high waist tied with a wide ivory ribbon—and it would, Becca thought with a shiver, look well on her. However, she was not so mad as to attempt to ride in such a thing. Rosamunde would have her on the ground in a heartbeat for such folly, nor would Becca blame her.

Before her, Nancy fluttered in midair, clearly agitated. She dropped the rejected frock on the floor, darted back to the wardrobe, and reappeared a moment later bearing a robe of diaphanous purple, stitched with hundreds of tiny mirrors.

"No," Becca said, keeping her voice firm and even, though she wanted to shout in frustration. "A *riding dress*."

Nancy threw the robe to the floor, where its mirrors

glittered disturbingly, dashed back and forth several times, then hovered bare inches from Becca's face, so that she could see the tiny silver face scrunched up in distress and the small hands twisting about each other.

"Never mind, then," Becca said, with an assurance she did not at all feel. "I'll fetch it myself." She closed her eyes, picturing the riding dress she had once owned, a lifetime ago, when being in town with Irene was the most excitement she had ever experienced, and the number of invitations tucked 'round the frame of her mirror was a matter of grave concern and no small amount of pride.

In those simple, happy days, her riding dress had been raspberry wool, with black frogs to close the jacket, and leather gloves dyed to match. She'd worn it with a high-necked ruffled blouse, and dainty black boots, shined until she could see her face in them, charmingly framed by a smart little hat with an ostrich feather curling along her cheek.

This dashing ensemble fixed before her mind's eye, Becca stepped to the wardrobe, and pulled open the door.

"Oh!" She could not quite contain that little gasp of surprise, though she had, she told herself sternly, hoped for nothing less.

She simply hadn't expected that it would work.

"Here," she said over her shoulder to her maid. "Help me with this."

Meri took his leave of Jack Wood, and struck off into the trees—not quite at random, for no one of the Forest Gentry was ever entirely random inside a wood.

Still, he did not willfully turn his steps to the north or to the east, but meandered as the short growth allowed it, listening the while for what the trees might tell him.

The floor of the wood was soft with old leaf, scattered with sticks and broken bits of branch. Shadow-flame and harper's-hood huddled under the protection of low shrubs, flaunting their bright petals. Overhead, a grey whistler gave note of his location and condition; he heard the call picked up a moment later, off to his right, and again, at the edge of his hearing, to the left.

Startled by his silent approach, a squirrel hurtled up a ralif, claws scrabbling noisily against the bark. A fallfox and her kits melted away from him, her eyes glowing golden among the winberige leaves as he passed.

In all of this he found only what he might expect of a elder, and somewhat sleepy, forest. He discovered no other fading, misty trees along his ramble, nor any signs of disease or predations other than those of old age. That this wood *was* old, he had no doubt. Broad trunks were warmly embraced by soft lichens; longhair moss wisped from the trembling fingers of conifers and the jagged ends of broken branches occasionally interrupted the symmetry of leaf and sky.

Meri paused once by a rotting stump, the tree laid out in broken segments along the forest floor, crumbling into the rich mold. He paused again by a tall pole of a tree, its bark polished away by the creatures who fed and sheltered inside its hulk, its once-proud branches now smooth stubs.

He paused a third time by a forest pool, and unwrapped the bread and cheese Elizabeth Moore had packed for him. As he ate, he listened to the birds, and the various sounds made by the small lives, and to the murmur of leaf against branch. Familiar sounds, and welcome to any Ranger who might find the way here, and rest a moment from wandering.

Indeed, thought Meri, as he bent to drink from the pool, all was as he might expect—saving one thing.

No single tree had spoken to him, either in welcome, or to ask his business among them.

⟨≈≈≈⟩

Her books were in the trunk under the window where she had left them, and what was left of her seeds, salves, and the little bag of duainfey.

"Get my shawl from the wardrobe, please, Nancy," she murmured, telling over these treasures with soft fingertips. These few things defined everything that remained of her dreams and hopes. She *was* an herbalist. A healer. A gardener. Those other things, that had been inflicted upon her, by her will or not—she was free of those things, as she was free of the collar and the compulsion of Altimere's will.

Free of everything, save memory.

There was a flutter at the edge of her vision. She turned as Nancy alighted on the bed, spreading out a crimson shawl gaudy with gold thread and long silk tassels. Becca sighed, quietly. It was not, after all, the shawl she had taken away from her father's house, but—'twould serve.

'Twould serve.

"Thank you," she said, and picked up Sonet's book, awkwardly one-handed. She placed it on the shawl, and had scarcely turned back for the rest when a flutter of wings warned her, and Nancy alighted with

Becca's own journal under one arm and the bags of
salves and seeds in the other hand.

She placed the objects with care, then rose into
the air, gathering the corners of the shawl into her
hands and knotting them.

"Thank you," Becca said again, reaching for the
packet. She snatched her hand back as Nancy darted
toward her, shaking her head from side to side, and
clearly expecting Becca to do—something.

"I—" She cleared her throat and inclined her head.
"I will be visiting a friend in—in another country," she
said slowly. "You are at liberty until Altimere returns."

Wings flashed, and Nancy shot toward the ceiling.
Another flash of wings and she was hovering bare
inches from Becca's nose, her face twisted in obvious
distress, hands gripped together as she were praying.

"Nancy, I am grateful for your service," Becca
said, tears rising to her eyes in response to the little
creature's pain. "I would take you with me, if I could.
But—Altimere made you, and it is him that you serve,
not me."

Nancy extended a hand and grasped Becca's collar, and now she could see that her abigail's face was
glistening as if with—but surely not! Nancy was a
construct! Surely a machine could not weep?

And yet it did seem as if Nancy were weeping—very
likely in terror of what would become of her, when
Altimere returned to discover Becca gone.

It was, Becca allowed, a predicament with which
she had some sympathy.

"Very well," she said softly. "I accept your service.
You may accompany me if you are able. Whatever
binds you is yours to break."

For a moment it seemed as if Nancy were frozen in air; then she bolted upward, turning a series of handsprings. She dove then to the bed, snatched up the shawl-wrapped packet, and darted toward the door.

"Yes," Becca murmured, sending one more glance around the sun-drenched room. "It is certainly time for us to go."

Sian was waiting in the hall below. Her eyebrows rose as Becca came down the ramp, but she made no comment, either on Becca's choice of clothing or the tiny naked woman who flew at her shoulder, bearing a bundle twice her size.

"Did Altimere's library pall?" Becca inquired, as she gained the hall.

Sian swept her an extravagant bow.

"In the sense that I was not allowed to remove any books from their places on the shelf—it did. One rapidly grows weary of admiring handsome bindings."

"In that case I am sorry to have kept you waiting so long."

"Please don't trouble yourself on my account," Sian told her with an earnestness Becca could not but feel was utterly false. "I exist to serve."

"You will then be relieved to learn that my horse is being brought 'round and that we may leave immediately your own has been saddled."

Sian gave her a sideways smile, eyes glinting, and Becca had a moment to wonder if she was quite wise to tweak the Fey woman. And yet, she thought rebelliously, she was Sian's prisoner, hostage to the Queen's command. Why should she pretend it suited her?

And if Sian were to place you into the sort of slavery from which you have only just recently won free? a cool voice murmured inside her head.

Becca's step faltered. Nancy, taken by surprise, bumped her shoulder with the bundle she carried, wings fluttering in agitation. Ahead, the door opened slowly, drawn by a pair of Gossamers, a tentative cast to their appendages. Becca bit her lip and quickened her step. She did not want to give the Gossamers time to think about her departure and their part in it. For the Gossamers were also Altimere's creatures, and who knew what punishments they might be meted, when the master discovered that she was gone.

"There is no need," Sian said at her shoulder, "to run, Rebecca Beauvelley."

Becca took a breath, a tart rejoinder on her tongue— then forgot everything: her fear, her situation, and the unlikelihood of her escape from either. She had eyes and thought only for the chestnut filly standing there, her reins in the keeping of a Gossamer, ears cocked forward at an interested angle, the star on her forehead blazing bright white.

"Rosamunde!"

Joy lanced through her, and she was across the courtyard, her arm around that elegant neck. Her hat had fallen off in her rush, or Rosamunde had pushed it away, so she could lip Becca's hair.

"Beautiful lady, I've missed you," she crooned, rubbing her cheek against the silken mane. Rosamunde whuffed, her breath warm and smelling of clover.

"We'll never be parted again," Becca whispered. "I swear it."

Rosamunde whuffed again, and there came the sound of hooves, walking purposefully.

Becca raised her head as a dappled grey with a mane like sea-froth strolled, riderless into the court-yard, reins loose along the proud neck.

"Well!" Sian said brightly behind her. "And here is my horse! We may leave at once." A low whistle followed. The grey whickered gently, strong ears flicking.

"Brume, old friend." The Fey woman's voice was soft now; tender, as if she spoke to a child. "Wilt bear me home?"

The grey blew and shook his head, as if laughing, then extended his right foreleg and bent his left, bowing, or so it seemed to Becca.

"Your spirit is wide and your heart is great," Sian murmured, moving past Becca and Rosamunde as if they were as tenuous as Gossamers. "There is no other like you."

She threw a long leg over the grey's back and settled herself in the saddle. Brume rose, and stood, the Engenium looking down at Becca.

"Do you require assistance to mount, Rebecca Beauvelley?"

Becca turned without answering, aware of a blur of color near Rosamunde's flank. Nancy still bore the bundle, though it must, Becca thought with a flash of guilt, weigh on her cruelly.

She turned, fumbling one-handed with the strap on the saddlebag. Something cool brushed her fingers—tentacles, she saw, deft and sure. The strap loosened, the flap came up and Nancy flittered forward to slip the precious shawl-wrapped bundle inside.

That done, the Gossamer pulled the strap tight.

"Thank you, Nancy," Becca said, and to the Gossamer. "Help me to mount, please."

She felt the pressure about her waist, and a moment later was settling into the saddle, the neat split riding skirt seeming a frivolous affectation in comparison to Sian's spare elegance.

"It is well," the Engenium said. "We take our leave now." Brume turned and moved out of the courtyard.

"Follow, please," Becca whispered into Rosamunde's ear. "We must do as she says until we can think of another way to keep ourselves safe, and together."

⸎

Meri finished his bread and cheese, washed his hands in the pool, and walked out to the center of the grove, his arms wide and his face turned up toward the leaf-shrouded sky. His chest was tight, his meager *kest* rising to cast dancing shadows among the lower plants. It had been many seasons since he had offered himself formally to a forest. Even after his long sleep, the trees had known him, welcoming him by name, respectful of his diminished power.

This wood, though... It was not merely that this wood did not know *him*. It was as if this wood knew *nothing*; as if it had dreamed itself out of the Vaitura entirely, leaving behind only empty trunks.

"I am," he said, his voice solemn, as befit this venerable and subdued place, "Meripen Vanglelauf, Wood Wise and Ranger. My purpose is to uphold the ancient covenant. Of my own will, I seek the trees. Of my own heart, I serve them."

His words rang for a moment against the air, then faded, as if swallowed by the forest's dream.

Meri took a breath, lowered his arms slowly, and stood, head bent. Disdained, his *kest* fell. He shivered in the absence of its warmth.

Sighing, he crossed to the pool, drank, and stood. He felt the veriest sprout, roundly ignored by his elders, and laughed wryly, recalling Jamie Moore's hot assertion that the trees spoke to him—and his wilting when Jack Wood had pointed out that the trees did not share their pain with him.

His thought snagged on that, and he frowned, frozen in the act of reaching for his pack.

The trees near the homestead had not only spoken to him, they had *known* him. Indeed, now that he cast his mind back, there had been tree chatter and a sense of regard this morning as he had walked out with Jack Wood, until—

Until they had come upon the larches, cloaked in their uncanny stillness. He must have been more distressed than he had understood, but yes, now that he thought, it was precisely as if the larches had marked a boundary between forests, as sharp and distinct as a wall between rooms.

Meri shook himself, grabbing up his pack and his bow.

All very well to pinpoint where the problem began. It was, he allowed, a step. However, his duty lay in the direction of discovering what the problem *was*, and doing his utmost to repair it.

Well.

Meri swung the pack up and settled it across his shoulders. Whatever it was that made this wood so strange and dreamy, it lay ahead of him. That, too, was a step.

"Steps enough," he sing-songed for his own amusement, "a journey do make."

He shook his head and moved off, with a Ranger's
ground-eating stride, one more silence among many.

Nancy settled on Becca's shoulder, one tiny hand
wound in the hair over her ear, pulling uncomfortably.
Becca began to speak—then stopped, suddenly aware
that her maid was trembling violently, her spasms
increasing as they came nearer the arched shrubbery
that marked the end of Altimere's garden.

Ahead of them, Sian and Brume passed through
the arch. Nancy's grip became excruciating; Becca
gasped, and bit her lip.

Rosamunde passed under the shrubbery. Becca took
a hard breath, tasting the lemony scent in the back
of her throat, and Nancy—

Nancy *screamed*.

Becca started, jerking the reins, Rosamunde danced,
steadied as her rider made a brief recover, then skit-
tered as Becca sagged, her shoulder abruptly ground
beneath an appalling weight.

Nancy's scream went on, high and hopeless, ragged
with agony. Becca pulled on the reins, and screamed
herself as the banshee on her shoulder spasmed, tearing
her handful of hair out by the roots. Becca pitched
forward, her braid snapping free of its pins, her heels
striking Rosamunde's side, and her horse *leaped*, hitting
the street with a clatter, charging Brume's flank. The
grey spun, ears back and teeth showing, while Sian
raised a hand shrouded in turquoise mist, and cried
out in a voice that brooked no argument, "Hold!"

Rosamunde slammed to a halt, throwing Becca forward, left hand tangled painfully in silky mane, right arm flung 'round a sweating neck while Nancy arced into the air like a stone from a catapult, scream trailing behind her—and cut off abruptly as she was surrounded by a turquoise-barred cage.

"Wrack and wind!" The bars solidified. Nancy threw herself onto her face, wings trembling.

"Release her at once!" Becca cried, pushing herself awkwardly up into the saddle, Rosamunde unnaturally still beneath her. "And remove your will from my horse!"

Sian raised haughty eyebrows. "Do you order *me*?" she asked, cold-voiced.

Becca shook the loose braid behind her shoulder and stiffened her spine. She ought, she knew, be afraid, but what she felt was anger, and a rising warmth. The day glittered at the edges, showing stipples of gold and copper.

"Do you infringe on my rights?" she snapped, hot to the Fey woman's cold. "My horse, Madam Engenium—and my servant!"

"The horse, I grant." A sweep of long white fingers and Rosamunde was moving, dancing nervously. Becca consciously adjusted her seat, and leaned forward to pat the proud neck.

"Gently, my lady," she murmured. "We have an agreement to reach."

"An agreement to *easily* reach," Sian snapped, and the bars enclosing Nancy contracted. "Surely neither of us desires one of Altimere's creatures by us on our journey."

"Nancy is *my servant*," Becca said, swallowing against the heat rising in her blood. "I told her that I would accept her service, if she won free of Altimere's influence." She moved a careful hand, startled to see a wisp of golden fog following her fingers. "I believe that she has done as much—as I have, myself."

Huddled on the bottom of the cage, the little creature nodded vigorously.

"You see?"

Sian shook her head. "Altimere's creature is under no geas to be truthful to you—or to me."

"I believe her," Becca said flatly. "And you harm my servant at your peril, Engenium."

There was a moment, a long moment, where the air seemed to heat uncomfortably, and sparks of gold, green, blue, and copper glittered like snowflakes in the sunlight. Becca heard a ghostly crashing, as if of waves striking rock, and a rumble as of a storm building . . .

Brume shook his head, frothy mane slapping the sides of his neck, and executed a sharp dancestep.

A damp breeze struck Becca sharply on the cheek, teasing the bars of Nancy's cage into mist. The little creature sprang aloft the instant the last wisp of turquoise had drifted away, did a double loop, and came to rest on the pommel of Becca's saddle. She knelt there and kissed Becca's hand. Her lips were cold and hard.

"You are welcome, Nancy," Becca murmured. "I trust we will have no more unseemly displays. Now, if you please, prepare yourself to ride."

Nancy leapt up. Following the flicker of color, Becca saw her settle on top of the right-side saddlebag, her hand gripping the leather strap.

"Very well." She licked her lips, tasting salt, and faced Sian firmly. "We are ready, Engenium."

"Not quite." Sian bent a stern, sea-colored gaze

upon her, and Becca felt a thrill of terror, that she had dared to set her will against this Fey, who was powerful beyond a mere woman's reckoning.

"If that creature behaves in any way that I find threatening to myself, my land, or my people, I will destroy it, Rebecca Beauvelley—and you will not be able to stay my hand. Do you believe me?"

Becca bowed her head, awed, and somewhat unsettled in her stomach. Had her time with Altimere made her mad, after all? How had she thought to stand against so puissant a lady?

"I believe you," she said submissively.

Sian might have snorted, or she might have laughed. Whichever, she did turn her horse, with a click and a lean, and moved off down tree-lined road, Rosamunde following before Becca gave the signal.

❧

If the path would not appear, he would make his own, as ever he had.

Altimere rose from his chair, shook out his lace, took a deep breath of warm, mist-tainted air, and took a single step forward.

It was as if he tried to push himself through a stone wall. He exerted his will, his *kest* rising in a blaze of silvered reds.

The mist around him flared sullen pink, gave—and tightened like a drumhead, flinging him back, off his feet, willy-nilly into the chair, ghostly hands around his throat.

"I do not permit!" The mist filling his mouth softened the shout to a whisper, but it would appear that in this, his will was, yet, sufficient.

The pressure around his throat faded.

He was alone in his chair, surrounded by mist.

Deliberately, Altimere sat upright, adjusted his collar, and closed his eyes.

He had not wished to do this; had not wished to place his pretty child in peril. But where was her safety, with him imprisoned?

Gathering his *kest*, he composed himself, and mentally told over those things which were bound to him. Not for him the gemstones and flowers braided into the hair, nor the knotted bits of silk. No; *he* was Altimere of the Elder Fey, and he had no use for such stratagems and tricks.

It was the necklace he reached for, showing blackly iridescent before his mind's eye. He did not like to endanger his child in this way, but, really, what choice did he have?

Altimere touched the necklace with his will, issued the command—

...and cried out as the image faded away into the mist, leaving an echoing emptiness behind.

Chapter Five

IT WAS IMPOSSIBLE TO TELL PRECISELY WHEN THE city became the countryside. Eventually, the road began to wind a little more among the trees, the shrubbery grew thicker and even less restrained, the now-and-then glimpse of an open window or the gable of a wooden roof grew rarer, and then ceased altogether.

They rode single file, and at a rapid walk, Sian in the lead. The road was wide enough for them to have gone side by side, but Becca wished to be alone with her thoughts.

Such thoughts they were! She had no notion of the geography of the Vaitura; indeed, she could not recall having seen a map of the land in the books she had struggled to decipher in the library at Altimere's country seat. There had not even been a map on the wall, which in retrospect was odd. Her father had a large and handsome colored map of the Midlands over the fireplace in his library at Barimuir House. She wondered at herself, that she had never noticed the lack in the library at Artifex. Surely, she thought, a great and elder lord living so close to the border would have maps at hand? Then she thought again. Perhaps there *had* been a map, after all, and Altimere merely willed her not to see it.

It came over her all at once, a longing for those days before she had fully understood what she had agreed to, in her ignorance and her folly. When she had believed herself safe, cherished, protected.

Loved.

Tears rose to her eyes, and she wanted nothing more than to be in her bath, ignorant and happy, Altimere lounging carelessly at the water's edge, his hair gleaming in the candlelight, the crimson dressing gown falling open over his smooth white chest.

Beneath her, Rosamunde's purposeful walk changed in response to her rider's inattention. Becca drew a shaky breath and adjusted her seat; Rosamunde's gait smoothed, and her ears flicked, as if to say, "Next time, I shall not be so gentle with you!"

"You are a marvel of patience and forbearance," Becca murmured, her voice choked with tears. "Indeed, *indeed*, I will try to deserve you."

Rosamunde snorted, and ahead of them, Sian looked back.

"We will rest after we have crossed Horn's land, Rebecca Beauvelley," she said. "Stay close and do not dawdle."

Becca swallowed a hot retort with the last of her tears, reminding herself that Sian had every reason to be doubtful of Becca's horsewomanship, after the display in Altimere's courtyard, but to assume her in need of rest after so short a time in the saddle as this!

Altimere had coddled her, unwilling in the extreme to try her physical strength. But he had never suggested that riding should exhaust her or that she might tire more easily than a three-year-old.

Sian does not know you, Gardener, and she is of two branches. On the one branch, she wishes to be away. Yet on the second branch, she would not risk your health.

"Because the Queen requires my testimony to strip Altimere of his honors and remove him from his place on the Constant, you mean," Becca muttered.

The concern we hear has to do with your health, Gardener. She considers that you have borne much, and before your roots were well set. This decision that you had taken, to end your growth, she fears it as a sign of a deeper malaise, which has not yet been cured. There was a pause, and then . . .

To end your own growth . . . that thought is unsettling, even to trees.

"Trees die," Becca muttered, as Rosamunde followed Brume 'round a corner in the path. "Certainly," she added, "Fey die." She shivered in the sunlight.

And sometimes trees and Fey too die at a time or in a manner of their own choosing, the tree said inside her head. *But to choose a death without first making a repository of what you have learned, and to make disposition of your kest—that is alien to trees and to Fey.*

Becca bit her lip and looked down between Rosamunde's ears. The voice in her head had sounded stern, censorious. Yet, what did trees know of subversion, lies—of betrayal? A tree was a simple thing; it grew or it did not. A tree could not be forced to murder a friend or be used as bait, to trap for the unwary.

Ahead, Sian raised her hand, signaling a stop. Becca obediently pulled up, raising her chin when the Fey woman turned in the saddle.

"We are fortunate that the Queen's artificer is elderly and prone to napping," Sian said. "The shortcut is still in place." She beckoned with long fingers. "Come here."

Becca urged Rosamunde forward until they were side by side with Sian. Rosamunde whickered as they drew up, and Brume turned his proud head to look down at her.

"Attend me, Rebecca Beauvelley," Sian said sternly, and Becca determinedly met her eyes. "Our journey from fair Xandurana to my own holding by the sea is made shorter and less wearing by use of a particular piece of artifice. To invoke it is expensive of *kest*, and some find it unnerving to traverse. But it is far less enervating than riding long days across the Vaitura. Look ahead and behold the construct of which I speak."

Frowning, Becca did as she was told. At first, she saw only trees, and the path, and a pair of redbirds playing tag in midair, twittering gaily to each other.

One of the birds dashed upward, wings flashing, and she saw it, beyond their bright busyness, like dark draperies moved by a slow, malicious wind.

"The *keleigh*!" she gasped, and turned to stare at Sian. "Is your home beyond the Boundary, then?"

"Beyond the Boundary?" Sian repeated. "How would that be?" She shook her head. "As to the nature of the artifice, you are both correct and incorrect. The substance and force are like unto the *keleigh*, but this is smaller, and transient. We shall ride but a small distance, yet cover leagues. This shortcut has been raised as a courtesy to the Queen's Constant, and will not maintain much longer."

Becca's eyes were drawn again to the bruised and billowing air. "I understand," she said.

"Good. Now, as I have said, some find the transition unsettling, though very few so much that they choose instead to ride the entire distance between Xandurana and their own lands. You may bandage your eyes, if you wish, and I will lead you."

"Why should I bandage my eyes?" Becca demanded, though in truth the movement of air against air was... disturbing. "I have crossed the *keleigh* itself, with my eyes open and my horse under my hand."

Sian's eyebrows rose. "Did you indeed," she murmured. Before Becca could reply, she inclined her head with every indication of courtesy. "I had no wish to offend you," she said, and took up reins.

"We go, before the gate is sealed. We will ride as hard as Brume allows, for he is the best judge in the places between. Keep hard by us. When we emerge, we will be on the border of Horn's land. Follow us closely; and *do not* for any reason dismount. Horn dislikes travelers, and has been known to harry stragglers on the road. We will rest once we have come under Sea Hold's branches. Do you understand me?"

Did the Fey think she was a child or a witling? Becca thought, a hot retort rising to her lips.

To Sian, as to us, you are the veriest sprout, Gardener.

Becca swallowed and inclined her head. "I will follow closely," she said, keeping her voice soft with an effort. "And I will not dismount until you give me leave."

"I have your word," Sian said, and it seemed that her voice echoed against the warm breeze, a thing of substance, and of portent. Becca tensed, expecting— what? she asked herself. A strike? A compulsion.

Apparently ignorant of the apprehension she had caused, the Engenium had turned away.

"By your grace, old friend," she said to her horse, and Brume walked deliberately forward.

"Now us," Becca murmured, dry-mouthed, into Rosamunde's ear. "This will be as nothing to you, brave heart." She glanced down to where Nancy sat on the saddlebag, her hands gripping the strap. "Stay there," she said sternly. The tiny creature nodded vigorously as Rosamunde stepped forward, toward the billowing curtain of power.

※

The wood grew darker, as if he had walked the day down into night. The voices of birds and the sounds of those others who lived among the trees faded into silence. Even the breeze stilled. The still air was surprisingly warm, and tasted of dead greenery.

Meri paused beneath the branches of an elitch, and pressed his palm against the trunk.

"I am Meripen Vanglelauf. Is there any small service which I might be honored to perform for you, Elder?"

Silence was his answer, stretching uneasily along the quiet air. At last, Meri took his hand away, stepped back and bowed.

"Elder," he murmured.

Straightening, he settled his bow, and touched the elitch wand in his belt. Thus comforted, he walked on, ever deeper into the dim, breath-caught wood.

◆≈≋≋≋≈◆

Brume vanished between one step and the next, sublimated into the chancy air. Becca took a breath, glanced down to be sure of Nancy, and prompted by a memory both compelling and confusing, tucked her crippled left hand between the saddle and Rosamunde's warm withers.

"Stay close," she whispered, something that felt like laughter and terror combined cramping her chest, then there was the veriest flutter against her cheek and they were in.

Heat struck her face, followed by a slap of cold; wind skirled, lashing Rosamunde's mane, and casting mist into Becca's eyes. She blinked it away and shook her head, trying to banish the persistent fizzing sound. Leaning forward, she sighted a horse-sized disturbance in the mist, outlined in a wash of turquoise, cantering.

She leaned forward, and Rosamunde increased her pace, though it seemed that the turquoise-dyed shadow was pulling ahead of them.

Becca could not hear her hooves strike over the clamor in her ears, and a man's voice, as plain as if he rode beside her—

"Rebecca! Come here; I want you!"

The mist swirled, the voice was lost, even as she turned her head, and surely there was a face, right *there*, inside the tricksy air? A man, his hair bright in the mist, and a long, white hand outstretched to—

Sunlight broke the vision, the mist ahead was sundered, and she could see green fields, with trees in the distance, and on her right hand a rolling hill.

Ahead, Sian, the Engenium of Sea Hold, pulled

her horse around, her face perfectly expressionless as Becca rode toward her.

"Look," she said, and nodded.

Becca looked over her shoulder, at the dusky curtains twisting in a turbulent, unfelt, wind. From somewhere, a chime sounded, so pure and sweet that tears rose to Becca's eyes. A blade of sheer silver light split the uncertain air; the curtains folded, collapsed—and vanished. Behind them was only a country lane, winding and pleasant, and the sun, high over the trees.

"What would have happened," Becca asked, her voice thin in her own ears, "if we had still been— in—there?"

"Why, then we would have become wanderers in the mist," Sian answered, her own voice somber. "Doomed to dwell in the places between."

Becca looked at her, but the Fey woman's face was as stern as her voice. "It is said that a rider may hear the voices of the heroes who fell to the *keleigh*, inside the shortcuts and the bypaths."

"This..." Becca swallowed to settle her suddenly rebellious stomach. "The path we took was *not* the *keleigh*, you said."

"It was not the *keleigh*, yet for the space of its existence it partook of the same energy, and existed in the same plane. What is lost at the Boundary may be seen in the mists of a conjure-bridge, far inland. But it may never be recovered."

Sian shook her head suddenly, as if she cast such dire thoughts behind her, and turned her horse. "Come. Let us put this place behind us."

It was hot in this place, and the mists were— surely!—thicker. Altimere shifted in his chair. His back hurt, and he was parched.

From time to time, he heard things. Chimes, hoof-beats, a glissade of harp strings, voices. He knew them all for phantoms, produced by his own ears in defense against the ongoing tedium of silence.

Enclosed by ghosts and mist, he grappled with his loss.

The necklace, the great artifact that tied his Rebecca to his will, kept her turbulent nature compliant, and her intellect confused—the necklace had been destroyed.

It was, naturally, possible for the necklace to give up its form and substance and return to the elements from which he had shaped it. He was no fool, to think that an artifact once found useful would undergo no future sea change which transformed it from favored tool to implacable enemy. One had only to witness the *keleigh* to see the folly in that.

However, it would have been rank folly to have built a wide vulnerability into so powerful an arti-fact. He had done all within his considerable skill to ensure that the only two persons who could break the necklace were himself—and Rebecca.

That Rebecca had found the fortitude and focus to overcome the disincentives that had been forged into the necklace at its making—was . . . difficult to encompass. And yet, he could conceive of no other, now that his own teacher, Sanalda, had passed on to greater wisdom.

His mist-stuffed ears could not hear his laughter, so he could not judge its temper.

Passed on to greater wisdom—that was what they

had said, back before the fall of civilization and the
sundering of the world. Now, those who would be
truthful might say, *who had been extinguished by her
pupil's ambition*.

Something had gone amiss, when he had used
Rebecca to—mincing no words!—*murder* Sanalda.
It had hardly been the best use of his tool, but
more—the bond between teacher and student was
not lightly sundered, nor was the act likely to leave
either unscarred. If—

He stiffened in his chair, caught by that last thought.
Surely, the bond between teacher and student was
potent, as was the bond between those others who
regularly shared *kest*.

Such as himself and his pretty Rebecca.

Scarcely had he articulated the thought than hope
blazed, his *kest* rose, and he flung his will against
the mist.

Rebecca! Come here! I want you!

Chapter Six

"THERE IT IS! STOP IT BEFORE IT FINDS THE TREES!"

The shout was followed by a horn blast, and howls of the sort that small boys are wont to make when they have the barnyard cat on the run, and beneath it all the sound of hoofbeats, pounding against the land.

Brume lengthened into a gallop, mane flying, Sian low on his neck.

Becca threw herself forward. "Follow!" she cried.

Rosamunde needed no more urging. She stretched into her silk-smooth run and was through the long corner in a flash, bursting out into a wide clearing.

Becca shook the hair from her eyes. Ahead, Sian and Brume raced, angling to the right, where three horses bearing three of the High Fey were at full gallop through the long grass, in hot pursuit of what Becca at first thought must be a rabbit.

Bandy legs flashed, a tufted tail slashed among the weeds. Becca urged Rosamunde to greater speed, angling as Brume did, to get between the exuberant riders and the desperate wild thing—one of the very wild things that Elyd had warned her against!

"What's this! They'll spoil the sport!" One of the pursuing Fey shouted. "Fendri, your cord!"

Becca looked up, seeing the rider farthest from her throw a long line weighted with stones into the air over his head. The cord danced between long white fingers, stones blurring. The quarry threw itself forward, the weeds catching at its scanty breech, cuts and scrapes showing on one hairy forearm. It carried one hand tucked into the opposite armpit, which put its gait off, and that hand was bleeding—profusely.

"Stop!" Sian's voice rang clarion across the clearing, echoing back from the trees they had just quit. She threw her hand out, and a turquoise wave burst from her fingertips, rolling across the grasses toward the three riders—

Who passed through it as if it were the merest nothing.

"*You* have no power of command here!" the middle rider shouted—and in that instant, the farthest rider loosed his cord.

Becca leaned; obedient, Rosamunde flung herself at right angles, making a turn that should have broken her back and her rider's too, and was flying over the hard ground, hooves thundering.

They would be too late, Becca saw with anguish. The spinning cord cut the air with horrifying quickness. Even if she and Rosamunde got between it and the fleeing creature, however would they bring it harmlessly down?

The cord whistled by, two horse-lengths ahead and

well above Becca's reach—there was a flash of jeweled wings, the cord stopped in midflight, spinning crazily in place as Nancy held on to the center, feet braced against the air, wings spread as the cord spun slower, and slower—and stopped altogether, hanging limp from tiny hands.

Becca pulled back on the reins and Rosamunde danced to a stop.

"Well done, Nancy!" she cried, even as the hunted creature threw itself to the ground and rolled between Rosamunde's hooves, where it cowered, its good arm over its unkempt head.

"*You* have no power of command here!" the center youth cried again, but his horse stuttered beneath him, as if unsure of its direction, then stopped as Brume pushed forward and Sian snatched the bridle.

"Warded land or no!" she snapped. "It is against the compact to hunt the Brethren, as well you know it, Narstaft!"

"I know that you are interfering in a private affair!" the youth shouted, petulantly, to Becca's ear.

Bright colors flashed at the edge of her vision, she looked up—and bit her lip to keep from laughing aloud. Two arm-lengths above her head, Nancy was solemnly skipping rope with the captured hunting-cord.

"That is mine! Return it!" Fendri, who had thrown the cord, commanded, his voice flattening the grasses. A whimper came from the creature trembling between Rosamunde's feet.

Up in the air, Nancy stopped her game and stood pensive, wings half-furled, hunting-cord held negligently in a diminutive hand, head tipped consideringly to one side. As clearly as if it were happening, Becca saw her maid toss the cord above her head, twirling it until it was less than a smear upon the air, and release it to its owner.

"No!" Becca cried out and raised her hand, sparkles of gold dripping from urgent fingertips. "Nancy, please take the cord over to that larch and loop it *gently* in the topmost branch."

"That is not acceptable!" the owner of the cord shouted. He took a breath, his outline beginning to show distinct flashes of red. "I demand—"

"Be quiet, you fool!" Someone snapped. Becca gasped, belatedly recognizing the voice as her own. "Or be sure that she *will* return it—and break your neck into the bargain! Go, Nancy."

"Is that a *threat*, Wood Wise?" The High Fey urged his horse forward two reluctant steps, his seat so stiff it was a wonder, Becca thought, that he remained horsed at all.

"It is a *statement*," she said, flatly.

"They do grow bold, don't they?" He looked to his companions, neither of whom seemed inclined to support him, then back to Becca. "What is your *name*?" He spat the last word as if it tasted vile.

Becca drew herself up, pretending not to see Sian's sharp sign of negation.

"My name is Rebecca Beauvelley," she said, into a sudden, perfect and windless silence. Sian shook her head.

"Rebecca— By the architecture of the sky!" the youth Sian held swore. "It's Altimere's pet!" His horse stamped, as it caught its rider's horror.

Rebecca pulled herself up—and this time heeded Sian's signal. Bad enough to have named herself. To assert that she was her own woman, free of Altimere's influence, would be fatal.

Might already have been fatal.

"Perhaps you would consider betaking yourselves back to the safety of your house," Sian said in a voice that was too soft to reach Becca as clearly as it did. "Before word reaches the Grand Artificer that you have been discourteous to one who accepted his protection."

It went hard against their grain, Becca could see that, for they were high-blooded young men, but prudence won out. The quiet rider, who sat closest to Becca, turned his horse first and walked sedately away, not looking back.

After a moment, Fendri the cord-thrower turned his horse and followed.

"Release me," the center youth, Narstaft, snapped at Sian. "I wish no quarrel with Altimere."

"Your father, who has attained wisdom, and old age, wishes no quarrel with *the Queen*," Sian told him. "Be assured that I will write to him that his youngest son believes it sport to hunt the Brethren, despite the covenant."

Narstaft licked his lips, but—credit where it was earned—he did not look away.

"There is no need for you to trouble yourself, Engenium," he said quietly. "I will tell him of this encounter myself."

Sian nodded, and loosed his reins. "Good."

The youth turned his horse and rode away in the wake of his companions. Sian waited, watching, and Becca did likewise. When they had all three passed under the shadows of the trees—only then did Brume turn and walk toward them.

"That was remarkably foolish," Sian said, with, Becca admitted to herself, a great deal of restraint. "If you cannot control that artifact—"

"I have no need to control her," Becca interrupted. "She does admirably on her own."

"Between the pair of you, we are fortunate that we came out of that encounter as well as we did." She closed her eyes, took a deep breath—and exhaled. "Come," she said, "let us ride on. There is a good resting place just a little further on."

Becca shook her head, and slid off of Rosamunde's back, staggering where she landed.

"What," Sian demanded, "are you doing?"

"This—Brethren," Becca said, moving around to where the creature yet crouched between Rosamunde's hooves—"is wounded. I am an herbalist and a healer. It is my duty to do what I am able to ease pain and comfort the infirm."

She heard a loud exhalation of breath from above her as she knelt next to the shivering creature, but the Engenium said only, "Of course."

❧❦❧

Meri walked deliberately onward, mindful of where he put his feet among the shattered twigs and spiteful stones. He slowed, the air pressing him down. His head felt stuffed with old leaves and it seemed as if his blood moved sluggish in sediment-clogged veins.

Still, he went on, drinking from the water skin Elizabeth Moore had insisted he carry, and which he had thought a slight against his skills as a Ranger.

Now, it would seem that the lady knew more than she had said, for he dared not stop, at all, in this leaden, unnatural place—and certainly he could not dare to drink, though he passed a stream that seemed to run fresh enough, and a pool so clear he could see the pebbles resting beneath the still water's surface.

He shivered, trying to think—to think of the calamity that could have caused this, for here was not merely an elder wood in the final segments of its life. No, there was something else at play here; something he could not name, and horrifying, which nonetheless tantalized and teased his feeble *kest*, and it seemed to him that there were Newmen—no! There was *Michael himself* with his clever blade, and seductive aura, half-tucked behind a drooping pine, smiling a promise of pain and desire...

"You are false! A dream conjured of shadow and dust!" His voice was louder than he had intended, sounding curiously flat on the dead air. Michael's phantom shattered, becoming merely a random pattern of leaves and branches.

Meri raised the water skin and took a meager mouthful. When the flask was resealed and hung back in its place, he called out again.

"I am Meripen Vanglelauf, Ranger and Wood Wise, here at the service of the trees!"

There was no answer.

Meri walked on.

"Well, I can't treat it if you won't let me see it," Becca said tartly.

Wounded hand still tucked close under its arm, the Brethren stared at her. Its eyes were dark yellow, ringed with black, not quite the eyes of a beast—and not quite the eyes of a man—framed by black lashes as stiff and bristly as a scrub brush.

It closed first one eye, then the other, and turned its face away. Slowly, the wounded hand crept from its hiding place, until it was out, curled in on itself, the bloody back half-extended to Becca.

She sighed in relief.

"Thank you. I will be as gentle as I may be, but I do have to examine it, and it may hurt you. Please do not think that I am attacking you, or willfully causing you pain."

Her patient made no answer. Indeed, Becca thought, as she leaned to examine the offered appendage, she had no reason to believe that it could speak.

The hand was gory, blood gluing the plentiful coarse hairs together. There was no evidence of crushing, however, and it showed a full complement of four fingers and thumb, each capped with a horny nail.

Becca lifted her canteen and poured water over the wounded member. Blood and mud sluiced away, showing two long cuts in parallel, shallow toward the knuckle and deeper toward the wrist. Both began bleeding again, but slowly. She put the canteen aside and leaned forward.

"I am going to touch you," she told her patient, and did so, probing along the cuts. The Brethren shuddered, and she froze, but it made no other move. Letting her breath out quietly, she turned the hand over to inspect the leathery brown palm.

"There does not appear to be anything lodged in either cut," she said, turning the hand back over and lowering it slowly until the palm rested on her knee. "And they are already starting to crust over. This is excellent. However, you would not want your hand to become infected. I am therefore going to put fremoni salve on it and wrap it with a clean cloth." She considered the creature's profile, its hair wild and tangled around its ears.

"Nancy," she said, turning to look for her maid, who was hovering at shoulder height. "Please bring me the white pot."

The little creature flitted to the various vials and pots Becca had asked her to lay out from the saddlebag, lifted the white one, and settled it by Becca's knee, uncovered and ready for use.

"Thank you, Nancy," Becca murmured, her eyes still on her patient's odd profile. "I will need one of the clean cloths in a moment."

Glancing aside, she scooped up a generous portion of fremoni salve, and said, "This will sting. That means the medicine is working."

She smeared the salve onto the cuts, coating them well. Her patient twitched, muscles bunching, and for a moment she feared—but it only sighed gustily, and stared steadfastly away from her.

"Very good," Becca said truthfully. "Now we wrap it."

The cloth was to her hand; she nodded her thanks to Nancy and bound the creature's wounds, taking care with the knots and hoping that the bandage would last a day.

"There!" she said brightly, as Nancy bore the pot away. "Keep this clean and covered and in a week you will scarcely know you had taken hurt."

"Keep shy of Narstaft's bird traps and you'll not take hurt again," Sian said, dryly. Becca jumped, having forgotten the Engenium's presence in the necessity of tending the wounded creature, and looked over to where the Fey woman lounged in the grass, her head propped on one hand.

"Not bird trap," came a low, growly answer from Becca's erstwhile patient. The creature turned its massive head, eyes wide and yellow and staring at Sian. "*Brethren* trap."

They shared a long stare, the creature and the Fey, before Sian sighed. "Is that true?"

"Is it a lie?" returned the Brethren.

"Very likely it is not," Sian conceded. "But I haven't the time to deal with it now." She leapt to her feet, light as thistledown, and bent to offer a long hand to Becca.

"Now that your duty is done, herbalist and healer, may I humbly ask that we ride on?"

"Of course," Becca said, coolly. She put her hand carefully into Sian's as if she, as much as the creature she had just treated, were a wild and unpredictable beast, and was raised to her feet.

"Nancy—" she began, turning.

But her medicines and books were already gone, and Nancy was pulling the belt tight on the saddlebag, her wings flashing brightly in the sunlight.

Becca nodded. "Thank you, Nancy," she said quietly.

Chapter Seven

SHE HAD COME! ASTRIDE HER QUARTER-FEY HORSE, her aura blazing gold, sapphire, and green, so potent, it burned the very mist away. He extended his hand. She turned her head; she saw him!

The hungry mirk gusted, riding an unruly, unfelt wind. Rebecca rode on, leaving him alone inside the mist.

⟡

They stopped beneath a ralif tree. Sian reached into her flat saddlebag, and paused, sending a sidelong glance to Becca.

"If you will allow your servant to wait upon us?" she murmured.

Becca felt her face heat, and ducked her head. "Certainly," she murmured. "Nancy—if you please?"

Her maid flashed to the Engenium's side, receiving from her hand a flat loaf, a packet wrapped in seaweed, a bottle, and two wineglasses that could not have survived the gallop at which they had traveled this last hour and more.

"Against the trunk, if you will," Sian murmured, and Nancy flittered away as if her burdens were nothing, while the Fey woman pulled a rug from the saddlebag, and stroked Brume's neck.

"Forage, friend," she said, and sent another glance to Becca, "and the little lady, as well, if you allow it?"

"Certainly," Becca said again, and turned to stroke Rosamunde's nose. "Forage with the gentleman, bold one, and rest."

Rosamunde blew lightly against her hair, and turned her head, as if she considered Brume and weighed his merits as a guide in this place. The big horse flicked a tall grey ear and moved off.

After a moment, so as not to seem too eager, Rosamunde followed.

Becca turned and walked to the base of the ralif, where the rug was already spread, and the loaf laid out, the seaweed packets opened to reveal dried fish, and wine in two glasses held in Sian's long fingers.

"Come," the Fey woman said. "Sit. Eat. Rest."

"Thank you," Becca said, and put her hand against the trunk, using it to steady herself as she sat clumsily, her dress ruched untidily under her. Again, she envied Sian her trousers and shirt—and sighed as she received her glass.

"Our journey is almost over," Sian said, sipping her wine. "This evening, you will sleep among your own kind."

Becca lowered her glass, the wine untasted.

"I had thought— Your pardon. Have you reconsidered the Queen's directive, then?"

"Not at all. However, there is no reason that you cannot be as comfortable as possible, problem that you are."

Becca tasted her wine, the first sip taking the dust out of her mouth, the second bright and fruity and cheering.

"You will send me back to—back across the *keleigh*, then? To my own people?"

"She sends you to her tame Newmens," a growly voice said from too near at hand. Becca gasped, and started, her fingers happily tightening on the glass, so that she did not lose it.

"What," she gasped, "are you doing here?"

The Brethren shook its horns. "You are here," it said.

"Indeed, I am, but there is not the least reason that you need to be where I am!" Becca said hotly. "Your wound is dressed and will be perfectly fine, so long as you take some care."

"*Care*," the creature crooned, its voice unnervingly like hers in tone and timbre. "Take *care*."

Becca turned to Sian, who had broken off a piece of the flat bread and helped herself to a morsel of fish.

"Send it away!"

Elegant brows rose. "The Brethren are their own creatures; they come and go when and where they please. An' it *dis*please someone else, why! all the better." She raised her head to consider the creature under discussion. "Is that not so?"

"The Fey are easy to displease," it answered, and Sian, astonishingly, laughed.

"Why, so we are, indeed! So we are."

Becca looked for place to put her glass down, and found a flat rock by her knee. Next to it was a

large leaf with a broken bit of bread and some fish
laid out and ready to eat. She hesitated, wondering
if Sian had—then saw a flutter of wings as Nancy
darted past, across the picnic, beyond the margin of
the rug, where the Brethren crouched in the taller
grass, its heavy head bent.

It looked up as Nancy approached and Becca felt
her heart rise into her throat. One swipe of that hard,
leathery hand would shatter Nancy like a snowflake,
and yet she approached fearlessly, holding out a leaf
like that at Becca's side, also bearing bread and fish.

The Brethren growled, too low for Becca to be
certain that there were words spoken, and accepted
the offering, daintily for so wild and rough-looking a
creature. It took a bite of bread while Nancy hovered over its shoulder, rapt, and entirely careless of
her danger.

Becca took a breath and turned resolutely to Sian.

"Tame Newmans?" she asked, her voice sounding
tight and breathless in her own ears. "With collars and
compulsions and obedience layered in, Engenium?"

Sian looked up sharply, crimson limning the high
arc of each cheek. "Certainly not!" she snapped. "That
is not the way thinking beings treat each other!"

Becca raised her hand to her throat, staring into
the other woman's outraged eyes.

"Is it not?" she asked icily. "The greatest artificer
among the Fey; son of an ancient house of artificers;
a man of letters, who sits on the Queen's Constant—"

"Altimere is not only of an old house," Sian interrupted. "*He* is old. His views and attitudes were
formed before the war. Only Sanalda is older." She
moved her hand, seemingly forgetful of the bread and

fish she held. "He is brilliant, studied, mannerly, and very, very powerful. But he *is not civilized*! Altimere is the author of the *keleigh*, and if you suppose *that* to be civilized, you are a naif, indeed!"

"I rode through the *keleigh*," Becca reminded her, "in company with Altimere. I must say that he did not behave very much as if it were his creation. In fact, he seemed to be quite sensible of its dangers. If he were its master, surely he would know how to pass through unscathed and untroubled?"

"*Author* is not *master*," Sian said, and sighed sharply. "I did misspeak, a little," she admitted, reaching for her glass. "Altimere was one of *three* persons strong in *kest* and learned, who together crafted the *keleigh*. Which worked a wonder for what it was made to do, but soon overgrew itself."

"Gobble, gobble, gobble," the Brethren said in its growly, eerie voice. "Fey. Brethren. Newmens." It made loud, smacking noises, and Becca felt her stomach tighten.

"What reason could there have been to tamper with such terrible forces?" she demanded.

Sian looked away. "Terrible reasons," she said softly. "The Fey stood on the edge of annihilation; many of the Elders—our best and strongest philosophers and artificers—had already fallen before the enemy. They were desperate times and desperate answers were crafted." She nodded at Becca's untouched lunch.

"Best have that," she said. "We'll ride without pause once we're under way—and we must soon be gone." With that, she rose, effortless, and walked off.

Becca looked down at her untouched meal. She did not feel like eating—anything, really, much less dry bread and fish. On the other hand, it would not do to faint, and shame herself before Sian and her "tame Newmans."

She picked up a bit of bread and some fish and nibbled on it.

The fish was salty; the bread sweet. Together, they conspired into an unexpectedly pleasing taste, waking the appetite she thought had languished.

In short order, the portion laid out on the leaf was gone. Becca reached for her glass—and jumped as a low voice growled into her ear.

"I can show you the way."

The glass escaped her fingers; jewels flashed in her side vision, and Nancy caught it, slipping it back into her grasp most gently. Becca paused to be sure of herself, lifted the glass, and sipped before turning to stare at the Brethren.

"Can you, indeed," she said icily. "And I suppose you can kill the Engenium, too?"

Nancy sped in a tight circle, whether in exuberant anticipation or horror, Becca could not tell. The Brethren shook its horns, and growled.

"I can show you the way," it repeated.

Becca sighed and sipped her wine, dampening her dry mouth.

"What is your name?" she asked.

The Brethren leaped up, snarling, tail lashing, blunt fingers curled. Becca gasped, raised the glass, and threw what was left of the wine into its face. It roared, but before it could attack—if, indeed, it meant to do so—a flurry of color darted at its face. The Brethren batted at its tiny tormentor; improbably, Nancy dodged each blow, darting in again, and again.

"Enough!"

Sian's shout shook the air; loosened leaves and cones tumbled out of the tree and into Becca's hair. The Brethren froze, then leaped across the blanket and ran. Nancy dropped down, wings beating furiously, and patted Becca's face with cold, tiny hands.

"Are you well?" Sian asked, crouching down at Becca's side, her arms resting on her thighs.

"Well," she acknowledged and shook her head irritably. "Leave over, Nancy; I'm perfectly fine."

Her maid dropped down until she was perched on Becca's knee, her posture one of continued worry.

"What did you do to anger the Brethren?" Sian asked.

Becca sighed. "I asked its name."

"Oh." Sian stared at her. "Well, you wanted to be rid of it." She rose, shaking out her sleeves. "Time to mount up." She moved away, leaving Becca sitting with her back to the tree.

"Well," she said determinedly, and rolled clumsily to her knees. The dress was bunched inelegantly and she wavered for a moment, almost falling—and her elbow was caught in a strong grip. Steadied, she rose to her feet, shook the bits of leaf and bark off of her skirt, and inclined her head.

"Thank you, Nancy," she said, with what dignity she could muster. The little creature mimed a midair curtsy and began to zip away.

"Nancy—"

The wings hesitated. Nancy twirled 'round to face her.

"It was extraordinarily brave of you," Becca said, bending down to meet honey-yellow eyes, "to leap to my defense. I wish, however, that you not risk yourself. Something like that—Brethren—could break you with a touch of its hand."

Nancy tipped her tiny head to one side, mimed another curtsy—and was gone in a flash of wings, which was, all things considered, not the answer Becca had been expecting.

"At your leisure, Rebecca Beauvelley," Sian called from the back of her mount.

Becca sighed sharply and went to mount Rosamunde.

Meri walked, and occasionally stumbled, but he did not fall.

He moved inside almost total darkness, his steps lit only by the feeble glow of his own *kest*. The trees he walked among gave off no slightest glow, and yet—they were not dead; they had not so much given up their essence as been separated from it.

A stick turned under his foot, and he very nearly lost his balance. His mouth was dry, but the water skin was long empty. Perhaps his luck would turn, he thought murkily, and he would fall into a stream.

Soon, he thought, he would have to stop. He was worn and feeble, his legs trembling with strain. It was not a decision he made willingly, but it was apparent that if he did not rest soon, he would fall—and where he fell, he would lie.

Best, he thought laboriously, to pick his spot, than leave it to chance.

As for choosing his spot—that was trickier. Every time he placed his foot, he struck a stone, or a stick. He was so tired.

Ahead, a smear of light beckoned, green and fresh. Meri blinked, squinting his shorteye. He had walked so long among these frozen, unnatural trees—was his vision creating a dream of tree-aura, to comfort itself?

But, it appeared not. The aura grew brighter as he walked, as if it were not one, but several. Meri felt his heart lift, and he walked more quickly. A breeze sprang from somewhere and kissed his hot cheek. Above, dancing beyond the reach of high limbs, were stars.

Meri threw himself into a ragged run toward those bright and welcome auras. A cry broke from his lips as he flung himself to his knees at the base of a pine, and pressed hands and forehead against the aged trunk.

Sleepy, half-absent comfort flowed into him from the tree, and he bit his lip to keep from sobbing like a sprout. When he had control of himself, he looked up and about him.

Behind, there was darkness; before him was the glow of a elder, somewhat sleepy, but wholly natural wood. To his right was a stand of larch, glad in the vermilion robes of age, their aura a thing of icy menace.

He had walked full circle, Meri thought, sagging back against the pine, and was back near the Newman village.

Chapter Eight

THEY RODE ON INTO THE DUSK, BRUME'S LEAD A BIT longer than it had been, as Becca urged Rosamunde to a more considered pace.

At first, Sian had glanced over her shoulder often, to be sure that she followed; lately, she had looked less often. And that, Becca thought, was precisely what she wanted.

What she did *not* want, so she had quite decided over these last few hours, was to remain in the keeping of a Fey *or* to be brought as a prisoner among her own people, who would rightly despise her.

She would, therefore, part from Sian's company, and before they came upon this village of "tame Newmens."

And, she thought, chewing her lip, as dark was quick approaching, it was time to put her resolution to the test.

The idea of venturing alone into the nighttime woods was daunting, but perhaps, after all, she need not be without a guide.

"Nancy," she said softly, as if Sian could hear her across the distance, and over the noise of the horses. An instant later, she felt a tiny weight on her right shoulder and the touch of cool fingers on her ear.

"I wonder," Becca said, all but whispering, "if you might fetch the Brethren to guide us away—at once."

There was a momentary pause, as if Nancy considered the wisdom of this mad request; then she was gone in a flash of silver and jewels, streaking off toward the trees at trailside, and vanishing among the shadow-limned leaves.

Becca sighed, and leaned forward to whisper in Rosamunde's ear. "Be ready, bold lady. You will need to be clever, quick, and silent, which I know you are. We must depend upon the Brethren, but it is not necessary, I think, to trust it."

A strong ear flicked, as if in agreement. Becca sighed again, and looked about her.

How magical the forest seemed, with this new sight of hers! The trees each sported their own pale aura, plainly visible in the growing darkness. Ahead of them on the path, Sian's shroud of turquoise light also glowed brighter, bathing Brume's flank with ghostly radiance.

Becca glanced down at her own brown fingers, outlined in palest gold. A glance behind showed Rosamunde's flank likewise gilded.

She chewed her lip, wondering if Nancy would be able to find the Brethren quickly, and if it would be willing to guide her. She had angered it, after all, and there was nothing save her own folly to support her uneasy hope that the creature still followed their small party.

What if she had put Nancy into danger? She would never forgive herself, if her order had brought harm onto her maid. Why hadn't she simply guided Rosamunde off the track and taken her chances alone?

Because she was craven, she answered herself bitterly. If had not been, she would have faced the marriage her father had made for her, and tried to change the future Altimere had shown her. Surely, there must have been some way to turn Sir Jennet from malice toward—if not friendship, at least a sort of comfortable neutrality.

Ahead, Brume vanished 'round a curve in the trail. This would be the time to slip away, if she dared to—

A flash of silver drew her attention to the right, and there was Nancy, turning handsprings in the darkening air, perilously near the horned head of—was it the very Brethren whom they had rescued from the High Fey's hunt or another?

As if it heard her unspoken question, the Brethren raised its hand, white bandage glowing in the dusk.

"Now, Rosamunde," she whispered, and applied the lightest pressure on the reins.

◈⣿⣿⣿◈

His pride would not allow him to return among the Newmen looking as if he had rolled down a mountainside. Indeed, his pride had taken a severe drubbing and needed to be coddled.

Meri stripped off his leathers, begged a few leaves from a near-at-hand soapwort, and waded into the darkling pool, disturbing the leaves reflected on its surface. A Wood Wise—nay, *a Ranger*—who had become lost under leaf? *There* was a tale to set Sian's court howling with laughter. He moistened the leaves, and scrubbed himself briskly, giving no quarter to aching muscles.

There was, of course, he admitted to himself, dunking his head beneath the cold water, something else, far more daunting than merely becoming lost.

He had been afraid.

Yes, there was the core of his shame. He, a Ranger, who had given his willing service to the forests of the Vaitura—he had *been afraid* of the trees under which he had walked. He had *run away*, to pile shame upon shame, and wept like a child on receiving the comfort of an elder.

Best for all if he returned to Sian immediately, and confessed his failure. After she was done laughing, she might send someone competent to mend...whatever was wrong. While he—

Well, he asked himself, ironically, *and what will you do? Offer yourself to the sea?*

Meri soaped himself a second time, submerged, and burst to the surface. He wrung his hair out and quit the pool. Shivering, he pulled his clothes on, and braided his wet hair, the memory of those cold, unnatural trees still in his mind.

In his years of wandering, he had never seen such trees, nor heard of their like from any other Ranger he had met on the trail.

"Of course," he muttered, shrugging his pack on and picking up his bow. "You were asleep for almost nine thousand nights, all praise to the chyarch of Ospreydale. Who knows what wonders may have sprung up in your absence?"

And, yet, the trees. Surely the trees knew of this affliction. And what the trees knew, they passed on to the Rangers.

Didn't they?

"What ails them?" he aloud, hoping that one, at least, of the sleepy elders might hear him—and answer.

He waited, eye closed and mind still, respectful of their age. When he opened his eye again, the early stars were flirting in the darkening sky.

A moment more he stood, considering his options. His instinct was to return immediately to Sea Hold and lay all before his cousin Sian. However, courtesy required he properly take his leave of Sian's Oath-held, and warn them to avoid the trees beyond the larch. Jack Wood might not have the eyes of a young man, or of a Wood Wise, but he clearly had access to other senses which had given him some small knowledge of the wood's strangeness.

Definitely, Jamie Moore, who was to all Meri's senses a proper Wood Wise sprout, should be told of the strange trees and warned away from the deep wood. Such trees had the power to confuse an experienced Ranger; he did not wish to consider what they might do to a sprout.

He settled his pack, took a breath, and bowed gently to the elders drowsing about him. Then, he turned his face toward the Newman village and began to walk.

⚬⚬⚬⚬⚬⚬⚬

"Quick! Be quick!" The Brethren darted ahead of Rosamunde, vanishing into the long shadows.

Scythe take the creature! Becca thought. How was she to follow when her guide disappeared? She dared not call out, nor urge Rosamunde to the speed her own nerves pled for. It was very true that Sian might miss her at any moment, and come thundering back on her big grey horse to snatch them under her so-called "protection." But she would not risk a stumble, or—worse!—a broken leg for her mount.

Before them, etched against the dark air, was a dazzling loop of garnet and green.

Nancy.

Becca touched her tongue to her lips, and leaned forward to whisper in Rosamunde's ear. "Follow, beautiful lady, but at your own pace. Do not risk yourself for me."

Both ears flicked, as if Rosamunde laughed at such faintheartedness. She moved forward at a measured walk, placing her feet so precisely that Becca scarcely heard a leaf rustle.

Proceeding thus, they followed Nancy's beacon, away from the path, and deeper into the trees.

Becca bent her head, allowing the branches they passed beneath to sweep harmlessly above her. They had been riding for some time, with no hint of pursuit, yet Becca kept craning toward the rear, expecting to hear the sound of hoofbeats and Sian's order to halt. It seemed fantastic that they could have gotten away so easily, and yet it appeared that they had indeed.

On they went. Though the shadows lengthened, yet they did not walk entirely in the dark, thanks to the tree-shine, and her own luminescence. Occasionally, they disturbed some branch-dweller, who complained with sleepy chirps or chitters and, judging horse and rider to be no threat, settled down again.

Ahead, Nancy darted into the heart of a shrubbery and disappeared.

"Not again!" Becca whispered sharply. "Rosamunde, stay—"

But Rosamunde did not stay. Ignoring word and rein alike, she pushed forward into the shrubbery. Leaves rustled, horrifyingly loud, a branch broke like a thunderclap, and there was an overwhelming scent of cedar.

"Stop!" Becca whispered frantically, but the noise was done. Rosamunde stood quite docile in the clear center of the plant, Nancy perched between her ears and the Brethren dancing in a tight circle on the ground, shaking its horns and growling.

"Be quiet!" it snarled, though it seemed quite shockingly silent to Becca. She tried to take deep, silent breaths, hoping that it wasn't the pounding of her heart that the creature objected to.

"Quiet!" it said again, glaring up at her with glowing yellow beast-eyes. "Stupid Gardener! Too loud! They'll see!"

They? Becca thought. Were Sian and Brume in pursuit, after all?

"I'm being as quiet as I can," she whispered, her voice so light she could barely hear it.

"This is not quiet!" The Brethren swept its horny hand up and out, fingers closing in the golden spill of her aura. *"Be quiet,"* it repeated for the third time.

Becca gasped. The rich light piercing the Brethren's fist faded, like the sun going behind a storm cloud, leaving only a pale wash of gilt behind. She raised her hand. If she stared, she could see the pale fires outlining her fingers. Rosamunde's flank was only a slightly warmer chestnut, as if she were bathed in dawn-light.

"What did you do?" she demanded, but the Brethren had turned away, its heavy head cocked to a side, as if it heard some sound too soft for her ears to discern.

"What—" she began again. Her words were cut off by the firm press of cold fingers across her lips. She pulled back, slightly, seeing Nancy as a blur of silver and jewels, emphatically shaking her tiny head from side to side.

All right, then, Becca thought. Nancy was plainly as

convinced of the necessity of quiet as the Brethren. Though she still did not understand how she should have known that her *glow* was too loud—much less what to do about it—she could keep quiet in... more traditional ways.

She pressed her lips tightly together. Seemingly satisfied, Nancy withdrew her hand, and drifted upward on lazy wings. She patted Becca's cheek lightly, then rose higher and was lost in the shine of the shrubbery enclosing them.

Ignored by her companions, she concentrated on what she could hear, which was precisely what she would expect to hear in a wood settling down for the night: branch-creak and leaf-rustle; the skitter of some small creature through the dried leaves that covered the ground inside her shelter; the call of a night bird.

Rosamunde tensed, noble head rising, ears at full alert. Becca's heart slammed into overaction, and she tasted the metallic tang of fear at the back of her mouth. Yet, she saw nothing.

Still, Rosamunde did not relax. Becca swallowed and sighted determinedly between those fine, upright ears.

Tree-glow was what she saw, and a glossy wall of blue-green cedar needles. Rosamunde had likely just picked up her rider's unease and, horselike, was on the lookout for goblins.

Becca took a deep breath, willing herself to relax. The Brethren, she told herself, was only being cautious, and hiding them until it could be sure there was no pursuit. Really, it was a wonder that it had led them so long before taking—

The wall of cedar framed by Rosamunde's ears broke inward, away from a massive head and snarling maw.

Becca screamed. Rosamunde reared, lashing out briskly with a front leg. The hoof caught the creature a glancing blow across its massive nose. It fell back with another roar, over which the Brethren's voice could be clearly heard.

"Run!"

It was Sian's voice the wind brought him as he came upon the Newman village, and Sian's aura he saw staining the new night with power.

"Well," Meri said conversationally, in case a tree or six might be listening; "I don't have to walk all the way to Sea Hold, after all." There came the sound of running feet, and the blare of Newmen auras. "Surely, this display is not on my behalf."

Sian has lost the Gardener, the voice of the elder elitch told him. *She is not pleased.*

"Certainly, Sian never took it well when she misplaced something," Meri allowed, slowing slightly while he sorted words out of the wind.

"...must have gone off the path at the long curve," Sian was saying, her voice sharp. "It is imperative that she be found—quickly—and brought here to safety! Where is the Ranger I sent to you?"

Meri sighed, and quickened his stride.

"Master Vanglelauf went into the wood this morning." Elizabeth Moore's voice was calm and unhurried, a notable feat in the face of a High Fey's angry panic. "We don't know when he might come out, Lady. He, himself, was unsure of what he might find."

"As much as it pains me to disturb Master Vanglelauf at his work, yet I must ask if you will have young Jamie request the trees to bid him come, and at once."

The two stood beneath the elitch's generous branches; he could see their auras clearly as he moved on, Sian's showing far too much turbulence, and Elizabeth Moore's a steady, if dangerously bright, copper. Sian must be distressed, indeed, Meri thought, to allow so much to be read; she was court-trained, as surely as he was, and certainly knew how to keep her aura calm, even—especially!—under stress.

"Don't trouble Jamie on my account," he called, and forcibly did *not* grin as Sian spun about to face him. "Good evening, Cousin."

"Cousin Meripen," she said, as if she suspected the existence of the grin, despite his efforts. "We are well met."

"So we are," he answered cordially, and bowed to Elizabeth Moore. "Good evening, Tree-Kin."

"Master Vanglelauf," she said composedly; "we had not looked for you so soon."

"I had not expected to return so soon," he said truthfully. "As it happens, I have news for the Engenium."

"Which will wait," Sian interrupted. "Meri, attend me. Diathen has put a Newoman, one Rebecca Beauvelley, into my care until such time as she is wanted at court. The trees call her 'Gardener' and appear to find her appealing. She was following me, but left the path between the long curve and the village green. A Gardener she may be, and holding the goodwill of trees, yet she must not spend the night, alone and unprotected, in the wood. Please find her and bring her back. I have asked Sam to rouse the others—"

Meri shook his head, remembering at the last

moment to swallow the sigh. If he must go and find this Newoman, he did not need the trees disturbed by the efforts of those who were—kindly—not Wood Wise.

"There's no need to send—to rouse honest folk from their beds," he said to Sian. "If Sam will come with me—?"

He looked to Elizabeth Moore, who gave him one of her roguish smiles and a cordial nod. "I'd wager you couldn't keep him in the village. I will do my best to keep Jamie here at least—unless you want him, Master Vanglelauf?"

In truth, the sprout would slow them, Meri thought, though he would need to practice his tracking, and it was an elder's duty to teach. He considered Sian, noting the anger tinting her aura. Sian had been court-trained. If she gave herself away by so much, the case was desperate, indeed.

"I look forward to hunting with Jamie on another occasion," he told the sprout's mother.

She laughed, her aura sparkling bewitchingly, and shook her head. "Always the courtier!"

"Indeed," Sian said; "it is always a pleasure to observe Meri in the midst of behaving himself."

He gave her a glance, eyebrow up, which she met with a frown.

"Now," she said pointedly, "would not be too soon to go. Cousin."

"Of course," he answered, keeping his voice smooth. Sian was in a chancy temper, indeed, and a wise man would not bait her. "Let me find Sam. We shouldn't be long."

Chapter Nine

DESPAIR MADE THE MISTS THICKER; THE AIR WARMER.
He would, therefore, not despair. There was no reason
for him to despair.

Indeed, there was reason for cautious optimism.
He had called; Rebecca had come. That the fickle
mists then rose to hide them from each other—the
mists were jealous; *that* was well known even of the
keleigh, which could not abide anything to thrive,
excepting itself.

The point to focus upon was that experimentation
had proved that he could call Rebecca to him, and
that she could recognize him amidst this tenuous
geography. That was well.

What was required, before he called her a second
time, was that he craft some way for them to connect
immediately, and before the mists intervened. He must
contrive to meet her at some point where the mists
were thin, and follow her back out. Whether she led
him to the Vaitura or to her own land, he cared not,

save that he was brought out from this mist-filled and treacherous place.

It was said that Drakin Fairstar sought her heart-mate inside the *keleigh*, when her duty was done and her hands were grown back. When she found him, so the tale went, she carried him far away into the mountains, and hid the two of them, until they forgot they were heroes, and, by degrees, the rest of who they had been, and so they had faded away entirely, rejoining the elements that had birthed them.

It was also said that the *keleigh* never relinquished that which it had claimed, but if anyone could have managed the thing, Altimere thought, closing his eyes against the monotonicity of the mist, it would have been Drakin.

The *keleigh* grew stronger on fear, on confusion, on pain. It melted away from power, confidence, and endurance. He had crossed the *keleigh* many times precisely by keeping his goal before his mind's eye, and riding on, refusing to accept any doubt of his safe arrival.

So, then, this substance, which was so like, and yet subtly unlike the *keleigh*. He had allowed himself to be vulnerable and it had attacked that vulnerability. Before he attempted another contact with Rebecca, he must gain and hold mastery over his environment.

He centered himself, feeling his *kest* warm at the base of his spine, and the tingle of banked power at his fingertips.

"I am Altimere, of the Elder Fey," he said, and the mist eddied away from his voice. He rose with studied calm, and with a hand-wave dispersed his chair back into the surrounding murk.

He took one step forward, another—a third.

And the mist parted to let him through.

Rosamunde was the wind itself, sweeping between trees and over low-growth.

From behind them came roars and other noises, that sounded like shouts, or laughter, or both. Ahead was darkness, lightly etched with tree-shine, and the blazing silver bar that was Nancy, scarcely beyond Rosamunde's nose, her wings a smear of color painted on the dark air.

Of the Brethren, there was no sign.

Becca lay almost flat, the reins long since lost, her strong arm around Rosamunde's neck, the fingers of her weak hand tangled in mad strands of mane.

Branches lashed her, as if they would unhorse her, but she clung to Rosamunde's back, and would not, *would not* fall. The sounds of pursuit fell behind, grew fainter, and fainter yet, until all Becca heard was the wind wailing in her ears.

"We lost them," she said—or tried to say. She loosened her hold 'round Rosamunde's neck and eased slightly upward, groping for the reins, whereupon two things happened at once.

The beast that had flushed them from their protecting bush roared out of the shadows toward which they were rushing, two creatures that looked as if they were made out of twigs shouting from its back...

...and Rosamunde stumbled.

"Stay close," Meri said to Sam Moore. "We will go quickly."

The Newman smiled, blue eyes glinting, ripples of humor flowing through the hectic disorder of his aura. "I heard our good Lady give that command," he said. "But why do I come at all? I'll slow you."

"You can run when it pleases you," Meri returned, settling his bow across his shoulders. "Besides, it will fall to you to take this Newoman in hand. It may be that she simply blundered from the path. But it also may be that she deliberately quit Sian's escort, in a reasoned attempt to escape. In either case, she may be more willing to come away with one of her own."

Sam frowned. "A prisoner? I—"

"Queen Diathen's prisoner," Meri interrupted, his attention more than half on the images beginning to form inside his head. "We neither of us wishes to disappoint *her*."

There was a pause, then a light snort, as if of laughter. "You're right there," Sam said. "Lead on, then, and I'll follow as best I can."

Meri nodded, took his direction, turned to the right, and leapt into a run.

It was a challenge to travel under the direction of trees. It required the ability to heed both the vision unrolling between one's ears, and the very real landscape through which one ran—and match the two.

Meri had often done such hunting before his long sleep, and it was only the matter of a few heartbeats before he had picked up the way of it again. It was rather like seeing from both eyes at once—dizzying, disorienting, and oddly energizing.

He did not worry about Sam Moore, whose woodcraft he knew to be equal to trailing, in the unlikely event that he fell behind. On the contrary, all his worry was centered on what the trees showed him, of a creature like some mad melding of horse and boar, accompanied by a handful of brown and stick-thin Low Fey. All were in pursuit of a chestnut mare, her rider clinging like a limpet to her neck, her tail streaming like water behind her.

Frighten the beast from the scent, he suggested to the trees as he ran. *Compel the Low Fey to abandon the hunt.*

We have tried, Ranger, a cedar murmured to him; *they do not hear us.*

Meri felt an icy stab in his belly. Low Fey that did not hear the voices of the trees? That was against all natural order.

Like the trees in the deep wood, he thought, leaping over a downed branch, *which do not hear the voice of a Ranger.*

Swallowing a curse, Meri ran on.

. . . Rosamunde stumbled.

The monster lunged, slashing with cruel tusks, one of the twig-man leaping from its back, screaming in a high, excited voice.

The horse-boar rushed by, and the twig-men crashed into Becca, its stick-fingers closing hard around her wrists, gibbering shrilly in her ear as it wrenched her from Rosamunde's back. The stick-man was beneath her as they hit the ground, the breath leaving her lungs in a scream, and ribbons of color distorting her vision.

She twisted, yanked her good arm free, and rolled away, sobbing in pain and fury. A angry snort warned her, she looked up to see the horse-boar charging her, and threw herself flat. The creature passed over her, and she rolled again, trying to get beneath the dubious protection of the small-growth.

Laughter sounded, her hair was yanked with a force that all but removed her scalp, and the twig-man was astride her, heavier than it looked, and utterly naked, her hair gripped cruelly in one long hand while the other tore her blouse from shoulder to waist, thorn-tipped fingers scoring her flesh.

Becca screamed, twisting, got her good arm free and struck out, only to have it caught in those same strong fingers, which were exerting pressure, while blood dripped from the scratches it had inflicted.

Somewhere nearby, a horse shrieked. She managed to turn her head enough to glimpse Rosamunde rising on her hind legs, exposing her belly dangerously to the horse-boar's tusks.

"No!"

Her captor struck her with the back of a hard hand. Becca's sight fragmented, the monster snorted, Rosamunde shrieked. Sight still confused, Becca twisted, not caring if she left her hair in the stick-man's grip. She struck out again, her weak arm connecting with twiglike ribs—and its weight was gone.

Free, she rolled, away from the sounds of angry hooves and furious hooting; branches scraped over her and leaves crackled against her ears. She dragged her hair away from her eyes and peered out upon the battle scene.

Directly before her, the twig-man was swatting at a tiny bedevilment, darting in and out, swift and bright as a needle. Nancy! Heart in mouth, Becca watched as her maid turned the twig-man, dodging his blows, while apparently landing no few herself. Beyond, the monster and Rosamunde faced off. Gore from half a dozen scrapes and scores marred the bright chestnut hide. The monster was not unscathed, and it displayed a certain respect as it faced its noble opponent, but it showed no intention of quitting.

Rosamunde bugled, rearing back, hooves dripping red sparks like blood. The monster answered with its terrible coughing grunt. Nancy darted in toward the twig-man's face; he dodged, twisting impossibly, his arm moved, the hard palm caught her square and slapped her out of the air.

She hit the ground, a dimming silver ember. The twig-man ululated, and raised his foot.

Becca rolled from beneath the shrub, throwing herself into the creature. Balance destroyed, he fell on top of her, but she kept rolling. Hooves thundered against the earth, and she thought she heard shouts, as she raised her hands and pummeled the twig-man.

Twigs broke beneath her hands, and still she struck, over and over, sobbing now, seeing again the hard hand flashing and Nancy smashed to the ground; feeling her hair twisted and her flesh scored, while Altimere stood by and did nothing—

Gardener! Have done!

The voice rattled inside her head. She raised her arm and struck the thing beneath her again, and again.

Very well, the tree said, *you may take his kest, if you so desire.*

The mare fought valiantly, and her downed rider had at last joined the fray, flinging herself on one of the two Low Fey, and punishing it with her naked hands. The other, forgotten in the melee, was creeping around to the rear of the rider, a rope-vine in hand.

Stop him! Meri flung his thought at the trees, zig-zagging 'round new growth. The mare's challenge split the air—and he leapt forward with renewed speed. So near, and yet not near enough!

Images unscrolled inside his head: The mare turned and struck, landing a solid kick in her opponent's ribs. On the ground, the rider continued to beat her now-quiescent enemy. Behind, the other moved, stealthily, too intent upon the scene before him to note that the branch he crept toward had of a sudden drooped. He eased forward, put his weight on the branch, and it snapped upward, slapping him into the tree's embrace, with a cry that Meri heard from very near hard at hand.

Two more leaps and he was at the edge of the battle, bow in hand and an arrow ready.

The mare was beset, now, her hooves planted firm and foursquare, as if she had determined to yield no more. Meri paused, concerned for a heartbeat it was her rider she protected. But, no, that one was yet astride the Low Fey, punching and striking with gore-dyed fingers.

Gardener! the voice of the elitch was so fierce Meri's fingers slackened on the string. *Have done!*

If the Newoman heard, she chose not to heed—and the horse-boar hurled into a charge.

The mare screamed, but held her ground. Meri pulled, loosed, and was moving in the instant the arrow left the string.

He vaulted to the back of the valiant mare, who

held firm though she could not like a stranger standing on her rump. The monster was dead, his arrow buried to its fletching in its right eye. Yet it was carried onward by its own weight, on course to strike the mare and smash her.

Meri raised a hand, drew his *kest*, and flung it into the ground directly before the mare's front hooves. Power flared, emerald and gold, splashed upward, and froze an instant before the monster's shoulder struck it.

His vision blacked, and all his bones screamed at the transfer of energy, but the barrier held. The monster fell not an inch from the mare's feet, and Meri slumped into the saddle.

The mare snorted irritably, muscles bunching.

"A little grace," he said, his voice none too steady. "I've just saved you a goring."

There was a pause, an ear twitched—

And a woman screamed, high and hopeless.

❧❧❧❧❧

Take his kest—Elyd was beneath her, his eyes dying even as he cried aloud in pleasure. Becca flung up and back, screaming, turned—and all but ran down a man in hunting leathers, callused hands held chest-high, fingers open, a bow and quiver on his back.

"Easy, then, Miss," he said in a voice so rough and commonplace that Becca nearly swooned. "I'm Sam Moore, out of New Hope Village," he continued, and the fires outlining him matched the blue of his eyes. "You'll be wanting somebody to look at those hands, and my sister's girl is a healer."

Scarcely understanding, she looked down at her hands, torn as if by brambles and dripping blood. She shook her head, and gasped, looking behind her—seeing only a pile of sticks among the disordered leaves.

"I think you've taken good care of him," Sam Moore said gently.

"He hurt Nancy," Becca explained. "She was trying to protect me."

"That's right," the man said, in the patient tone one uses with those caught inside a fever-dream. "She's fine, and a brave horse she is." He jerked his chin to the right.

Rosamunde! How could she have forgotten? Becca spun, and there she stood—ears up, eyes bright, but—there was blood on her flank, on her shoulder, and just beyond her, the monstrous horse-boar, an arrow in its eye.

"Scythe!" Becca flung forward, raising her torn hands—and lowering them, her laughter not—quite—convenable. "Rosamunde! Brave, bold lady! I left you to fight alone!"

"Each of you had your enemy," Sam Moore said from behind her. "Both acquitted well." She heard him move slightly.

"Best we get on, Miss. The sooner those hands are tended—and the lady's wounds, too—the quicker they'll heal."

"We do not leave until we find Nancy," Becca said, flatly. She looked about. There! That was the bush she had hidden beneath. Nancy had darted between it and the approaching twig-man, and been dashed down . . .

She looked down at the scuffed and marred ground. How could she hope to find one small person among the churned leaves and gouges?

"Nancy!" she called, her stomach cold with dread. "Nancy, come here! I want you!"

No quick silver body framed by bright-flashing wings appeared. Becca swallowed and looked down. She would search every inch of the Vaitura, then, until she found her.

"Happen she hid herself?" Sam Moore asked. "We can send out more searchers, from the village. You need care, Miss. Those hands'll be hurting soon."

"You may go, if you like," Becca said absently, her attention on the ground. "I appreciate your assistance, but I will not leave until we have found—"

There! Between Rosamunde's forefeet! Was that a feeble silver glow among the dead leaves and detritus?

Becca knelt, and carefully brushed the leaves away. "Nancy?" she whispered.

There was no answer; the little body did not move.

Lower lip caught between her teeth, Becca tried to think. Nancy was so tiny! How could she find what was broken, if anything? Would whatever hurt she had taken be made worse by lifting her and carrying her to Sam Moore's healer-niece?

And yet—they could not remain in this place. What if there were more monsters in the wood?

Gently, Becca slid her fingers beneath the little body, and raised it, cushioned by fallen leaves. Cradling Nancy to her breast, she thrust clumsily to her feet—and would have fallen, had Sam Moore not caught her arm.

"Thank you," she said, her attention for her burden. So still, her glow so dim...

"That's all right," Sam said. "I can carry that for you, if—"

"No," she said shortly. "*I* will carry her."

There was a slight pause, then Sam nodded.

"Fair enough. Can you hold her while I put you in the saddle?"

Becca shook her head, and glanced up at him. "Rosamunde is wounded. I wouldn't ask her to carry me. We can walk to your village."

Sam Moore's eyebrows lifted, and his glance down at herself was frankly dubious, but all he said was, "'Tisn't far."

❧❀❧

The captive Low Fey had slipped his trap. Meri sighed and leaned briefly against the tree. He had very much wanted to talk to that one.

Well.

He watched Sam lead Rebecca Beauvelley and her horse out of the savaged clearing in the direction of New Hope Village before he ducked out of his shelter to recover his arrow. The Low Fey the Newoman had beaten was gone, leaving a few scattered twigs in his wake. Meri shook his head and passed on. He retrieved his bow, turned, and gave one last glance behind him at the dead monster cooling upon the ground.

I've never seen its like, he commented to whichever tree might be listening.

Nor have we, Ranger, said a nearby ralif. *Nor have we.*

Chapter Ten

ALTIMERE WALKED THROUGH INDISTINCT LANDSCAPES, neither hurrying nor dallying, but with much the air of a gentleman taking a ramble through his garden of a peaceful afternoon. After a time, he grew fatigued, and thought he might rest himself and partake of some refreshment.

He paused and looked about him, spying phantom trees coquette in the flowing air; and indeterminate clusters of rocks, or flowers—or neither. Not, in truth, a very pleasant aspect, but he would contrive. As he always did.

A gesture brought a thread of mist to his hand. He placed his will upon it and shaped it, almost absently, into marble bench. When it was formed to his satisfaction, he caused green grass to carpet the insubstantial ground. Behind him, a ralif tree sprang into being, gnarled branches dividing the tricksy air, leaves cooling the bench at its base.

Altimere seated himself, back against the trunk,

smiling when he felt the rough bark rub against his jacket. His smile faded as he considered the grass—too green, too uniform, too...boring. He lifted an eyebrow and violets appeared, shy and charming among the bright blades.

"Very nice," he said, and raised his hand.

A wine glass appeared between his fingers; claret glaring balefully at the mist.

Altimere sipped—and sighed. The flavor was off; the red flat, rather than rounded, the peppery aftertaste all but nonexistent.

"It will not do," he said. The wine steamed out of the glass; the glass melted from his fingers.

Altimere settled his back more firmly against the ralif, pleased with its solidity, composed his mind, and raised his hand as if to receive a wineglass.

⚜

Fear had subsided, leaving room for pain, of which there was a surprising amount. Not just her gashed and misused hands, but her back, her knees and her shoulders—all doubtless bruised and battered in her fall from Rosamunde's back and subsequent rolling about on the forest floor.

Sam set a brisk pace through the woods, though by no means as quickly, Becca suspected, as he might have gone on his own. After assuring herself that Rosamunde moved freely, that her wounds did not begin to bleed a-fresh, and that she did not object to Sam leading her, Becca dedicated herself to keeping up, despite the protest of her own injuries. She had borne worse, she told herself; and she had not by any means taken the worst wounds.

Her head did hurt, and walking seemed to exacerbate the pain, which was slightly worrisome. What worried her more was that there seemed to be a shifting fogginess at the edge of her vision. If she were concussed, she might be raving, or unconscious, by the time they reached Sam's village—but there, Sam's niece was a healer; she would surely know what to do.

More frightening than these commonplace injuries was Nancy's condition. The little creature lay unmoving among the dead leaves and bits of moss in Becca's palm. She did not breathe—but Nancy never did breathe. How was she—or Sam Moore's niece—to treat such a patient? Becca worried. How were they even to discover what had been broken? If Nancy would wake, she might provide some clues as to her needs, but if she persisted in this state of seeming unconsciousness...

At least, Becca thought, Nancy's silvery light persisted, though, alarmingly, her wings had faded from bright jewel-tones to a forlorn and muddy grey.

"Trees," she said, not caring if Sam Moore heard her. "What shall I do for Nancy?"

An artificer must repair an artifact, Gardener, a soft voice told her. *The wisdom of trees does not grow in that soil.*

Becca bit her lip. Altimere had told her that Nancy was an artifact. She had forgotten—or, very well! She had never really believed it. Machines did not exhibit irony, or temper; haughtiness or gladness. Machines did not scream in agony when they willfully separated themselves from their maker's influence. Those were the actions and reactions of a living intelligence, and if that intelligence were encased in a gem-and-silver body, it was no less alive.

Perhaps Sian will know, Gardener, the soft voice suggested—and Becca stumbled to a halt.

"Sian!" she cried aloud.

"Miss Beauvelley, are you hurt?" Sam caught her shoulder—carefully—his hand an unwelcome weight holding her against the ground.

"Your—village!" she stammered, staring up at him. "You are one of Sian's tame Newmans!"

Sam's lips pressed together tight, and it seemed to Becca that his hand became momentarily heavier, before he replied, in a perfectly level voice.

"New Hope Village owes allegiance to the good lady at Sea Fort. In exchange, we live as lightly as we might on her land, and keep the accord my mother made with the trees. There's nothing *tame* in that, Miss. We're not Lady Sian's pets!"

That last was tempery, after all—and why shouldn't it be? No man liked to be accused of being less than he was. She had not escaped Sian at all, nor avoided the judgment of her own kind; she had only made her position even more untenable. Sian was not a fool; furthermore, she was under the direct order of her Queen. For the first time, Becca wondered if Fey might compel Fey, and if the Queen in particular had compelled Sian's obedience in a matter she plainly felt was ill-judged.

Becca sighed. Compelled or freely obedient, it was unlikely that Sian would allow her prisoner another chance to slip away. Becca could likely look forward to a guarded room in Sam's village of New Hope, if Sian didn't simply put the sleep on her until the Queen demanded her presence at court.

"I cannot go with you any further," Becca said, her voice quavering. "Please leave us."

Sam shook his head. "Lady Sian was worried for your safety, Miss. She sent us to find you, quick, and bring you back safe." He sighed. "We didn't manage that too neat, I guess, but—"

"But if you will," a light voice interrupted from the shadows beyond Sam, "waken the ire of creatures unknown even to the trees, you must expect to have something to show for the encounter."

Sam turned his head. "I thought you'd run back to the village ahead of us," he said. "I made a wager with myself whether you'd sit down to dinner alone, or wait for us to join you."

The other woodsman snorted. Becca could make out a tall shape—taller than Sam, and slender, with tatters of green luminescence fluttering about him— which was probably, Becca thought, only the blare of Sam's greater aura, bleaching the color from his friend's.

"Call me a fool," the other hunter said, "but I didn't like the notion of returning to Sian without her truant in hand."

Sam grinned. "There's that," he acknowledged. "Well, then, now that you've caught up, you can help guard against any more of whatever that was."

"I will certainly do what I might," the light-voiced man said placidly. "But I think we may not see any more trouble tonight."

"I wouldn't be disappointed if you were right," Sam said, and looked down at Becca. "Do you want one of us to carry your—your Nancy, Miss? You don't look half steady on your feet, and it's still a bit to walk."

She was trapped. It might have been possible,

though not, she admitted, likely, to run away from Sam. But now that they were joined by Sam's hunting partner—another missed opportunity.

Tears pricked her eyes. She blinked them away, and shook her head, gasping at the dazzle of pain.

"I will carry Nancy," she said determinedly. "Please, lead on."

~~~⚬⚬⚬~~~

"Better," Altimere said, and tasted the wine again. Yes, definitely better. Pleasing, in fact.

"Now," he said, casually twisting a side table out of the mist. "Cheese, and some crudités."

~~~⚬⚬⚬~~~

Meri confined himself to the pace Sam had chosen, which, while doubtless slower than Sian would have wished, showed respect for the wounded.

He had heard the Newoman's refusal to be lifted to the saddle, in consideration of her mount's injuries. Walking beside the mare, on Sam's right and a few steps to the rear, he inspected her more carefully than he had a chance to do earlier. She had taken three cuts, none as deep as he would have supposed, given the nature of her opponent. He had wondered if she had lamed herself during the battle, but her gait was smooth, and her aura was calm, unlike her rider's, which was shot with red and orange bolts of agitation and pain.

"I did not expect to find a war-mare in these woods," he murmured, a small gallantry for the lady's ear alone, so he was startled to hear the Newoman answer, from beyond Sam's protective bulk.

"Rosamunde is bold and greathearted," Rebecca Beauveley said, her voice thin, but steady. "I am honored that she allows me to ride her." There was a small pause, and a rattle of stone, as if the Newoman had missed her footing. "She is quarter-Fey."

Quarter-Fey? Meri looked at the mare's lines, the tall sturdy ears and sapient eye. "You surprise me," he said truthfully.

"She was bred on the—the other side of the *keleigh*," Rebecca Beauveley continued, and it seemed to Meri that the words spoke themselves, without much direction from the speaker. "Her grandfather was one of Altimere's stallions, that he sold to Lord Quince, who bred him to his prize mare. He intended the offspring for his own mount, but Lady Quince put her foot down. So he bred that one, too, to another of his mares, and the result was Rosamunde."

"And a fine horse she is, too," Sam said. "I'd wager that most would have bolted from that . . . thing. Your Rosamunde gave battle."

"She is very brave," Rebecca Beauveley agreed, and fell silent.

There was, Meri thought, walking shoulder-to-shoulder with the brave Rosamunde, much in that little story worth thinking on. The fact that the mare traced her lineage back to the stables of Altimere the artificer—who had sold her grandsire to Newmen on the *other side* of the *keleigh*—that alone was enough to raise the hairs on the back of his neck.

"We're almost home," Sam said, though Meri thought the cheerful note in his voice was forced. "See those lights over there through the leaves? That will be our house, I don't doubt. My sister's girl will take good care of your hurts, Miss, and Elizabeth—my sister—is the best cook in the village!"

"Rosamunde will need care," the Newoman said. "And Nancy."

"I'll take care of the bold lady," Meri heard himself say, to his considerable surprise. "You needn't worry there."

"Thank you. Nancy will need to be tended—immediately. If Mr. Moore's niece will allow me the use of her supplies."

"I think," Sam interrupted, thereby saving Meri the need, "that Lady Sian is very anxious to see you, Miss, when you return. The—the Nancy. I'll take it—she—to my niece and let her try her skill. I don't know that she's had much chance to patch up Hobs, though every now and then one would come out of the woods and ask my mother to wrap a cut, or splint a broken bone."

"Nancy is not a Hob!" That came out sure and strong, Meri noted. "She is—she is my friend."

"Fair enough," Sam said soothingly. "But you have to own, Miss, that she isn't like you or me."

Good of the Newman to have left him out of that particular equation, Meri thought, though he didn't think Rebecca Beauvelley had noticed.

"She may not be *exactly* like you or me," she said, still strong and snappish, "but she is alive, and fearless, and—and good. I will *not* have her injuries ignored."

"No one said that," Sam protested, the lights of the village quite near now, and it was not, Meri thought, only Elizabeth Moore's house that spilt light out into the night.

The sprout lies in wait, Ranger, an elitch commented, but Meri had already seen the flicker of the boy's aura.

"Jamie," he said, half in warning and half in command.

Laughter rustled the leaves and the sprout dropped out of a larch a few paces ahead.

"There you are!" Jamie said exuberantly. "What took you so long?"

"There was a battle royale engaged when we arrived, and we were obliged to assist in the vanquishing of the foe before we could continue," Meri answered, just ahead of Sam's avuncular, "Jamie, make your bow to Miss Beauvelley and offer your service, please."

"Yes!" Jamie stepped respectfully into their group at Rebecca's Beauvelley's far side, his quiet greens and curious yellows immediately hidden by the noisy blare of her aura.

"Good evening, Miss Beauvelley," he said, politely. "I'm Jamie Moore, Sam's nephew. Is there anything I carry for you? You look tired."

"Thank you," she said distantly. "I am not so tired that I cannot carry my friend another few steps. However, it would be very kind in you to run ahead and let the healer know that there will be wounded for her to tend."

"I—"

"That's well-thought," Sam interrupted. "Do that errand, will you, Jamie? And also let Lady Sian know that Miss Beauvelley has asked that her wounded be treated before anything else goes forth."

Jamie sighed, lightly, but perfectly audible to Meri's ears.

"Sam, Lady Sian sent me to tell you that Miss Beauvelley should be brought directly to her."

"Fine!" the object of this discussion snapped. "Tell Sian that she may meet me in the healer's room, then! I *will not* have Nancy's life endangered!"

"That seems a reasonable compromise," Meri said into the stunned silence that followed this pronouncement. "Pray carry that message, as well, Jamie."

"Master—"

"Go," he interrupted, letting sternness be heard. Jamie went.

Sam led them to the house that Meri had seen in his longeye look from atop the spystone. A tree, shaken off its roots by an earthdance, had struck the roof. In the meanwhile, the tree had been removed and the roof mended. The small room built off of the main house had not been harmed at all; and Violet Moore stood in the open doorway, her face set and her aura a confusion of yellow, orange, and grey.

"Good evening, Healer," Rebecca Beauvelley said firmly. "I have an unusual patient for you."

"My brother said you carried a wounded friend," Violet answered, her voice much surer her aura had predicted. "He also said that you were wounded yourself." She stepped aside. "Please, come in."

The Newoman hesitated, glancing behind her. "Rosamunde . . ."

"I had said I would care for the lady," Meri said from the shelter of the mare's shadow. "My word is good."

"Thank you," Rebecca Beauvelley said, and with no more argument stepped through the lighted doorway.

Sam hesitated for an instant, and looked around. "I should have been quicker off the mark to offer care for her horse," he said resignedly.

"You are better suited to guard Diathen's hostage," Meri said, slipping the reins out of the Newman's fingers.

"Because she'll trust me," Sam said with unexpected bitterness. "I don't have much heart to stand as jailer."

"Nor do I," Meri answered, truthfully. "Nor, I suspect, does Sian. Trust me, Sam Moore, you do not want the Queen's eye to fall upon you. Best you do as your sworn lady bids, and think no farther than duty."

Sam snorted. "That's advice you take yourself, is it?" he asked.

Happily, he did not wait for Meri's answer, but strode through the open door, toward the two Newomen bent over a small form on the table.

"Well." Meri sighed and stroked the mare's elegant neck. "Rosamunde, is it? Let us get you on the mend." He looked about him, noting the signature of several beneficial small-plants along the side of the house.

The Elder Healer kept those low-growers that she made use of most often close to her hand, the elder elitch told him, and once again offered the images of the old woman bent over her work of grinding, drying, and combining.

"To each his own custom," Meri said, though the old woman's way seemed unnecessarily complex. He stroked the mare's neck once more, and moved toward the glow of the small-plants. The mare walked companionably at his side, pausing when he did.

"Here," he murmured, crouching down beside the golden-glow. "Of your kindness," he said to it, as he had learned to do very long ago, when he was scarcely older than Jamie Moore. "Of your kindness, would your share your virtue with a friend?"

For a moment, nothing happened, and Meri wondered if, perhaps, the plants over which the elder had placed her hand could not heed a stranger. Then, the glow began to solidify into a sphere, as if the plant produced a berry of *kest* for his use. He extended his hand and it dropped, warm and smooth as a pebble, into his palm.

"Thank you," he said politely. "I pledge that your gift will be used to heal, and in no way to do hurt."

He rose, the tiny gem of *kest* cupped in his hand. His ears brought him the sound of voices, moving closer, as he stepped to the mare's side.

Sian comes, the elitch remarked. *She is not best pleased with the Gardener.*

That was scarcely surprising, but Meri had more important matters than Sian's temper to concern him at the moment.

Careful to keep his own meager *kest* confined, he stepped before the mare, and raised his hand, letting her see what he held.

"A gift," he said, which a Fey horse would know, but that one bred beyond the Vaitura might not. "To mend your wounds."

A strong ear flickered. The mare whuffed thoughtfully, and bent her proud head.

"Yes," Meri said encouragingly. He raised his hand to press the golden gift of *kest* against the white blaze of her star.

Power flared, sparking briefly as virtues met and meshed. The mare's coat shone, as if every chestnut hair were lit from the outside. The gash on her shoulder faded, and the worst one, on her flank. Meri stroked her nose, murmuring gently while the healing ran its course. She stood firm, and perfectly calm under his hand, and when the melding was done, he ran his palm down her shoulder, and smiled.

"Not even a scar," he said to her. "You are blessed, indeed."

The mare blew lightly, and he felt his grin grow.

"There you are, Cousin Meri!" Sian's voice was brittle. He sighed, and leaned his forehead briefly against the mare's shoulder. "If you're done resting, perhaps you would attend me?"

It was not, he thought, going to go well for the Newoman Rebecca Beauvelley, not with Sian in *this* temper. Nor would it go well with him, to refuse to attend her.

"Surely," he said, keeping his voice even. He turned away from the mare, spotted the sprout in Sian's train, standing between his mother and the elder Jack Wood.

"Jamie Moore," he said. "Unsaddle the mare, and see to her comfort."

He had expected the sprout to demur, but to his surprise, Jamie stepped forward with the alacrity of relief. "Yes, Master," he said, sturdily, as he received the reins, and added, lower, "thank you."

Chapter Eleven

"PLEASE, PUT YOUR—YOUR BURDEN ON THE TABLE," the girl said, her voice as tight as her face.

Becca did as the healer requested, gently placing Nancy in her bed of leaves and moss atop the scrubbed wooden table. She gasped as she flexed her fingers, and again as she looked down at her hands. Seen in the light, they looked—very bad, the right, which had cradled Nancy, especially, with bits of grass and leaf stuck to the drying blood.

"I'll need to clean those," she said, and looked up at the girl, her slim figure soaked in brilliant yellow and orange. "If I might ask your help?"

"You might," the other said, and it seemed to Becca that the tight face eased somewhat. "I am Violet Moore." Her eyes moved to the door, and Becca turned her head to see that Sam had come into the workroom and was seated on a bench by the door. "Sam's niece."

"Yes, he had said. I am Rebecca Beauvelley," she

continued. "I am very glad to meet you, Miss Moore. I fear that Nancy is . . . very seriously injured. In my—in my own country, I am a healer, but Nancy's injuries may require all of our combined skill."

"That may indeed be the case," Violet Moore said, motioning Becca to follow. "I'm glad to hear that you are a healer yourself. While the headman has said that I'm now village healer, two days ago I was a half-trained apprentice."

Becca looked at her, the compressed lips and the dark shadows beneath her eyes.

"My sympathies. Am I to take it that your teacher has . . . passed on to a brighter land?"

The girl's brown eyes filled. She turned abruptly and picked up the kettle, splashing hot water into the waiting basin.

"Wait a moment," she said harshly, and went over to the neat shelves, her movements graceless and hurried. She returned with a twist of dried easewerth, which she sprinkled into the water before testing it with the back of her hand.

"It will not burn," she said, "but I fear that it will *hurt*, Miss. What did you do to mark yourself so?"

Becca looked down at her gore-stained fingers, took a breath, and plunged both into the steaming water.

It *did* hurt. She bit her lip and kept her hands submerged, watching the bits of leaf and other rubbish float to the surface, feeling the water dissolve the dried blood and open half-sealed cuts.

"I'm afraid that I . . . beat . . . a creature made out of dry twigs and thorns," she said, and raised her head to meet Violet Moore's eyes. "It had set a monster against us, knocked me off my horse, and struck Nancy down when she tried to protect me. I—" Suddenly, she could not meet those eyes. She looked down again, at the rusty water, trash swirling on its surface. "I wanted to kill it."

"And rightly so," Sam said from across the room. "When we came on the scene, it looked like they were doing their best to kill you. That...*creature*, whatever it was, wasn't just playing with your horse, Miss Beauvelley, and as you say, the Hob didn't mind hurting your Nancy, there."

"That's right," Violet said, suddenly brisk. "If Sam says that you did right, Miss, then you can depend on it that you did."

"Now, there's good advice!" Sam said, with a glib earnestness that put Becca suddenly and painfully in mind of her own brother. "I'm glad to hear that you've come 'round to my point of view, Violet!"

His niece ignored him, and brought out a cloth. "Here, Miss. Let's dry you off and see what we have to deal with."

"Nancy—" Becca began, looking over at the still form on the table. Had her glow dimmed? "Her state is very bad, I fear."

"It may be," Violet said briskly. "And if that is the case, she will certainly need your skill more than mine. Give me your right hand."

There was some sense in what the girl said, especially if she was herself not an experienced healer. Becca lifted her right hand out of the murky water, shook it carefully, and allowed Violet Moore to enfold it in the cloth. Her touch was gentle, but Becca found it necessary to bite her lip so as not to cry out.

"Now the left," the girl said, holding out the pink-stained cloth.

Becca raised her left hand slowly, blinking at the damage there. How had she found the strength to strike the creature hard enough to produce such damage to her crippled hand? She looked up into Violet Moore's frown.

"Have you hurt your arm?" the girl asked, wrapping the towel gently around Becca's left hand.

"A long time ago," she answered. "My hand is very weak and I do not have a full range of motion. I wonder that I was able to strike at all, much less so strongly."

"Anger sometimes lends strength," Sam said from his seat near the doorway, and gasped, boots scraping on the floor as he leapt to his feet. Becca and Violet turned, Becca pulling her hand free of the towel and allowing it to fall to her side, as Sian walked in, attended by a sturdy woman outlined in copper fires, an old man leaning on a stick, and a slender man in hunting leathers. Others crowded behind those four, but Sian raised her hand and they stopped short of entering the workroom.

"Miss Beauvelley." The Engenium's voice was brittle, her movements so sharp she seemed to cut the air as she walked forward. "You summoned me, I believe?"

~※~

The room was too small, and overfull with power. Meri hung back, his hand pressed hard against the dead wooden walls, the open door at his back not as much comfort as he had hoped, blocked as it was with craning Newmen.

Rebecca Beauvelley's hands had been cleaned; in the absence of old blood, the lacerations seeped new. He wondered that the healing had not yet taken place, unless the damaged Nancy had taken precedence?

But no—a glance at the table between Sian and the two Newomen showed a small silver-limned form curled among a handful of forest-floor trash. It showed no aura, and it did not breathe, yet there was no sense of death about it.

An artifact, Ranger, the elitch told him.

An *artifact*, Meri thought, and leaned harder against the wall. And it was Altimere the artificer who had sold a horse to a Newman across the *keleigh*, which had been the grandsire of the mare who permitted Rebecca Beauvelley to ride her.

Whence came this Newoman? he asked the trees, but if they answered, it was lost in the blare of Sian's anger.

"Well, Miss Beauvelley? Did you dare to summon the Engenium of Sea Hold?"

Rebecca Beauvelley's chin went up, her aura reflecting Sian's anger.

"If it comes to that," she said icily, "I am the daughter of an Earl. While I don't suppose I outrank you, certainly neither of us is the servant of the other. What I asked was that you speak to me here, so that both of our necessities could be met."

That was well-said, Meri thought, and it might even have answered, had she had the wit to moderate her aura, and modulate her voice. Temper would only draw temper, as *kest* drew *kest*, and no good could come of either.

"Your *necessities*," Sian said, her voice edged and her aura stitched with red, "included leaving the path and losing yourself in the woods, making a mockery of my protection—"

"Does it occur to you that I might have had quite enough *protection* from the Fey?" Rebecca Beauvelley interrupted hotly. "It seemed best to throw my lot in with the trees, who are at least kind to me."

Sian rocked back on her heels, her hands tucked in her belt. Elizabeth Moore slipped by her and went to stand at the foot of the table, while Jack Wood planted his stick on the dead wood floor midway between Sian and the door.

"Placing yourself in the care of trees seems to have worked well for you," she observed.

Rich color mantled the Newoman's brown cheeks, but she took a hard breath and answered, with a credible attempt at calmness, "It did not, as it happened, but it was scarcely the fault of the trees that we were purposefully led astray and then fallen on by bandits."

She looked down, as if suddenly recalling herself, turned slightly, and held her hand out to Violet Moore.

"If you please," she said, "the rag."

The girl handed the pink-smudged cloth over, and Rebecca Beauvelley blotted her hands with it absently, as she stepped to the table.

"The trees," she said, looking up into Sian's face, "suggested that you might know how to...heal...Nancy."

"*Heal* it?" Sian repeated, disbelieving. "It's an artifact, as you well know, and has no precedence over my business with you!"

"I disagree," the Newoman said flatly, and used the cloth to gently clean the tumbled bits of forest debris away from the small silver body. "Nancy broke her tie to Altimere in order to serve me, and she fell protecting me. Whatever else she may be, she is my *friend*, and I have too few in this place to allow her to fail!"

There was a rustle and a shift in the crowd blocking the doorway. Meri turned his head as Jamie Moore wriggled into the room. The sprout sent a quick glance toward his mother, stern and alert at the foot of the table, and slipped over to stand next to Meri.

"That—thing—" Sian said, and Meri heard the rumble of surf beneath her words, "is a danger to you, to me, and to the Queen. I spared it once, out of courtesy to yourself. I can no longer allow it to exist."

Kest flared, turquoise and aqua, arcing from Sian's fingers to the tiny figure on the table.

"No!" Golden power washed the room, straining against the wooden walls.

Meri cried out, his *kest* leaping to answer the outflow of power. Beside him, the sprout shouted, his aura afire as he moved blindly toward the glory.

"Jamie!" Meri lunged, one knee banging painfully against the floor as he caught the boy and held him, pressing the small face into his shoulder, feeling the thin body tremble with the buffeting of forces too strong for him.

Cringing, his *kest* yearning, Meri stared up at the confrontation. The Newoman's *kest* was considerable, but she was obviously untrained in its use. Sian, on the other hand, had had a great deal of training, her *kest* was considerable, *and* she stood upon her own land, among folk who had accepted her protection. Even as he watched, the flow of Sian's *kest* shifted, and began to twine itself around Rebecca Beauvelley's *kest*. Meri swallowed, suddenly ill. If she succeeded—and he thought she could—she would tie the Newoman to her, *kest*-to-*kest*, overriding the other's will.

Sian must not subsume the Gardener, the elitch thundered into his head. *You must stop this, Ranger!*

He must stop it? Meri thought dizzily, his meager *kest*

burning in his veins. And yet, he thought, feeling the boy's body shivering against him—who else was there?

Meri lurched to his feet, and thrust Jamie into the arms of a woman hovering at the door.

"Hold him!" he snapped, and turned, reaching Sian's side in two long strides.

"Sian! Have done!"

She ignored him. Indeed, she might not have heard him.

"Sian!" He dared to put his hand on her shoulder, felt the thrill of her *kest* along his nerves.

Rebecca Beauvelley was going to lose this contest; she had no control, nothing but untamed power. Worse, her already fragmented focus was disintegrating, as fear crept in to replace anger.

She was right to be afraid, Meri thought, and too unschooled even to disengage. If she simply dropped her defense, Sian would bind her before she could stop herself.

If, inside this state of exalted anger, she wished to stop herself.

The Newoman needed a distraction, something to draw her attention and her *kest*, something that Sian would recognize, even in her anger, as untouchable.

Scarcely had he formed the thought, than his fingers were in his pouch. The sunshield, that the sea had given him so many days ago. A chancy gift, as the sea's gifts often were—and something against which Sian, the Engenium of Sea Hold, would *never* contend.

He felt the intelligence within the sunshield take note, felt sea-*kest* wash through his blood.

"Subdue the Newoman," he murmured, and tossed the sunshield directly at her.

As he had hoped, she jerked back, her *kest* flaring wildly, even as her right hand rose. The sunshield flashed in the instant before her fingers closed around it. Sian's *kest* fell so quickly Meri winced in sympathy for the headache she had doubtless just given herself.

On the far side of the table, Rebecca Beauvelley swayed slightly. Meri breathed deeply, as if to prompt her, and was faintly gratified to see her inhale, as well, her *kest* visibly falling. Two more breaths and she was nothing more than a bedraggled and exhausted Newoman bathed in a dangerously brilliant aura. She shook her head, and raised her hand to look at the sunshield.

His heart jolted, and Rebecca Beauvelley lifted a face as pale as linden leaves, eyes wide and hopeless as she stared into his face. She shook her head, though what she denied he could not say, and her lips parted.

Softly, he thought, anxiously—and to the trees. *Tell her to speak Sian sweet, and apologize for contending with her.*

The Newoman blinked, her face going vague. She nodded, and cleared her throat.

"Sian, please forgive me," she said, her voice trembling slightly, which was not, Meri thought, a bad thing. "I should not have challenged you. But, truly, Nancy is not a danger, and—and I wish you would help me to mend her. The trees said—that you might."

He felt Sian stiffen beside him, and for a heartbeat feared that she would come the haughty High Fey. The moment passed, however; Sian's stance softened, and she inclined her head.

"All you need do is renew its *kest*," she said. "Artifacts do not continue forever without a renewal of power, and this one has undertaken some . . . significant exertions of late."

Meri had not thought it possible for Rebecca Beauvelley's face to pale further. Watching her, he felt ill himself, and shivered as if with a sudden chill.

"Renew her *kest*," she whispered, staring down at the tiny figure. It seemed to Meri that it was significantly less bright than it had been, and he wondered if it would cease to be altogether, once the glow went out.

Slowly, the Newoman approached the table, and slowly bent over the small object there. Meri fancied he tasted silver and grit as Rebecca Beauvelley kissed the thing tenderly on its cold lips.

No one in the room or outside of it spoke. No one moved.

On the table, the artifact named Nancy began to glow, bright, brighter, brightest. Her wings flushed red and green, and suddenly she was up, flashing a long silver loop around the room, and turning handsprings on the air.

As suddenly as she had risen, she dropped back to the table, and knelt. Taking Rebecca Beauvelley's bruised and bloodied hand in both of hers, she kissed her fingers.

Rebecca Beauvelley sighed. Meri swallowed around the lump of emotion in his throat.

Sian nodded, and crossed her arms over her breast. "There," she said briskly, "what had I said?"

Chapter Twelve

SHE WAS BURNING; SHE WAS MELTED; SHE WAS LIQUID gold, formless and flowing. Even as she flowed, she felt something contain her; glimpsed a rope of living turquoise coolly dividing her heat. More heat built, enough to burn the world, and yet the fluid rope remained untouched. It divided, forcing her to flow into smaller and smaller pockets, ineffectual ...

... and frightened.

Becca tried to step back from the flowing heat; tried to shake away the confining strands, but she was confounded by the blare and sizzle of power.

Something arced into her vision, as cool and calming as snow. She reached out and caught it, heard a roar, a crash, and tasted salt on her lips.

She felt her body, her hand, fingers closed about something damp and cool, but the fire, she was on fire—no, she *was* the fire! She breathed in, as if she would cool herself, astonished when the heat did subside, a little.

Deliberately, she inhaled. Again, the heat decreased.

A third breath, deeper than the first two, and she was merely herself, somewhat unsteady on her feet; her head light with pain and fatigue.

She raised her hand to see what it was that she held—and gasped, her heart stuttering in terror, as she saw in memory what she had not made sense from in the midst of the fire.

The object in her hand—a bone-dry disk from which the thinnest possible thread of blue emerged, wafting delicately across the table, until it became part of the ragged cloak of greens and blues drifting about the slim woodsman. She saw him plainly now—not a man at all, but Fey, his face stern and scarred; his uncovered eye as green as new leaves.

Bound again, she thought, and shook her head in despair. *Rebecca, you fool!*

Gardener, the tree addressed her with gentle urgency. *You must not shame Sian before those who shelter under her branches. Apologize for challenging her, and ask her aid sweetly.*

Becca blinked. The tree offered good counsel, she admitted to herself. The Landed were courteous to each other; to be otherwise was to encourage misbehavior among the subordinate orders. She cleared her throat and looked to the Fey woman, standing taut and grim just across the table.

"Sian, please forgive me," she said, hating the way her voice shook. "I should not have challenged you. But, truly, Nancy is not a danger, and—and I wish you would help me to mend her! The trees said—that you might."

For a moment, she feared that she had not been

sufficiently respectful, and if Nancy was to lose her
life because of Becca's ineptness, when she had given
so much—

Sian inclined her head.

"All you need do is renew its *kest*," she said, as if
it were the most obvious thing in the world.

Becca stared at her, stomach knotting. Renew Nancy's
kest! she thought wildly. Did the Fey expect her to
mount the tiny silver body here and now? How—but
wait! In gentler times, Altimere had taken *kest* from
her with a simple kiss.

"Renew her *kest*," she whispered, looking down at
the tiny figure. Was—no, *surely* the silvery glow was
dimmer now! Would Nancy cease to exist, when her
light died completely?

That was by no means an experiment Becca desired
to make. She bent down and pressed her lips gently
against Nancy's hard mouth.

She felt a wash of warmth, and a connection, as if a
hook had seated firmly in its eye. Dazzled, she stepped
back, and Nancy rushed into the air, a shooting star
in reverse, turning exuberant handsprings in the air.

Becca smiled; she heard someone laugh, and someone else sigh. Nancy dropped to the table. Kneeling,
she raised Becca's weak and battered left hand and
tenderly kissed her fingers.

Tears rose. Becca blinked them away with a sigh.

"There," Sian said briskly; "what had I said? Now—"
She looked about her, and nodded to the woman limned
in copper standing at the foot of the table. "Elizabeth,
this is, as you have heard, Rebecca Beauvelley. With
your permission, I would leave any further discussion
until we have all eaten and rested."

Elizabeth inclined her head gravely. "I think that's wise, Lady. We all want our beds, I think."

As if he took her words for a command, Sam Moore moved toward the door, his big hands making absurdly delicate shooing motions.

"Go on home, now," he said, comfortably. "Let Miss Beauvelley get settled in and have her hurts looked to. There'll be plenty of time for questions and talking on the morrow." He paused to look at the old man leaning on his stick, who in turned looked to Elizabeth.

"Thank you, Jack," that lady said. "I'll have just another word or two with Lady Sian."

"That's well, then," the old man said, and nodded briefly to Sian. "Lady," he said, and looked across the table, meeting Becca's eyes firmly. "Daughter of an Earl, are you, Miss?"

"Yes," she said, and hoped most earnestly that the old man would not ask her *which* Earl.

Happily, he did not ask, but smiled and gave her a nod. "Not many in New Hope know what an Earl is. You rest easy, here. It's good land."

Becca felt tears sting her eyes, and managed a smile. "Thank you."

He turned, stick striking the floor, and went out the door ahead of Sam, who closed it firmly behind.

Becca drew a hard breath, raised her hand and pointed at the one-eyed Fey with his ragtag aura blowing about him. "What is your name?"

He raised a disdainful eyebrow. "Meripen Vangle-lauf," he said, his voice light and cool.

She glanced down at the flat, round bone in her hand, looked back at him, and threw it as hard as her aching muscles allowed.

"I refuse this!"

He leaned—no, he *flowed* forward, scooping the thing out of the air. It vanished among long brown fingers as he inclined his head.

"Meri," Sian said, "is the cousin of whom I told you, Rebecca Beauvelley."

"As unpredictable and as willful as one might wish," Becca murmured, remembering, and saw the Fey's eyebrow rise again.

"Master Vanglelauf has kindly come to help us with our trees," Elizabeth said, her calm, commonplace voice drawing Becca's eye. She smiled and stepped forward, her gaze dropping briefly to Nancy, kneeling yet on the table before Becca.

"Welcome you, Miss Beauvelley," she said softly. "I am Elizabeth Moore, Sam's sister. Now that your friend has been mended, it would be best if you let Violet tend to you. There's a bed here, and Violet will stay with you. I will send over food, and ale, and we'll talk—" She looked to Sian, but more, Becca thought, as one issuing an order, than asking permission—"on the morrow. Lady?"

"I bow to your arrangements, Elizabeth," Sian said with a blitheness that made Becca shiver. "Thank you." She gave Becca a perfectly cheerful grin. "Sleep well, Rebecca Beauvelley. Violet—I thank you."

"Lady," Violet said softly, from behind Becca.

Sian nodded, and turned, slipping her hand 'round the other Fey's arm. "Come, Meri, you must be starved yourself."

The door opened, and they exited, followed, after another smile and an earnest look, by Elizabeth Moore, who drew the door closed behind her.

"Now," Violet said, on a long exhalation. "Let's bind those hands, Miss."

"Master Vanglelauf, please allow me to thank you for . . . what you did for Jamie." Elizabeth Moore's voice was grave, her aura casting a bright copper shadow before her.

"No thanks are needed," he said, truthfully. "It was no good place for a sprout."

"I . . . see." They walked a few paces in silence, the Newoman, the Engenium, and himself. He held the sunshield inside the curl of his fingers, its dry surface prickling his skin.

"Would it be possible to tell me," Elizabeth Moore said, and he heard the sharp edge beneath her delicate tone, "what it was that endangered Jamie?"

Sian said nothing. Meri swallowed his sigh.

"His *kest*—you understand that a sprout has very little, and is naturally not skilled in its uses—his *kest* was drawn to the . . . contest between Sian and Elizabeth Beauvelley." He paused, weighing what he had just said, and judged that something more was needed. "You mustn't think him inept; it was an . . . unconsidered display by persons of strong *kest*. I was nearly drawn in, myself."

"My apologies, Elizabeth," Sian said softly. "My failure to rule my temper endangered your son. It is not how I treat those who live within my honor."

"I know that, Lady," the Newoman said, as if her mind were on something else. "Many tempers were drawn thin tonight. Master Vanglelauf."

His eyebrows twitched upward in surprise. "Tree-Kin?"

She made a light sound somewhere between a sigh and a laugh. "I see that the wood has told you all. Palin, who is Jamie's sire, promised me two children— one to follow me, and one to follow him. It was Palin who told me that *kest* is the ability to draw upon the strength of one's soul."

Meri blinked. *Soul?* he queried the trees, and the elitch answered immediately.

The inner fires, Ranger. Palin and the Old Woman were fast friends and spent much time disputing this point.

"I am assured that this is an apt description," he told Elizabeth Moore.

She laughed outright this time. "How convenient to talk to trees without the need of a translator!" she said, as they came to her door. "Please, thank them for their care of us, Master Vanglelauf." She turned. "Lady, will you come in?"

"Thank you, no," Sian answered. "I think I have disturbed your peace quite enough for one day. We will talk tomorrow, Elizabeth."

"As you say, Lady." She turned—and turned back again.

"Miss Beauvelley," she said. "She speaks to trees and she has the ability to draw upon the strength of her soul."

"That would seem to be the case," Sian said dryly.

Elizabeth Moore nodded. "Then isn't she Fey?" she asked, and stepped into her house, closing the door gently behind her.

✳   ✳   ✳

"That was well done, Cousin, I thank you." They were beneath the central elitch, Sian with her back against the trunk and her feet drawn up on the bench; Meri reclining in the grass.

"Catching the boy before he was engulfed?" he said drowsily. "It *was* well done, and I accept your thanks. You might have bound us *all*, Sian!"

"So I might have. Rebecca Beauvelley has the art of trying tempers well in hand. She will *not* believe me her friend, though I have done everything possible— did I bind her will?" She moved a hand in a wide, shapeless gesture. "I did not! And she repays me by running away! But, no—I compliment you upon your timely rescue of Elizabeth's son, but I thank you for binding Diathen's prisoner."

Meri felt abruptly cold.

"I bound her for a moment, to disarm her, and allow you to disengage," he said.

"Is that so? Perhaps you had best consult your ally, Sea Ranger."

Root and branch! *Bound* to a Newoman? To *that* Newoman, who could subsume him with a careless thought?

He shivered, suddenly ill, and snatched the sunshield out, seeing the thin strands of *kest* drawn into it—one a familiar tangle of greens and blues, the other an ungiving shine of purest gold.

"No," he said aloud. "I refuse this!"

"Cousin, think!" Sian cried from her seat on the bench. "This solves the conundrum of how to respect Rebecca Beauvelley as the covenant directs. Bound to you, she may remain awake and in pursuit of her own necessities. Except as they involve running away and attempting to hide herself from Diathen's summons, of course."

"Of course," Meri said, staring at the sunshield, the two threads drawn into it... "There is, however, a problem."

"Meri, do *not* say that you are afraid of her! She is *a child*, without the least education or understanding of her power. You—"

"Yes, yes, I am old in guile, though my fires are banked. But that is not...precisely the problem, Sian."

She stirred on the bench. "What is it, then?"

"Why only that it seems we are not so much bound to each other, as we are both bound to the sunshield."

⋘⋙

She had, Becca thought, groggily, amassed an astonishing number of bruises and contusions over the last day. Violet had undressed her, sighing over the stained and torn riding dress, and probed for broken bones. Discovering none, she sponged and treated the various scrapes, and wrapped Becca in a blanket.

"I am going to brew you some aleth tea," the girl said, "to help with the pain. Dinner ought to be coming soon. Is there anything else you would like?"

"A bath," Becca said, her eyelids heavy.

Violet sighed and shook her head. "You are *not* to get those hands wet tonight, Miss! You know as well as I do that they need time to heal. In the morning, after you've had a full night of sleep, we'll look at what we have."

"Nancy can bathe me," Becca protested. "And I can hold my hands above the water."

"*Not* tonight," Violet returned firmly. "Now, you sit right here while I brew the tea."

Her own mistress Sonet must have sounded just this way when she had been a new-made healer, Becca thought, and smiled.

"I will sit right here," she assured the girl. "I will not take a bath, and I will," she added, wincing as her shifting on the chair woke protest from half a dozen bruises, "welcome the aleth tea."

Violet smiled shyly and touched Becca quickly on the shoulder before darting away.

Becca sighed and looked about her approvingly. The bed and chair were separated from the larger workroom by a wooden screen that could be moved, or even removed, if the healer wished to keep a closer eye on her patient while she worked. Sonet had a similar arrangement in her workshop, for those patients who required her close attention.

On the other side of the screen, she could hear Violet Moore moving quietly, the slosh of water being poured into a kettle and the rustle of dried leaves. It was, she thought, sighing, all very homey. How easy it was to forget that she was *not* at home, but across the *keleigh*, and once again the bound prisoner of a Fey.

She bit her lip as a wave of desolation rose, and closed her eyes. It was no matter, the tears leaked beneath her lashes and dampened her cheeks. Becca swallowed, hard. She did not want Violet Moore to see her cry, and yet, she was so tired. She wanted to sleep, and to wake up and find that—from the moment she had accepted Kelmit Tarrington's invitation to ride in his phaeton to this very moment where she sat, weeping ashamedly—to find that it was all and nothing more than a bad dream. She would wake, and rise, and put on her dressing gown. Her cousin's maid would comb out her hair and dress it with a pretty ribbon, and she would meet Irene in the breakfast parlor, to drink chocolate and tell over their plans for the day.

Becca bent her head. "Nancy," she whispered.

There was a *poof*, as if a small wind had manifested in this protected corner, and cool hands patted her cheek. Becca opened her eyes and beheld her maid, tiny head cocked to one side, as if awaiting orders.

Well... and she had *summoned* her maid had she not? Becca thought. She drew a hard breath.

"Nancy," she said, keeping her voice low and calm. "I would like a nightdress. And I wish you would comb the leaves and twigs out of my hair."

Nancy stood utterly still for the space of two heartbeats.

Then, she vanished.

The tears began again, hot and fast. Becca looked down, blinking. It was true that she had nothing—

"That is *not* so," she whispered, licking tears off her lips. "You have Rosamunde, and Nancy, and your books; your seeds and your salves. You have your wits and your training as a healer."

All true, and—and so what if she had no nightdress? she asked herself rebelliously. She had often slept naked beside Altimere before—

She gasped, shocked tearless by the intensity of pain, and raised her head.

Nancy swirled into existence no more than a hand-span from her nose, a packet under each arm. She flitted to the bed and put the comb and brush on the coverlet, then dashed upward, shaking out a nightdress in spotless white, its sleeves deep with lace, and ribbons at the throat.

"Where—" Becca began, but Nancy gestured impatiently, clearly meaning her to get onto her feet. Becca stood, swaying slightly, and, encouraged by the small homey sounds still coming from behind the screen, let the blanket fall away.

Nancy patiently worked the wide sleeve over the crippled arm, tied the ribbons primly, and pressed her back down into the chair. She picked up the blanket, and draped it tenderly over Becca's shoulders, fetched the comb and went to work.

By the time Violet Moore came 'round the screen, carrying a cup of aleth tea, Becca was drowsing and Nancy was braiding her hair loosely, for sleep.

⌀∞∞∞⌀

"Bound to a sunshield?" Sian put her feet on the ground and snapped forward, frowning. "That's—"

"Impossible? See for yourself." Meri held it up, the threads glowing bright against the dark air. "Inconvenient? Definitely so. Horrifying?" He shook his head, speechless.

"I would have chosen insupportable," Sian said, her voice surprisingly moderate. "I have never seen, nor heard of such a thing. Does the sea reclaim you, Cousin?"

"*That* choice was mine, and long made," he said, staring at the thing in his hand.

One did not bespeak a sunshield as one might a tree, by asking a question and receiving a—most times—cogent answer. Communication with the sea's children was more fluid than that, and subject to many levels of nuance. Still, what he had to say was simple enough.

Carefully, feeling his way along paths he had walked too little of late, he arrived at a place where he felt the tide move in his blood, and, bearing full upon him, the attention of the sunshield, like the plash and play of water among beach stones.

I refuse this binding, Meri let the thought flow out of him. *The sea long ago released me to the trees.*

Waves lapped the shore, and set stones clattering against each other.

The Vaitura is not just trees, the stones clattered. *The Vaitura is not only the ocean.*

You cannot claim what is not yours, Meri answered.

The stones clattered, briefly loud; perhaps the sunshield was laughing. The sound of surf faded, and Meri shook himself back to the night, and blinked stupidly at Sian, sitting on the grass next to him, a wooden mug of ale in one hand and a piece of bread in the other.

"Elizabeth sent the boy out with food," she said, putting the bread on her knee. She reached behind her and produced another wooden tankard, which Meri accepted with gratitude.

He had not expected more than a few heartbeats to have passed during his exchange—unsatisfactory as it had been—with the sunshield. However, as the poet wrote, the sea kept its own time. He supposed he ought to be pleased that he had not been detained longer.

The ale had a pleasing nutty flavor; he drank deeply, and took the bread Sian offered with a nod of thanks.

"If you will forgive me, Cousin, it seems as if your

powers of persuasion were not equal to the task you set yourself."

Meri sighed and had recourse to the ale once more.

"The sunshield appears to be making its claim for the Vaitura entire," he said, settling the tankard into the crook of his knee and breaking off a bit of bread. He chewed thoughtfully, wondering whimsically how many out-of-the-common-way events one day could contain.

"Oh." He turned to Sian, who lifted her hand, as if to ward him.

"I'm not certain I like your tone," she said.

Meri sighed. "Nor should you. Will you hear the report of your Wood Wise *now*, Engenium?"

"It would appear that I must," she answered, waving permission. "Report, by all means, Meri."

"I spent the day lost inside a wood," he said baldly. "It may be only luck that I wandered out again—or it may be that ... whatever intelligence holds the trees grew tired of its sport."

Sian was watching him attentively, her aura showing an edge not unlike a knife.

"A Ranger who has become lost under leaf is very nearly as strange as a sunshield that seeks to bind Fey."

"That is precisely the path that led me to recall this now," he acknowledged. "The trees had no awareness, no curiosity; their *kest* was—silver. Cold. Possibly not *kest* at all. I had no sense of anything alive—even the birds shunned the place."

She nodded, absently chewing bread.

"Sian," he said abruptly, "where are Sea Hold's Rangers?"

"Sea Hold's Rangers?" She laughed, if so grim a

sound could be termed laughter. "Would that I knew. They wandered away, each in receipt of a charge—you know what Rangers are, Cousin!—and have not yet been released to their other duties.

"I did send one to find one, but nor did she return. You were good with your numbers—how long might I continue to spend two when one had gone unreturned?"

"Even a Ranger on charge may send a message by the trees," Meri said, stomach tight. "What are their names?"

"Joda Meerlauf, Varion Fanelauf, Skaal Meerlauf, Cai Vanglelauf, Dusau Meerlauf, and Kluka Xanlauf."

Meri nodded, and belatedly brought his hand up to cover the yawn.

"I will inquire," he said, "but not tonight." He finished his ale, and reached over to lean the tankard against Sian's knee.

"Your Wood Wise has had a most exerting day, Engenium, and now seeks his nest."

Sian shook her head, eyes wide in bogus wonder, her aura admitting a ripple of mischief.

"Your manners are fair, indeed, Cousin Meri, when you choose to display them."

"I look forward," he said, rising to his feet, "to the moment when I may say the same of yours, Cousin Sian. A peaceful nighttide to you."

"And to you, Cousin," she answered softly.

Chapter Thirteen

IT WAS WARM, AND THE AIR WAS SILVERED WITH FOG.

Becca looked about her, identifying the trunks of trees, and flowers in stern, ordered beds, reminiscent of the grounds at Artifex. She did not remember rising from her bed in Violet Moore's workroom, though she must have done so, nor walking out into this shrouded garden, clad yet in her chaste, white nightdress. Her feet were bare and the bandages were still wrapped around her wounded hands.

Where was she? She turned 'round about, trying to identify a landmark—or even a flower—but the mist made everything strange. Music moved on the hot, sluggish breeze, and the fog danced about her, stroking her face with wanton fingers. She shook her head, and took a breath; it seemed that the cool pleasant taste of duainfey touched her tongue.

She was, she thought, inside a dream—or, perhaps not precisely a dream. There was real danger here.

"I will awaken now," she said, but the mist she

had inhaled cottoned the inside of her mouth and vanquished her voice aborning.

"Rebecca," a whisper, softened by fog, but she knew the voice. She would never forget his voice.

"Rebecca. Come to me, *zinchessa*."

She meant to stand firm; indeed, it seemed that the uncertain geography moved more than she did, the impish mist leaping at her side, plucking at the ribbons of her gown. It was so *warm*. Scarcely thinking, she pulled the ribbons, and allowed the fog and the turgid breeze to tug the opened gown down her arms and waft it away.

The fog continued to flow, wantonly stroking her nakedness, waking such desires that she nearly lay down on the unseen ground and allowed the phantom fingers to have their way with her.

"What have you done to your hands, foolish child?" The fog covered them, shaping itself around Violet Moore's careful bandages. "You must take better care of yourself, *zinchessa*. Had I known you would be so careless, I would not have considered leaving you alone."

"Altimere?" Her voice was sticky and warm, like the air, and her thighs, and the long strands of hair that the mist had teased loose from her braid.

"Altimere, what do you want?"

"I want you by my side, pretty child! It is what I have always wanted. Come to me, now. I know that you are able."

By his side, she thought, and felt a longing so intense she thought it would murder her on the spot, with the mist making sport of her breasts. But—had she not been by his side when his teacher Sanalda was slain, by his will and her hand? Had he not withdrawn his protection and exposed her to violence, shame, and agony?

She remembered; she remembered it all, so clearly. Looking down she saw golden light dripping like blood from her fog-locked fingers. Where the light touched, the fog burned away; and she saw in the flickering flames the blasted carcasses of trees. "No," she whispered. "No. I won't come to you."

The mist blew apart in a scalding blast; cruel fingers dug into her softest parts, and she screamed, gagging when the mist filled her throat with a taste like rotting flowers. The burning wind flung a white wraith into her arms—her nightdress, writhing like a mad thing. She clung to it and ran, the fog beating her now, until she fell, twisted, and sat up—

Whimpering and shaking, her limbs twisted in a blanket strongly scented of lavender, and a single rosy ray of sunlight creeping beneath the screen.

She focused on that sunbeam—clear and clean, and completely unlike the murky, disturbing fog of her dreams. And Altimere! What could it mean, that she dreamed of Altimere inside the *keleigh*?

Or had it, indeed, been a dream? *Could* he call her, even now, when she had rejected him?

Becca bit her lip. Surely, she thought, it had been a dream, born of the stresses of the day, and—and had she not only yesterday seen—and heard!—ghosts in the mists of *keleigh*? It was not wonderful that she had dreamed of it—nor that she should dream of Altimere. She suspected that he would figure in her dreams for the rest of her life.

She licked her lips, tasting blood.

"Nancy," she said softly, so as not to wake Violet Moore, should she still be abed in the next room. "Nancy, I would like to bathe and dress, please."

There was a moment of perfect stillness, while the sunbeam stretched along the floor, then three *poofs!* of displaced air in quick succession.

The first produced a stand and a pitcher at the far corner of the little alcove. The second, a wooden tub, steaming gently, sitting on a bright rag rug.

The third *poof!* produced Nancy herself, her arms filled with bundled clothing, and a pair of sturdy country shoes dangling from one delicate hand. She unburdened herself and flashed over to the bed, tugging the covers down with a will and harrying Becca out of her warm nest.

"Brute!" Becca laughed in spite of herself, pressed her fingers to her lips and looked guiltily at the screen.

"Yes, I'm up!" she continued in a whisper. "Now, attend me—*gently*, if you please, Miss!"

She slipped out of bed and approached the tub, pausing at its side. The rag rug was soft and comforting beneath bare feet, the steam rising from the water scented with mint and rosemary. Becca raised her left hand and clumsily used her bandaged right to unknot the dressings. The cloth fluttered down to the rug, revealing a smooth brown hand, the fingers long and well-formed—and not a scratch nor a scar to be seen.

She unwrapped her right hand with fingers that shook, and found a similar state of complete healing. It was as if, she thought, wondering, turning her hands over, she had never been wounded at all.

"It was only fremoni that she used to dress them,"

she whispered to Nancy's impatient flutter. "Easewerth in the water, to dull the worst of the pain, fremoni on the wounds before wrapping, and aleth tea to put the patient to sleep." She shook her fingers, imitating impatient wings. "Those should have been days a-healing."

Nancy's wings fluttered again, expressive of boredom, or possibly irritation. Becca felt her lips curve into a slight smile.

"Yes, I was the one who called for a bath," she said; "and the water is doubtless growing cold while I stand her and moon about. Your pardon, Nancy." She raised her unmarred hand and pulled the ribbons of her nightdress, shivering suddenly as she remembered her dream and the liberties taken by the mist...

The nightdress fell to pool on the rug about her feet. Becca stepped into the tub, and sat down, Nancy steadying her right elbow. She sighed in heartfelt contentment as the warm bath embraced her—and squeaked as water cascaded over her head.

She shook the hair out of her eyes in time to see Nancy replace the pitcher on the stand. The tiny creature twirled, plucked a bar of soap from the air, and approached with such an air of determination that Becca could almost see her shoving up sleeves she did not possess.

She denied him!

He leapt to his feet, dashing the glass away, anger dissolving wine and glass before ever they were swallowed by the mists.

After all his planning, his care, his—

Anger.

Deliberately, Altimere calmed his rising *kest*. The boiling mists withdrew somewhat as he did so, and that calmed him further. He had been close, oh, so very close to another entrapment, for the mist was greedy for *kest*, and for anything else that would fill up its nothingness and give it weight, form, being.

It was said that those who wandered the mists changed, which at first thought was only rational. A living being who becomes a mist-wraith has surely changed. But it seemed that there was something more to that commonplace than he had considered.

He moved his hand, recovering his glass and its wine from the mists. Anger was not an emotion of which he often partook. Oh, his Rebecca had moved him twice to mighty rages, but, in main, he was a rational man. As an artificer, his nature tended to logical thought, to problem-solving and experimentation.

Altimere sipped his wine, frowning into the mists, seeing something beyond the wearisome sameness.

Perhaps, he thought, he had one more string to his bow.

Nancy did not bathe one as gently as the Gossamers, but she was certainly thorough, Becca thought some while later. She had been briskly dried and her hair wrapped up in a towel. The tub, stand, and pitcher were gone, though the rag rug remained comfortably underfoot. Becca shivered slightly in shift and bloomers while Nancy shook out a canvas split skirt, and a long-sleeved blouse demurely figured with honey-cups. Those, with the sturdy shoes and wool stockings also to hand, were precisely what Becca wished to wear, while remaining troublingly similar to certain articles of clothing she had last seen hanging in her closet in her father's house, far beyond the *keleigh*.

"Where did these clothes come from?" she asked, as Nancy did up the long row of tiny mother-of-pearl buttons. Of course, there was no answer. Becca sighed and suffered herself to be pushed down onto the chair. Stockings and shoes went on with brisk efficiency, while, abandoned, the rag rug blinked out of existence, returning, so Becca devoutly hoped, to wherever it was that Nancy had...borrowed...it from.

Her hair had been ruthlessly dried, the towel vanquished, and the braid almost done when Violet Moore peered 'round the screen.

"Well! I can see that I needn't worry about waking my patient!" the girl said. Her cheeks were rosy, whether from exertion or embarrassment, Becca could not determine. She stepped into the small space. "Let me see your hands, please."

Becca extended her right, and Violet Moore took it gently, subjecting it to a minute examination.

"This has healed very well," she said at last, releasing the member to its owner.

"Not only have my hands healed *well*," Becca said, "but they seem to have healed with remarkable quickness. Can you tell me, is this...usual? Or was there something else beside easewerth and fremoni and aleth in the cure?"

Violet stared down at her, lips parted, and Becca wondered what she had said to earn such a look. The girl shook her head and forced a smile.

"I remember, now. Gran had said that—on the other side of the hellroad—an injury might take a week and more to heal, even with the proper application of cures. Here at New Hope, healing is more rapid, as long as—" Her face shadowed and she glanced aside. "As long as," she continued, her voice lower, "the correct cure is applied."

"I . . . see . . ." Becca said, frowning.

Violet cleared her throat, straightened her shoulders deliberately, and raised her chin. "Did you sleep well?" she asked, determinedly civil.

"I slept until I woke," Becca told her, which was one of Sonet's old jokes. But, really, there was no reason to burden this innocent girl with the sorts of dreams a ruined woman had earned as her nighttime companions.

"I do apologize for not having been on hand when you did wake," Violet Moore said. "I was out in the garden and lost track of time."

"No need for apologies," Becca said, feeling the tug of Nancy tying off her braid. "I was well-attended, though now that you are here I will admit to being hungry. Thank you, Nancy," she added as the tiny creature came 'round to hover before her. "You have been very helpful this morning. I will call you when I need you."

Her maid braced her feet against the air and executed a broad bow before vanishing entirely.

"Where does she go?" Violet Moore asked softly.

Becca shook her head. "I have no idea. It cannot be far, however; she always hears me when I call."

"That's useful," Violet said. "And an artifact, so the Good Lady said. Did you create it?"

Becca glanced aside, face heating. She stood, and bought another moment by shaking out her skirt.

"I am not an artificer, alas," she said, managing to keep her voice firm and light. "Nancy was . . . created . . . by a Fey, whose allegiance she rejected. She now serves me."

"I understand," Violet Moore said, though what—or how much—she understood was more than Becca could say. "And you must forgive me, Miss! You're wanting your breakfast and here I am keeping you talking! There's tea, bread, and jam in the kitchen, if that will serve?"

"That will serve very well, indeed!" Becca said warmly, her stomach noisily agreeing. She blushed, and Violet laughed.

"Come along, then," the girl said. "I could have another cup of tea, myself."

∽≫≪∾

"Good morning, Lady Rosamunde." Meri leaned on the gate of the lean-to, watching the mare with approval. She flicked her ears, perhaps with something less than approval, and glided up to him.

"That's gently done." Meri stroked the soft nose and sighed. He'd woken sticky and disoriented from a dream of mist-walking and unlocalized lust. Such things were unsettling, though they came rarely to a Ranger. He'd left his nest for a look at the dawning sky and a breath of the new day's breeze. The dream clung to him, though, waking longings that were surely nothing short of madness in one who stood soft of *kest* and surrounded by heady Newmen auras.

Unwilling to return to his nest and tempt another

such dreaming, he had strolled into the near trees and breakfasted on bonberry, vinut, and spring water so cold it took his breath.

Fully awake, and satisfied, the dream finally fading, he had leaned against a ralif and sent a good-morning to the trees.

Good sun, Ranger. That was the voice of the ralif he rested against, though he could feel the attention of other trees, all about him.

"I am in search of a branch of Rangers, who passed under leaf some number of days ago. It is reported that a charge came to each, save the last. None have sent word of their condition, and she to whom they owe duty begins to wonder after them."

A Ranger under leaf is in no danger, said a larch.

Meri shivered and forcibly thrust aside the memory of the trees under whose undead branches he had stumbled, lost and blind and disregarded, beside which the monster his arrow had taken receded to a mere novelty.

"I have myself walked among trees that took no note of me, nor of anything living," he said slowly. "And there are strange things a-move, under leaf."

True, said the larch.

And—*What are their names?* asked the ralif.

He gave them; six names. Five Rangers who had received a charge, and the sixth, who had gone seeking.

The trees will search, Ranger, the ralif said, and he felt the agreement of others, as the names made their way into the thought of the forest.

He'd thanked them, and took his leave, walking back to the village for lack of a better direction for himself, and so had found himself at the lean-to sheltering Rebecca Beauvelley's quarter-Fey horse.

He stroked the mare's nose again, hearing the slight sound of young steps behind him. Rosamunde snorted, and danced away, perhaps not wanting to be seen accepting his caresses.

"Good sun to you, sprout," Meri said, turning sideways, with his foot still on the rail.

"Good sun, Master," the boy said with his accustomed good cheer. "The Lady sent me to find you and say that there will be a Speaking under the Hope Tree at the next half-hand."

Meri sighed to himself. At least he would not have to endure the auras of the entire village while confined by dead wooden walls.

"I will be in attendance," he said to the boy. "And yourself?"

"Oh, the whole village will be there!" Jamie said blithely. "Lady Sian sent me 'round to everyone." He grinned. "I'm to tell Miss Beauvelley now, and escort her to the Speaking."

Meri felt his eyebrow rise. Send a vulnerable sprout to escort that one? What was Sian thinking?

As if she heard the slight to her rider, Rosamunde snorted and stamped.

"She is a very... beautiful... lady, isn't she?" Jamie asked. Meri blinked down at him.

"Who?" he asked, around the tickle of cold dread in his belly.

"Miss Beauvelley," Jamie answered. "So... bright."

"Oh, aye, she's bright." Meri reached out and put his hand on the boy's shoulder. "Jamie, mind me."

The sprout looked up, winging brows rumpled.

"Rebecca Beauvelley is—you may think her beautiful. But her aura—she is not like the others here in the village. You must take care not to come too close to her, lest her brightness burn you."

Jamie frowned, then smiled.

"I'll be careful, Master," he said, and slipped out from under Meri's hand. "I'll fetch Miss Beauvelley now."

Meri shook his head, watching the boy run down the grassy lane.

"May I ask," he murmured, "what the trees told the sprout just then?"

Why, only that you were harmed by wretched and evil Newmen across the hellroad, said the elitch at the center—the Hope Tree itself. *And that you are justly wary since.*

"That will not help him to protect himself," Meri said irritably. "Last night, he might have been immolated, or bound to her, or—"

Ranger, these Newmen have sheltered beneath my branches for many sunrises. They are not the same as those who treated you so cruelly.

"Cruelty need not be deliberate," Meri argued.

There was no answer from the tree.

He sighed, and staggered, as Rosamunde pushed him firmly with her nose.

"It was an earthdance," Violet Moore was saying, staring hard into her teacup. "We all ran out into the green. Gran... We were in the workroom. She sent me out, and—she said she was coming right after! And then—the tree fell. It struck the house, not the workroom. The dance kept on, and Gran never came out—maybe she didn't trust herself to walk on the land. When it was over, I ran back—she was on the floor, no mark, as if she were sleeping. We took her to Mother's house and put her to bed."

She swallowed, raised the cup, and sipped, blinking hard.

Becca sipped her own tea, put the cup down, and picked up her bread and jam.

After a time, the girl took up her tale again.

"She didn't seem to be hurt—" Violet raised her hand, unconsciously, Becca thought, and touched her right cheek—"a scrape, here, from when she fell, I thought. I looked in the books, but— She had some trouble breathing. I gave her air nettle tea, by drops. I thought—I thought that had eased her, but she didn't wake up. Sam came back from Sea Fort—and still she hadn't woken. I gave her a tiny dose—three grains, no more!—of kaen. It seemed to do nothing. Sam sat with her, and I did. She began to sweat, and show some restlessness, and I thought, *Good, the kaen is working on her*, and then she—she took a deep breath and just—she was gone..."

She closed her eyes, but that didn't stop the tears. Becca put down her uneaten bread and reached across the table to put her hand over the girl's.

"It is...very hard...when a patient dies," she said, slowly, trying to think what Sonet would say, in her infinite, practical wisdom. "Especially a patient who shows no mark, or any reason to fail. It must be—I can imagine that your grief is made worse, Miss Moore, by the fact that it was your own teacher who died. It must feel as if you failed her."

The girl bent her head, the tears coming in earnest now, and nodded bleakly.

"Yes," Becca said. "But, you know . . . I think you did well."

"Well!" Violet gasped, pulling her hand away. "Gran died!"

"Yes," Becca said again. "She did. But that was not the fault of your treatment. You were conservative and thoughtful, and I do not know that I could have done anything better." She paused, recalling Sonet's words upon a particular occasion. "One of the sorry truths of our calling is that sometimes, for what appears to be no reason at all—someone will die. The elderly often slip away from us this way. It's as if they just—become tired. It's not the healer's part to prevent them from seeking their rest. We treat the ill and the infirm, set bones and stitch cuts." Becca took a breath, Sonet's words echoing inside her head.

"We do our best, Land helping. But we must never forget that we're part of the cycle of growth and death, too."

She leaned back, biting her lip, suddenly ashamed of her presumptuousness. Who was she to advise this girl, who had lost the guidance of her teacher and the love of her grandmother? Who—

The garden door burst open, and the boy Jamie stepped into the kitchen with a smile that faded as he beheld his sister's distress.

"Violet?"

She turned her face away, and bent, using her apron to mop up. "It's all right, Jamie," she said, breathlessly. "Miss Beauvelley and I were talking about healing."

"Oh." He cast a doubtful look at Becca, who did her best to smile for him.

"Good morning, Jamie Moore," she said.

"Good sun, Miss," he answered, and cleared his throat. "The Lady sends me to escort you and—and Violet to the Speaking."

Becca frowned. "Speaking?"

"I expect Lady Sian will be telling us her plans and orders," Violet said, her voice hoarse, but her damp face approaching composure.

"That's right," Jamie said. "Under the Hope Tree, and everyone's to come." He turned and glanced outside at the sky. "Now."

Becca shook her head. "I need to tend my horse first. I should have done it ere this," she added, around a sudden stab of guilt. Rosamunde had protected her—had taken wounds for her!—and she had not even thought—

"She was hurt last evening," she said pushing back from the table, and rising.

"She's fine, Miss," Jamie said, smiling up at her. "Master Vanglelauf tended her wounds last night, like he promised you he would. I found him with her just a few minutes ago. I'm sure she's well looked after."

It seemed to Becca that a dark wing passed over the sun. Master Vanglelauf! The one-eyed Fey with his cold demeanor, who had bound her to him with a bit of bone, and was now ingratiating himself with her horse!

"I—" she began, and found her elbow in a strong grip. Startled, she turned her head and met Violet Moore's determined brown eyes.

"Miss Beauvelley, your horse is well cared for," the

girl said forcefully. "You can check on her after the Speaking. In the meantime, I don't know how such things are done beyond the hellroad, but here in New Hope, when our Lady calls us to a Speaking, we do not dawdle and we are not late."

"That's right," Jamie piped up from her other side. "It would be disrespectful."

Becca swallowed. "On the other side of the . . . hellroad . . . when the Landed called folk together, that call had the force of law."

"Well, then," Violet said, stepping forward, and urging Becca with her. "That doesn't sound so different from home, now does it?"

Chapter Fourteen

SIAN STOOD UNDER THE BIG ELITCH TREE, BRAVE IN her leggings and shirt. She appeared, to Becca's eye, well rested and in possession of her temper. On her left stood Meripen Vanglelauf, hands behind his back and legs braced wide, and on his left Sam Moore, arms crossed over his chest. On Sian's right stood Elizabeth Moore, face calm, and hands folded before her.

Gathered in a loose semicircle before them were perhaps three dozen folk, ranging from the greybeard with his stick to a babe in a sling at his mother's breast.

Good morning, Gardener, a deep voice echoed inside her head. *I am called the Hope Tree. You are welcome to shelter beneath my branches*.

"Thank you," she whispered, feeling tears start to her eyes, as Sian looked up and saw her.

The Engenium inclined her head gravely, and raised her hand, beckoning with long, elegant fingers. Becca went cold, her feet rooted to the ground. Sian wanted her *up there*, in front of the *entire village*? She—

*Peace, Gardener. Sian means to arrange for your
protection. And a new seedling in the grove is known
to all.*

True enough, she thought, swallowing. True enough.

Still, it was—hard, harder even than walking through
Altimere's garden, past the flowers on which she had
been raped, through rooms where she had serviced
Altimere's guests. Her stomach twisted, and she was
abruptly sorry for her simple breakfast of tea and bread.

Somehow, she made it to the little group at the
front of the crowd. Elizabeth Moore smiled at her
and took a step sideways, making room for Becca to
slip into position at Sian's immediate right.

"Good sun, Rebecca Beauvelley. I trust you slept
well?" Sian sounded positively courtly. Becca looked
up into intent, sea-colored eyes.

"I slept well," she acknowledged, which was true, if
not *entirely* true. "Thank you," she added, belatedly.

The Fey inclined her head and turned to face
the assembled villagers. Slowly, the gesture rich with
meaning, she placed her fingertips together, raised
her arms to the height of her shoulder, and spread
them wide, as if offering an embrace to all of those
gathered.

"Good sun, people of New Hope. I am Sian, Engenium of Sea Hold, keeper of your oath, protector of
your land. Today, I bring you a duty, and a warning."

There was a little stir at this, though none of the
faces Becca saw expressed dismay. Curiosity, rather,
and a little intrigue. Sian lowered her arms, slowly.

"First, your duty." She extended a long hand, caught
Becca's wrist, and stepped forward. Becca, perforce,
went with her.

"This is Rebecca Beauvelley, who crossed the *keleigh* in company with a High Fey. Queen Diathen in fair Xandurana requests on her behalf the boon of your hospitality, until such time as she is required at court. Rebecca Beauvelley is a healer and a Gardener."

Speak to them, Gardener, the Hope Tree urged her.

"Good sun," she said, her voice thinner than she liked. She cleared her throat, and raised her chin, meeting the eyes of the old man who had spoken to her last night, and told her that there were not many in New Hope who knew what an Earl was.

"I am pleased to offer my skills for the greater good," she said, the words coming somewhat easier off her tongue, "and in return for the care of myself, my horse, and my servant."

The old man gave her a toothy grin, and an easy nod. "That's right, Missy," he said. "And the trees talk to you, don't they?"

"They do," she answered. "The trees have been very kind to me."

"That's well, then. Ye can help young Master Vanglelauf to figure out what's gone amiss with ours."

Becca swallowed bile, refusing to think of the one-eyed Fey and what service he was likely to require of her.

"I will do everything in my power," she said faintly, "to assist the trees."

The old man gave her another nod. "That's right," he said again, and pointed his long chin at Sian. "Is there other news, Lady?"

"In fact, Jack Wood, there is. I must warn you all that strange Fey may come into your village. They may say that they are sent from the Queen, or from me. Direct all such visitors to Master Vanglelauf, who will remain here as my emissary and the instrument of my will."

That created something more of a stir among those who stood in deference to their Lady's word. Indeed, Becca felt a frisson along her own nerves, and wondered if Sian had touched them all with her power.

"I have," Elizabeth Moore said from her place behind Becca, "asked the trees to call Palin and Vika in to us, as well." There was a pause, as if the woman had smiled. "After all, Master Vanglelauf must sleep sometime."

"These strangers are enemies of the Queen?" a sandy-haired man called from the crowd. "Should we arm ourselves, Lady?"

"With the permission of the headman and the tree-kin." Meripen Vanglelauf's cool voice sliced effortlessly through the minor babble arising from this question. "With their permission, I will set wards, and request that the trees be vigilant for us. It should not come to fighting."

"Indeed," a woman cried from very near to Becca, her voice thin and shrill, "it *ought not* come to fighting! Fey can enslave with a look! The best answer is to hide yourselves in the wood!"

Becca gasped, belatedly recognizing her own voice, and pressed her fingers against her lips.

The green was silent, saving the movement of a breeze through the branches stretching above them all.

"In fact," Sian said, calmly, "that is not ill advice. It is better for Fey to deal with Fey, especially when there may be, as John Culdoon surmises, opposing political goals in play. You are of the land, by your oaths and by your actions. The land will protect you, and the trees will shield you. Use these gifts wisely, and all will be well."

She looked out over those assembled, to the right, and to the left.

"I hold your oath," she said and it seemed to Becca that the very air shimmered with the force of her words. "I carry your lives next to my heart. You may be at peace, under my protection."

Becca shuddered, tasting the ghost of peppered wine score her throat. *Protection.*

Sian's word is good, Gardener. She does not hold her duty light.

Becca swallowed, stomach roiling. Beside her, Sian raised her arms to shoulder height and curved them inward until her fingertips touched, then lowered her joined hands to her waist.

"Good sun. Good growth. Good travel," she said. "Until we meet again."

"Good sun, Lady!" "Until again!" "Travel safe, Lady!" The chorus of well-wishes washed over Becca, leaving her feeling limp and strained. Blindly, she turned and walked away from Sian's side, past Elizabeth Moore and away.

No one tried to stop her; no one joined her. She had no clear notion of where she was going, only that she had to get away, to be by herself and order her thoughts.

"Hope Tree?" she whispered.

Gardener. What would you?

"Do you know where Rosamunde—my horse—is?"

There was a pause, in which she still somehow felt the tree's presence, though it did not speak. Slowly, she became aware of a picture growing inside her head, of a lean-to sheltered by a larch tree. Inside the lean-to, shoulder pressed against the gate—was Rosamunde, ears perked forward as if she had seen Becca approach.

Becca felt her heart lift. She blinked, disoriented by the vividness of the picture inside her head. Another blink brought the world around her into focus. Behind her, she heard voices—Elizabeth Moore and Sian—and the sounds of people returning to their daily business. Ahead of her, she saw the green, and Gran Moore's house, with its attached workroom and side-garden. To her left...

To her left, and some distance past Gran Moore's house, along a sort of grassy avenue, she saw the hint of a fence covered in winberige blossoms, and the corner of a roof, shrouded in larch leaves.

"Thank you, Hope Tree," she whispered, and began to walk down that grassy avenue.

A dozen steps along, she heard a whinny, and an emphatic snort, as if Rosamunde were scolding her for being so slow.

Laughing, Becca began to run.

There was, Altimere admitted to himself, a degree of risk involved in what he planned to do—risk to his liberty, to his continued survival, and to his plans for the Vaitura, and the *keleigh*. Still, an artificer did not falter because of risk. Indeed, as his teachers had carefully instructed him, risk was the heady land that lay between *can* and *cannot*, where all things are possible. Still, the mists had not yet succeeded in making of him a fool, and he had prepared as well as he could. A bell jar wrung from the sticky mists sat upon a similarly constructed worktable. It was like enough to the arrangements previously known to his subject that he felt it would not rail against its confinement—out of habit, if nothing else.

It did trouble him, that his sole raw material remained the mist. He had reasons—compelling reasons—not to wish the mists to taste what he would draw to him.

He checked his precautions once again, and flicked his finger against the bell jar, smiling slightly when it rang.

The bond between those who had shared *kest* was strong, and the bond between student and teacher.

But the bond between the creator, and that which was created—that was a special and potent bond, indeed.

Altimere shaped the thought of his artifact—his great work, though it seemed so small. He shaped the thought lovingly, building detail upon detail, until it stood in his mind as vividly as if the actual construct hovered before him.

When he was satisfied with his detail and his concentration, he flicked his finger once more against the glass, and spoke a single word.

"Come."

∽≫✕≪∾

"It would have been mannerly," Meri said, "to have allowed me to know beforehand that I was going to be burdened with your will."

Sian gave him a sidelong glance. "Perhaps it would have been, Meri, but a moment's thought would surely have shown you that I had no other options."

"I think you have another option," he said, as they

walked beyond his nest and toward the threshold to the forest.

"Do I? Teach it to me, by all means."

"You might take Diathen's hostage to Sea Hold. Indeed, I would call *that* your only option, rather than leaving her here 'mong Newmen, with no protection save one ill-used and befuddled Ranger."

"I think you give yourself too little credit, Meri! It is hardly like you. As to taking Rebecca Beauvelley to Sea Hold—I dare not."

"*Dare* not?" He stopped to stare at her. "You *dare not* burden *Sea Hold*, which has stood in the teeth of storm and sea, and weathered not only the last war, but two before that—with *one* Newoman?" He raised a hand to Sian's elevated eyebrows. "I grant her untrained and heedless, but she certainly mounts no threat to Sea Hold. To this village, however, and to those whose oath you hold, she is a threat, indeed. And that *before* we come to the matter of 'strange Fey' who may have an interest in her failing to return to Diathen's hand." He laughed, mirthlessly. "Who shall be shown to me, shall they?"

"Meri, you must have slept poorly; you are not usually this humble of your abilities. There *may be* strange Fey. Equally, there may be no one at all. And in any wise, I still do not dare bring her to Sea Hold—not while she is bound to a sunshield."

He opened his mouth—and closed it with a sigh.

"Precisely." Sian bowed, put her fingers to her mouth, and whistled.

"At least tell me," Meri said, as they stood awaiting the answer to her call, "if it *is* Altimere the Artificer that I may expect to entertain on behalf of the lady."

Sian sighed. "Cousin," she said softly, "I cannot say. Altimere the Artificer has disappeared, and Councilor Zaldore with him. Their lack is the reason the Queen's Constant was put to recess."

"Zaldore..." Meri frowned. "She who sent the geas to me under your name."

"That very Zaldore," Sian agreed, as the shadows shifted, and grey Brume ambled up to her.

"My very good friend." She reached out to stroke his nose tenderly. "Wilt bear me home?"

The stallion blew, and bowed. Sian threw a leg over his back, settling as he rose. She smiled down at Meri.

"You are a hero, Cousin."

"It pleased some to say so, based on a single action, taken many sunrises ago," he returned. "It bears recalling that there has been much that I might have done better, since."

Sian laughed, and Brume turned, moving from a walk to a canter with seamless grace.

He waited until they were out of sight, then turned back to the village, sending his thought ahead to the elitch.

Where might I find the Gardener, Elder?

"Not a mark on you!" Becca ran her hand wonderingly over Rosamunde's shoulder, across her barrel and flank. Horsehair flowed like silk beneath her palm, no tears or rents apparent. Rosamunde blew and stamped, twice, the muscles moving sweetly, with no hitch or grab.

Becca laughed. "Yes, all you like and more! But you must allow me to be amazed—and so very grateful."

She stroked Rosamunde's flank again. "You must not take such terrible risks for me," she whispered, her voice choked with tears. "You and Nancy—I do not deserve either of you."

She moved forward. Rosamunde bowed her head, allowing Becca to stroke her soft nose. "I wonder if Nancy can saddle you?" she murmured. "Perhaps she can; there is nothing she has not been equal to, yet. Perhaps I will even be allowed to ride you, in between sleep and servitude." The tears, conquered once, rose again. She leaned her forehead against Rosamunde's neck and bit her lip. "You will think me the greatest goose alive," she whispered, "but I have allowed myself to be bound again."

Rosamunde muttered, perhaps in irritation, for which Becca could hardly blame her. Surely it was not ridiculous to hope that one's rider could preserve her liberty for more than a day?

Rosamunde trilled a welcome. Becca stiffened, then turned, expecting perhaps Violet Moore, come to cajole or bully her errant patient into taking a nice nap.

Meripen Vanglelauf—her new protector! Becca thought bitterly—leaned against the gate, his arms crossed on the top rail and one booted foot braced against the bottom.

He was, Becca saw, with a catch in her throat, as brown as Elyd had been. Her friend's face had been rugged and weary, but someone, she thought, had used Meripen Longeye hard.

The sun fell full on his dark face, illuminating a stern study of hard lines and hollow cheeks. A scar slashed pale and shocking across his left cheek, and another, through his right eyebrow, across the stern

brow, vanishing into his hair. The patch over his right
eye was leather; the left eye was as green and giving
as glass. As he had been last night, he was dressed
in woodsman leather, breeches and vest over a shirt
that was all the colors of the forest. His hair hung in
a loose tail over one shoulder; the breeze toyed with
locks of brown, auburn, and black. There was a knife
sheathed on the right side of his belt, and an elitch
branch thrust through it on the left. His tattered aura
was all but invisible in the bright sunlight.

Rosamunde trilled again and walked out from under
Becca's hand, thrusting her nose at the Fey, as if his
caresses were not only her due, but welcome.

"Lady, we have celebrated each other once already
this day."

Rosamunde thrust her nose again. The Fey paid
the required toll, absently, and looked beyond her.
Becca's stomach cramped, but she kept her chin up
and met that green glare firmly.

"You have no high opinion of Fey," he commented,
his light voice expressionless.

"I am certain that it must reflect poorly on me, to
have formed a low opinion of persons who enslave
others, and hunt those they deem to be their inferi-
ors." Becca heard her voice shake, as if she were ill,
and indeed, she did *feel* ill, weak and uncertain of
her balance. She walked forward, though it brought
her closer to him, and put her hand on Rosamunde's
flank, hoping to draw courage from contact with that
high-hearted lady.

"Unbind me," she said to Meripen Vanglelauf. "I
refuse you."

He sighed, and tipped his head, perhaps so he

could see her better from his single eye. "Yes, so you
had said. Believe me, please, when I say that the last
thing I would wish to do is bind a Newman."

"Then why have you done so?" she snapped.

"I have *not* done so," he snapped back, rapier quick.

"Oh? And I suppose you didn't throw that bit of
bone at me last night when Sian was trying to murder
Nancy—"

"When you had angered Sian to the point of nearly
binding you herself?" he interrupted. "Which she would
have instantly regretted—not to mention that it would
have been no good thing to have done before her oath-
sworn?" He straightened from his lean on the gate, his
right hand dropping to the hilt of his knife. "*You* were
provoking a disaster, which I attempted to disarm."

"By binding me." Becca was shaking, her nerves
clamoring with fear, anger, and disgust.

"I have not bound you! Do you wish a demonstration?" He straightened, and flung his left hand out, as
imperious as Altimere himself. "Rebecca Beauvelley,
come here."

Becca fell back a step, tasting peppered wine along
the edge of her tongue.

Meripen Vanglelauf smiled, grimly, and swept her
a sarcastic bow.

"Thank you."

Becca shook her head. "Am I," she said slowly, "a free
woman, utterly in control of my own will and destiny?"

Astonishingly, he laughed. "Oh, certainly! As much
as I am!" His hand moved more swiftly than her eye
could properly follow it, seeming only to touch his
pouch and there—as last night!—the white bone was
tumbling through the air at her.

Becca stepped aside, right hand fisted at her side. She would not be tricked twice! she thought as the object tumbled closer. Of itself, her crippled left hand rose slightly, palm up, fingers cupped.

The bone dropped gently onto her palm.

Becca moaned, and stood staring at it: a perfectly white, circular bone, with...petals, perhaps, embossed in a circle 'round its center. Snagged at the center were two lines of spiderweb, twining lazily together—one green-and-blue, very like the ragged aura that blew about Meripen Vanglelauf; and the other bright gold, just like the light that sometimes dripped from her own fingers.

Shivering, nauseous, she forced herself to look back to him.

"The last time I was bound to a Fey," she said, her voice high and unsteady, "it was through the means of a necklace. Now I am bound by a bone. The difference is, if you will pardon my saying so, immaterial. Release me."

"*You* are not bound," Meripen Vanglelauf told her, and it seemed to Becca that his voice was more panicked than haughty. "*We* are bound! Can you not see it?"

She stared at him, then down at the object in her hand, with its meager adornment of silken light. Aura-stuff, she thought. Very well.

"*We* are bound," she said, keeping her attention on the thing she held, "by this object?"

"The sunshield. Yes."

Becca weighed it, feeling the prick of tiny dry spines against her palm. It was, to all of her senses, dead; whatever intelligence that had once informed it had long fled. How it could bind anything was beyond her ability to know. However, a healer did not need to know precisely how easewerth worked upon the nerves to know that it dulled pain.

She closed her fingers around the . . . sunshield, feeling sharp edges cut into her skin. There was a roaring in her ears, and she felt as if she were about to swoon, but surely, surely, there was only one thing to do?

The roaring grew louder as she turned her hand over and opened her fingers.

There was a flash of green and gold as the sunshield tumbled to the ground. She marked its landing place well, raised her foot, encased in its sturdy shoe . . .

"No!" Meripen Vanglelauf's shout reached her even over the thunder in her ears; a tree's *Gardener, do not!* rattled the inside of her head.

There was a flare, a cold snap—and her back was on the ground, her vision a spangle of silver and turquoise, and Rosamunde was lipping her skirt. The air moved, and she turned her head to the right in time to see Meripen Vanglelauf snatch the dead whiteness of the sunshield from the grass at her side, and scuttle away, as if she were some fearsome beast that he had approached too nearly.

"Are you mad?" He was on one knee, back against the gatepost, fist pressed over his heart. His voice was shaking—*he* was shaking, Becca saw, and his brown face looked muddy.

"If I am, it's no small wonder," she returned. "Help me to stand."

"No," he answered starkly, pressing even tighter against the post. He held his fist out to her, as if she could see through his fingers to what he protected. "This is a *sunshield*! You *cannot* destroy it."

Becca twisted, and fell, panting, her limbs too weak to support her. "You say that it's bound us—this sunshield. The only rational thing to do is destroy it." She tried to sit up again, braced against her crippled arm, and again fell back.

"This is absurd. Help me up."

"No," he repeated, looking faintly ill. "You do not snare me that easily."

He came to his feet, fluid as a cat, his fist down at his side. With his other hand, he touched the elitch branch thrust through his belt, and visibly took a breath.

"You are a danger to this village and to yourself," he said, clearly and quite calmly. Then, he turned and was gone, as if he had walked from the sunlight into shadow.

Becca closed her eyes, feeling tears gather. Rosamunde blew against her hair.

"Yes, no doubt I do look ridiculous," she said. "Oh..." She took a hard breath.

"Nancy," she whispered. "Help me up, please."

First, she baited Sian, then she tried to destroy the sunshield. Meri reached the central elitch and all but collapsed against it.

"Rebecca Beauvelley has a will to die," he said, staring up into the dense branches.

Ranger, that was so, but she has learned better. The thought of the trees is that she requires training, and the opportunity to grow with her own kind.

"There is no one here to train her," Meri said, closing his eye, and leaning his head back against the wide trunk. The sunshield... He shuddered, seeing her raise her boot, hearing again the crash of the invisible wave that knocked her off her feet, to lie helpless, the sunshield less than a handspan from her side.

It had taken every bit of his courage to dart over and snatch it up to safety, skittish as a tree-mouse and just as sensible. Her aura had drawn him, brilliant and horrifying, and there had been a moment—scarcely a moment—when he had thought himself caught by her influence, as unfettered golden strands wafted toward his poor protection.

"Hero, indeed," he muttered, and laughed, weak and wobbly.

There is yourself, the elitch said, interrupting these shameful memories.

Meri blinked. "Eh?"

To train her, the elitch said. *Someone must, for you spoke sooth when you said that she is a danger to herself and to those who shelter beneath my branches.*

"I cannot train her!" That dazzling aura, so warm and compelling... "She would drink me dry and not even celebrate the vintage."

Not so. You can teach her better, Ranger.

Oh, yes, he could teach her better, Meri thought bitterly. But to do so would require a closeness—not quite a melding, but a willful sharing of *kest*, the thought of which simultaneously excited and disgusted him.

"No," he said, and pushed away from the support of the tree. The sunshield, he replaced in his pouch, after another long glare at the threads of *kest* captured at its heart. To his left, he heard Newman voices, and also to his right. His stomach cramped, and he shook his head, angry with his weakness.

He needed to go out, he thought, among the trees,

where there were no Newmen with their brilliant, seductive auras. He needed, in fact—

"Wards," he said, recalling the pledge he had so recently made. "I must set wards."

If the tree—any tree—heard him, they vouchsafed no answer.

⚬⚬⚬⚬⚬⚬

Despite his best efforts, the bell jar remained empty. There had been not even the faintest flicker of *kest* to indicate that his command—tied to the artifact with the strength of a geas, for of all the things he would willingly lose, this was very nearly the least—there had been indication that his command had been heard.

Altimere closed his eyes and waved a hand, vanquishing table and jar. With his other hand, he fingered a handkerchief out of the warm mists and blotted the moisture from his face.

He had, he thought, allowed Rebecca too much freedom, amused as he had been by her foolish antics. Who better than he knew the power of a name?

It would perhaps be worth wondering, once he was free of this place, just who was the bigger fool.

Chapter Fifteen

BECCA PAUSED ON THE THRESHOLD OF THE WORKROOM, taking time, as she hadn't done, last night or this morning, to look about her. It was an ordered and orderly place, with cords of drying leaves, braids of wild onion, and clusters of lavender hanging from the rafters. Other ingredients were sorted meticulously into drawers and baskets on the shelves over one worktable, while more shelves held pots of salve, tonics, tinctures, and twists of herbs.

It was all so familiar and comfortable that she felt her eyes prick again. *Really, Becca,* she scolded herself, blinking the tears away, *when did you become a watering-pot?*

A small sniff came from inside the room, followed by another. It would seem, then, that she was not the only watering-pot at hand.

Violet Moore stood at the worktable against the far wall, her back to the door. She was pulling down baskets and peering into drawers, touching twists of this and branches of that—doing inventory, Becca thought, stepping carefully into the room—or mourning.

"Gran always kept ahead," Violet said, though she did not turn her head. Perhaps she was speaking to herself. "I'll need to go out tomorrow for more cadmyon and marisk."

Becca came 'round to the girl's right, watching as she stretched to take down a basket. "Cadmyon *or* marisk, I would think," she said. "One blooms in spring, the other in fall." No sooner were the words out of her mouth than she wished them back. How foolish—

Violet turned her head with a smile.

"You must know seasons!"

"Indeed, I have been long enough in the Vaitura to recall that *here* there are no seasons," Becca said, irritation sharpening her voice. She smiled, to show that her anger was for herself, and not for Violet. "I had been trying to teach the garden at Xandurana to heed a proper cycle, but I fear it was an uphill road."

"It seems to me that seasons only make some things rare when they are most wanted! Surely it is better to have everything available at all times, so that supplies may be replenished as they are needed, rather than hoarded and told over."

"Perhaps it is," Becca said slowly. "In Xandurana, it had seemed to me that the plants constantly risked themselves in the crush of everything growing at once, but it may be that I am wrong—or that the benefits reaped outweigh the risk. Certainly, I have *never* seen such results as you achieved here." She raised her unmarked right hand.

"The land is rich with virtue on this side of the

hellroad," Violet Moore said, shyly. "Gran said that. Even seeds that were sung into the land, and so grew more potent plants—over there—she said, didn't have half the virtue as wild gathers do on Lady Sian's land."

"Certainly, there is no overnight healing on the other side of the *keleigh*," Becca said, "no matter if the seeds were sung over!"

"Well," Violet said, pulling down a basket and frowning into its depths. "Much depends on the injury. Your hands were cut, but the bones were whole. If I'd had to splint your fingers or your arm, you would not have seen so swift a healing." Stretching high on her toes, she put the basket back. "We need corish root, too. Well." She gave Becca a sidelong glance. "Let me show you the rest of the house, then we can do a survey of the garden."

"There's no need for me to see the rest of the house, surely?" Becca protested, though she followed Violet through an interior door and into a wide room.

"Indeed there is!" the girl said, briskly. "If you are to be our healer, then this will be your house."

"Stay! Sian did not bring me to be your healer!" Becca cried, stopping in midstep.

Violet turned to look at her.

"You were at the Speaking," Becca told her, sharply. "I am here only until the Queen sends for me." Seeing the girl's eyes widen, she softened her voice. "And, besides, I would not wish to usurp your place, Miss Moore. *You* are the healer here."

"I don't know enough!" Violet wailed. "Gran had not released me; I was still her 'prentice when she—she—"

"No one ever knows enough," Becca said, as Sonet had once said to her. "We do as much as we can, as well as we can do it. And we learn, from our mistakes even more than our successes." She sighed at the girl's stricken face. "I will teach you as much as I can while I am here. But I cannot think that I will be here for very many days." And who knew, she thought bitterly, what Meripen Vanglelauf's *sunshield* might require, other than the right to knock her to the ground and hold her helpless at whim.

She sighed. Nancy had helped her up, straightened her clothing, and made her presentable again. There were only the bruises on her rump and her pride to testify to her misadventure.

Becca shook herself, and looked about for a happier topic of consideration.

"This is a very pleasant room!" she said to Violet Moore's anxious eyes. "I would be very happy to guest here, but—"

"You must stay somewhere," Violet interrupted, "until the Queen wants you. It might as well be here. I live here, after all, and it will be—be convenient for you."

Ah, Becca thought, and smiled to herself. "That sounds a reasonable plan," she said to Violet. "I will be pleased to stay as your guest, though you will have to bear Nancy, who I own is odd."

Violet nodded seriously. "I'll be glad to have you and your servant," she said, and this time Becca did not smile. For here was a way to fill the house with voices and motion, and to keep at bay the malicious whispering shadows of guilt.

Violet moved her hand, showing Becca the door opposite them.

"The kitchen is through here," she said, beckoning Becca to follow her. "And the garden just behind."

"You know," she said, after Becca had duly admired the pots hung on their hooks and the neat cooking hearth. "There's a saying we have here—'I'll do it in a Fey's hurry.'"

Becca tipped her head. "And that means?"

"In the sweet by-and-by," Violet said, pushing open the door and stepping out into the garden. "The Queen may not call you as soon as that."

<hr />

Setting wards is a tricky business at best. Factor in monsters from beyond the ken of trees, and it approached impossible.

Meri took his time walking back along the track. He noted the near-invisible traces of Brume's passage, but saw no signs of another horse until he had passed beyond a wide curve that put New Hope Village out of sight.

There, he found signs a-plenty. He followed what must be Rosamunde's hoofprints off the path and into the brush, frowning when he found wisp of fur and a misplaced clod. Rebecca Beauvelley had let them understand that she had designed and executed her own escape, and yet here it would appear that she had enlisted aid.

Or had she?

Meri crouched down, the better to study the signs. Brethren were as curious as cats. It could have been that one had dawdled nearby, enchanted by the Newoman's aura, or the novelty of someone riding blindly into the wood after dark.

So. The Brethren had waited, here, and then had followed—?

Meri raised his head, seeking, found the sign again, farther on, and rose, finding the place where its path intersected the horse's route—and where the Brethren took the lead.

"Well," he murmured, "it would appear that Rebecca Beauvelley has allies."

The Gardener dressed his wounds, a ralif offered. *He was obligated to come, when she sent for him.*

"*Obligated*," Meri muttered. The Brethren were usually more canny than to allow themselves to become *obligated*. Still, it could have happened—and especially if there was blood in it.

He followed the trail, admiring its essentially linear tendency—Brethren in the lead, horse following, dainty of her footing, but clearly moving in haste, but with no attempt to conceal themselves. That seemed odd to him. Had they thought that Sian would not come after? Or had all the care gone to putting distance behind them before they went to ground? If the Brethren had a lair nearby—but would it lead a Newoman there?

It was then that he found the frizenbush, and understood the Brethren's plan.

Straight into the heart of the bush went the tracks, and so did Meri. At the hollow center, he shook his head in disgust at the wreckage of twigs and leaf, the hopelessly muddled ground, and the broken gap in the sheltering branches, already beginning to weave themselves tight.

Meri hunkered, needles sticking into his back, and considered what he saw before him. The Brethren had thought to hide them in the frizenbush, trusting it to shield them from Sian. Which it might have done though Meri thought Brume would not have been so easily fooled. Also, there was the question of Rebecca Beauvelley's cursed brightness. Even the natural dampening powers of the frizenbush might have been overcome by such a display.

He frowned down at the hopelessly churned soil. Had they found the monster hiding in the heart of the bush, waiting for prey?

No, he thought, after a moment. That rupture in the basket of branches had been made from something thrusting *inward*. Meri leaned forward, spying a fan of bloody drops across blue-green branches. Someone, he thought, had scored a hit. His wager was that it had been Rosamunde, though that might have been his newfound affection speaking.

He came to his feet, scrutinizing the branches for a sign of the mare's departure. A glitter of dusty gold drew his eye upward, to a long strand of brown hair caught among the needles. No need to ask to whom that belonged. Carefully, he reached up, untwisted it from the needles, and slipped it into his pouch.

"She has," he said to nothing and to no one in particular, "less wisdom than a seedling."

There was no answer, which was, he supposed, just as well.

He stepped through the branches and considered the options available to him. The end of Rosamunde's flight, he knew, and though it was probable that he should follow it, if only to be sure that the mare's idiot rider hadn't left any other ragtags of *kest* strewn carelessly about, it would seem that backtracking her pursuer's route would be the more . . . instructive.

It was hot.

It was always hot in this place. No matter if he sat, or walked or slept or thought, the heat did not abate.

If he wished, he could indeed produce a breeze, but it failed to cool unless he invested more of his thought and energy than he wished to give, and in the end he was just as uncomfortable for all that he was master of himself.

He had begun to wonder, recently, if this unremitting heat were a deliberate, and vital, segment of Zaldore's plan of betrayal. His preference for comfort and order were well known. Perhaps she had confused *preference* with *need*, and plotted that he would use all of his time and expend all of his *kest* seeking comfort, rather than rescue.

That he had turned his thoughts first to rescue proved yet again that he was Zaldore's superior, in all ways. That he had failed in his attempts to secure that rescue . . . well. He was not defeated yet.

If only it were not so hot.

He did miss his Rebecca, not only for her *kest* that he might draw on to his own benefit, or for the additional small comforts that she might offer, but for her naïve observation. One to whom everything was strange must naturally ask questions of an elder. And he had found Rebecca's questions—very often— illuminating. It was a matter of thought and direction.

For example! It had been he, Altimere, who had realized that the very rotation that contained the *keleigh* created a spiral that might be traveled by those of good fortitude and a strong mind, and since the first one or two dispatched to attempt this theory had not returned, he had gone himself to prove it.

He done much walking between the worlds. While he was not so foolish as to think that he knew the *keleigh* in all its changeable faces, yet in his travels there, he had seen torrent and snowstorm, wind, anomalous fogs, and, yes, heat. Nothing endured, within the *keleigh*; all and everything was subject to change.

This heat, changeless and unremitting...

He shook a kerchief out of the mist and mopped his brow, noting that he was leaning against a ralif, and trying to recall if he had caused it to be there.

That was one of the known dangers of traversing the *keleigh*, after all; its nature clouded not only vision, but also thought and recall.

Heat.

He was no ordinary adventurer, to have so often ventured into the other world, but a seeker after truth and insight. To some he was a philosopher. But no, that would not do. Altimere was no mere philosopher, observing and analyzing, only to write a report which was bound into a book, of interest only to other philosophers.

No, *he* was a creator of the first water, an artist of artifice.

He slipped his hand into his pocket, feeling for, and finding, the top he had used in his demonstration of *kest* and motion. Top in hand, he stood there, recalling the party, and Zaldore's interest. It seemed very long ago.

Waving his hand to inform this odd world that a glass cube now existed on the generosity of his will, he spun the top onto the cube and watched it, absorbed, thinking of the heat.

The artificers—they named themselves *mechanics*— of the world beyond the *keleigh* were fine craftsmen; he admired their ability to work with objects of stern form and gain understanding of their peculiar natures. He marveled at their ability to build *new* devices that were based, not on generations of lore, but on self-acquired knowledge and perception. Those *mechanics* and *chemists* and *mathematicians* were much closer to him in thought and practice than the courtly philosophers who never dared venture into danger to prove their cherished theories.

The top twirled slower and slower, till, at last, it toppled over.

Heat!

In that other world, he had seen demonstrations, theoretical and practical, regarding the nature and workings of heat. Heat was the key to moving things, heat was the key to melting things. Heat could be added, but the act of compression could also produce heat. Constraining and shrinking the room available to a gas concentrated it, and made it hot.

Sometimes, to the point of explosion.

Now he snatched up the top, now he grabbed away the table of glass, now he stared into the mist, recalling experiments going well, recalling the glorious explosive failure of the steam wagon.

He sat down at the base of the ralif.

There was not one wall between freedom and himself, but two.

Zaldore had much to answer for.

The monster's trail was more subtle than he had expected, given its entirely unsubtle attack on Rosamunde. Meri followed with interest, marveling at the creature's lightness of foot. Perhaps it had assistance?

"The Low Fey who were partners in the attack against the Gardener and her allies," he said to the trees. "Are they known to the trees?"

There was silence while he backtracked his quarry around a clutter of brush and low-growers.

Such arise from time to time, Ranger, a culdoon said diffidently. *The eldest think their kind is recent and not well rooted.*

This was hardly useful, but culdoon were not wise. And it was notable, Meri thought, that it was one of the lesser trees who had made answer, while the great ones remained silent.

"Thank you," he said. "It would be . . . of interest of me, to hear when the trees next notice another branch of this Low Fey."

We will watch, Ranger, the culdoon promised, which Meri knew that it would do, until it forgot.

The ground sheltered by the low-growers was damp; Meri clearly saw the imprint of the monster's hooves, growing more defined for the next half-dozen steps, as if it had leapt in and landed hard—

From nowhere.

Meri stopped, staring at the ground. Directly before him the hoofprints were carved into the damp soil, precisely as if the monster he backtracked had leapt down from a height, and landed firm, an illusion made more compelling by the fact that there were no prints, nor any other sign of passage beyond.

He cast along the angle, looking up, but there were no trees in the proper place or of necessary height to produce those prints. The wood here had given over to low-growth for a space, as if there had been a fire, or—

A gleam of silver beyond the bowing fronds of a tall weed captured his eye. His belly froze, but he forced himself to creep forward, as if stalking dangerous game, and keeping the good green of living plants all about him.

There, only a few steps past those green fronds under which he now sheltered, was the flat shine of silver against the air, and the cold sense of something neither alive nor decently dead.

Meri shuddered. The...apparition hovered twice his height above the floor of the forest—a flat rectangle of dead air, boiling with languid grey mists.

It was, he thought, glancing behind him for another look at that first, impossible pair of hoofprints, high enough to account for their angle and depth.

Meri sat back on his heels and closed his eye.

"Did they—the Low Fey—accompany the beast out of this... thing...?"

Yes, Ranger, the culdoon answered. *They rode on its back.*

"Is that object—of—the *keleigh*?"

There was no answer.

Meri opened his eye, glaring at the rectangle. Its edges seemed to be becoming less...definite, smokier, and he had a moment's dread, that the mists it enclosed would, unconfined, pour free out into the unsuspecting wood.

The edges continued to fade, and the mists, as well, until—abruptly—it was gone, leaving behind a disagreeable taint on the air.

"How," Meri asked the wood about him, "am I to ward against that?"

There was no answer.

After a time, he rose and, taking care with it, crafted a simple repulsion ward. He reasoned that it did no good to spend a great deal of *kest*—even had he a great deal of *kest* to expend—to ward a road that faded in and out, and might never manifest in this exact location again.

When the ward was in place, and he had rested, he spoke to the wood.

"It would assist me, a Ranger in the service of the trees," he said formally, "if I were informed of the manifestation of such beasts and Low Fey as attacked the Gardener yestereve."

His words echoed slightly, as if they traveled a great distance. Meri waited, and at last came the thin, papery voice of a very old elitch, indeed.

We will be vigilant on your behalf, Ranger.

Violet had decreed tea and bustled off to make it, leaving Becca blessedly, if temporarily, alone on the bench beneath the bitirrn tree to overlook the garden.

It was a pleasant place, with neat rows of cultivated herbs, clusters of vegetables, and a border of mary's gold; winberige grew with abandon over a low arbor, heavy fruit nestled amid alternating leaves of dark green and parchment. The air was a-buzz with honeybees, and gay with flutterwisps, their wings almost as brilliant as Nancy's.

Becca sighed. Though she had been long months in the Vaitura, the mingled dry leaves and green among clusters of the same plant struck her eye—and her Gardener's heart—as wrong.

"Was the Vaitura always without seasons?" she

asked, expecting no answer, nor did she receive one for the space of time it took a flutterwisp to drink its fill from a mary's gold bloom and rise on the back of the sweet breeze.

There were seasons, a voice—a very old voice, so it seemed to Becca—said laboriously. *There were seasons, and great storms of rain, and lightning, and snow.*

"Why did it change, then?" she asked, when it seemed clear that the tree was not about to speak further.

It changed ... the old voice wavered, as if uncertain of the meaning of either her question or its answer. *It changed*, it said again, more definitively.

"But something must have precipitated it," Becca argued. "Change does not simply occur."

A light step and the clink of pottery warned her. She pressed her lips firmly together. It would not do to be seen talking to herself, she thought.

"Thank you," she said, as Violet Moore set a cup on the bench next to her. She picked it up so the girl would have room to sit, and sipped cautiously.

She smiled as the simple taste cleansed her mouth: fremoni tea, sweetened with honey. Comfort in a cup, as Sonet had used to say.

"Well," the girl said, with a brightness that sounded forced to Becca's ear. "What do you think of our garden, Healer?"

"I think it a very fine basic medicinal garden," Becca said truthfully. "All of the healer's friends are present, saving those—such as marisk, cadmyon, and corish root—that do not thrive under cultivation. I wonder ..." She paused, and sipped her tea, considering the sudden thought. But really, she said to herself, why not?

"I wonder," she continued, "if I might plant something of my own here?"

Violet opened her eyes wide. "I don't see why not,"
she said, and without a doubt the bright tone was
forced. "After all, this is your garden."

Rosamunde's trail was considerably less subtle than
that of the monster which pursued her. She had simply
attempted to outrun her attacker, and thus preserve
her rider's life. Meri could hardly fault her; indeed,
the simple strategy might have served her well, had
she been a full Fey horse, rather than a quarter-breed
accustomed to the very different horrors that prevailed
on the Newmen side of the *keleigh*.

Or, if she had been pursued by a creature bound
to the laws of the land.

He marked the moment that the monster left off its
pursuit; it had paused, and sunk back on its haunches,
the action driving its hooves deeper into the ground,
and from that ungainly position it had leapt, small
stones and crumbs of soil rolling away from the scars
in the ground.

Afraid of what he might see, Meri nonetheless
sighted along the line of that jump, but if there had
been a similar fog-filled rectangle overhead last evening, it had since dissipated.

Unsettled, he continued, following Rosamunde's trail
alone, now, until he came to the place where they
had been beset, the enemy that should have fallen
behind suddenly appearing at the fore.

He stood there for a dozen heartbeats, surveying
the scene, the torn trees and trampled ground a fitting

setting for the monster that his arrow had dropped not a hand's span from Rosamunde's front hooves.

The monster was not where he had left it. He had not, by this time, expected that it would be.

In the interests of thoroughness, he searched the area until he found the place where it had leapt into reality again, and he searched again, with his back against a ralif tree, for any untoward workings or unclaimed *kest*, but all he found was another strand of Rebecca Beauvelley's pretty hair, sparkling gold among the disordered grasses.

He untangled it and and put it with the other one in his pouch, his thoughts on darker matters. Deliberately, he crossed back to the ralif and put his back against its trunk.

"There was the carcass of a beast here," he murmured, tipping his head back and closing his eye.

Ranger, there was. It went to mist. They all do.

"All?" Meri opened his eyes in startlement. "How many have there been?"

Ranger—across how many sunrises? The elders believe that they have become more common.

"Will it aid anything to set wards here?"

There was a pause, not long enough for him to grow restive.

The elders believe that a simple ward, such as you have constructed once this day, will suffice. A much shorter pause, then, *You may draw upon my* kest *for the working, Ranger.*

Meri sighed.

"Thank you," he said softly, regretting the necessity, yet unable to deny the need.

He centered himself carefully, brought the image

of the ward to the front of his mind, and drew a
green draught of the ralif's *kest*. His blood sparkled,
the air tasted of brandy, and the wind filled his ears
with seductive music. The image of the ward faded,
and he panicked, terrified that he had drawn more
than he could administer in his reduced state.

Will is the master of power, his mother's voice
told him sternly from memory. *Apply your will, Meri
Wooden Head, or learn to enjoy subjection.*

He took a deep, intoxicating breath, and concentrated his will. The ward wavered to the front of his
thought; he touched it with the tree's rich *kest*—and
shouted wordlessly as it blazed into actuality, spitting
green fire; shouting dismay and distress.

Meri shook his head, not terribly surprised to find
himself on his knees. He pushed to his feet, shivering in the absence of the tree's power, and made an
unsteady bow.

"My thanks," he said to the ralif.

Our thanks, Ranger, the tree replied. *You serve
the trees well.*

"What *is* this?" Violet unwrapped the cloth to reveal
the gnomelike rootlings. "I don't think I've ever seen
anything like."

"It's called duainfey," Becca said, from her seat on
the bench. Violet had refused to allow her down in
the dirt, and had claimed the planting as "'prentice
work." Becca tried not to let her disappointment
show, while vowing that she would soon give herself
the pleasure of working among Lucy Moore's plants.

"Those were given me by *my* mistress, on the other

side of the *keleigh*, with her own 'prentice book. The entry there claims it a rare plant, even in its home land. I had planted some at—in my garden in Xandurana, and they took well to the soil there. It may be that they will flourish here, too. I would like to have a supply, for it has its uses."

Violet picked one of the rootlings up, turning it over curiously.

"Mind your fingers!" Becca cried. "They exude an oil, which will raise blisters." She held out her hand, showing fingers innocent of any mark, and Violet laughed.

"Yes, very good," Becca said, with a smile of her own. "But, truly, Violet, I was burned; my fingers would still show the scars from the blisters, if your superlative healing not reft them from me."

"Well." Violet put the rootling briskly on the ground, and studied her own fingers. "I don't appear to be burnt," she said, holding her hand out to Becca with a smile. "But I will be careful. How are these planted?"

"Roots down and spread, and buried only halfway," Becca said. Violet nodded and reached for the handspade.

"What are its uses?" she asked, her attention on her work.

Becca hesitated, which was, of course, ridiculous.

"It has several uses," Becca said slowly, wondering at her reluctance. Violet was learning the healing arts, and there were several plants hanging in Lucy Moore's workroom that gave surcease from pain.

"One leaf-tip, taken by mouth, is said to bestow clear sight. A tea made from dried leaves purifies the blood. The fresh leaves, taken by mouth, give release."

Violet looked up at her, brown eyes wide. "Release?"

"Surely you have been taught that healers have a duty to see that needless suffering not occur. Sometimes, release is all that we can give."

Violet nodded, looking down again, though she did not immediately continue with her work. "Gran did teach me," she said softly. "But, I don't, that is, I haven't—"

"Release is a gift," Becca said gently; "terrible, but a gift, nonetheless. It is not given often, and that is as it should be."

Violet finished planting the first rootling and reached for another.

"Have you," she asked, "ever given the gift, Miss Beauvelley?"

Becca closed her eyes, remembering the feel of the leaf in her mouth, the pleasant wash of warmth in her blood.

"No," she said softly, "I have not."

Chapter Sixteen

IT HAD REQUIRED THE EXPENDITURE OF *KEST*, AND
A careful examination of his memory, for he did not
dare to allow a false or fog-born fact to thwart him
now. However, all was at last in readiness. Soon, the
heat would cease to trouble him.

Soon—oh, very soon—Zaldore would be brought
to a full and complete understanding of her error.

Complete, yes.

Smiling, Altimere wound his watch with a paternal
air, glancing away into the mists. He dismissed the
utensils from his meager luncheon, and gave the ralif
tree leave to dissolve.

For this endeavor, and taking into account his
dependence on the very mists that ensnared him for
his materials, he had decided to return to the most
basic forms he could recall. The very crudeness of the
symbol-bound working would mark out any attempt
of mist-shaped—or other—intervention.

There was some singing involved, not unlike that

with which his Rebecca's people encouraged their
seeds to grow, in the land across the *keleigh*. His
voice was thinned by the mist, and made an unhappy
creak, but 'twould serve.

Also required was the drawing of lines, which had
been problematic until he had managed to freeze a
thin rectangle of mist, and call a scalpel to his hand.
He created and lit several cone-lights so that they
flickered in the star patterns favored by the ancients;
then he recited the words from his memory, carefully.

The star he had scribed on the frozen mist was
his own height twice, and as exactly drawn as one
might; he stood within the inner circle's circumfer-
ence, breathed deeply and confidently, and began
the working.

He called all the sound within this worldlet to him,
and he called all the light that was not of his own
will. He marked that the dial of his watch gave off
eight spots of light; and further marked that dropping
a pebble created no new sound.

From his pocket, he withdrew a hand mirror, and
held it up.

The light dimmed, first the dial-points on his watch,
then the rest, from whatever sources they came.
Dark grew slowly at first, then faster, and yet faster,
as the light fell into the depths of the mirror, now a
reservoir of power held in his left hand. The place
around him palpably shrank, and the heat grew even
more stultifying.

He spake a word, shrinking the bubble of stuff
nearer about him, deliberately concentrating all of
the *kest* it had—on him.

As the dark increased, he folded the watch away,

tucking it carefully into his pocket and out of harm's way. His feet were getting hot, as if the ground below his boots was hotter. His ears felt warm, his face flush, his *kest* peak.

He spoke the word he had formed, for the unmaking of walls, spoke it with all the will within him, and all the dark, silent power teeming at the edges of his star.

For a breath, nothing happened.

Sound returned in great crashing rhythms.

The song he had sung crashed outward and the mirror became a blazing beam stabbing into the emptiness.

The heat fled from his body so quickly he feared for his consciousness. His throat ached. He swallowed and swallowed again, while his ears were assaulted with an agony of sound.

Around him, the starlines blazed. The mist-shrouded world tilted, and he fell, his mirror disappearing into dust.

He landed, hard, on his knees, the breath going from him in a shout.

Shakily, he stood.

The first thing he noticed was the blessed coolness— and even a breeze! to ruffle his hair and kiss the sweat from his throat.

The second thing he noticed was that the sky was hidden by a low ceiling of unending cloud.

The third thing he noticed was that the horizon, if there was one, was shrouded in mists.

He had, he told himself carefully, won through.

Into the very *keleigh*, itself.

Putting his hand into his pocket, he withdrew the watch, and opened it. It ticked, the hands moving as they should. Relief washed through him. So much, then, had gone right.

For the rest—well, then. It was fortunate that he had been here before.

Meri set wards until he could scarcely stand—paltry things; mere warn-aways. Tomorrow, he would have to do better, for he felt in his heart that the boundary with the shadow-wood ought to be well warded, indeed. If his concern with that particular boundary had more to do with the safety of the slumbering elder trees than that of Rebecca Beauvelley, well—he was a Ranger, and his first concern must naturally be for the trees.

At the moment, hard truth told, it was the Ranger who was first in his care, light-headed and drifty as he felt. He paused for a moment, leaning into the comfort of a young elitch, and took stock. His *kest*, which had been rising, slowly but steadily, had under the strains of the last few days fallen to worrisome levels. He would need to take care—very close care—for it would profit the trees not at all if he were to drain himself dry.

In care for the Ranger, then, he gathered culdoon, vinut, and morel, which he ate, slowly, beneath the kindly branches of a ralif, by the side of a spring-fed pool. When his meal was done, and having secured the tree's consent, he climbed it and settled on a broad branch some distance above the forest floor.

He set no wards for himself—it was necessary to conserve what *kest* he possessed for the protection of the trees—but he trusted the ralif to rouse him, should a woodscat or a denilar or a Brethren bent on mischief locate his resting spot.

"Good moon," he murmured, which was, after all, only courtesy.

Good moon, Ranger, the ralif in whose branches he sheltered responded. *Sleep well, dream wisely.*

Meri sighed. He would, he thought muzzily, be glad of no dreams at all. As for wisdom...

The thought faded, and Meri slept.

"Good night, Miss—Rebecca," Violet said shyly, they having decided over the course of an evening spent companionably by the hearth, that they would address each other by their given names.

"Good night, Violet," Becca returned with a smile, and stepped into her room.

She pressed the door closed behind her, and stood with it against her back, staring.

When she had quit this chamber prior to dinner, it had been simple—perhaps even austere, with a plain table to hold a basin, and a shelf above it. The straw mattress had been covered in good linen, and a worn but serviceable patchwork quilt. Now, within the space of a few hours at most, it was—altered out of all recognition.

A rug patterned in bright yellows and deep browns lay on the planed wooden floor; curtains of matching yellow dressed the window. A wardrobe stood in the far corner of the room, brass handles gleaming, and a small vanity table sat beneath a chaste mirror, her comb and brush set neatly to hand.

The bed was swathed in a coverlet the color of elitch leaves, across which a half-dozen small bright pillows bloomed like flowers. A table sat between it and the far wall, holding her books, a water jug, a cup, and the lamp.

"Nancy—" Becca's voice wavered, indistinct. She cleared her throat and spoke again, more firmly. "Nancy."

A spot of color swirled into being, spinning larger, and her maid was hovering before her on jewel-toned wings.

"Nancy, where did these...*things* come from?"

The little creature spun 'round, as if she were looking for something, then darted to the wardrobe, pulling the doors wide. Becca pushed away from the door and crossed the room to peer inside.

The wardrobe was not, as she had feared it would be, empty; her nightdress—she supposed it to be the same dress she had worn last night and which Nancy had whisked away this morning while Becca was having her bath... Her nightdress hung chastely from a hook, and on the floor at the back were Rosamunde's saddlebags, Nancy sitting pertly atop them.

"*All of this*," Becca demanded, pointing backward into the room, "came out of those saddlebags? That's preposterous."

Even as she said so, she recalled Sian pulling crystal and wine and fresh food from the depths of *her* saddlebag—but no, she told herself. Sian was a Fey, a creature of *kest* and mystery, who could shake snowflakes from a fire, if she wished to do so.

"Those saddlebags are—enchanted, aren't they?" Becca asked. "Like the wardrobes at ho— at Altimere's houses." Nancy leapt into the air and turned a handspring, blazing like a star in the dark depths.

"There is no need for sarcasm," Becca murmured, She turned from the wardrobe and walked to the bed, tossing a corner of the coverlet back. The sheets were linen, cool and smooth. She pressed on the mattress, which sank delightfully beneath her palm; it was as she had feared—goose down.

Who would have thought Nancy had so much initiative? Becca thought, feeling a little wild as she looked about her. What if she wished for a coach-and-six? Would that come out of the saddlebags, as well?

Her head hurt.

Turning, she went over to the vanity table, and fingered the brush—silver, heavily cast with wheat sheaves, precisely like the set she had left behind at Barimuir, long months ago. How odd. But perhaps the saddlebag read her mind, as well.

She sighed and rubbed her forehead.

"Nancy," she said. The tiny creature flashed out of the wardrobe and stood a few inches from Becca's nose, her feet braced against the air, and her hands on her nonexistent hips.

"I wish you to be as frank with me as you are able," Becca said. "*Where* did these things come from?"

Nancy tipped her head, as if considering the question closely. She nodded once, firmly, and dropped slightly downward. Darting forward, she placed her hand on Becca's breast, over her suddenly pounding heart.

"From me?" That tale was even more preposterous than the saddlebags, she thought, and sighed lightly. It was probable that further questioning would elicit progressively more outrageous stories from her maid; besides which, she was tired.

"Very well," she said; "we shall talk about this again,

later. In the meanwhile, if it is quite convenient, I would like to be made ready for bed."

※

The dream began with candlelight; rich puddles of yellow light splashing across a dark cloth, waking glitters that were disturbingly *kest*-like from a tumble of silver and faceted stone.

From his comfortable recline on the ralif branch, Meri moaned, far too softly to wake himself.

It was the necklace that drew his eye and his desire, drawing his *kest* as if it were a living thing, and powerful, too. He tried to move his eyes, to step back, away from its immediate influence. His resistance was futile—pitiful. He might as well have resisted the tide. Shivering with desire, he watched his hand move forward to touch the glittering stones.

※

She knew it was a dream, but try as she might, she could not waken herself. It was as if the she who had escaped Altimere's influence and lay safe in New Hope Village hovered a hand's span above the shoulder of the she in the dream, foreknowing horror, yet powerless to change one detail of what went forth.

Horrified, she watched herself walk down darkened hallways and out into the night, breasts bare and wanton, her body rosy with lust. It was only a short walk, really, from the house to the barn, and the room where Elyd, where she—

No! She must do something, she must—she would not kill him a second time! But she needed so much... Desire heated her blood, burning—burning her hand.

She cried out, and the dream-Becca, wanton murderess, vanished, dissolving into now-Becca, crouched shivering in Lucy Moore's herb garden, her nightdress muddied beyond redemption, and a duainfey rootling clutched in her left hand.

Weeping, she opened her fingers one by one. The rootling fell to the ground, silver and gold against the darkness. Ignoring the agony in her hand, she scrabbled in the dirt with her fingers, desperate to replace the duainfey before it took harm from her use of it.

"I'm sorry," she whispered, her burned hand tucked against her thigh, and tears sprinkling the soil liberally. "I'm sorry, I'm sorry, sorry..."

"Miss Beauvelley?" The voice was soft, rough along the edges, and carrying a weight of concern. "Are you all right, Miss? Can I help you?"

"What?" Becca started, looking up into a brown face—young, too young to be here, to be with her, and about him those cool greens, just as Elyd must have—

"Miss?" His eyes were pale blue, wide, and dazzled. He held out his hand to her, and she snatched herself back, screaming even as she toppled gracelessly onto her side. "Go away!" she heard herself shriek across a night suddenly rent with crimson and gold. "Walk away from me now and never come back!"

Thunder rolled, and somehow she saw his face, the start of shock, and the moment when the blue eyes lost some of their brightness, and the green glow outlining his form faded...just before he turned—not as if he wished to do so—and walked directly away from her, heedless of plants, detouring grudgingly around the trellis, and walking on, until she lost the glow of his diminished aura inside the darkness.

The dream dissolved in a confusion of desire and pain. Meri half-woke with a start, one hand pressed flat on the branch that was his couch, shivering with unfulfilled need.

Two such dreams in as many nights, he thought muzzily, was worrisome. Perhaps he had been too long between meldings.

"But who," he muttered, settling his head again and closing his eye, "would I meld with?"

The breeze danced, rustling leaves on all sides of him, as if the night itself exerted itself to soothe him. Meri smiled—and slipped into a doze.

Jamie Moore! The voice of the Hope Tree knocked Becca back into a planting of mint, and sent ripples of pain through her head. *Jamie Moore, you have given your service to the trees! The trees do not release you!*

Jamie Moore!

Becca whimpered and raised her arm to shield her ears, as if she could soften the tree's shout.

Gardener, you must remove your will from him! Another, softer, though no less urgent voice crept into her abused head. *Quickly!*

"I . . . I . . . no," she whispered. "He mustn't come near me. It would be terrible—"

Gardener, it may already be terrible. He is only a sprout, and you have overridden his will. Release him!

Becca cringed. Overridden his will—just as Altimere had overridden hers. And yet—

"I don't know how," she moaned.

Ranger! Awake!

"You don't need to shout," he muttered with a sigh for the loss of the comfortable drowse. "What's amiss?"

The Gardener has put a geas upon Jamie Moore, the ralif told him, its thought very rapid, indeed. *He walks toward the shadow-wood, and the trees cannot turn him.*

Chapter Seventeen

HE HEARD THE TREES WHISPERING EVEN BEFORE HE saw the sad flutter of the boy's aura, ahead of him, and bearing steadily toward the baleful silver gleam of the shadow-wood.

Meri stretched his legs, ignoring the unsteadiness in his own stride and the conviction that there was little enough he could do for the sprout, even when he caught up, except turn him from the wood, and, perhaps, bear him company.

The trees regard you, Jamie Moore, an elitch murmured. *We marvel at a sprout so brave and true, and stand in awe of the Ranger you will grow to become.*

You may stop, sprout, and rest, a ralif urged, 'round the croonings and caresses of the culdoon and the larch. *The Gardener's geas is not that you must walk forever.*

What precisely is the geas? Meri asked that one. The sprout was steps away, now; he could hear ragged breathing, which told him that Jamie Moore was

215

weeping. He swallowed a surprisingly potent jolt of anger. *Yes, very good!* he thought angrily. *Enslave a child and blight his spirit!*

It is believed that the Gardener imposed the geas in error, the ralif told him.

I'll grant it an error, indeed, Meri growled. *But the geas—?*

Go away! Rebecca Beauvelley's voice screamed inside his head. *Walk away from me now and never come back!* Even as a reflection from the memory of trees, the blast of power that accompanied that doom made Meri gasp and snatch after his own feeble *kest*.

"Root and branch, no wonder the sprout weeps," he muttered. "His head must still be ringing!"

Ahead of him, the boy went to the right, around a fallen branch too tall for him to go over and too low to duck beneath.

Meri drew a burst of energy from the very core of his bones, leaped the branch, and caught the child as he came back to his path.

"Jamie." He put a light hand on a thin shoulder. The boy tried to walk on, but he exerted pressure— sufficient to hold him in place against the ground.

"I can't," the boy whispered raggedly. "Master, she sent me—I have to—but I don't want to go away and never come home again!" he wailed.

"I know." Meri crouched down, a hand on each shoulder now, lightly, lightly, and his face level with the boy's wet face, looking into the wide and miserable blue eyes. "Jamie, listen to me, eh?"

"Ye-es, Master. But I have to—"

"You are under a geas," Meri interrupted ruthlessly,

"and it is very true that there is something that you cannot refuse to do. Were you charged to walk constantly with no rest, and without food?"

"I—" The sprout took a deep breath, and Meri marked how he trembled even as he centered himself. "No," he said, though tentatively. "I—I am to walk away from her and never come back."

"Well, then," Meri said, keeping his voice light, "there's no harm in stopping for a meal with a friend, then, is there?" He rose and lifted his hands from the boy's shoulders.

Jamie began to walk.

Meri spun 'round ahead of him and again put both hands firmly on his shoulders. "Jamie!"

"I—" He hiccuped in distress. "Master, I must keep walking."

"No," Meri said sternly. "That is not the geas upon you."

"But—"

"Heed me, sprout! A geas will fill you up with itself, if you allow it. You would be wise not to allow it. You *can* stop walking, whenever you will. Do so." He lifted his hands.

Jamie jerked forward half a step—and stopped, hands fisted at his sides, his aura shot with determined threads of brown.

"Good," Meri said approvingly. "Now, seat yourself, please, and gather your strength. Would you like a culdoon?"

"Yes, Master," the boy said. "Thank you." Wisely, in Meri's estimation, he folded his legs and sat where he stood, his hands pressed flat on his thighs, as if to keep his legs from moving.

Meri slipped over to a nearby culdoon tree, which willingly gave of its fruit, and returned to sit cross-legged on the ground, his knee pressing companionably against the boy's.

Jamie devoured his fruit as if he hadn't eaten in days, and sighed when it was gone. He looked around him, his eyes losing focus. Meri felt his knee jerk, and gestured with his culdoon.

"So, how did you happen to find yourself with a geas on your head, Jamie Moore?"

The blue eyes sharpened, though the boy rocked forward, as if he meant to rise, then thought better of it.

"I was night-walking," he said, keeping his eyes on Meri's face. "Mother doesn't like me to do, so I don't go far afield, only 'round the village, and the trees who know us."

Meri nodded, and did not say that a sprout of tender years ought not to go night-walking without an elder at his elbow and that Elizabeth Moore was wise to dislike her son's solitary nighttime rambles. Instead, he allowed that the night was very agreeable and inquired if the ramble had been a good one.

"It—until. That is," the boy stammered and shook his head. "I had only been out for a little while, wandering the green, watching the stars dance and listening to the trees dream. I drifted over toward Gran's house, to—to see how the bitirrn fared." He gave Meri a sidewise glance. "I know it's ill-tempered, but it does like a visit now and then, and it isn't too much for me, so—"

"Of course," Meri said smoothly, though he had never known a bitirrn to care for anything a Ranger or a Wood Wise might do. "What happened in the garden?"

"Well . . . Miss Beauvelley was there, and her aura was bright and so—strange. She was crying and kneeling down in the dirt in her nightdress. I thought she might be hurt, or—so I asked her—very gently!—I asked her if she was in need of assistance."

Meri finished his culdoon and nodded encouragingly.

"I—it was if I had woken her. She—she fell back and she screamed at me, and I had to turn and walk away—*had* to, Master!" The blue eyes were filling with tears again.

Meri reached out and patted Jamie's knee. "I'm certain that you did have to," he said seriously, "for that is the nature of your geas." And, he thought privately, a very poorly crafted geas it was. *Never come back* was fairly—or unfairly—plain, but the injunction to *walk away* wanted some care. How far was "away"?

"Do you think you've walked far enough?" he asked Jamie. "Perhaps we might build a nest here, as we are true brothers of the wood." The notion of trying to sleep so near to the cold shine of the shadow-wood appealed to him not at all, but he doubted his ability to turn the boy from his path. Only Rebecca Beauvelley could do that, he thought. *Away from me*, indeed!

Meri sighed. He could feel Jamie vibrating as the geas worked on his muscles. Soon, he would have to rise, to walk. It was not a matter of will against will so much as will being bludgeoned by sheer, brute force. Rebecca Beauvelley's geas might have no finesse, but she had loaded it with frightening amounts of power.

"Master, I—"

"Stay." He put his hand on the boy's knee, pressing

him down, feeling the geas warm his hand, though it was nothing to do with him. To hold the boy, he needed to break the geas—and only the binder, or the one bound, could do that.

"Master?" Jamie's voice was high, shaking with need.

"Fight it," he said, desperation clawing at his heart. "Jamie. Deny it."

"I—cannot!" the boy wailed, and came to his feet as if jerked upward by a string.

Meri rose rapidly, and ran two steps to catch up with that rapid walker, his route as straight as a plumb line, toward the eerie silver sheen.

"Jamie, you do not wish to go under those trees," he said.

"I don't," the sprout agreed miserably. "I want to go home."

"Hold on to that desire," Meri urged. He caught the boy's arm and hauled him to a stop. "Focus your will. I—" He extended his hand. "I will help you. My *kest* to yours, sprout. Willingly."

The boy hesitated, his feet shuffling against the forest floor. His hand rose, and Meri held firm, though his heart quailed. He had so little—and yet he could not allow—it would be murder or worse to send the boy into that wood. If there was a chance . . .

The small, grubby hand wavered; fell. Meri swallowed relief strongly flavored with shame.

"Jamie?"

The boy shook his head. "What if it traps both of us?" he asked, his voice dull and unchildlike. "The trees need you, Master."

He turned and began again to walk, though it seemed to Meri that his steps were slower.

There must be something—*some*thing he could do, at least to turn the lad's steps, if not to break the geas entire. If—

...*away from me*... The tree-memory of Rebecca Beauvelley's voice screamed inside his head.

Away from *her*.

The thought had scarcely formed than his hand was in his pouch. They crackled against his fingertips as he withdrew them and carefully separated one from the other. The first he replaced in his pouch. The second, he stretched between his fingers: a long strand of glossy brown hair, crackling with golden *kest*.

Her *kest*, he thought, leaping in front of Jamie Moore.

Away from *her*.

The shadow-wood breathing cold against his back, he bent and put the strand atop the forest floor litter, directly in the boy's path.

Jamie screamed.

"How far?" Becca asked.

Her nightdress was an irredeemable rag, and her bare feet were possibly in the same case, but those things did not matter. What mattered was that she had done the unforgivable—what she had once thought was impossible. She had imposed her will over the will of another person and forced him to act as she desired.

She was a monster, no better than Altimere—worse! for at least Altimere had possessed a plan, a *reason* to make some sense of her suffering. She—she had planned nothing, but had senselessly struck out at a child, and if she died this night, it would not be until after she had found Jamie Moore and repaired her error.

"How far?" she panted again.

This time there was a ready answer.

Very near, now, Gardener.

She nodded and ran on, sobbing for breath, her side on fire. Ahead, she saw a silvery gleam, which she thought might be the moon, lost again as she ran through a stand of slender new-growth.

On the far side, she realized the glow was not the moon at all, but a hard shine obscuring the forest ahead, while it illuminated two figures.

One of the figures screamed, high and hopeless, spun about and began to walk, rapidly, unsteadily, in a straight, uncompromising line. The silver light snagged on tumbled brown hair; the breeze brought her the sound of soft sobbing.

"Jamie!" She altered her own path, running directly toward him. "Jamie!"

He screamed again, did Jamie Moore, and collapsed to the ground, where he lay, curled into a ball, his arms folded over his head, as if to protect himself from the blows of an enemy.

She took another step, suddenly afraid that he was having a fit. Had her mistreatment driven him into an epilepsy?

"Jamie—"

"Stop!" *That* voice was all too familiar.

Becca stopped from sheer surprise, and stared over the fallen boy into Meripen Vanglelauf's ravaged face.

"Break the geas," he said, each word falling as hard and distinct as a pebble.

"He's ill," she said, in agony for the boy's distress. "I need to—"

"Break the geas, woman! He'll be well enough then."

On the ground between them, Jamie Moore whimpered.

Becca dropped back a step, shaking her head.

"I don't know how," she whispered. "I don't know what I did."

There was a long pause. Becca swallowed, took a step forward, and jumped back again when the boy cried out.

"He's in pain," she said then, her eyes on the crumpled figure. "I did this. Please, if you know how to undo it, teach me."

"Withdraw your will," Meripen Vanglelauf said, slowly. Becca opened her mouth, but he raised his hand, forestalling her protest.

"Look at him—at his fires. Do you see where they are dimmed?"

Obediently, Becca looked down at the boy. His aura—his "fires"—were pale, cool greens, as fine and as flowing as silk, excepting one blotch of tarnished gold along his left side.

"I see it," she breathed.

"Your fires overlay his," Meripen Vanglelauf said, the cool calmness of his voice steadying her nerves. "This is subjugation; he neither accepts nor welcomes it. In time, if they are not withdrawn, your fires will erode his, until it is your *kest* alone that informs him."

Becca shuddered, and sank to her knees, her eyes on the blight that lay so heavy upon the fresh green colors.

"What must I do?"

"To break the geas, you must remove your influence—reclaim your fires."

Horror shook her. "I— The only way I know is to—is to lie with—" Her voice choked out and she wished nothing more than to run into the forest and hide herself. She kept her head down, and her eyes on the boy's pitiable form.

"You do not seek a melding here," Meripen Vanglelauf said, as matter-of-factly as if they discussed the weather. "What you performed was no act of sharing, for the betterment of both, but a selfish act of power. Call your fires to you. Accept your action, which is yours alone."

She leaned forward, staring at the area of tarnish, like rot, she thought, and extended her hand, seeing the golden light drip from her fingertips.

"I reclaim my *kest*," she said slowly.

Was it some trick of her new vision, or did the blight on the boy's aura change shape?

"Again," Meripen Vanglelauf said softly.

"I reclaim my *kest*," Becca repeated. This time, the change was obvious; the golden spot floated above the cool green fires.

"It must be three times," he said inexorably.

Becca drew a breath, tasting the heat that wavered in the night air.

"I reclaim my *kest*."

There was a boom, as from a sudden thunderstorm, and a flash of molten gold light, piercing her from belly to brain. Crimson stained her vision; she swayed on her knees, shook her head—and there was Meripen Vanglelauf, kneeling on the ground beside Jamie Moore.

"Well done," he said coolly, putting his hand on the boy's shoulder.

Jamie flopped over onto his back, so loose and graceless that Becca gasped.

"Not again!" she cried.

Sian's cousin looked up, his single eye cold.

"He's fainted," he said, "and no wonder. It was a heavy burden for a sprout to carry. You might have been kind, and merely immolated him. What were you thinking?" The last was not calm at all, though it stopped short of a shout.

Becca hung her head, feeling drained and near to swooning herself. "I thought that I was a danger to him, and that it would be best if he never came near me."

"And so you proved yourself a danger to him," Meripen Vanglelauf said. He finished arranging the boy's limbs to his satisfaction, gathered him up, and stood.

Becca struggled to her feet, gasping at the protest of cut flesh. Her burned hand was screaming for treatment. She cast about her, seeing the familiar shape of easewerth in the silver glare from the—

She straightened, squinting.

"Are those," she said, not believing, "trees?"

"In a manner of speaking, they may still be trees. Certainly, they were once."

"That's—wrong," Becca said.

"Yes," Meripen Vanglelauf agreed from behind her. She turned to stare at him and he lifted one shoulder in a defensive shrug. "It's wrong. And no—I don't know how to make it right."

He turned, the boy in his arms, and began to walk back toward New Hope Village.

Becca snatched up a handful of easewerth and followed, crushing the leaves in the palm of her burned hand as she went.

Chapter Eighteen

THERE WAS A COPPER GLOW AHEAD, LIKE A HEARTH fire comfortably banked for the night.

"Beneath the elitch," Becca said, though it was more for her own comfort than her companion's interest. Meripen Vanglelauf had not addressed a word to her since they had begun the walk back to the village, nor acknowledged her presence in any way.

While she could scarcely blame him for not wishing to associate with someone who keenly felt herself to be beneath contempt, still it would have been... comforting to have had some conversation.

The easewerth had numbed the pain in her hand, and she had managed to snatch up a few leaves of fremoni along the way. She did not really want to think about the state of her feet, which had worrisomely stopped hurting some while back, nor the spectacle that she would present to Elizabeth Moore, who was even now calmly awaiting their arrival.

Meripen Vanglelauf walked beneath the elitch

branches, knelt at Elizabeth Moore's feet, and lay the boy across her lap.

"He lives, Tree-Kin," he said, his voice cracked and wavering.

"Thank you," Jamie's mother said, and though her voice was even, it was not, Becca thought, *quite* calm. "He knows the dangers of night-walking, Master Vanglelauf."

"It was not the night that did this," Becca said, stepping up to stand beside the Fey. "And Master Vanglelauf abases himself for no reason." She swallowed. Meripen Vanglelauf rose and moved three good paces to the side, leaving her alone before Elizabeth Moore, watching wretchedly as she smoothed her son's hair off of his forehead.

"I—the error, the anguish, any hurt he has taken—" Tears stung her eyes and ran down her cheeks, doubtless, Becca thought disjointedly, increasing her aspect of wanton madness.

"I am so very sorry," she whispered. "It is all my fault."

"Perhaps not *all*," Elizabeth Moore murmured surprisingly, her eyes on her son's face. "It cost you a number of years of apprenticeship, and a great many mistakes to become a healer, did it not, Miss Beauvelley?"

Becca blinked. "Of course," she said slowly. "It is a complex craft, and there is much to learn."

"So my mother often said," the other woman said softly. "Master Vanglelauf, our good lady tells me you were schooled for a time at the Queen's Court."

"So I was." His voice, though cracked, was sardonic. "Nor may I tell you at this remove which lessons were the more difficult—statecraft, of which I am an indifferent practitioner at best—or philosophy, of which my tutor granted that I had learnt just enough to prevent my burning down Xandurana."

"So it may be," Elizabeth Moore murmured, "that... whatever...befell Jamie this evening was not *all* the fault of Miss Beauvelley?"

Becca heard Meripen Vanglelauf sigh.

"We will commence her schooling—tomorrow," he said, not with the best grace. "For tonight..."

"For tonight," Elizabeth Moore interrupted, "we could all use some sleep." She rose effortlessly, her son lolling in her arms. "May I call on you, Miss Beauvelley, if Jamie wakes to need healing?"

Becca's throat closed. "Of course," she whispered; "though it is more than possible he will not wish to see me."

"Sleep heals much," Elizabeth Moore observed, and inclined her head gravely. "Thank you both, for fetching him home. I know I'll not have him much longer, so every day is precious to me. Good moon to you both."

"Good moon, Tree-Kin," Meripen Longeye murmured, bowing.

"Good moon," Becca whispered.

She watched until Elizabeth Moore had entered her house. When the door had closed behind mother and child, and Becca looked about her, it was to discover that she was alone.

Sighing, she turned and limped toward Lucy Moore's house. She would, she thought, go to the workroom, and call Nancy to bathe her. After, she would dress her own hurts, and perhaps take a drop or two of bitirrn cordial, to insure a dreamless sleep.

The estate at Tarsto had been his entry point, but surely, Altimere thought, that had been a matter of convenience for Zaldore and not an indication of where his hot pocket prison had been located with regard to the geography of the Vaitura.

The *keleigh*, after all, rotated. That had been the insight he had provided himself when the *keleigh* was incepted: without that rotation the stability of the protective wall would be minimal and variable. *That* was his artifice, and it had come from his long interest and study of the strange rules of physical objects. Rotation gave duration. He had little doubt that the mock-*keleigh* he had been trapped in had a motion also, else it would have required *kest* at a far higher density than the *keleigh* in order to maintain it.

It was the rotation of the *keleigh* as a whole which was behind the unpredictable nature of the interior, for it was not as glass nor stone nor wood, but rather a smoke—a dream—of *kest*, constantly in disarray.

Their first attempt at protection from the forces they had unleashed upon the enemies of the Vaitura had resulted in a wall impenetrable and deadly to Fey and foe alike—and insupportable for more than a few heartbeats by any energy source they knew, save perhaps the very oceans.

The second attempt had been much closer to the *keleigh* now in the world, but it, too, pulled energy at too rapid a rate. That problem being solved by the application of a dimensional spin, it became the *keleigh* which even now protected the Vaitura. That it existed on *kest* had been a fact so basic that it need not be stated, much less discussed; everything existed on *kest*, after all.

The bitirrn cordial gave her dreamless sleep, though not so deep that she failed to rouse when Violet Moore came into the workroom in the early morning. It had been set at dinner the evening before that she and Becca would go foraging for marisk and the other low supplies. There was no possibility of that now, of course, not when Becca had almost murdered the girl's brother.

She kept very still in the little bed behind the screen, lashes down and breathing slow, even when Violet put a callused hand against her cheek, and then put her fingers against the heart-point under the jaw.

"Sleep is the great healer," Violet muttered, which Becca thought might have been something her grandmother had used to say. All she really cared about, though, was that the girl left her alone.

After Violet's departure, Becca lay still, sleepless now, her stomach knotted with shame; tears leaking weakly from her eyes.

Last night—the dream, which had so vividly recalled the details of her willing enslavement, and the moments leading to Elyd's death. She had escaped that nightmare, only to find the boy, whose features were so similar—he had seemed to her confused mind to have *been* Elyd, and in deadly danger from her. She had thrust him away with everything that was in her— surely, that had been—if not a noble act, then born at least from a benevolent desire?

Becca hiccuped, and pushed her damp face into

the pillow. In truth, she thought bitterly, it had been fear that had motivated her—fear that she had not banished the dream, but only driven it into a horrifying new channel; fear that she would, given the opportunity, and entirely free of Altimere's compulsion, act precisely as she had done before.

You might have murdered that boy, Rebecca Beauvelley, she told herself bitterly. *You might murder him yet, and all the good folk in this village. Sian was right to have put the sleep on you. She ought never to have woken you at all.*

"What shall I do?" she whispered.

Becca turned over on her back and stared up at the ceiling with its dried bunches of mary's gold and rosemary hanging from the eaves. She thought, tentatively, of the duainfey rootlings growing in the garden. In another day or two, at the rate that plants grew in the Vaitura, they would put forth leaves. She might, if she wished, soon complete that which had been interrupted.

To her considerable astonishment, she found that she did not want to die. The calm acceptance of the inevitable that had accompanied her former decision to take her own life was absent. More than that—she had made promises. She supposed that Rosamunde might find a willing rider in Meripen Vanglelauf, who seemed utterly besotted. But even if she were of a mind to accept him, that did not absolve Becca of her promise that the two of them would never be parted. And Nancy, who had risked all to leave Altimere's service, and enter her own! Who would care for Nancy's interests, and, and renew her *kest* when she ran down?

Who, indeed, would teach the fragile young healer, and help her find faith in her skill and intuition?

No, no. She could not die, not now. It was entirely out of the question. And yet, something—she must do something. She was a danger to those who were innocent, or weaker than herself.

She—

We will commence her schooling—tomorrow.

Becca sat up. "Will he?" she demanded. "Will Meripen Vanglelauf teach me?"

He said so, before tree and tree-kin, the elitch pointed out, sounding, just slightly, amused.

Becca chewed her lip. After last night, she would rather—well, no, she had already decided that she couldn't die, now hadn't she?

Meripen Vanglelauf might loathe her, but he had promised to teach her, before tree and tree-kin. She gathered that held a certain potency, for one who was a Ranger, and beloved of the trees.

Becca nodded, and threw the blanket back.

"Nancy!" she called.

"Good morning," she said, when Elizabeth Moore opened the door. She couldn't quite manage to lift her head and meet the other woman's eyes. It had taken all of her courage to come here and stand in place like a civilized adult, until her knock was answered.

"I wonder," she said to the door-stone, "how Jamie does?"

"He roused at dawn, ate some bread-and-jam and drank water, then went back to his bed. I'm thinking he'll be just fine by evening, Miss, after he's gotten caught up."

"I'm sure he will be," Becca said hoarsely. She cleared her throat. "Well. Thank you, I just thought—"

"Would you like to see him, yourself?" Elizabeth Moore asked, standing aside. "For all my mother was a healer, and Violet becoming, I never learned the lore, myself."

Becca's heart froze in her chest. *See* him? She could never face—but he was asleep, and he had suffered a shock to his system, and she was a healer.

It was her duty, if nothing else.

"Yes," she said faintly, and forced herself to raise her head and meet Elizabeth Moore's ironical blue eyes. "I would like to see him. Thank you."

The first thing she thought, seeing him abed, with his hair tumbled against the pillow and his face slightly damp with sleep, was that he looked not at all like Elyd. Certainly, his skin was brown, as Elyd's had been, and as, to a lesser degree, hers was. There, however, the similarity ended. Elyd's face had borne the marks of years of—Becca blinked at the thought—of perhaps years, she continued carefully, of having been bound against his will, denied even the solace of walking among the wild trees that he loved.

Becca shook her head. She had been so dazzled by Altimere's *regard* that she had been unable to see the suffering of a man she had called her friend.

"Miss Beauvelley?" Elizabeth Moore's voice was soft, perhaps worried that the healer had already seen something amiss that a mother's hopeful eye had overlooked. *A fine healer you are,* Becca scolded herself, and came to the side of the bed.

She put her hand against the boy's smooth cheek,

and happily found no fever. A touch to the heart-point detected only the easy rhythm of rest. His breathing was deep and even, and he snored a little, like the burr of a happy cat.

"I think you are correct," she said, smoothing the boy's pillow before turning to face his mother again. "He was exhausted by last night's...misadventure... and is regathering his strength. If he does not wake of his own will by twilight, wake him yourself and insist that he eat a meal. A walk—in company with yourself or his uncle!—would not be amiss, followed by his usual night's rest."

Elizabeth Moore smiled. "Jamie's usual night's rest is as little as he can manage," she said, waving Becca into the hall ahead of her. "That child loves the night woods like no one I've ever known." She paused, her head tipped slightly to one side. "Saving his father."

"Perhaps this evening you can prevail upon him to stay in," Becca said carefully, "and rest."

"Perhaps I can, perhaps he will," Jamie's mother said with a small sigh. "His nature is beginning to firm. It's not that he means to be disobedient, but that he can't help himself."

Becca considered that. "You had said—last night— that he won't be with you much longer," she said. "Is he for 'prentice?"

"In a manner of speaking." Elizabeth Moore paused with her hand on the door. "He'll be going with his father into the wood, to learn his duties as a Ranger." She shook her head. "One for me and one for him, that was our bargain, and Palin never meant to be

cruel. Neither of us counted on a mother's heart."
She sighed. "Still, it's best to let him go. He'll never
be happy bound by walls."

"One for you and one for him?" Becca repeated.
"How— Forgive me!"

"How peculiar?" The other woman gave her an
ironic smile. "So it must seem to you, or to anyone
who had not listened since her cradle to Palin and
her mother argue the difference between Fey and
Newman and wonder if we were to marry, then
would our children bear the best of both, and serve
the land more fully.

"When I came to think of marrying, Palin proposed
his bargain, and I agreed, with my mother's full
approval. It was a marvel to bear those two children
and see how different they were." She smiled again,
the irony vanished. "One for him and one for me . . .

"Well!" She shook herself suddenly, and pulled
the door briskly open. "Thank you, Miss Beauvelley,"
she said, reaching out to touch Becca lightly on the
hand. "Thank you for coming by. It must have been
hard for you."

Becca nodded. "It was hard," she admitted, "but it
had to be done." She took a breath and deliberately
stiffened her back. "Besides, now there is something
harder I need to be about."

"That will be your lessons with Master Vanglelauf,"
the other woman said wisely, and gave her a nod. "Be
of good heart, Miss."

"Thank you," Becca said, stepping out onto the
path. "I will do my best."

Something was operating...not quite as it ought.

Three times now Altimere had brought the image of Artifex before his mind's eye, raised his *kest*, and attempted to leave the *keleigh*.

Three times, he had failed in that simple process, though his will was as firm as ever.

He sat himself down by the ghost of a culdoon tree and produced a glass of wine from the mist. Though it was mist, still, it was easier to work, without that unpleasant and recalcitrant stickiness that had characterized the mist filling his late prison.

Sipping his wine, Altimere took stock.

It was apparent that he had not come out from Zaldore's prison unharmed. He had expended more *kest* than he had realized in combating the mists, and had of course gathered no more to him.

Though his will was firm, it was possible that his low levels of *kest* were interfering with his timely escape from the *keleigh*—a significant difficulty, as the *keleigh* consumed *kest*. The longer he remained within, the more would he be consumed by his environment, until he was but a memory of himself, wandering the mists.

He was therefore wise to have made his best attempts of escape before his power was depleted. And now that he had established himself already too low of *kest* to break free on his own, he must seek assistance.

Happily, assistance was to hand.

There were three anchor points for the *keleigh* inside the Vaitura. One was at Sea Hold—on the far side of the Vaitura from Zaldore's estate of Tarsto. The second was in Rishelden Forest, hard by Xandurana. The third was at Donich Lake, in the mountain country. Altimere had been to all of them, and could picture them clearly in his mind.

By their very nature, *kest* tended to pool at the anchor points. The pooled *kest* at some times was so large that it threw a shadow across the *keleigh*. That shadow could be followed, and the accumulated kest absorbed.

Once he had absorbed sufficient *kest*, he would be able to step out of the *keleigh* and into the Vaitura.

In theory, he thought, it should work.

Chapter Nineteen

THE GARDENER COMES, RANGER.

Meri stepped back into the shadow of the friendly culdoon tree and shook his head.

"I cannot do this," he whispered, hating the cramp of fear in his belly and the weakness in his knees. Teacher and pupil shared a special relationship—not a full melding, but yet an easy sharing of *kest* and knowledge. It had not been unusual, during his own tumultuous schooling, for his tutor to imbue his *kest*, so that he might learn the correct architecture of a particular subtle working from the inside. To engage with Rebecca Beauvelley in such a wise...

His stomach twisted, and he slumped against the culdoon, pressing his cheek to its foolish trunk.

Despite what he had told the sprout last night, will alone was not sufficient to survive. Oh, a will rigorously trained, and partnered with a...moderate...amount of *kest* was certainly enough to perform wonders. Alas, while his will was strong, he had not

238

taken a philosopher's course; and to acknowledge his present levels of *kest* to be *moderate* was to indulge in dangerous deception.

He could not teach Rebecca Beauvelley. The trees had first call upon his service and his duty. Rebecca Beauvelley could, could—

Burn down New Hope, in her ignorance? the elder elitch inquired politely. *Enslave a grove of sprouts with a word, and with another bind them to a second doom?*

Meri shuddered. The single geas she had laid on Jamie would have surely been the end of him before he had walked through another night—and that assuming that he had not strode headfirst and heedless into the shadow-wood!

Meripen Longeye, the charge comes to you.

Cheek against the culdoon, Meri shivered, then straightened as a flicker of gold disturbed his senses. *The Gardener comes, Ranger.*

～※※※～

The trees had guided her to a quiet spot just outside of the village proper, a circle of woven grasses sheltered by pine, culdoon, and larch. Becca stepped lightly, peering into the odd nest, seeing a bow and quiver laid neatly to hand, and a light indention among the grasses, vanishing even as she watched.

"Master Vanglelauf?" She spoke softly. Respectfully. After all, she reminded herself, she was here to ask for a kindness—a considerable kindness—from someone who found her despicable at best.

"Master Vanglelauf, the Hope Tree said that you were about."

She looked 'round, seeing the trees with their still

branches, and the bright fruit peeking shyly from
beneath the culdoon's leaves. A bird sang overhead,
its high, sweet voice putting her momentarily in mind
of Diathen the Queen. She shivered with the thought,
and glanced back to the grassy nest.

"Surely," she said to the trees, "he wouldn't have
gone far without his bow?"

There was no answer. She hadn't really expected
one, though it would have been nice to know why
the trees had led her here if the object of her quest
was absent.

Sighing, Becca turned roundabout, looking for
something—some sign of his direction, perhaps, or—

"Oh!" She gasped, hand rising to her cheek.

Meripen Vanglelauf seemed to step from the very
heart of the culdoon, and stood before her, arms
crossed over his chest and a formidable frown on his
scarred, austere face.

Becca curtsied, wobbling somewhat, and straightened, aiming her eyes over his left shoulder, so she
did not have to meet his cold green eye.

"If you please," she said, her cheeks hot with
embarrassment. "I would value lessons from you in . . .
in philosophy."

There was a long moment in which he did not
answer. She bit her lip and recruited herself to patience,
watching his tattered green fires blow in an unfelt
wind, certain that he was about to pour abuse on her
head for her callous and brutal treatment of a child.

But no, it would appear that he had merely been
thinking, after all.

"What," he asked, his voice so cool that she shivered, "is *kest*?"

Becca straightened her back. This at least was familiar to her. Every trade had a catechism. Though her first answer would undoubtedly be wrong, yet it required some thought, for it would aid the teacher in learning how much, and what sort of, work needed to be done.

"*Kest* is an . . . informing humor," she said slowly. "It may be taken, or given, and it may be worked, after a fashion." She bit her lip, considering. "It is generally invisible to, to those who live across the Boundary. Fey possess it, and use it to provide themselves with all manner of things."

"How does one acquire *kest*?" came the second question, and Becca felt her skin heat from the roots of her hair to the bottoms of her feet.

"One acquires *kest*," she began, and felt tears start. She closed her eyes and took a breath.

"One acquires *kest* by lying with or performing sexual acts with those who are well supplied." Her stomach cramped, but she would not, she thought, tears dampening her cheeks, she *would not* shirk the question. She had asked for instruction, and whatever Meripen Vanglelauf might ask of her would be nothing to what she had already done.

"*Kest* may also be taken by . . ." She cleared her throat. "May be taken by one who has compelled another to gather it in . . . in the manner previously described."

She drew a ragged breath, and waited, eyes closed, while the silence stretched, and stretched . . .

. . . and was broken by a sigh.

"*Kest*," Meripen Vanglelauf said, his voice betraying nothing of his thoughts. "*Kest* is the fire that informs the world, and everything that moves within the world. Fey possess it, and Newmen also. Trees, small-plants, the birds in the sky, and the creatures among the grasses—all are informed by *kest*.

"*Kest* may be shared, it may be given away, and it may be shaped. *Kest* is the great healer. *Kest* is never lost."

There was another pause, very slight, during which Becca found the courage to open her eyes.

Meripen Vanglelauf stood with his legs braced, and his hands tucked into his belt, gazing into the evergreen branches above her head.

"One acquires *kest* by living," he said; "by walking up and down in the world and partaking of it. One may meld with another, in order to share, change, and grow. We are a part of all those with whom we meld, and they are a part of us, for *kest* is never lost."

He moved his gaze down from the branches and looked directly into Becca's face.

"You were under the protection of Altimere the Artificer." It was not a question, but Becca answered as if it were.

"I was," she said, hearing her voice quaver. "He... required me to, to meld, and to steal *kest*, which he then...took from me."

His mouth, which had lost some of its frown in what had surely been a soothing recitation of well-known material, tightened again.

"When the will of the Elders informed our lives, such subjection was common," he told her. "The war altered the way we—*the Fey*, as you have us, as if we were all one—live, for very few of the Elder High survived it. The Queen in Xandurana decreed, with the force of her Constant, the Vaitura, and the trees, that henceforth our law would change. No more would the stronger dominate the wills and the lives of the weaker, but all Fey would live together, each according to their service, whether it be low or high."

He lifted an eyebrow.

"Diathen having spoken in full, that covenant is, albeit sometimes indifferently, obeyed. The Brethren are most often at risk, but to say truth they delight in provoking others."

"Altimere," Becca said, hearing the bitterness in her voice, "did not appear to know that there was such a covenant."

The firm lips twitched, as if Meripen Vanglelauf had captured a smile inside the curve of his frown.

"Altimere knows the Queen's Rule full well," he said gravely. "It is merely that he is Elder and High and holds to the old ways." He hesitated, then inclined his head. "Those things that he taught you may be . . . untrustworthy. Strive to set them aside and learn better."

"He taught me nothing, save that Fey are not to be trusted, which seems to be a lesson to hold close," Becca snapped, before she had quite realized that she was angry.

"Perhaps he taught you that Altimere is not to be trusted, which is a very different thing, though worthy, as you say, of a place in memory." He tipped his head, as if taking counsel of himself, and nodded, once.

"You are, so the trees say, a healer."

"Yes," Becca acknowledged temperately, "I am a healer."

"Despite this, you have not healed your arm. What are your reasons?"

Her temper, roused, now flared. What had her arm to do with...philosophy lessons?

"It is well to note," Meripen Vanglelauf said coolly, "that strong emotion casts its shadow upon the aura, which is the reflection of the inner fires. One's enemies may therefore gain a significant advantage over one merely by observing the state of one's temper. Happily, and with practice, one may learn to control one's emotions and thus shield oneself on that flank."

Becca glared at him, then, remembering the control she had enforced upon herself after the accident, she took a deep breath, and another, deliberately cooling her temper.

"Very good," her teacher said, distantly. "Now, if you will: Your reasons for refusing to heal your arm."

"Why do you believe that I *refuse* to heal my arm?" Becca asked hotly, and felt her temper flicker. She took another breath and was able to continue, with tolerable calm. "Indeed, many were at pains to heal it, but it is crippled beyond repair." Another impulse flickered, and she looked up into Meripen Vanglelauf's eye. "Altimere had said it made me more desirable to Fey. Do you not find it so?"

"No." Perfectly composed, that reply, and if, Becca thought irritably, there had been any alteration in the ragged aura that billowed about him, it was too subtle for her to perceive.

"There are, however," he continued after a heartbeat, "a certain sort of Fey who may find such stratagems attractive. Fey are...accustomed to measuring *kest* by the power and beauty of the aura. Recall that the aura is the reflection only of the inner fires. Therefore, one who displays an aura that is...rich and sensuous...

may be supposed to harbor much *kest*. Among certain
of the High, there is a...craving for *kest* merely for
the sake of accumulation. Those would find one who...
calls attention to her abundance of *kest*, desirable. By
allowing your arm to remain withered when clearly
you possess the power to heal it, you announce that
your *kest* is sufficient to all things. There are very
few who have so much, and those must be sought-
after as melding partners, by those who wish to...
increase themselves."

Becca stared at him. "The—those—they thought
they were taking power *from* me?"

Meripen Vanglelauf considered her gravely.

"That's preposterous!" Becca cried—and then, without warning, began to laugh. "Ah, *that* is where he
turned the tables on them! While they thought they
had gained an advantage through me, he was robbing
them of power—through me!" She shook her head,
took a breath, hiccuped, and managed to fight the
laughter down.

"I do not think," she said to the Fey's lifted eyebrow,
"that—Newmen, as you call us—possess *kest* in the
same manner as Fey. It may be that the aura—is all
we have. Certainly, I've never known anyone in—on
the far side of the *keleigh*—who could use *kest*."

"Fey and Newmen are different," Meripen Vanglelauf said with cool courtesy. "Certainly, it is possible
that Newmen have not the skill to manipulate their
kest—especially if there are no teachers on the other
side. For now, however, you have the attention of one
who may teach you...some few things. However or
wherever you may have acquired it, certainly you have
accumulated *kest*. Heal your arm."

Becca stared at him in frustration. "It cannot be healed," she said, speaking slowly and distinctly. "I am crippled and have been for years."

He looked bored and a little impatient.

"You are a healer. You have *kest* enough. Do you have the will?"

Her temper broke lose from the bounds she had set upon it.

"Will has nothing to do with it!" she cried. "If it were *will* that would do it, I would have been cured ten thousand times! The muscles were torn, then burned, then ignored. *I am a cripple*, Master Vanglelauf! There is no cure!"

It was, she thought in the midst of her anger, very warm of a sudden. The breeze brought her a taste of smoke and of leaf-burn. Gasping—coughing—she looked 'round. The grass between her and Meripen Vanglelauf was on fire, the flames leaping higher as she stared, horrified.

The Fey snapped a word that slid past her ear, and raised a slim, brown hand. Mist formed in the air, thickening rapidly, until raindrops splashed down upon the flames, quenching them with a hiss.

"I—" Becca began, and darted forward with not a thought for her skirts along the steaming ground, and caught Meripen Vanglelauf's elbow, thinking only to steady him as he staggered—

"Do not touch me!"

He tore away from her, face pale and posture uncertain, but it was neither of those that caused Becca to stare, and to shiver.

The thin rags of his aura had—diminished.

If one's aura was the reflection of the inner fire,

she thought wildly, then Meripen Vanglelauf's fires were dangerously low.

"No, please—" She extended her hand. "I—Master—*kest* can be given—as a gift?"

"Yes." His voice was thin, as if he were short of breath.

"Then," Becca said, speaking rapidly, "allow me to make amends. I would replenish what you spent to mend my error."

"No!"

The shout took her to her knees, and when she looked up, Meripen Vanglelauf was gone, vanished—melted into the culdoon, perhaps, or spread out along the wind.

Becca bent her head and struggled not to cry.

"He's ill," she said to the trees.

He is diminished by his sorrows, Gardener. Leave him to his duties now, and come for another lesson on the morrow.

"If we keep on at this rate, my lessons will kill him," she objected, staggering to her feet.

Tomorrow, come again. He will teach you; you will learn.

That had the weight of law behind it, Becca thought, and composed herself as well she might. The fire, she saw, with relief, had not come near his nest. She hoped that the smell of burnt vegetation would not be too unpleasant for him.

"Trees," she said, softly. "Please tell Master Vanglelauf that I will try to be a better student."

Certainly, Gardener, the Hope Tree made answer. *Go, now.*

By the reckonings of his watch and his sleeps, he had been inside this second, larger, prison, a ten day plus three. In that time he had found rock-strewn paths and trees without vigor, lifeless dust basins, streams without flow, and light that neither increased nor diminished.

Several times he had seen footprints in the dust, but their direction was lost on the stone that ridged out of the fundamental mist.

What he had not found was the anchor point at Rishelden Forest, nor yet any significant pool of *kest* nor any clue to the direction and condition of the Vaitura.

Twice, he had nearly convinced himself that the Vaitura no longer existed, that all and everything had been swallowed by the mists. The third time the panic rose, he snapped paper and pen out of the aether and began to draw a map.

The map had grown and was now quite detailed. He had returned willfully to his starting point twice; he made notes of his measurements and compared them, seeking to learn—something that would be of use to him in his extremity.

Everyone knew that there were heroes in the mists. Altimere by no means aspired to that estate. However, it came to him, as he walked and measured and mapped, that it might in fact be of some use to him to locate such a one.

Soon after he had that thought, he found a small stream of what ought to have been spring water. Rather than a cool, fresh odor it held nothing he could smell. Throwing a stone into it produced dull splashes; throwing a very large rock into it produced nothing larger.

Finally he dared touch the liquid, which was opaque to his *kest* and held none of the virtue water should know. It very nearly ran around his finger: none of its expected dampness clung to his hand.

There was more geography present now, and as he walked the mist felt thinner. The stream was a convenient path; like a well-mannered stream in the Vaitura there was some room between the banks and the nearest obstructing trees or rocks, as if from time to time a cleansing flow pushed back against things that encroached. He felt a continued disconnect between the world and himself, an oddity...

The oddity was that though there were trees and plants, they showed, like the water, none of the normal attributes of *kest*. They seemed to live, and yet they did not. They ought to have been dead, at least, or, in keeping with theory he had himself postulated, subsumed into the *keleigh*. That they were neither was...worrisome in a way that nagged at him, but which he could not articulate further.

Chapter Twenty

FOR THE THIRD WARD, HE ASKED PERMISSION OF the abundant mosses carpeting the floor of the sleepy forest, and drew its *kest*, careful not to take more than he could control.

By the time it was done and the ward in place, he was feeling so thin and unsteady that he sat down with his back against a sleepy, ancient pine, and closed his eyes so that he would not have to see the unnatural wood that lay beyond his wards, and acknowledge how inadequate they were.

Who hears me? he asked, wearily.

I hear you, Ranger, the unmistakable voice of the elder elitch that called itself the Hope Tree said strongly. *The Gardener asks me to tell you that she will strive to be a better student.*

Meri laughed weakly. *She could hardly be a worse one.*

Did you learn tree lore all in one day? the elitch asked.

Nay, and I own that my knowledge remains inadequate. I made no claims to being an apt pupil.

The Gardener expresses her judgment, as a healer, that you are ill, Ranger. Is that so?

He sighed. *Certainly, I am light. If there were another present to take this charge, I would ask the boon. What news, indeed, of those Rangers I had asked of?*

There was a pause, long enough for him to nod off, his back warm against the sleepy pine.

They have passed from the memory of trees, Ranger. The elitch's voice was somber.

Meri sat up, chilled to the core. Passed from memory of trees? But the trees recalled everything! All and each of them, and their actions, good or ill. When their *kest* was spent and they had returned to the elements which had formed them—they lived on, in the memory of the trees.

Elder, how can such a thing be?

The trees remember much, Meripen Vanglelauf, but they cannot remember all, the elitch said sternly. *The trees do not number those who wander the mists, and the wood that you attempt to ward away from us is beyond our thought entirely.*

Meri looked down, trying to order his thoughts. Certainly, it was true—the trees could not recall those who had been taken by the *keleigh,* for if *kest* were never lost, yet it could be transformed. As for the shadow-wood—such a thing was beyond his experience, though it was . . . disquieting to hear that the trees found it so, as well.

Until you walked beneath those strange branches, we had no knowledge of it, save as a void; an absence of trees, the elitch told him.

An *absence* of trees? Worse and worse, Meri thought, and lay back against the pine again. The pine's sleep was deep, and he was so very tired. There were many more wards to be set. A nap, to recruit his strength and regain his focus... A nap would not at all...be...amiss...

"So there you have it," Becca murmured into Rosamunde's ear. "Apparently I need only marshal my will and direct my *kest* to heal my arm. What a fool I have been, Lady Rosamunde, to believe myself forever a cripple!"

Rosamunde snorted and stamped a foot.

"Yes, you are doubtless correct. The study of such matters beyond the Boundary is far different." She sighed and leaned against Rosamunde's warm shoulder.

"I wonder..." she murmured. "If *kest* informs all things, including the small plants...might it not be possible to—to draw the healing humor directly from the plant?" She chewed her lip. "I think I would very much like to meet a Fey healer," she said. "And certainly I would like to hear why our methods are so much more...efficacious here in the Vaitura."

Rosamunde flicked an ear.

"Yes," Becca said, holding her left hand out under the soft nose, revealing the patch of shiny pink skin across her palm. "It's entirely healed. The scar may fade, or it may not—but, truly, it is as good as it needs to be. There is no pain, and I have not lost any...more...strength or motion."

Rosamunde blew an interrogatory.

"Well, yes, I suppose I might consider it a practicum," Becca said. "And, as you say, if I succeed, many things will be made easier..."

The list unrolled before her mind's eye: to be able to cut her own meat, brush her own hair, do up her own buttons, take off her own shoes, tie a bow, bathe...

"I wonder..." she murmured, stepped away from Rosamunde's side. "I wonder how it might be done..."

If it were one of her patients, she thought, she would begin by examining the area, by touch and by sight. She unbuttoned the sleeve as she walked over to the edge of the corral and leaned against the fence. Pushing the sleeve up as far as it would go, she considered the withered member, not as a shameful thing, but as a problem in healing.

Carefully, she ran her fingers up the ruined arm, identifying wasted muscles, and clicked her tongue. It was difficult to believe that anything—even *kest!*—could rescue this, and, yet—Meripen Vanglelauf had been certain that the thing could be done and she must, she supposed, bow to his superior understanding.

So, then.

She braceleted her left wrist with her strong right fingers and closed her eyes, seeking—and finding the pool of molten gold at the base of her spine. No sooner had she identified it, than her blood began to warm. Determinedly, Becca gripped her own wrist, trying to imagine the golden warmth flowing to her fingers and into the ruined muscles.

Heat built; the very air tasted hot, and yet there was no sensation in her ruined arm at all.

Rosamunde screamed.

Becca's eyes flew open, and she echoed the scream, staring at the flames at her feet, greedy tongues licking along the grass.

"Rosamunde!" she cried out. "Run!"

The mare reared, front hooves cutting the hot air, and screamed once more.

Her skirt was smoldering; golden light dripped from her fingertips.

"Stop!" she cried, but the flames she had created no more heeded her command than more mundane fires.

Meripen Vanglelauf had said a word, and raised his hand. Mist had formed, thickened to clouds and rain had fallen, extinguishing the flames she had kindled.

"What was the word?" she cried, but the trees did not answer.

Becca bit her lip, tasting blood, hearing Rosamunde's hooves drumming against the ground.

Defiantly, she raised her hand, thinking of—*reaching for*—the moisture in the tree leaves, and in the grass, and in the trough at the far side of the corral.

Mist swirled 'round her fingers, thickening, darkening into swollen purple. Lighting flashed, gold and crimson, and thunder rolled.

Rain exploded from the roiling clouds, turning the ground in her immediate vicinity into a quagmire, drowning the greedy yellow tongues.

"Enough!" Becca gasped, and folded her fingers closed, breathing in and willfully imagining the molten gold retreating along her veins, pooling at the base of her spine, cooling, cooling.

Cool.

Becca looked around at what she had wrought; the water draining slowly away into the scorched soil, her soaked skirt splattered with mud, and Rosamunde, mincing toward her between the puddles, shaking her head so that her mane slapped the sides of her neck noisily.

Becca sighed and raised her hand to stroke the soft nose. Rosamunde blew emphatically into her ear.

"Yes, I don't doubt at all that I look a fright," Becca sighed—and then laughed. "But, Lady Rosamunde, did you see? *I put it out!* Even without the word! Perhaps I *will* learn to use *kest*! I will be able to protect us all and we need fear nothing—not from Altimere—not even from the Queen!"

⚬~∞∞∞~⚬

"What's that you've got, Vika, a dead one?" The voice was low, gritty, and sounding not particularly interested in a dead one.

Something pointed and damp shoved against Meri's face.

"G'way," he muttered, while what felt like a particularly rough piece of bark scraped his cheek.

"Still alive?" The voice was, perhaps, slightly more interested in a live one. Meri wished that whoever it was would leave him to sleep, and take the rasping bark with him.

"Here, let me have a look." The scraping stopped, and Meri felt warm fingers against his forehead.

"Let be!" he snapped, and heard a faint growl from somewhere nearby.

"Bit of spark in 'im yet," the voice said approvingly. "Here, then, lad, have a drink. Nay, nay, I'll hold the bottle."

Water, tepid and tasting of the skin, splashed into Meri's mouth. He reached, suddenly desperate for more, choked, swallowed, gasped, and cried out when the stream was withdrawn.

"You want to rest a bit before you take more," the

voice told him. "Which you'd know, if you had your wits about you."

Meri licked the last drops of water off his lips, opened his eye, and glared into a face as brown and seamed as elitch bark beneath a shock of hair the color of old wheat.

"I *have* my wits about me," he said, his voice little more than a raddled whisper.

The other Wood Wise nodded approvingly, eyes the merest leaf-green slits in his worn face. "Certain you do! Which is why Vika and me found you sleeping snug against an Old One, and looking to be sharing the Long Dream."

Meri blinked, and sat up, turning to stare at the pine he had reclined against so comfortably. An Old One, indeed, and on the edge of its final sleep, but strong enough, still, to overwhelm a thin-*kest*ed Ranger and pull him down into the dreaming.

"Oh." He closed his eye. "You'd think I was just sprouted." He sighed, and looked to his rescuer. "My thanks, Brother." He got a knee crooked, pushed himself awkwardly up—and would have toppled right over again if the other hadn't grabbed his shoulder and steadied him.

"No need to rush matters," he said. "If it were me, I'd take a bit to savor my luck."

"Luck?" Meri shook his head, carefully.

"I'd call it luck that you've enough *kest* left to warm yourself." The other jerked his head toward the lowering shadow-trees. "That wood's no friend to our kind, nor to any other, I'll warrant."

"I allow you to be right," Meri told him. "Have you been inside that wood?"

The other laughed and settled back on his heels, withdrawing his hand slowly. "No, nor will I! There's too much that's precious riding my shoulders, and it's a burden I'll risk for nothing you can name."

"I wonder you walk so close, then."

That earned him a crooked smile and a sideways glance from those vivid, half-closed eyes. "We just skirt the edges, Vika and me. Shortest route from someplace to someplace else. Why go inside, yourself?"

Meri took a breath and carefully drew his legs up, one at a time, until he sat cross legged and erect.

"Have you some waybread to spare?" he asked.

"Here you are." A broken bit appeared between two gnarled fingers.

"My thanks." Carefully, he gnawed off a corner. Now that his limbs were strengthening, he felt *kest* beginning to warm at the base of his spine. "I was sent by the Engenium at Sea Hold to help the Newmen at New Hope Village learn what was amiss about the wood that sheltered them," he told the other Wood Wise. Something moved at the edge of his vision. He turned his head and stared into the slitted red eyes of a sizable woods cat, its brindled fur making it all but invisible against the grass.

"Vika?" he murmured.

"That she is," the other said, and gave Meri a nod. "I'm Palin Nicklauf—and you'll be?"

"Meripen Vanglelauf." Meri cleared his throat. "I've met your sprout, Jamie."

Palin laughed, and offered the water skin again. "Had all sorts of ill luck, haven't you?"

Meri drank, prudently, and put the skin aside. "I found him likely, and well schooled."

"There's praise, coming from the Longeye," Palin said. His face shadowed. "I heard the boy's plea to the trees. Has young Lucy given up her *kest*?"

"She has," Meri confirmed, and paused to chew more waybread. "Her apprentice blames her own lack of skill."

"Aye, well, that's Violet in the shell." He shook his head. "It's hard for the young to accept the failures of youth."

"Of Jamie—" Meri began. Palin raised a hand.

"The trees tell me the sprout was under a geas last night, and won free by your kindness."

"It's . . . somewhat more complicated than that."

"What isn't?" the other said rhetorically. "I'd hear the tale if you've a mind to tell it."

Meri recruited himself with another sip from the skin. "You'll have heard of the Gardener."

"Will I? The elitch and ralif scarce speak of anything—or anyone—else."

That was, Meri thought, chewing a bit of waybread, a detail that had escaped him. Trees often babbled of their favorites—but it was mostly the culdoon and the larch and the other more foolish trees. Elitch and ralif were not only more sensible, but saw further.

"They do see something," he acknowledged, giving Palin a nod. "What it is, I don't know, even after having some dealings with her."

"Asked?"

"Not in so many words."

Palin grinned. "Nor have I. More fun to guess it out, though I might change my mind on meeting her. Why put a geas on the boy?"

Meri looked him in the eye. "It was an accident."

There was a pause, while Palin traded him glance for glance, then nodded, just once.

"An accident," he said, his voice utterly bland. "Might've befallen anyone."

"She displays an aura like...Newmen," Meri said slowly. "Unlike the Newmen of—of my acquaintance, who seem...unaware of the inner fires, and blind to the auras of others, she—Rebecca Beauvelley—is aware of her own power and of the auras of others. She has, however, not been trained in the slightest. Jamie frightened her, so I make it out to be, and she shouted at him to go away from her and never return, never realizing..."

"Never realizing that she was no more like Violet or Eliza or even Lucy—hot, brilliant, and powerless—if ever she had been."

"Why is that?" Meri asked suddenly.

"Eh? No talent for it, and no one to teach them, I expect. As for yon pretty Gardener—"

Palin's voice chopped off, and he became so still he seemed to vanish into the forest air.

Meri froze where he sat, scarcely breathing. The constant undertwitter of birds and other creatures had died away; not so much as a flutterbee moved.

From inside the shadow-wood came...sounds, as of something...hunting.

Vika flowed through the scant grass like a whisper-breeze, ears back, tail low. She paused some distance from the place where living forest became undead wood, and Meri saw her hackles rise.

With infinite care, and not half so much grace, Meri crept forward until he was at the woods cat's side. He was not particularly surprised to see Palin on the cat's other side.

The sounds within the shadow-wood continued, but nothing showed itself.

"I don't like that," Palin breathed.

"Nor do I," Meri answered, thinking of the creature that had beset Rebecca Beauvelley, and trying very hard not to think of the amount and kind of damage such a monster might do at New Hope Village.

His wards were pitiable things, Meri thought. They would protect nothing. And the Elders drowsing here could hardly be expected to rouse—

Warmth at his side, growing rapidly warmer. He moved his arm slowly, his eye on the shadow-wood, and pulled the elitch wand out of his belt.

Will you watch, he asked it, *and warn?*

Aye, it whispered, and Meri smiled. He brought it 'round before him, unsurprised to find a fresh hole in the mold, into which he slipped the slender branch. He pressed the hole closed with his fingers and then went back, pushing with elbows and knees, until he was under the branches of the sleepy pine, Palin and Vika with him.

"That'll do," the other Ranger said, and rose to his lanky height. At his knee, the woods cat stretched, her yawn exposing a mouthful of needle-sharp teeth.

Palin held a hand down, and Meri was not too proud to take it.

"Try your legs, Brother, and see how you stand."

Meri came to his feet, feeling the crackle of *kest* against their joined palms.

"Nay..." he protested, slipping his hand away.

Palin tipped his head. "What's amiss? It's nothing

more than you were willing to do for the sprout, so the elders tell me. I'm hale, and you could use the aid, Brother."

"The last one to give me her *kest* died of it," Meri said slowly, feeling the black edge of that moment, when he knew that her gift would be her doom—and knew that he would accept it...

"I'm hale," Palin repeated, and nodded toward the village. "Best we go on, if you're able. Eliza'll take a piece out of my bark, if I don't show myself soon."

Chapter Twenty-One

"AND THAT," BECCA SAID, MEETING VIOLET'S EYES firmly, "is what happened. I will perfectly understand if you do not wish me to live in your grandmother's house, or to subscribe to my teaching in anything."

The girl glanced down at her lap, which was filled with gathered marisk, and Becca bit her lip, recruiting herself to patience. This was Violet's decision to make and *truly* she would understand if the girl did not wish to have the almost-murderer of her brother under roof.

"It must be difficult," Violet said slowly, "to have had these virtues thrust upon you without receiving training in their use." She expertly stripped the blossoms from a marisk stem, frowning as they tumbled down into the basket.

"Father believes that a race of halflings might serve the land best." She gave Becca a slight, sidewise smile. "Which is where you'll see Jamie and me."

"Your mother had said as much this morning, when

I went to see how your brother did," Becca admitted, sorting the corish root according to size. "Have you received training in the use of *kest*?"

Violet shook her head. "I'm Mother's child. The trees do not talk to *me*."

Becca frowned. "That seems less halflings and more half," she observed, and Violet giggled.

"It does, but that was their bargain. And who is to say that, when I'm ready to marry, that I won't bear a Ranger-to-be? I think..." She paused while she stripped another stalk. "I think that, *over time*, as more intermarriages happened, that fewer children would be born either tree-wise or not." She slanted a sideways glance at Becca. "Father takes the long view—Gran used to say that he was practically a tree, himself."

Becca laughed, and it seemed that she heard an echo inside her head.

"I wonder," she said, then; "have you ever spoken with a Fey healer?"

"The nearest I've come to a Fey healer is Father," Violet answered. "Mother called for him to come, so you might ask him any questions you have." She grinned. "He might even answer.

"For that matter," she said after she had put her basket down and piled the stripped marisk stalks to the side, "Master Vanglelauf will know as much as Father, since they are both Rangers. All I know is that a Fey in need of healing merely asks a particular plant for some of its virtue."

Becca blinked. "Is your father prone to jokes?" she asked.

"Sometimes. But I've noticed that when he most seems to be joking—then he is speaking nothing but the truth. Gran said that some of what he said sounded like tall tales because he didn't have our words."

"And the rest of what he says perhaps only sounds outlandish to those who are not . . . intimately knowledgeable of the Vaitura?" Becca guessed.

Violet nodded, shaking out her skirts. "Would you like some tea? I think that—"

She stiffened, as if she'd heard something—and a moment later Becca heard it, too: a high, weird wailing sound that seemed to echo off the branches, then die.

"Father's home!" Violet cried, and ran toward the bottom of the garden.

Becca set aside the corish root and rose, following more sedately, reaching the end of the path in time to see Violet throw herself into the arms of a disreputable-looking fellow in worn leather. He caught Violet up and spun her around as if she were a child in nursery, his laugh echoing hers. A little behind him stood a large brindled cat, tufted ears cocked alertly, one shoulder companionably against Meripen Vanglelauf's knee.

He . . . looked slightly more robust than he had when they had parted earlier, which relieved her considerably. The pale tatters of his aura seemed a deeper and more subtle green; the comparison with the rich brown and orange of Violet's father's aura was, however, telling.

"Good evening, Master Vanglelauf," she said politely.

The green eye speared her. "Good evening, Rebecca Beauvelley," he answered, distantly. He nodded down at his companion. "This is Vika."

Since it seemed that he wished her to do so, she bowed slightly to the cat. "Good evening, Vika. I am pleased to make your acquaintance."

"And she's pleased to make yours," a strong, rough voice assured her.

She turned to see that the other Ranger had set Violet on her feet and stood with his arm around her waist, considering Becca from leaf-green eyes. He smiled, easily, but without impertinence, and gave her a nod.

"I'm Palin Nicklauf. You'll be the one the trees have named Gardener?"

"Rebecca Beauvelley," she said, returning his nod. "Yes."

"Then I'm as pleased to meet you as Vika is," Palin Nicklauf said.

"Perhaps . . . not," Becca said, with difficulty. "I'm afraid that I have been the . . . agency of some harm befalling your son."

"So the trees told me."

Becca braced herself for anger, but Palin's voice was perfectly easy and calm.

"Master Vanglelauf tells me there was no malice in it, and that he's charged to teach you better. Is that so, Longeye?"

"That's so," Meripen Vanglelauf said composedly, though Becca felt a spark of anger for the casual cruelty. "Palin."

"I hear." The other Ranger gave Becca a grin. "The Hope Tree tells us the sprout's awake, Gardener, wanting both his dinner and a walk under leaf. I think we'll find his hurts to be only what any sprout might find, in the process of setting his roots." He turned to look at Violet.

"I'm to your mother, now, sweet flower. Are you coming?"

"Yes!" Violet exclaimed, and gasped in the next breath, throwing Becca a conscious look. "I—that is..."

"Go." She waved her hand with a smile. "I have a good deal of thinking to do, and it's been too long since I've had leisure to putter in a workroom."

"Thank you!" Violet darted forward and kissed Becca on the cheek. Turning, she caught Palin's hand and the two of them skipped diagonally across the garden, Vika the cat flowing like silk beside them.

Face warm, Becca touched her cheek, as if her fingers could find the shape of the girl's kiss. A simple, chaste kiss of friendship, she thought—and took a hard breath against a chest that was tight with tears.

She remembered then that she was not alone, and turned toward Meripen Vanglelauf, likewise abandoned.

But the Ranger and his tattered aura were gone, withdrawn to his own devices while she stood, confused.

"Well," Becca said, and went resolutely up the path. She had said that she wanted to putter in the workroom, had she not?

At the bench, she paused to pick up the basket of marisk blossoms that Violet had stripped before marching on to the kitchen door.

~❊❊❊~

Meri dropped into his nest, arms wrapped around himself, and concentrated, on the smell of the grass, the muttering of a tree-mouse, the creak of limb and trunk...

"Root and branch," he whispered, and rubbed his cheek against the cool grasses that made up his couch. "She is too beautiful."

Slowly, his *kest* subsided; slowly, the clamor to meld

and lose himself in her brilliance faded. Slowly, he began to think.

Ranger, are you well?

"Becoming well, Elder, thank you," he muttered, flopping over to his back. A breeze wafted through the culdoon's branches and skipped over to dry the sweat from his brow. "I have simply... forgotten... what it is like to be... vulnerable to the power of others. I have not been so thin since I was a sprout."

Perhaps you should meld with the Gardener, the elitch said.

"No!" He sat up, then collapsed again to the grasses, one arm flung across his eyes.

You would gain much, the elitch persisted, un-treelike, unless one recalled that the trees of one's home forest often guided a sprout's first few meldings. *Truly, Ranger, the trees fear for you.*

"The trees need not fear," Meri tried to say, but the falsehood stuck in his throat. In truth, the trees were right to fear; and yet—to meld with Rebecca Beauvelley; she would be a part of him forever, as Faldana was. He could not...

He could not meld, he thought wearily. He could not set worthy wards. He could not solve the shadowwood. Verily, the forest was littered with his couldnots! The wards, at least, might be solved, but Palin had refused to assist him.

Will you speak with him? he asked the elitch.

Palin carries his charge, the answer came, surprisingly sharp. *We do not ask more of him.*

Elder, if I do not have some help, someone to set—

Behind the shelter of his arm, he blinked, seeing in memory the extravagant beauty of her, golden flames traced with green, scarred with crimson. An aura such as the Vaitura had not seen—possibly in the length of a memory as long as that of Altimere the Artificer. An aura and the ability to use her *kest*.

"I will take her with me tomorrow," he said, speaking aloud so that he could measure the words against the twilight. "She can set the wards. I will show her one of mine—she has eyes to see!—and bid her follow the pattern. It will be a lesson..."

Indeed, he thought, well pleased with himself; it would be a lesson, and a stern one. Nor would it require any intermingling of the teacher's *kest* with the student's.

It may be that the Gardener can riddle the wood you saw for us, the elitch added, which Meri chose to hear as further approval for his plan.

Smiling, he curled over on his side, settled his cheek into the crook of his arm—and plummeted into sleep.

<hr>

At noon, or midnight, according to his watch, Altimere was attacked by a winged creature with a woman's head. It shrieked insults at him, and drove sharp talons at his face.

He threw a dart of *kest* at it and it blew apart into mist and feathers, leaving behind the echo of a scream.

An hour after the attack, he came across footprints in the soft material by the stream's edge. Some were boot-clad, some barefoot, and some were a vague smudge as if who walked there was unused to leaving tracks, or too little in the world to do so.

Altimere paused, chest tight, with an odd sparkle at the edge of his vision. In a moment, he was again master of himself, and walking once more.

Following the footprints, Altimere came to a pile of five goodly stones. Wedged between the stones was a flat bit of silvery wood with short names and marks scratched upon it.

It was a strange record he looked at, and showed a certain intelligence and certitude of purpose. Studying the cryptic notes, Altimere pieced together a history.

One Dusau Meerlauf, wandering through the strange mists, had come by the stream and followed it . . . and at some point had come across his own steps, as it were. Having undertaken, like Altimere, an attempt to record time and place, Dusau Meerlauf had been the first to inscribe his name on the wood—perhaps he had created the primitive tablet and gathered the stone splinters that served as pens. In any case, Dusau Meerlauf inscribed his name as D. Meerlauf, and left two slash marks. At some point, Kluka Xanlauf and Cai Vanglelauf came by together: C. Vanglelauf and K. Xanlauf, and added a slash each . . . and two stones to the pile.

Then came Varion Fanelauf, solitary . . . and perhaps between, extra visits by the original D. Meerlauf, whose record now was nine slashes, while Cai and Kluka showed five, Varion Fanelauf showed four, and Joda Meerlauf, last comer, showed two.

Wood Wise or Rangers all, Altimere thought, which was no bad thing, saving they seemed as trapped as he was.

Still, they showed amongst them a certain native ingenuity and an understanding that their plight might be ameliorated if they could band together with others: precisely the understanding he had lately come to!

Hope shuddered painfully through Altimere's chest.

Five others. The *kest* of five, even five depleted Wood Wise, plus his own surely . . . might . . . be sufficient to win out of the *keleigh* and back into life.

He must, he thought, meet these intrepid Wood Wise—very soon, indeed.

He drifted on a raft of ralif branch and elitch leaf, borne up by salt waves, and soothed by a tender breeze. There were sweet nuts and tart culdoon to dine on, and wine made from dawnderi blossoms. He knew he was asleep, and that the sleep was a gift; he sighed and pulled it more tightly around him and sank deeper into the—

Ranger! 'Ware! 'Ware! The wards are breached!

The stars were out and Violet had not yet returned. When Becca stepped into the garden, she heard excited voices, laughter, and a glissade of notes from a stringed instrument. Light blazed from Elizabeth Moore's house, supplied equally by candles and the fanciful fires of auras. It seemed the whole village had turned out to welcome Palin Nicklauf back home—though, perhaps, Becca thought, New Hope was not so much Palin's home as a place where friends and kinfolk could be found.

She hesitated, wondering if she ought to join the crowd of well-wishers and merrymakers. It was a situation that required nice judgment and she had never been more than moderately proficient at this sort of social equation.

In the end, she turned away from the noisy, glittering

party and walked to the bottom of the garden, where it was quieter, and where she might perform her experimentation in peace.

✧✦✧

Silver stood among the living, and a cold glow crawled along the ground. Meri slammed to a stop, his arm around a thin birch, and stared at the elitch wand that he had planted a dozen paces out from the edge of the shadow-wood. Between him and it there was now a grove of undead trees, glowing cold and unnatural against the night.

His wards—were gone, unmade, he supposed. The elitch wand stood where he had planted it, aura hectic, a shadow-tree not three handspans away.

"Elders, wake and know your peril!"

His words fell like stones out of the dead air. Not even the birch he embraced stirred.

Who hears me? he sent, hoping that his thought at least would be unimpeded.

I hear you, the answer came back, prompt and strong, but the voice belonged to none of the trees he knew.

Show yourself, Meri sent.

Very well.

Directly before him, perhaps eight paces out, was the silvery seeming of a ralif. The voice seemed to originate there, though it was unlike that of any ralif Meri had ever conversed with. Perhaps it followed, he thought, that trees so unnatural would find even their voices altered beyond recognition.

Carefully, he loosed his hold on the slumbering birch and stepped away from it. Before him, the ralif glimmered balefully, growing uncertain in outline, until it was as insubstantial as mist.

A figure stepped forward, to stand with legs braced inside the tree's foggy outline. The mists obscured his form, and the hard silver shine hid his fires. Still, Meri felt a tug, as of kinship, or memory.

I am Meripen Vanglelauf, he sent; *Ranger.*

The indistinct figure bowed slightly, and straightened, hands tucked into his belt.

I am Vamichere Pinlauf, Ranger.

Meri shivered.

Vamichere Pinlauf went into the keleigh *with his wood during the last days of the war,* he sent. *He is a hero and his name one to conjure with.*

They begged me to leave them! The anguish in the other's thought was raw enough that Meri felt a scream build in his chest. *My trees! I to continue while they were unmade? No, a thousand times, though the Elders would have their damned boundary despite us—an it cost every life in the Vaitura!*

Meri swallowed. There could be no doubting that this...shade...was Vamichere Pinlauf. Though how it was manifest, and what it was about...

What do you here, Vamichere Pinlauf?

There are heroes, the other told him, his thought now eerily calm, *in the mist.*

So my betters have taught me, Meri acknowledged. *They taught me also—what is lost to the* keleigh *is never recovered.*

All honor to your masters, Meripen Vanglelauf, we have found a way. The other motioned with a mist-softened hand at the shell of the tree he stood in. *We have found a way to remove those things which are lost to the keleigh—to push them out again into the daylit world.* He gestured again. *My trees live again.*

Horror shuddered through Meri. *No,* he sent. *No, Ranger . . . they do not live.*

They must! We have liberated them!

The shout nearly split Meri's head. He went back a step, caught himself, and took two steps forward, feeling the unnatural shine that was neither aura nor *kest* cold against his cheek.

Perhaps they have been too long within the keleigh, he said, pity filling him. The silvered trees were terrible—wrong—and yet—if Vanglewood were to slide into the *keleigh,* would he not bend every effort to succor it?

The trees you have liberated have no kest, Brother, he sent as gently as he could. *They have no voices.*

My wood is not dead!

No, Meri answered; *but neither is it alive.*

Silence. The figure in the mist seemed to shrink in on itself.

Perhaps, Meri suggested. *They require . . . you.*

A ghostly laugh echoed through his head, discomforting.

We have together pushed all manner of life from out of the mists, yet—heroes that we are—we cannot ourselves step free.

Meri looked about him, at the dying trees and the undead, and back, again, to the mist-shrouded figure. He took a deep breath, and forced himself forward—one step, two steps . . . three . . . the cold energy burning his skin . . . and held his hand out.

Perhaps what you need . . . is someone to pull.

Easewerth's aura was a dim indigo, difficult to distinguish from its leaves. Becca knelt down carefully beside the small planting at the bottom of the garden, and considered what she saw. By those signs she knew to look for—leafing, stem-strength, color—the plants were exceedingly healthy. Sonet might have complained that they were leggy, but Sonet liked her plants bushy and low to the ground.

"Best they keep their virtues close than waste them in trying to fly" was what she had used to say, and then look sour when Becca pointed out that they were each abjured to turn their faces to the sun and grow as straight as they could.

By those signs she knew less well—color and depth of the aura—it seemed that the easewerth she studied was goodly and strong. She extended her hand, slowly, and felt a thrill along her fingers.

"Please," she said, "may I have some of your virtue?"

Nothing happened; she neither heard a voice inside her head, as she had half-expected that she might, nor felt a seepage of slow indigo into her blood. She *did* feel the molten gold at the base of her spine begin to warm, and rise.

Mindful of her earlier misadventures, she dropped her hand, closed her eyes, and concentrated on breathing until the warmth subsided.

There must, she thought, be some art to regulating the flow of one's inner fires. With her, it seemed to be nothing or conflagration—which Meripen Vanglelauf, his aura in tatters, then extinguished with a word.

"Very well." She took a particularly deep breath, hoping to cow her eager fires, and extended her hand once more.

"Please," she said, and came to her feet with a snap, precisely as if Altimere had suddenly imposed his will over hers, only this time she did not have the blessed confusion bestowed by the collar to soften the experience.

Without any input from her own will, she began to run, awkwardly, then all at once with the fleet, effortless grace she had observed in Meripen Vanglelauf.

"No!" She tried to stop, she tried to throw herself to the ground, she tried to divert her steps so that she would run into a tree—but whatever held her in thrall did not allow her so much as one step taken under her own will.

"I won't!" she screamed, feeling the ever-ready inner fires flare.

Gardener! The voice of the Hope Tree shook the thoughts in her head. *Run as you have never run before! Meripen Longeye fades!*

"Where?" she gasped, as the *other* pushed her into even more speed. She might, she thought, gain the nest before the pace she was driven at broke a leg.

The sunshield will guide you, the Hope Tree said. *When you run past, take up the twig that is on the bench at my feet.*

The Hope Tree loomed. She was dimly aware of people, of shouts; compelled, she ran on, her hand going out of its own accord to snatch the stick up.

Run! the tree thundered, and run she did, the elitch twig gripped in urgent fingers.

Chapter Twenty-Two

HIS *KEST* ROSE, EXULTANT, MEETING AND MELDING with silver. He cried out, his voice strange to him, and tried to pull away, but the other was too strong—no melding of equals, this, but a power so vast that *every*thing must rise to it, become part of it, lose...

...lose...

Silver...cool and clean. Green and blue fluttered, fading, at the edge of his vision, and he cried out again, both eyes open now, and seeing, near and far, away into the roiling silver mist, seeing faces, row on row—Fey and Newmen, shoulder-to-shoulder, at one with the mist and the undead trees.

Meripen Longeye!

The voice was so strong the mist shivered, and those standing among the front ranks went back a step, as if compelled.

Meripen Longeye! The trees do not release you!

He fell then, or thought he did, but it was so hard to know with everything going to mist, and it was

silver ... silver dimming his eyes, silver mixing with
his blood, silver so cool, so cold ...

... so ... cold ...

~~~≈≈≈~~~

Her body was beyond her; she ran until her thoughts
whited, and still she ran. She dared not close her eyes,
and it seemed to her frantic senses that sometimes
she ran *through* trees, rather than between them, and
that she felt her soul catch and leave threads on the
rough inner barks.

Meripen Longeye! the Hope Tree thundered. *The
trees do not release you!*

Perhaps it was the force of the shout, or perhaps
the sunshield pressed her into even greater efforts.
The trees she passed blurred into silver—and then
became green, and brown, and silver, as the sunshield
withdrew its will from her.

Released, she staggered, and fell, her head hitting
the ground hard enough to throw a spangle of stars
across her vision.

Gardener, arise! He fades, he fades!

Whimpering, she pushed herself to her knees,
looking wildly about—

Meripen Vanglelauf lay not three handspans away,
at the foot of a hard silver ralif. His scarred face was
composed and peaceful, his lips tinged just slightly with
blue. He had lost his patch; both eyes were closed,
long lashes lying lightly along stern cheekbones; his
hair was tangled with dead leaves and green. The
lines of his limbs as he lay there among the forest
floor litter were clean. He appeared to be whole,
hale, and unwounded.

Saving that the tattered green rags of his aura—
were gone.

"No..." Becca crawled to his side, lifted her hand
to the heart-point, and blinked at the twig she yet
clutched in her hand.

Give it to him. The Hope Tree's voice was quieter
now. *My gift, given freely, from the top of my crown
to the deepest roots.*

Becca dropped the twig on the still chest, barely
attending what she did, fingers already on the heart-
point, her own heart stuttering in horror.

If Meripen Vanglelauf's heart was beating, it was
doing so very quietly, indeed.

"No..." Becca whispered again. "You can't live
without *kest*."

She had so much that she couldn't control it. And
here he lay, so cold, when the Hope Tree itself wept
for him.

Becca took a breath.

Bending, she placed her mouth against his blue
lips, and deliberately reached to the pooled gold of
her power.

◦≈≈≈◦

Power flowed to him. The heartfire of the Vaitura
itself rose through his roots, green, brown, and amber,
pulling him tall and taut. Branches burst from his
body, reaching toward the benediction of the sky, and
golden light poured upon his greedy leaves, burning
the mists from his eyes, heating his blood, and melting the last cold crystals of silver.

Warm and comforted, he lay listening to the small
sounds of the wood. In a moment, he thought, he

would open his eyes and see what strange new world he found himself inhabiting. In a moment, he would surely do just that. But for *this* moment, it was more than sufficient to lie still, and listen, and rejoice in being alive.

Gold fires and green danced with brown and amber. Becca clung to Meripen Vanglelauf, unable to end the kiss, unwilling to disrupt the play of powers. It seemed that the cold lips softened against hers. Beneath her, his chest moved as he took in a deep, shuddering breath; and the pulse under her fingertips staggered, stumbled, and began a steady beat.

Enough, Gardener. We have done what was needful.

She raised her head, the trees—silver and green— swirling unpleasantly around her. *You have given him everything*, she thought, as she allowed herself to slide to the ground.

You have given what was needful, and no more. The trees honor you, Rebecca Beauvelley.

"Thank you," she murmured, warmed and comforted by the tree's voice. She closed her eyes.

"I can show you the way," a deep, growly voice whispered, hot breath against on her ear. Something sharp poked her firmly in the side. "Wake, silly Gardener."

Becca sighed. "Go away."

"I can show you the way," the voice repeated, slightly louder. "The hole in the hedge."

Becca started up, suddenly very awake indeed. "You!" she cried. The Brethren dodged back, but she was quicker; her good hand darting out and seizing the creature around the wrist.

"Release! Release!" the Brethren shouted, yanking against her fingers.

"Betrayer! You tried to kill us!" Becca shouted back. The creature tried to free itself again; she twisted 'round, letting the force of its efforts pull her to her knees.

"Stupid Gardener was too bright!" it cried. "Called bad things down on us!"

"You led us to them!"

Her fingers slipped on the Brethren's wrist. It yanked again, breaking her grip. She threw herself forward and grabbed its tail.

"Stop! Stop!" it screamed, but she held on grimly.

"We'd given you nothing but kindness," she panted. "And you led us to those things . . ."

"No! Let go! I know the way! No monsters if stupid Gardener will be sensible!"

"On the surface, that seems excellent advice," a light voice commented. Becca, her heart in her mouth, looked over her shoulder.

Meripen Vanglelauf sat cross-legged on the forest floor, both eyes open and plainly sighted. The left eye was as green as new spring leaves; the right was ocean blue. His scarred face bore a look of faintly amused interest. Outlining his slim form was a cloak of woven greens, shot with gold and umber. It shimmered and flowed about him, informing his least movement with grace and beauty.

"If the lady releases your tail, will you stay and speak with me?" he asked.

"Rude, stupid Gardener lets *go*," the Brethren muttered.

Meripen Vanglelauf moved his head slightly from side to side. "Your agreement...?" he suggested.

The Brethren growled, and shook its horns. Becca held onto its tail for all she was worth.

"I agree," the Brethren said abruptly. "Let *go!*"

The Ranger nodded. Rebecca let go.

The Brethren snarled, muttered, shifted—and crouched on its haunches.

"Thank you," Meripen Vanglelauf said calmly. "Now, you offer to show the Gardener 'the way'—which *way* would that be?"

"The way through the hedge," the Brethren growled.

Becca settled her chin on her arm and kept still where she was, flat against the ground.

"Everyone knows the way through the hedge. Not all are foolish enough to take it."

"Longeye doesn't know everything," the Brethren said.

"Now that," Meripen Vanglelauf replied, "is very true." He raised his hand and fingered his brow above the sea-blue eye. "Will you bring me my patch, Little Brother? I think it may have fallen by yon silver ralif—mind you don't go too close."

The Brethren snorted, and darted away. The Ranger moved his attention to her.

The aspect of his face with both eyes uncovered, Becca thought, was—unsettling. The blue eye focused, and surely saw—but upon objects and events far beyond her, while the green eye was sharp upon her face.

"Sit up," he said. It sounded like a command.

"I cannot," she answered, "without someone to assist me, or at least a great deal of flailing about. I did not wish to disturb the conversation."

He frowned, which expression had lost none of its direness, then glanced aside as the Brethren approached, the patch extended on one horny paw.

"Those trees comfort no one," it commented.

"That they do not. My thanks." Meripen Vanglelauf took the patch.

"Where do they come from?" Becca asked, while the Ranger placed the patch over his blue eye and fussed with knotting the cord. "The silver trees? They—it is as if they have been frozen."

"I am told, and by one who should know, that they come from out of the *keleigh*," Meripen Vanglelauf said. He finished with the cord and glanced between Becca and the Brethren.

"You had heard of this hole in the hedge previously," he said to her.

"The Brethren had mentioned it before," she admitted; "and offered to show me the way."

He nodded thoughtfully and looked back to the Brethren "Will you show *me* the way?" he asked it.

The Brethren hesitated. "The other ones fell," it produced eventually.

"I see. I am touched by your regard for my safety."

"I am *not* touched," Becca said hotly, "by its disregard for mine!"

The Brethren turned its heavy head and stared at her.

"It's the Gardener's land, beyond the hedge."

"That is true, but I assure you that the hedge—the *keleigh!*—is no less inimical to me than it is to you, or to Master Vanglelauf!"

"The trees—" the Brethren began, then growled, lowering its horns.

"Peace, Little Brother," Palin Nicklauf said easily. He stepped out from—surely, Becca thought, *from behind*—a birch, Vika at his knee, two packs and a bow distributed about his lean person. "You're looking well, Longeye."

"I'm feeling well," Meripen Vanglelauf told him, rising with heartbreaking grace. He slid one pack from Palin's back and took the bow, tipping his head when the other Ranger dropped the second pack by the first.

"You're coming with me? I'll be glad of your company, Brother, but I believe it needful that one of us remain here." He turned and nodded at the cold silver trees.

"These are come out from the *keleigh.*"

"Are they now?" Palin looked thoughtful. "And the manner of their coming?"

"They are pushed out of the mists by the efforts of heroes. I myself spoke to Vamichere Pinlauf..."

Palin said nothing—pointedly, Becca thought.

"...and nearly died of it," Meripen Vanglelauf concluded. "Warn folk neither to go among nor have intercourse with the trees. If someone calls to them from the mists, they are wisest not to answer—and they must not by any means offer their hand in succor."

"I'll keep the sprout close by, and consult with the Hope Tree, and others," Palin said slowly. "Eliza's folk don't quite see as we do, Brother, but there's Eliza herself, who's given herself as tree-kin..."

"And Sam," Meripen Vanglelauf added, "who bears the oath to Sian."

"Well." Palin looked about him, his gaze eventually lighting on the packs at his feet.

"As it happens, Brother, you will be having company,

but it won't be mine. The trees had it that the Gardener should walk with you."

"I," Becca said, "am clearly not going anywhere."

Palin grinned and stepped over to where she reclined yet on the ground. "Need some help, Gardener?"

"If you would be so kind. I would also take it kindly if you would then escort me back to the village."

"First thing first." He extended a wiry hand. Becca took it in her good hand and let his strength guide her up, first to her knees and then to her feet.

"There you are, then," he said. "I'll just be helping you with the pack..."

"I am going back to the village," Becca said, speaking slowly and distinctly. "I am not going traipsing around the Vaitura with a pack on my back, looking for—for a *hole in the hedge!*—that has apparently defeated several experienced Rangers! I would only—as I am sure he will agree—be in Master Vanglelauf's way."

She turned to look at that gentleman, certain of his warm agreement, but he was gazing abstractedly upward, as if he were sighting the stars through the branches.

"The trees have said it's you and the Longeye going together with the Younger Brother, here," Palin said cheerfully.

Becca frowned. "The trees may say what they will," she said firmly, "but there are reasons why I must return to the village. I have a horse—"

"Aye, and I'll be pleased to care for her while I'm there—which will be a time, since my charge is to wait there for any strange and unwelcome Fey who may arrive to endanger Sian's oath-sworn."

"I also have," Becca said, around a feeling of desperation; "a servant. She is—that is, she requires a renewal of *kest* from time to time in order to—"

"I've heard something of that one, too," Palin said slowly. "An artifact, is it?"

"So everyone seems to insist," she said icily. He raised his hand, showing her a callused palm.

"I'm pleased to do what I can for that one, too, Gardener, but artifacts are tricky, and I wouldn't want to do it harm. I'll take a look at it when I get back to the village. Between the sprout and me, we'll figure out what's best to do. Where do I look for it?"

Becca bit her lip. "I—am not entirely certain where she goes when she is—when she has no duties for me," she admitted, one eye on Meripen Vanglelauf, who had given over staring into the treetops and was busily adjusting his pack. "She . . . appears . . . when her name is spoken."

"Might be we'll have something to talk about, after all," Palin said with a grin.

"She cannot speak," Becca said repressively. "Her name is Nancy."

"Then I'll do what I might, Gardener." He looked down at her gravely. "Best you get your pack on."

"I am not going," Becca said flatly.

The charge comes, Gardener. The Hope Tree sounded, Becca thought, tired. Certainly, it had reason. As did she.

"I have this evening run a great distance through the forest and assisted in the healing of someone in a crisis of *kest*, and who has yet to be cured of a deficiency of courtesy! I am very tired. Therefore, I am going back to the village and I am going to bed.

I am not the least use on a journey to see a hole in the—"

"The charge has come," Meripen Vanglelauf said, his light voice echoing the tree. He tipped his head. "It is true that the charge has come to me, and not to you. But, it is felt that the . . . bond . . . we share through the sunshield will insure that you accompany me." He hesitated, and gave a reluctant nod. "It is not what I would have, Rebecca Beauvelley, but I suggest that sunshields are chancy at best. Behind them is all the power of the sea. It would be best to put on your pack and accompany me willingly, for if you do not, you will accompany me nonetheless." He considered her. "Perhaps you find subjugation is what you like."

"It is not!" A brief shower of golden sparks reminded her to take a hard breath and cool her temper. Feeling somewhat less incendiary, she turned her back on the lot of them and began to walk.

Half a dozen steps toward the village, her legs locked, her feet seemingly rooted to the ground.

"Stupid Gardener," the Brethren said, clearly.

"You see?" Meripen Vanglelauf added. "Resign yourself and at least you have the boon of traveling under your own will. It will be easier, for all."

Chapter Twenty-Three

THE NIGHT WIND WAS LIGHTLY EDGED WITH CHILL, AS if promising the snow he had not seen fall since first he had walked under Vanglewood's sweet branches. Above, the stars were rich and frolicsome, and the dreams of trees made fantastical shapes against the dark.

Indeed, Meri reflected, it was just the sort of night that might tempt any Wood Wise from out of his tree, to dance with the shadows, sing with the stars, and race the manic breezes toward morning. Stern and weary Ranger that he was, yet he might have tried a jig or two himself on such a night, were it not for cold shine of the undead wood on his left hand, the Brethren at the lead of their small party, and Rebecca Beauvelley, walking badly in her cumbersome skirts, her aura showing flickers of temper like lightning between high clouds.

He could scarcely blame her. She had said aright— she was more of a burden to the expedition than an aid—but there! It was best to think of Rebecca

Beauvelley as little as he could manage, with her walking directly before him. If he considered her overmuch, then he would begin again to think of other matters which were best left unconsidered.

The Gardener is also a healer, the Hope Tree told him, its voice already thin with distance. *She could not see you fade, Ranger.*

It seems, he sent carefully, *that you also gave much, Elder.*

How not? the tree answered. *For many sunrises, you served the trees, Meripen Vanglelauf. A touch here, a word there; a healing, a quick release. Your kest is woven into the kest of entire forests. Should we not return some small portion to you, in your extremity? It is no small thing that you give us, and we do not hold your service lightly. We regard you, Ranger.*

Elder, I thank you, Meri sent, chest tight. *My service is my life.*

There was no answer, nor, he thought suddenly, did there need to be one. It was very true that his service was his life; that was what it was to be Wood Wise and Ranger. And if the trees judged that his service was yet needed, then what was it but their right to revive him and snatch him back from—

He shivered, recalling the cold seep of silver along his veins. *Truly, you would have ended*, he told himself, *had she not given the gift. And as for whether she should have withheld it—the sunshield compelled her and the elitch advised her. What would you, Meripen Woodenhead?*

As for the manner of his near-return to the elements that had borne him . . . Kind enough to say that he had been made foolish with pity. That kindness begged the question of whether the shade of Vamichere Pinlauf had aimed to entrap him, to pull him into the *keleigh* to join with the other heroes; whether it was simply mad with loss, or was nothing more than an accident of the mist, recalling for an instant that there had been a Vamichere Pinlauf, once . . .

The effort to extract the trees—and, root and branch!—*other living things* from the *keleigh* would seem to be madness of itself, Meri thought. Yet, if there were heroes trapped in the mist, would they *not* attempt to defeat it, to be true to their service, and to rescue those in peril?

The terrain had changed, the ground becoming stonier as they bore away from the border with the undead wood. The Brethren increased the pace, and Rebecca Beauvelley increased hers, though he felt shoulder muscles and back complain. He blinked, breath-caught, and forced his own shoulders to relax.

He had, he reminded himself, received a great gift from Rebecca Beauvelley, and though they had not melded, yet they were linked by that which they had shared. As they accumulated *kest* from other sources—which they surely would do—the awareness each had of the other would become less . . . intense, but for now at least, he would know her pains and her sorrows—as she would know his.

Ahead, a stone turned under her foot. She cried out, staggered, snatching one-handed for balance—and fell, striking her knee with a force that sent a shock of pain through Meri's body.

"Stop!" he called ahead. The Brethren, its clay-colored aura displaying flickers of what might be irritation, circled back, as Meri knelt beside the Gardener.

"We can rest, take some waybread and water," he said, keeping his voice even, so that he did not add the burden of his impatience to her other dismays. "But we will need to walk on, after."

"Fix it," the Brethren said, and added, in her own voice, "This will sting. That means the medicine is working."

She shook her head, wearily. "There is no medicine that will fix it," she said dully. "I know that I walk off-balance for it, and am more susceptible to stones." She sighed and raised her head to meet Meri's eyes, her own a soft and weary brown. "Master Vanglelauf, is there nothing you can say to the trees to make them see the folly of this?"

"It is not the trees that compel you, but the sun-shield," he reminded her.

"Yet you said it was the trees who compelled you."

"The charge has come to me," he admitted. "It is not . . . quite the same thing as compulsion, for no Ranger will refuse a charge." He shook his head. "Say if you will that it is our nature that compels us—but you are neither Wood Wise nor Ranger. The trees can lay no charge on you." He rose and held down his hand to her.

"Come, let us rest. You'll feel better for a bit of waybread."

⚬~∞∞∞~⚬

The night was intoxicating, exciting senses she scarcely knew she possessed—and perhaps that she had not, before her wild run through trees and forest and the desperate gamble for Meripen Vanglelauf's life.

Sunshield, she tried, forming her thought very carefully. *What do you want of me?*

If the dried bit of bone heard her—and she very sternly forbid herself from wondering how it might—it did not choose to answer, which was, she thought irritably, all of a piece.

Her skirt had picked up night dew at the hemline and the wet fabric clung to her ankles, making it difficult to walk. The pack was an unnatural and uncomfortable burden; her back was already beginning to ache—another pain added to a growing list. The sunshield had not been particularly gentle in its use of her; she had a myriad of bruises, as well as cuts and scrapes on her hands and face. Surprisingly, though her legs hurt, they did not refuse to bear her, as she had half-thought they might. The sore muscles even eased somewhat as they walked on, which gave her some hope for her back.

The skirt slapped her ankles, hampering her stride. She sighed, wishing after Sian's sensible leggings. Perhaps if she called Nancy . . . but Nancy wouldn't be able to hear her, would she? Not away out here in the woods, moving farther and farther from New Hope Village.

Ahead, the Brethren, their guide, bore right, away from the eerie, ice-clad trees. The bushes gave way to a sort of sharp, scrubby grass, growing amid plentiful rocks and free-rolling stones. Becca tried to mind her footing, but a stone moved, the dress clung, and she was down, feeling utterly foolish, and the pain in her knee added to her list of complaints.

She stared for a long moment at Meripen Vanglelauf's brown, capable hand, held down in an offer of aid, then looked up into his stern face.

"I thought that I would not snare you so easily," she said, hearing the petulance and distress in her voice.

He pressed his lips together, but gave her a curt nod.

"We are now more equal in *kest* than we were," he said evenly. "As I have been trained and you have not, you are more at risk in this transaction than I." He raised an eyebrow. "Will you dare it?"

Dare it she did, feeling a slight and not unpleasant crackle of energy across her skin in the instant before their hands met. He lifted her easily to her feet and guided her to a ralif tree, offering his assistance once more, so that she sat down with some modicum of grace.

It was the Brethren, surprisingly, who slipped the pack off her shoulders and dragged it around onto her lap. She had barely begun with the laces when the Ranger sat down beside them, a waterskin on his knee and a bit of cracker in his hand.

"Here," he said, breaking the cracker into three and handing them around.

Becca nibbled hers, surprised by the burst of nutty sweetness. She was surprised, too, by evidence of a new...gentleness in Meripen Vanglelauf. His care for her well-being seemed genuine, with no appearance of his previous ill-concealed disgust.

Her bit of cracker was gone, leaving her well satisfied. She leaned back against the ralif and sighed.

"Drink," Meripen Vanglelauf said quietly.

She stirred to take the water skin from his hand; sipped, and passed it to the Brethren, who drank as if unused to such niceties before giving it back to its owner.

"Before we go on," Meripen Vanglelauf said, turning

so that Becca must look squarely into his face, "it is time to heal your arm."

"I—" she began; and closed her mouth, pressing her lips tightly together.

"Yes?" he inquired.

"I tried—after you—after our first lesson was over. I tried to heal it and—I almost set Rosamunde on fire!"

Both eyebrows rose, though Becca thought he looked more amused than horrified.

"I gather, however, that you avoided this doom. Tell me how."

Becca sighed, and settled herself more firmly against the ralif, feeling a not unpleasant warmth soothing her tired muscles.

"I asked the trees to tell me the word you had used," she confessed, "to put out my previous fire."

One corner of the stern mouth twitched, then straightened.

"Did you?"

"I did, but they did not tell it to me," she said. "I—I suppose you would say that I *reached out* and gathered up water from the trough, and the grasses, and it rained down—quite a lot, I'm afraid; nothing so neat as yours!—and put the fire out."

"I see." He looked down, busying himself with hooking the waterskin to his belt. When he looked back up, his face was as austere and serious as ever.

"The word I spoke was . . . a construct, in which the process you describe—of calling water to your hand—had already been stored. It needed only the speaking of the word to set the work into motion." He paused. "Those of us who are philosopher-trained learn such things, which are, occasionally, useful."

"But the word," Becca said, thinking about what he had told her; "it would have done me no good, even if the trees had told me, because I had not ... prepared it beforehand."

"That is correct. Now," he said briskly, with a glance aside. "If the Younger Brother will grant us the gift of his patience for few heartbeats more ..."

The Brethren growled, and came to its feet.

"I will come back," it said, and walked away, to Becca's eyes vanishing into the darkness.

"Brethren are shy of such workings as we are about to undertake," Meripen Vanglelauf said to her look of inquiry. "Tell me how you tried to heal yourself."

She told him, quickly, and felt her face heat as he shook his head.

"*Kest* is the fire within," he said, with a return to his former asperity. "Why draw it outward, only to push it inward again?"

"Now that you say so, it seems utterly nonsensical," she said. "I suppose I was thinking in terms of applying a cream—easewerth, perhaps—rather than ingesting a tea or tinsane."

She sat up, determined to learn what he had to teach.

"Though you still doubt that it can be done," he murmured, as if in counterpoint to her thought. He frowned. "You are a healer ..."

"I am. But Violet tells me that Palin—and, we assume, yourself!—need only ask the appropriate plant for its virtue in order to be healed, with none of our chopping, or drying or brewing to be done! It seems to me that we are about very different businesses and simply call them by the same name."

"That is possible," he said, his brows pulled together in thought. He sighed. "Elizabeth Moore had asked a question, for which I had and have no good answer: If a Newman can accomplish a Fey's service, and precisely as the Fey would do it, is that person Fey or Newman?"

"Or one of Palin's half-breeds, perhaps," she said, chewing her lip. "That would be a question close to her heart, would it not? Given her agreement with her—with Palin?"

"So it might," he agreed, and lifted a finger. "Attend me, now, and draw your *kest—softly*—upward, toward your center."

"My—center?"

He placed a brown hand over his heart, and inclined his head, one eyebrow well up.

Becca took a deep breath, and felt after the molten glow pooled in its resting place at the base of her spine. Gingerly, she pictured it rising along her backbone. For a moment, she felt nothing, then all at once the too-familiar flush of desire, and the slow movement of hot honey along her veins.

The night faded away, the cool breeze stroking her hot skin went unregarded. All of her attention was directed inward, her entire will focused on the slow, contained rise of her fires...

"Good." Meripen Vanglelauf's cool voice seemed to come from very far away. "Now, direct it along your wounded arm; your will is sufficient to this, and to direct the healing..."

She was dimly aware that she was shaking; that her clothing clung to her wetly. Her blood was consumed with *kest*, and it was burning its way into her arm.

She imagined the wasted muscles regaining vigor, the blasted nerves regrown, strength and motion...

Her arm was on fire; she screamed and convulsed, straining against the straps as the power crackled through her, burning, destroying—

"*Healing* power!" a voice shouted, and an echo rang inside her head, "Heal!"

"Rebecca—*your will* is what decides between destruction and healing!"

Her arm—she could not—but no! This time, it would be different! The fires would act upon her as they had been meant to do; the spasms would exercise atrophied muscles, bringing them back to full health. This time, it would work. She would be healed. She would rise from this place whole and beautiful.

She *would*.

"Enough." His voice was like a long draught of cold water. "Withdraw your *kest*."

She gasped and concentrated, picturing the fire retreating, flowing up her arm and down, down, quiescent now, and cool.

"Rest now," Meripen Vanglelauf told her. "You've done well."

She stirred and looked up into his face; she was, she understood after a moment, lying flat on the ground, with her head resting on one of the packs. He nodded to her left and she looked, at first seeing nothing but the ruins of her sleeve, only then understanding that the brown, firm flesh showing between the scorched fabric belonged—to her.

"I did it," she gasped, raising her hand to her face, turning her wrist this way and that...

"Indeed. You did it." For all its coolness, his voice did not sound precisely steady. "Rest now."

"But—" She could scarce move her eyes from the marvel of it. "The Brethren..."

"I will speak to the Little Brother," Meripen Longeye said, firmly. "You will rest, and recover yourself." He leaned forward slightly, as if he would kiss her forehead, and whispered, *"Enayid."*

A wave of weariness washed through Becca; her eyes drifted shut, and she slept.

Chapter Twenty-Four

"WE REST HERE," MERI SAID TO THE CULDOON, "until the Gardener is recovered from her healing."

There was a rustle in the mid-leaves, and the Brethren appeared, a fruit in each hand. It dropped one, and Meri caught it.

"My thanks."

"The tree gives it," the Brethren growled. "One for the Ranger, and one for you, too, Little One."

Meri grinned and bit into the fruit, savoring the sharp taste. "These . . . creatures that surprised you when you were guiding the Gardener . . ."

"Stupid Gardener is too bright!" the Brethren snarled.

"She is certainly very bright," Meri agreed, and had another bite of culdoon to cover his shudder. Bright *and* willful. He was not at all certain that he could have endured the healing she had just imposed upon herself—the shadow-pain he had received through their *kest*-bond had all but set *him* to weeping. He shook the thought away and looked back to the Brethren.

"I wonder where they come from, these creatures, and if you think we might encounter any on our way to the hole in the hedge."

The Brethren was silent for so long Meri thought that he would get no answer at all. Then came a soft growl, and a sharp rustle, as of a tail snapping irritably among leaves.

"There is much of the Gardener in you, Longeye."

Meri froze, the culdoon suddenly tasting of ash. Deliberately, he swallowed, and rested his head against the tree's trunk.

"The Gardener gave a great gift," he said evenly. "I am in her debt."

"There is more," the Brethren observed, "of the Alltree."

Meri laughed slightly. "The Alltree is a story for sprouts, and for the Little People, snug in their holes."

"Silly Brethren," the creature crooned, and growled again, as if in debate with itself.

"The Brethren see many things," it said slowly.

Meri waited.

"We see roaming mists, dead trees, and creatures even stranger than we. There is a hole in the hedge, Meri Longeye, and the wyrd is blowing through."

Altogether, Meri thought, that was a very un-Brethren-like speech. He cleared his throat, but there was a rustle of leaves above him, and when he looked into the culdoon branches, the Brethren was gone.

<hr />

The dream was of dappled leaves, scented breezes, and bright flowers; a child's happy woodland. Becca, curled sweetly on silky grasses, knew it for what it was—a sleep imposed upon her—and felt a small golden ember of anger begin to smolder.

Deliberately, she brought her attention to one single honeycup blossom. Concentrating, she altered it, pulling it tall and giving it a copper beard, until it was a penijanset blossom blowing there. Emboldened, she pushed at the fabric of the dream, feeling it give way under the assault of her will, the bright day darkening, the dappled leaves becoming shadows, and the flowers fading.

Becca opened her eyes, and sat up.

She was alone with the packs, tucked cozily against the ralif. It was, she thought angrily, not enough that she had *again* been thrust into sleep by a Fey, she must be left vulnerable and unguarded, too!

Not unguarded, Gardener, a mellow voice said inside her head. *I had you under leaf.*

"Thank you," she said, putting her hand against the tree's trunk—and gasped, staring at the strong supple hand delicately outlined in gold, pressed against the rough bark.

"I *am* healed," she whispered. She had half feared, but no! On impulse she threw both hands into the air and waved them wildly over her head. She jumped to her feet, spun—staggered as the wet skirt snarled around her ankles. She saved her balance by windmilling her arms, and laughed aloud.

"I *am* healed," she said again, loud enough that her voice came back to her from the surrounding night. She pressed her fingertips to her lips, took a step back—and stumbled as the skirt caught her up again.

"That is *quite* enough of that!" It was the work of

a moment only to unbutton the spiteful garment, and step away, leaving it lying on the forest floor.

"Which is all very well," she told herself, "but you cannot walk naked through the wood."

Her eye lit upon the packs. Perhaps Palin had packed extra clothing. The thing had certainly weighed enough to have held a whole wardrobe.

The laces came apart easily under nimble fingers and she quickly set out on the ground a rope, an axe, a tin of tea, several leaf-wrapped packets of waybread, and a wooden cup. Whereupon, the pack was empty.

"How can so little weigh so much?" Becca asked the wood rhetorically. "Surely, there must be something—"

She reached inside again, thinking that she might have missed something balled up and shoved into a corner, wishing against hope that the something might be a pair of sharkskin leggings and a wide-sleeved shirt.

Her fingers touched something soft.

Her fingers touched something rough.

She pulled them out, first the one, then the other, and stared at them as they spilled over her lap—a shirt in flowing forest green; sharkskin leggings, tight and tough.

Becca bit her lip and took a careful breath. "I would like a belt," she said aloud, though that, she knew, was foolish. "And a good knife."

She reached into the pack and withdrew those items.

"Sturdy boots," a light voice suggested from behind her. "And a vest."

Becca gasped, embarrassment warring with anger. Anger won.

"How dare you put the sleep on me!"

He moved out of the darkness to lean a casual

shoulder against the ralif trunk, green and gold silking about him.

"You needed to recruit your strength," he said mildly.

She glared at him. "I will *not* be put to sleep whenever you or any other Fey wish it! Sian thought nothing of putting me to sleep, without so much as a by-your-leave, and Altimere—!" She bent her head, pressing her fingers to her lips.

"Go away," she whispered. "I want to get dressed."

He said nothing. After she had composed herself somewhat, she raised her head.

She was alone under the ralif, her clothes and goods strewn all around her.

Meripen Vanglelauf was gone.

The ralif whispered when he returned, while she was finishing her braid, using the comb she had last seen in Violet Moore's grandmother's bedroom, and, before that, on her own dressing table at—across the *keleigh*.

"Where do they go," she asked, by way of a peace offering. "When they are returned to the pack?"

"They fade," he answered, his voice also neutral, "unless they are required to remain. After all, they're only shadows."

Becca turned to frown up at him. "Shadows? But..." She held up the comb, showing him its solidness.

"Think it into something else—a necklace, perhaps, or—"

"No!" Becca recoiled—and stared as the comb melted out of her fingers and was gone.

"How—"

"We draw upon the heart of the Vaitura for such

things," Meripen Vanglelauf said, as if he were delivering another lesson, which, Becca supposed, he was.

"We are children of the Vaitura," he continued. "We each have our service, and we are cared for according to our need." He knelt, and pulled his pack to him. "There is no need to make a comb for you, and one for me—" Smiling slightly, he withdrew his hand and showed her the same silver comb—"when the thought of a comb will groom us all."

"But do you make nothing?"

He tipped his head. "Did I not just make a comb?"

Becca sighed. "I—don't know," she confessed. "I—surely New Hope Village makes what it needs—and not out of thin air, sir!"

"I don't doubt that they do," Meripen Vanglelauf said carelessly. "They are Newmen, and have their ways." He rose effortlessly, shrugged into his pack, and settled the bow.

"The Brethren awaits us at the culdoon tree," he said. "It's time we were walking again."

◆◆◆◆◆◆

"The trees here, they aren't real. They won't talk, they don't grow, and they'll steal all your *kest* in a eyeblink if you don't watch close."

"The heroes are like them, all silverlight and gone. Sometimes they'll give you words, and sometimes you can hardly see them, or hear them."

"The trees are like shortcuts—I saw a sprout come in through one. And then it closed, and the sprout screamed . . . and her *kest* just . . . blew away."

"They're working though, the heroes, shades though they be. We can't figure, quite, what it is they're doing. They're chary of us, because we're here, but our trees are still thriving in the Vaitura."

All of the Rangers had their say, four of them sitting in a semicircle around the pile of marked stones, drinking ale that Altimere had produced out of the hanging mists. He listened, and questioned pointedly, arriving at an improbable description of long-dead heroes thrusting *keleigh*-kissed trees out into the Vaitura.

"Why?" he asked.

"What would you?" That was Cai, the restless Ranger who had not yet spoken. "This is a curious place you have built for your amusement, Elder."

Her voice put her behind his left shoulder. He turned, courteously, to face her, and pretended he did not see the serviceable leather truncheon in her hand.

"Forgive me, but I do not believe I understand you."

Cai swept her free hand out, encompassing the *keleigh* entire. "The creatures of this place are mis-shapen and desperate, the heroes long gone mad, the forests dreadful and dangerous. All of us here—the poor, mad heroes; the ghastly trees; the monstrous creatures; ourselves—why, even the weeds!—all long to be elsewhere. You made this place—you and the philosophers. Can you not solve it for us now, as you snatch good ale out of the very mists that bind us? Can you not unmake this place?"

"The *keleigh* may be unmade," he said, which was truth, if a simple one; "but not from within it."

He rose then, carefully, taking a pace back, which allowed him to include all the Rangers in a glance, and left him out of range of a quick blow, were Cai mad, rather than weary and ill with grief.

"Think of the *keleigh*, which one might liken to a wall, or, more properly, to a storm coming from the sea, all in motion in a great swirl, with winds and lightning."

Here he demonstrated the inner and outer spiral, by animating a passing thread of mist.

"What we did in defense of the Vaitura was to create such a form of chaotic materials, that stretches and shrinks time, steals energy; material that confuses and leaches life. When the material was gathered and the forms imposed, we set what we had made into motion around the Vaitura, sealing us away from the devastation that had been visited upon our enemy.

"Such a storm is not an easy thing to build; it required much *kest*, much energy, and a very great deal of will, as well as crafting beyond rapid description."

"And who bade you build this great and terrible work?" Dusau asked.

Altimere inclined his head. "We acted as required, at the behest of the Queen and the Constant."

He paused again, then went on, speaking as much to himself as his listeners.

"We accomplished what was asked of us, losing many of ours, and many more trees, and then, perforce, we rested and moved on, those few of us who were left, for the Vaitura was safe.

"Yet the action of the *keleigh* is not just in the plane of growing things. This we saw as we worked, assuming that the motions and equations were of theoretical interest at best, since they required energies far above those we intended to work; and thus what we overlooked was that we were not dealing with something as simple as the light of the sun on a warm day. We had assumed the trees of the forests we used for power, and the lives of those heroes who stayed with their trees as we worked, we assumed that these were destroyed, consumed by chaos. *Gone*."

He paused, then waved at a misty hilltop crowned with silvered trees.

"Alas, as we now see, *kest* cannot be so simply eliminated. The trees we thought destroyed have not properly subsumed and returned to the Vaitura, but linger on in this unnatural form. Since the *keleigh* continues to spin, and continues, therefore, to suck *kest* from the world, the *keleigh* continues to grow."

"And we can do nothing, any of us?" Cai challenged.

"There is that which can be done, but it cannot, as I said, be done from here. I am the last of the artificers who built the *keleigh*. I know what needs done to stop it."

"You, and no other?" Skaal's question was low and potent.

Altimere nodded, sober and firm.

"This seems likely. No one else in the Vaitura has the keys to the building. No one in the Vaitura can call on the *kest* I have available there."

He looked at them, one by one by one, seeing their service etched on their faces, and their desire to do something in their eyes.

"You say the heroes have devised a way to evict their trees from the *keleigh*?"

"That looks to be what they're about," Dusau agreed.

"Then I think it is decided," Altimere said briskly. "We must go to the heroes at once, and have them put me across. Once I am in the Vaitura, I will—on my *kest* and my honor—bring the *keleigh* down."

Chapter Twenty-Five

"THE FEY MUST MAKE THINGS," BECCA SAID WHEN they stopped next to a spring for waybread and tea, and to refill the water bottles.

She raised her cup, and pointed at the tea tin. "There is a trade market at Selkethe, and another at Lunitch!"

She felt a jolt of distress, and blinked at Meripen Vanglelauf's stern face.

"Assuredly, the Fey make things, and there has always been trade. Do you think that the clothes you wear are woven only from *kest*?"

"But—"

He took the cup from her hand, filled it with spring water, and handed it back to her.

"This is not tea," she said.

"It will be when you add the leaves and heat the water," he answered, filling his own cup. He glanced at the Brethren, apparently asleep on its back across the spring. "Would you like tea, Little Brother?"

"Tea," the Brethren said, mimicking the Ranger's voice. "Would you like *tea*, Little Brother?"

"I'll take that as a no," he said, and reached for the tin. He sprinkled a few dry leaves into the water. Becca felt a brief warmth, saw a flash of green above his cup, and smelled spicy tea.

"We are children of the Vaitura," Meripen Vanglelauf said as Becca dropped a pinch of dried leaves into her cup. "If I wish to make a cup, I will find a piece of fall wood and shape it."

Becca frowned, drawing her *kest* carefully to the cup. The water boiled, and she withdrew the heat immediately, proud of her control.

"Would you," she asked, "use a knife, or *kest* to form it?" She looked up at him. "Your cup out of wood."

He tipped his head, as if it were a fair question to which he must give proper thought. "I would by preference use a knife, for my father taught me the pleasures of carving when I was a sprout. He carved his arrows by hand, as well, with only a veneer of *kest* to finish them, and to ensure that they flew true."

"The Fey I saw at the market at Selkethe was dealing in fabric," she said slowly, recalling the day as one might recall a pleasant dream. "A...friend... told a story of her grandmother, who had a pitcher from a Fey at market. Whatever went into it stayed fresh and never soured."

"Do you ask me how such things are made?" He gave her a faint smile. "Why not work out how it was done, yourself? Who knows when you might need a pitcher?"

Becca gave a small, and perhaps not quite ladylike snort. "For the pitcher... let me see. I would dig the clay and shape it, and fire it with my *kest*."

"I," Meripen Vanglelauf said, "would dig the clay, afterward shaping and firing it with *kest*, for my hands have not learned to make pitchers. Then a veneer of *kest*, to preserve whatever is placed within."

Becca sipped her tea, finding it pleasant. She lifted the cup. "Why drink or eat at all, then? Why not simply ask the plant to give you its essence?"

"Because drinking tea is pleasant," Meripen Vanglelauf said repressively, "and there is no harm in pleasure, so long as it harms none." He sighed. "Do you always have so many questions?"

Becca laughed. "I was a trial to Elyd, too," she said, and swallowed suddenly, lifting her cup to hide the sudden rise of tears.

"Who is Elyd?"

She cleared her throat. "He was . . . he cared for the horses, at Artifex," she said slowly. "I—he was my friend. Elyd Chonlauf. I think that—I think he may have been . . . subjugated. There were things he could not seem to remember, and when he looked at the trees beyond the wall . . ."

"If he was out of Chonist Wood, then it is probable. That land falls within Altimere's honor—or had done, before I slept."

"But—the Queen's Rule . . ."

Meripen Vanglelauf shrugged. "Altimere would not necessarily bide by the Queen's Rule. It is, however, just as possible that your friend had fallen to his will before the Queen's Rule was lain down."

"He—" Becca shivered, remembering. "Elyd. I had asked him if he had been in the war, and he—but he didn't know how long he had been in Altimere's service."

"Do you recall everything of your time under Altimere's protection?"

She blinked tears away. "Apparently, I was often asleep."

"We share another bond, then," he said, with forced lightness.

"I wonder that one who was pressed into sleep imposes it upon another so lightly," Becca said, snappish in her distress. She leaned across his knee to rinse her cup in the flow from the spring.

Fire crackled, green and gold. Becca gasped, her body aflame with desire, as if Altimere's will rode her of old. She moved, slowly, feeling the stroke of power along her flesh. Yearning, thoughtless, desiring, she reached for Meripen Vanglelauf, seeing in his scarred face a pure and infinite beauty; feeling the play of his *kest* against hers, knowing that he, too, desired.

"No."

Horror shuddered through her, and a tangled vision of pain: knives, corrosion, and a woman's hopeless scream.

"No!" Meripen Vanglelauf cried, revulsion in his voice.

Becca twisted, falling back onto her elbow. Pain lanced, scarcely noted in the greater pain of self-loathing. Shivering in mortification, she turned her head away, and wished that the ground would split open and swallow her.

Peace, Gardener. It was, she thought, an elitch tree that spoke. *Ranger, peace.*

Foolish as it no doubt was, she was comforted by the tree's voice, and—even more foolish—she thought that the Ranger was, as well.

Keeping her eyes steadfastly on the ground, she pushed herself to her feet, retrieved her fallen cup, and packed it away. From the corner of her eye, she saw Meripen Vanglelauf rise, shrug on his pack, and pick up his bow.

"We should go on," he said, perhaps to her, or perhaps to the Brethren, who seemed to still be slumbering in the grass.

"So soon?" it asked, leaping to its feet. It shook its horns, whether in frustration or amusement, Becca could not tell.

"Not far now," it said, and moved off at a brisk trot.

Fool, Meri berated himself. *You already carry the burden of her* kest—*must you meld with her, too; make her a part of yourself forever? As Faldana is—or was . . . Your* kest *was guttering; the Gardener filled a vessel all but empty.* He moved on, following Rebecca Beauvelley, who followed the Brethren. That was the worst cut. Faldana had given up her *kest* to him in that terrible land beyond the *keleigh*, for had she sublimated there, she could not have returned to her own beloved trees. No, Faldana's doom was to give all that she was and had been into the keeping of Meripen Vanglelauf.

Who had lost her, finally and forever.

A branch caught on the Gardener's pack and whipped back, very nearly slicing him across the cheek. Which would, he acknowledged, have been only what he deserved. He had been stumbling through the wood like a Sea Wise, scarcely minding what he saw.

Not that what he saw was much more cheering than his thoughts. The trees had been dwindling for some while, in numbers and in vitality. Those they walked among now were scarcely distinguishable from bushes, with a few yellowish leaves clinging to their spidery branches. He raised his head, and fancied he saw the purple sneer of the *keleigh* across the bright midday sky.

There was a rustle among the dead leaves and withered grass. Meri looked down in time to see a long, naked tail disappear into a broken trunk. It was no sort of animal he recalled, and he stretched his legs in order to come to the Newoman's side.

"Rebecca Beauvelley," he said.

She looked up at him; her face was wet with tears. The sorrow that this caused him filled him with horror.

"I wish," she said hoarsely, "that you would call me Becca—or Gardener. To be using my whole name, when we are to come under—under the influence..."

He understood her concern all too well; one kept oneself close, in such country, under the scrutiny of such forces.

"Very well, Gardener," he said. "And I will be Ranger, here. I wished to caution you that this land has been altered by the forces of the *keleigh*. You may see strange animals; certainly, you will see a dying off of the trees and small growth."

"I crossed the *keleigh* once," she reminded him. "I remember the country between Selkethe and the Boundary itself looked as if it had recently burned over. I don't recall it as so...wide...a patch. We are not near yet, are we?"

He pointed to the purpling sky. "Approaching," he said. "Be alert. The care of the trees is thin in such places."

"Why?" she asked, as they passed beside a elitch that had been split and blackened, as if by lightning. "Why was the *keleigh* built?"

Astonishingly, it was the Brethren who answered.

"The Old Fey built it to save themselves from their own folly," it growled. "They cut the ties that bind us to the world."

Becca the Gardener looked up to him, brown eyes wide.

"In sum," Meri told her, "that is precisely why— and how. The complete history is more complex, and encompasses half a dozen wars and games of dominion, such as the Elder High delighted to play."

"The Old Fey," she mused. "Like Altimere."

"That one," snarled the Brethren. "Kin-taker. World-breaker. Changer. Caught now in his own trap."

"Caught?" she asked, as a shadow moved at the edge of Meri's eye.

He spun, saw the horn, the rolling red eye, and danced sideways, narrowly avoiding the thrust at his chest.

"Run!" he yelled, as it stormed past, tangling the horn in a tumble of dry branches, and trumpeting frustration. Perhaps, Meri thought, breathlessly, the care of trees was not...completely dead in this place.

The creature screamed again, and reared. The knotty twigs resisted...one broke.

Meri turned, saw the Gardener standing as if transfixed, her eyes wide and her lips parted, and grabbed her arm, dragging her along with him until her feet began to move under her direction.

"Run!" he shouted again.

Hooves pounding behind them, they ran.

❦ ⋘⋙ ❧

The unicorn burst from the brush and charged, missing the Ranger by less than a finger's width. Becca stared as the mad whiteness thundered by, its horn momentarily entangled in a knot of dead sticks. *A unicorn*, she thought. There seemed to be room for only that one thought in her head. She stared, her feet rooted...

...and uprooted as Meripen Vanglelauf yanked her along with him, very nearly twisting the arm from its socket in doing so. Once she was running, the unicorn out of sight, she could think again—and she could be afraid.

"Run!"

Becca ran. From behind came a scream of pure fury and the pounding of hooves. Ahead, the path twisted and turned between the blasted remains of trees. She ran, pack pounding bruisingly against her back.

Was the sound of hooves from the rear getting louder?

The path ahead twisted—and vanished into a confusion of deadfall and scrub trees.

Becca twisted to the right—the hoofbeats *were* louder; and she could hear angry snorts. Ahead—ahead the path narrowed into a tunnel, branches and shadows woven together overhead.

"In there!" the Ranger panted, but she needed no urging to dive into the tunnel and run on, shoulders bent and pack scraping the indistinct ceiling.

From behind came a shriek of utter fury, reverberating along the walls of their sanctuary. Becca sobbed and clapped her hands over her ears, stumbling on as the walls of the passageway grew thinner and the light faded to black, starless night.

She was not running now; she was groping her way, hands before her, glad of their golden glow, though the light pierced the dark barely a step ahead.

"Can you," she gasped, when she felt she had regained enough breath to power her voice, "see in the dark?"

"Somewhat," came the winded reply. "But not in this."

"If we should come to a precipice..."

"Hold a moment, and I will take the lead."

"So you may have the honor of falling to your death first?" Becca asked. She heard a gasp from behind her, and was sorry that she had not seen how the laugh had altered his face.

"Wait," he said, then. "There's light ahead."

She squinted. "I don't— Yes. I do see it. Let us hope that there isn't a unicorn waiting for us at this side."

"What," Meripen Vanglelauf said as they inched onward, "is a unicorn?"

"A storybook creature, on—the other side of the *keleigh*," she said. "Have you never seen one?"

"This is my first," he admitted. "What is their service?"

"They honor maidens," she said. "Mind! The tunnel turns downward."

The slope became more pronounced, running down toward a toothy oblong of light. Becca ran the last bit, to keep her footing, and burst from the cramped darkness, her pack scraping on thorns and rock, into a wide sandy field pocked with weeds.

Meri crouched at the end of the tunnel, staring out at a bleached and dying land. There was not a single tree within the sight of his shorteye, and the air tasted of sand. In the near distance, a structure loomed, built of stone and murdered trees. He leaned back into the comforting darkness and swallowed against the surge of sickness. Newmen! Had they killed every tree on the land in order to build that terrible dwelling?

Becca the Gardener was on her knees, taking up a handful of sandy soil as if she hoped to learn something from it—perhaps, he thought, she sought after the manner of its doom. For himself, he had seen enough. There was indeed a hole in the hedge.

"Gardener," he called. "Let us return."

She looked up at him, her face vague, as if she had forgotten him entirely.

"Return?" she repeated. "No, we cannot."

"There is nothing more to see," he said, keeping his voice sweet. The emotion quivering along the *kest*-bond was something akin to pain, and, though he did not understand her service, certainly he could imagine that a gardener would only be distressed by this wasted place. "The Brethren told true. We take it now to Sian, and she to the philosophers."

"No," she said again. She dropped the handful of sand and pointed at the monstrous structure of wood and stone. "That is—that is my father's house! I grew up here!" She turned to stare at him where he sheltered yet inside the tunnel.

"What has happened?" she cried. "How could the land have died so quickly? I have only been gone a matter of months—perhaps, perhaps a year. This—" She waved a despairing hand, indicating, Meri thought,

the desolation surrounding her—"what could have
caused this?"

"That is why we must take this to the philosophers,"
he said, reasonably. "Come, Gardener."

"You may go," she told him, rising to her feet
and turning her face away. "Your service is not here.
Mine is."

With no further ado, and without a word of fare-
well, she walked off, away from him and toward the
house that she claimed as her own.

Meri watched her leave, walking balanced and
determined, very much, he thought, like a Ranger
returning to her own wood after a weary wandering.
For himself, he would no sooner set foot on this
tainted, terrible land than—

His muscles twitched and he was jerked up uncer-
emoniously, banging his head on the ceiling of the
tunnel.

"No," he whispered, but the sunshield heeded his
plea not at all. Bound, compelled, he walked after the
slim, determined figure, stiffly for the first few steps,
as horror induced him to fight the compulsion, then
at a light run, as he accepted his doom and raced to
catch her up.

Chapter Twenty-Six

SHE WOULD GO 'ROUND BY THE KITCHEN, BECCA decided, and she would ask Mr. Janies to bring her to Dickon. She would ask him not to mention her visit to Mother, and, most especially, not to Father. Not until she had discovered the nature of the calamity that had overtaken them. A surprise, she would say. A surprise visit. Mr. Janies had been her friend, before. Perhaps he still was.

The front gate was open, the proud spearheads in desperate need of paint. How, she wondered, had all this happened so quickly? Surely, she was looking at the result of years of neglect, not mere months, and yet—

Panic closed her throat; gasping, her heart squeezed with horror, she almost fell, threw out a hand and braced herself against the gate.

From behind her came a sound—as of a choked-off scream. She shook her head, turning, and found Meripen Vanglelauf on his knees in the dust, one shaking hand extended to her.

"That metal..." he whispered hoarsely. "Come away."

"Metal—?" She stared at him. "It's only iron."

"It burns, and the wounds do not heal." He shivered, and turned his face aside, as if the very sight of the gate pained him. "Root and branch, Becca! *Come away!*"

Carefully, she let go of the gate, and looked down at her palm. Satisfied, she walked back to his side, and knelt.

"Look," she said gently, as she would speak to a raving and frightened patient. She dared to touch his shoulder, pained to feel him shiver so. "Meripen. I'm not hurt."

Slowly, he turned his head, stared at her unmarked hand. His face was damp with sweat, horror etched along the austere lines...

Becca raised her hand and touched his face, tracing the pale scar across his left cheek. "You crossed the *keleigh*," she said softly, knowing it as surely as he had told it out. "And someone—one of my people—did this to you."

He closed his eye and bowed his head; she felt a flare of agony, saw for a confused moment limbs bound in iron chain, the corrosive wounds weeping; a stone floor and a woman's naked body convulsing, an iron bar thrust inside of her—

Her stomach rebelled. She swallowed—and again, forcing the sickness away.

"I'm sorry," she whispered, inadequately. "I— Why did they do this?"

"Is there some act that we might have performed that would justify it?" he asked, bitterly. "Faldana died of their treatment, and I, too, had she not given up the last of her *kest* to me." He gave a shuddering sigh. "They wanted to learn how we had made the gold piece the market woman demanded as payment for a loaf of bread."

"A gold piece for a loaf of bread?" Becca asked, but—it would have been obvious that the two were strangers. And what plain woodsman had such hair as Meripen Vanglelauf? A canny woman might make of such strangers what she would, and gold was more certain wealth than a pitcher.

As for making the coin—that she thought, dismally, would have been no trick at all for one trained in Fey philosophy.

"No," she said to Meripen Vanglelauf's bent head. "There is nothing you could have done that would have justified such treatment." *Nothing?* she asked herself. *What of Altimere?*

"I am ashamed for my people," she said, and that was true, whatever had befallen her at different hands.

He shook his head. "The trees were at pains to remind me that the folk at New Hope Village were not the same sort," he said, his voice sounding only weary now. "It is the same with us—as you know to your sorrow."

She cleared her throat. "Why are you here?" she asked him. "I had thought you on your way back to Sian."

He made a soft sound; it might have been a laugh.

"The sunshield binds us, even here."

Becca sat back on her heels, and glanced over her shoulder at the house.

"Meripen, I must go into this—into my—home, and speak to my brother. I—the land here was bountiful when I left it, mere months ago. The Landed—we are stewards of the world! I must know what has happened, and if there is—if there is anything I might do to repair this..."

He nodded, though he did not look up.

"There is iron," Becca persisted, "in the house. Will the sunshield allow you to wait for me here?"

He sighed and raised his head, his face calmer now. "I doubt that it will allow us to become far separated," he said. "And I would rather not be forced." He looked past her, to, she thought, the gate. "All is well, so long as I do not touch it."

She looked at him sharply. "Is that true?"

"As true as it can be," he answered. "I will stand behind you and keep my hands close."

"I'm sorry," she said. "I—"

"It is your service," he interrupted, rising to his feet with a fraction of his usual grace. He held his hand down to her, and after a moment she took it and allowed him to raise her to her feet.

The kitchen garden at least was well planted, though the plants were not as lush as she recalled. Perhaps, she thought, her time in the Vaitura had altered her sense of what a proper garden ought to look like.

Or perhaps, she thought, it had not.

She paused with her hand on the latch of the kitchen door. "This is iron," she said softly. "The room we are coming into—"

"I will keep my hands close," he assured her, "and my wits about me." A twisted smile accompanied that last.

Becca nodded. "I will—it may be that my brother will be angry, at first. If he says anything that—please remember that he is largely ignorant of the Vaitura, and has . . . much cause . . . to be displeased with me."

Meripen inclined his head. "I will be meekness itself," he assured her.

The latch worked and the door came open, quietly. A glance at the hinges showed them in better repair than the front gate, but there! Cook would never have tolerated anything slovenly about her kitchen.

The kitchen . . . that was dark, the fire cold, without so much as a string of onions hanging from the rafters. Cook's worktable was littered with dirty dishes—the house crest, Becca saw, that was brought out only on grand occasions.

Becca stood by the table, feeling ill and not a little puzzled.

"Mrs. Janies?" she called softly. "Cook?"

No one answered her.

Surely, she thought, they would not have just *gone out* with the kitchen in such a state? She tried to imagine the scope of the disaster that would permit dirty dishes to remain on Cook's worktable for more minutes than five—and failed utterly.

"Well," she said, for Meripen's benefit. "I suppose we had best look in the library, then."

She was uncertain now, and growing more deeply distressed with every dead and dusty room they entered. Meri followed her closely, trying to ignore the taint of *iron* in the air, and to keep his wits about him, as he had promised.

Certainly, it was a melancholy enough place that they wandered, but free—thus far—of active dangers.

He hoped, for the ease of Becca's heart, that she found her kinsman soon, but that event was becoming to seem less likely with each door she threw open.

"The ladies' parlor." Her murmur was surely for herself. He followed, mindful to step lightly on the scarred wooden floor, and was only two steps behind her shoulder when she turned the knob gaily painted with honeycups and pulled the door wide.

Unlike the other rooms they had opened, this one was bright with sunlight, and overfull with furniture, books, and a bewildering array of objects. A man sat behind a table piled high with textile, his aura an unfortunate glare of orange and grey—the whole flashing into crimson as he leapt to his feet.

"Thieves! Enter at your peril!"

Meri's hand dropped to the hilt of his knife. Becca stood where she was, alert, but to his eye unalarmed, so he did not draw, but waited, his wits very much about him.

"I am Miss Rebecca Beauvelley, the Earl of Barimuir's eldest daughter," she said, with a haughtiness very nearly approaching that of a High Fey. "Pray let my brother Richard know that I am here and desire to speak with him."

"Richard." The Newman standing behind the table at the center of the cluttered room tipped his head to one side. "That would be Richard Beauvelley?"

"It would," Becca said coldly.

The Newman laughed. "You gypsies have no end of gall! *I* am Richard Beauvelley, madam! What d'you make of that?"

"Only that you are obviously in your cups, sir, and therefore of no use to me. Pray call for someone who is less disadvantaged. I would like to speak to my brother today."

Another laugh, some grey edging the scarlet. Meri shifted, his fingers tightening on the comforting hilt of his knife. In his judgment, this Newman traced his kin-lines more closely to Michael and his lord than Elizabeth Moore or Jack Wood.

"Certainly, Your Highness," the Newman sneered. He brought his hand up from behind the table, and pointed a cylindrical object at Becca. "Go, now, or I *will* kill you."

Becca lifted her chin, her aura showing significant flares of anger amid the swirls of confusion.

"Tell me what has happened here," she said. "I have been away for some ... little ... time. Some calamity has befallen the land and I would learn what it is. Are the whole of the Midlands afflicted?"

"You must have gone away from the world," the Newman commented, and if his hand did not waver, yet he made no more threatening movements.

"I have been far enough away that news of the Midlands did not reach me," Becca repeated.

"The Governors have said the Black Wind blew across the entire world—the Corlands were least afflicted, there being so little there in the first wise. So ..." He made an indistinct motion with the object he held. "... should I happen to allow you and your buck to leave here alive, Your Highness, you'd best be from the Corlands at the next house you attempt."

"I will remember, thank you," Becca said, her voice soft and soothing, as if, Meri thought, she spoke to one bent under a burden of pain or grief. "In the meantime—what is the Black Wind?"

"It blew across the the world, and sucked the virtue out of the land," the Newman said, singsong, like a student saying back a particularly tedious lesson. "The soil dried, the trees fell, the crops withered in the fields. My grandfather, for whom, as Your Highness doubtless recalls, I am named, saw half his fields go to sand before he died. My father saw the last trees fall in the park before he hanged himself in the wild garden." He laughed then, and the hackles rose on the back of Meri's neck.

"*Wild garden*," the Newman repeated, sounding eerily like the Brethren. "He hanged himself from the elitch, the last living tree on our land." He inclined his head. "Is there anything else your humble servant may tell you?"

"What has caused this affliction?"

"Why, no one knows! It might be a bobble in the rotation of the planet, or a condition at the solar center. Might as well say it was magic, Your Highness. Someone pulled the cork from the bottom of the world and all the life ran out." He shrugged, and fingered the thing in his hand worrisomely. "The Governors sent to New London—that was before Grandfather died. New London does not answer."

He paused, an arrested look in his pale, mad eyes. "Grandfather *had* a sister named Rebecca. She eloped with a Fey. That was the start of all our troubles."

He took a step, coming 'round the table, the object held before him with new purpose. "*Did* you come from out of the world, Your Highness?" he said softly. "Now, are you the bastard daughter of my great-aunt and her Fey? Not the woman herself, I think, for she was by family report a cripple and hideous to see."

The Newman took another step, surprisingly firm, and Meri saw his fingers tighten on the object, while Becca stood as if rooted, her aura such a blare of distress that he thought it likely she did not recognize her danger.

Meri swept the knife from his belt, leapt forward, snatched Becca's arm, and pulled her back. The knife he loosed as a distraction; it struck the Newman's shoulder hilt-first. His arm jerked, there was a sound like thunder, punishing the ears, but Meri was already running, and Becca, too, back the way they had come, with the mad Newman bumbling after.

"Thief, whore, bastard! *Fey!*"

They reached the kitchen with its multitude of horrors, the stink of iron so thick he could scarcely breathe, and there was the latch, smoldering balefully. He took a breath to brace himself for the agony, put out his hand—and hers darted beneath, slapping the latch down, and they were out, into free air tasting of sand and death.

Another thunderclap, and more shouted insults, fading. They sped past the iron gate so quickly Meri barely felt its burn inside his long-healed wounds.

Down the field they ran, and there—there was the tunnel, the route back to the Vaitura, to his trees and to—

Becca.

Two steps from the mouth of the tunnel, Meri spun and looked about him.

Becca the Gardener stood by the wilting and *kest*-less plants, her own *kest* rising in a spiral of golden motes, rising, until she seemed a woman on fire. Rising, pouring from her fingertips...

. . . and into the needy ground.

She was full of power, but the soil had been denied for too long. Her *kest* drained away like a spring shower, running uselessly into the sand.

Her aura faded from sun-gold to dust-tan. She wavered and went to her knees, swaying, even as he stripped her pack down and off, and caught her up in his arms.

"No," she whispered, as he raced for the tunnel, past his own abandoned pack. "I can heal it . . ."

"You cannot heal it," he answered, ducking into the darkness. "That is for the Fey to do."

Chapter Twenty-Seven

SHE WEIGHED LESS THAN HIS PACK HAD, HER *KEST* guttering but not yet gone. Meri threw himself along the dark tunnel, his own aura a green-and-gold smear, barely discernible through his tears.

He should have known . . . he should have watched, he should have understood that she would *try*. He knew she had less wit than a sprout, and a hero's sense of her own service.

There was light ahead of him, and he gasped in relief, though he knew that what he would come out into would be the blasted landscape of the badlands. Still, it would be the Vaitura. There would be some virtue in the land at least, and he might breathe a mite of *kest* into her until they could come under the care of trees.

Briefly, he considered stopping here, inside the tunnel, for the *kesting*, but rejected the notion. He did not know the virtues that made up this strange construct, and he could not take the chance that they would be inimical to *kest*.

The light ahead grew brighter, tinged with green, as if filtered through leaves. For a moment, he allowed himself a fantasy, that they would emerge not in the badlands, but under the branches of his own beloved trees. A sprout's imagining, but warming for a moment, as he ran onward, the Gardener dying in his arms.

She moaned, her *kest* blowing and thin; and there—there was the end of the tunnel—he leapt, hit the ground on his shoulder, and rolled, Becca's limp body cradled to his chest, and the benediction of trees overhead. He put his hand on her breast—she was cold; the last brave flame extinguished—and his *kest* rose in blare of power, pouring forth, until she was limned in green fires, and still he gave more, until the two of them blazed like fallen stars against the grass, and a stern voice directed—

Enough!

His *kest* fell, and he did, strengthless, to the ground beside her, staring up into a ralif, and feeling the very air caress him.

Welcome, Meripen Vanglelauf, the ralif told him. *You have been too long away.*

Meri took a breath, and smiled. However it had happened, they had arrived in Vanglewood. He would question and puzzle later, he thought, his eyes drifting shut. For now, he and Becca were safe.

They were home.

There were voices murmuring just beyond her ability to hear. It seemed rather a number; the overall tone one of curiosity, and yet—*should* there be voices?

Becca stirred, groping after memories. Had the lunatic with the pistol apprehended her, after all? She remembered...she remembered pouring *kest* into the needy land, much as another gardener might pour water on a dry kitchen patch.

She remembered feeling weak, and a numbness in her extremities. She remembered wondering if she had been struck by a bullet.

She remembered hoping that Meripen Vanglelauf had escaped. She had seen him...seen him well on his way. Surely someone so fleet would have—

Welcome, child. You have wandered long.

The murmurs fell away into silence, respectful of this new speaker, her voice warm and mature. A grandmother, Becca thought, and sighed, soothed and comforted.

I have wandered far, a new voice, as brilliant and bracing as a draught of spring water, made answer. *Now that I am home again, I wish nothing more than to remain.*

And yet you know, as we do, that this is not possible, the grandmother said sadly. There was a small pause. *Good sun to you, Gardener. Be at peace beneath within this wood.*

Becca stirred, and opened her eyes to a leafy canopy so lush, the sunlight that filtered through the leaves was tinged with green. It was, she thought drowsily, like resting underwater.

"Where are we?" she asked.

"Vanglewood," Meripen's light, cool voice answered her.

She turned her head, unsurprised—pleased!—to find him seated cross-legged on the grass by her right hand. He appeared unscathed; more, he appeared rested, and...younger than he had been.

"Vanglewood," she repeated. "Meripen Vanglelauf. This is your home, then?"

"My own wood, yes." He smiled, a tender expression such as she had never before seen from him.

"Thank you," she said slowly, "for bringing me here, but, tell me—what happened? I remember him—Dickon's grandson? how could he be? Dickon is only thirty!—chasing us, and I remember the land... I was going to heal the land..."

"The cure for what ails that land is not so simple as pouring the *kest* of one woman upon it," he told her soberly. "All the Wood Wise of the Vaitura could cross over and give up their *kest* to the land, and still it would not be healed."

"But—" Becca stared at him. "What is wrong with it?"

"The *keleigh*," he said, with a momentary return to grimness. "Just as it is the *keleigh* that ails the Vaitura. This is something for the Queen and her Constant, and nothing that can be parsed by a Ranger and a Gardener, no matter how well traveled."

He leaned forward then, and took her hand in his. Becca felt her stomach tighten in equal parts anticipation and fear, while her *kest*—but, what was this? The power coiled in waiting was green more than gold; cool and perhaps a little cautious. She looked up into Meripen's face. He sighed.

"You had given all but the last flickers of your *kest* to that—to the land beyond the hedge," he said gently, as if he wished to soften a blow.

"So you did—what I had done for you." She

frowned. "I understand, and I—I thank you for your care of me. It could not have been an easy thing for you."

He laughed slightly, and looked down at their joined hands before meeting her eyes again.

"Truth told, I scarcely thought, save that it must be done." One more glance at their hands before he withdrew his and rose. "Now that I am home at last, I must pay my respects, and give my excuses. Will you come with me?"

Becca rose, nearly as lightly as he had done, and paused. She could hear the trees murmuring to each other, and feel the land as a living thing beneath her feet. The breeze was laden with a thousand scents, and was as heady to the senses as brandy.

"Is it always like this," she asked, closing her eyes and drinking down the air. "For you?"

There was a small silence, while she stretched high on her toes and raised her arms, allowing the breeze to sway her poor branches.

"I had almost forgotten," Meripen Vanglelauf said, very softly, indeed.

She dropped down from her toes, and opened her eyes to look at him.

"Is it—rich—for you now?" she asked, carefully. "Again."

He smiled slightly. "That it is," he answered and raised his hand to point out their direction.

"Where do we go?" Becca asked, moving swift and light at his side.

"To the heart of Vanglewood."

It was a blessed thing to walk again among his own trees, and to hear their beloved voices once more. He ought never to have ventured out from this safe canopy, he thought, his heart full near to bursting, and his face turned up toward the leaf-laced sky, basking in their welcomes.

Alas, he had been sent forth from the trees, to his mother at Sea Hold, and from there to Xandurana, for the polish befitting a prince. Thence back again to Sea Hold, and the learning of shiplore and the ways of the wave, and to pay the three voyages he had sworn to the sea. And at the end of the third voyage, he made his choice and returned at last to Vanglewood—only to find that his life beyond its trees had marked him. He was not, if ever he had been, a simple Wood Wise, content inside the forest of his birth; bewildered and a little foolish beyond them. No, Meripen Longeye must wander, so he took up service as a Ranger, returning to his home trees infrequently. There was no taint upon a Ranger's service, after all, and much honor to gain. But, in the end, Meripen Vanglelauf had wandered too far.

He glanced at Becca the Gardener, fair dancing with joy beside him as she took in the benediction of Vanglewood's affection, and scarcely knew whether to laugh or weep.

He had forgotten. He had been so depleted and ill that he had refused the aid of those who regarded him, and *he had forgotten* what it was like, to fully walk among one's own dear trees.

The air was beginning to brighten, and Meri felt his steps quicken. Perhaps he danced, too, in counterpoint to Becca, and if he did, who might blame him, returned from his journeys, cured of his ills, home, *home*, and almost—

The trees brightened ahead of them. Becca hesitated and extended a tentative hand, precisely as he had done, the first time his father had brought him here.

And, as his father had done for him, he took that hesitant hand in his own, and led her into that sacred place.

From the joy and brightness of the sentinel trees, they stepped into a pure lucent beauty, sunlight like liquid gold gilding leaves as bright as emeralds. Peace wafted on the sweet breeze, and before them stood an elder tree gently wrapped in lichen, its red branches so broad that New Hope Village could easily have sheltered beneath them. Birds flew between the branches, and a streamlet wound, silent and silver, around its roots.

Vanglewood, I am home, he sent, feeling Becca's hand warm and relaxed in his. *I have one more duty to perform in the name of the Vaitura. When that is done, I wish to return and never more to roam.* He paused, feeling a pang, then took a breath of lucent air and bowed his head. *I ask it, Vanglewood.*

There was a pause, then a rustle of the perfect leaves, sounding almost as a sigh.

Long have you served the trees, Meripen called Longeye. *The trees would reward you as you have asked.*

Meri shivered...

However, Vanglewood continued, the word like a knife to his heart. *You have been chosen for another, and greater, service. Vanglewood is no longer yours.*

"What?" In his shock, he cried aloud, his voice

ruffling the flow of the stream. *Vanglewood, what cruelty is this?*

The breeze caressed him, and Becca's fingers squeezed his. He grew calm, and yet—

The mark of the Alltree is upon you, son-Meripen, and on the Gardener as well. Vanglewood is no longer yours.

Despite the rich air, he could not breathe. Vanglewood—his trees were denying him, but—

Vanglewood, the Alltree is—

The mark of the Alltree, Vanglewood interrupted, its thought sharp, *is upon both of you. Vanglewood relinquishes its claim.* There was another pause, then, infinitely gentle. *Vanglewood remembers, son-Meripen. You are not lost, while these trees endure. Go, now.*

Altimere felt the cold glow well before the Rangers began to show signs of disquiet; eventually it was Skaal who came to him requesting that he walk "very quietly, very quietly on all fronts," if he could.

He damped his questing *kest*, felt it vibrate in resonance to power. His whole body informed him that nearby was a well of power the like of which he had not seen since he had stored the energy of Rebecca's magnificent triumph in Xandurana.

The Rangers followed their own advice, stepping with care as they climbed a grey hill toward a grey sky. They approached the hillcrest cautiously, Skaal whispering.

"They are raising power. They are returning the forests that gave up their *kest* to build the *keleigh*, returning them to the Vaitura."

All thought stopped; his breathing caught, his hands went still.

Only long experience kept his horror out of his face and stance. The thought that he could not form before. Now—*now* he remembered.

This was a paradoxical situation; the trees ought to be gone entire, their memory as nothing, the heroes who had given them over dust and less than dust.

He tried to do the equations in his head and failed.

"Come, Altimere. Soon enough they'll know we watch. Best to see what you will before they amend seeing!"

Seeing was unsettling: Skaal whispering the names of forests and groves, pointing to this section or that section of the grand plain below was the more unsettling.

The equations jumbled and came together twice, three times:

If these trees were returned, the very fabric of the world would collapse. *Kest*, which could be neither created nor destroyed, would become chaos. Thought and will would die.

He looked below and saw the folly of the *keleigh*, and knew it to be his own.

Chapter Twenty-Eight

THEY WALKED AMONG SILENT TREES IN SILENCE. THE air was no less rich, though it failed, in the face of the tragedy that had befallen Meripen, to intoxicate. Becca walked quietly, and tried to think what she might say to soften the blow he had received. To lose at one strike his home, his family, and the hope of his future? Truly, there was nothing to stanch such a wound.

The heart-tree though . . . she frowned. The heart-tree had said that he had the mark of a greater service upon him. Perhaps he was looking to his hurt, first, forgetting the second portion of the tree's message.

"What," she asked tentatively, "is the Alltree?"

That gained her a stinging glance from a hard green eye. They walked on, with birds singing and scolding, and flutterwisps dancing along a bank of honeycups. Becca had resigned herself to being a silent tourist among these beauties, when Meripen Vanglelauf sighed.

"The Alltree," he said slowly, "is a myth. A story to lull sprouts to sleep."

Becca thought about that as they passed under a culdoon. Meripen raised his hands, and she heard his thought, *May two eat from your bounty?*

Eat well, the tree answered, as two fruit dropped into the waiting hands. *Eat joyfully*.

Thank you, Meripen sent, and Becca echoed him, not wishing to be rude.

Thank you, culdoon.

You are welcome, both. Be at peace in this wood.

Meripen swayed a very slight bow, handed a fruit to Becca, and continued onward.

Holding the culdoon between her two hands, Becca walked with him, thinking still.

"How could you—and I!—bear the mark of a—a myth?" she asked, which was possibly an impertinence. "Surely the heart of Vanglewood is wise beyond even—"

"Perhaps," Meripen interrupted, apparently following his own line of thought. "Perhaps Vanglewood mistook the—essence—of the world beyond the *keleigh*—which must seem strange and disturbing—"

"For the Alltree?" Becca shook her head. "*Must* it be a myth?"

"If it is not, then it has been holding itself aloof for—why, since before the *keleigh* was made! It—" He paused, the culdoon halfway to his mouth, and stared at her.

"The Brethren," he said.

"The *Brethren*?" Becca shook her head. She'd been told that the race had a reputation for mischief, but—"Surely even a Brethren would not go so far for mischief as to—"

"No." He held up his hand. "The Brethren said to me—you were resting from your healing. He said that there was much of the Gardener in me—meaning your gift of *kest*—and more, of the Alltree. I thought it a bit of foolery, but—" He extended his hand to her.

"Tell me," he said, "please, precisely what you did, when you renewed me."

Becca stared at him, feeling her face warm to the roots of her hair.

"I—your lips were blue, and, and you had stopped breathing," she stammered. "And I recalled that Nancy had—when I had renewed—" She cleared her throat and looked away. "I kissed you. That and the twig from the elitch—"

"The twig from the elitch," Meripen said softly. "Which elitch?"

"Why..." She raised her fingers to her lips. "The Hope Tree. But—"

He closed his eye. "What became of the twig, after?"

"I don't know. I fell into a swoon, then the Brethren woke me, and you came awake—"

"Yes. And I don't recall any twig particularly, but—"

"It said—it said, 'My gift, given freely, from the top of my crown to the deepest roots,'" Becca murmured.

Meripen sighed, opened his eye, and gave her a wan smile.

"Well, and the Brethren had said that Longeye doesn't know everything," he said wryly. "The Hope Tree, eh? That shelters Newmen beneath its branches, and accepted Lucy Moore's oath—and Elizabeth's. Does it make you wonder, Becca Gardener, if the Newmen came there by chance?"

"Since I don't know where they came from..." she said, turning with him and continuing to walk.

"They came from beyond the *keleigh*, which they

call the hellroad. The place they left, so Palin tells me, was called Hope Village. Their lord was at war with another of his station. Lucy Moore convinced the folk that it was better odds in the *keleigh* than staves against bows, and led them here, where they founded New Hope Village, and Lucy gave her oath to the trees."

Becca bit into the culdoon, considering.

"You think," she said eventually, "that the Hope— your pardon!—the Alltree, guided Lucy to itself. But—why?"

"It is said that the roots of the Alltree bind the world together," Meripen said. Kneeling, he pushed the culdoon pit into the soil and covered it with leaf mold.

"Does the *keleigh*," Becca wondered, "cut the world in half?"

"I believe my philosophy tutor would have it that the *keleigh* separated the Vaitura by one handspan—not merely a wall, but a discontinuity of time and effect."

Becca blinked. "Forgive me," she said. "I will need to think on that."

"By all means. On the rare occasions that I revisit the issue, it continues to baffle me." Meripen shrugged. "I am no philosopher, nor an artificer." He glanced up at the sky beyond the leaves.

"There is someone I should speak with," he said suddenly, "ere we," his voice caught and he cleared his throat, his head bent so that he seemed to study something of note on the forest floor. "...ere we— quit—this wood."

Becca waited.

After a moment, Meripen nodded, as if coming to an agreement with himself, and set off a brisk trot.

Becca bent and pushed the culdoon pit into the soil and covered it. That done, she dusted off her hands, rose, and ran after.

"Ranger." The Wood Wise slipped out of her tree and bowed, which was bold indeed for Wood Wise, saving that Meri marked how her hands trembled and how she stood rooted scarce a step beyond the trunk of her tree. "What is required?"

After one quick look at his face, she kept hers averted, and did not acknowledge Becca at all. Meri thought of insisting that she honor the Gardener, then decided such insistence would discommode both the Wood Wise and Becca herself, who stood to one side, wide-eyed in amaze.

"I have discovered in my wanderings a new and dangerous tree," he told the Wood Wise. "Though they have the seeming of ralif, elitch, or other familiar tree, these strangers are silver, and they have no voice. One that I saw seemed to become a portal for a mist-wraith, which drank of my *kest*."

The Wood Wise swallowed and nodded at the ground. "We have knowledge of these trees, Ranger," she whispered. "We have lost—we have lost Nim, and also Ralix, who was only a sprout. We shun them, but it grows difficult, for more and more of them come to be amongst the true trees, and we—we have our service, Ranger."

"Have you sent—" Meri asked, around a dread so great it seemed to freeze his very *kest*—"to the heartwood?"

Another nod. "I went myself, Ranger. Vanglewood..."

She raised her face and Meri could see tears and a lurking horror in her eyes. "Vanglewood had no knowledge of these trees, Ranger, and no advice to give us. Ulo—very nearly we lost her, as well, for she took an axe to the tree that swallowed Ralix."

"Did she? What happened?"

"The axe bounced on the first strike, and the second. On the third, Ranger, it broke, and—and the tree consumed the *kest* so released. Ulo said, later, that it seemed as if a shadow had come between her and Vanglewood, and she felt a . . . a desire to offer service to this tree. She remembered, though, what it had done to Ralix, and she ran away, into the deep wood. I—the trees say she is with a ralif, sleeping."

"It is with the trees," Meri said, with a firmness he did not at all feel. "That is well. Now, can you tell me where these silver trees are?"

"Where?" Her brow furrowed and he felt a pang for forcing so difficult a question upon her. "I—they are along all of our paths, Ranger," she said slowly; "but more plentiful, in the West."

"In the West," he repeated, numb now with dread.

"Yes, Ranger," the Wood Wise said humbly.

Sea Hold lay to the west.

"Thank you," he said and extended a hand to touch her shoulder, wincing for her trembling.

"Will you not aid us, Ranger?" That was bold, too, despite her fears. Her wet face showed an uncertain hope. He was, after all, a Ranger; it was his service, to aid them, and, thus, to aid the trees.

But Vanglewood had failed her.

"I go now," he said gently, "to find those who will aid us all. Be wary; keep the sprouts close; ask the trees to root you, if it seems you are being drawn too close into danger." It was nothing she would not do without his saying out the list, but it was all that he had for her, now.

"I go to the Engenium at Sea Hold, to beg her help," he finished, watching the hope die out of her face. "This is nothing that Wood Wise can mend; nor even a Ranger."

"I understand," she said, staring down once more. "Travel quickly, then, Ranger," she whispered, and added, so soft it was barely louder than a thought, "Gardener."

She took a single step backward, and vanished from sight, though he could feel her curled with her tree, taking sore-needed comfort.

❧

He marked out the pattern, and confirmed with his Rangers that it was always the same.

"They get larger," Cai told him. "It seems, the more trees they evict, the more they *can* evict, if you understand."

Cold with horror, Altimere understood very well.

The power that they raised—potent, cold and silver— that was something else again. Focused chaos, he thought, and suitable, perhaps, for moving the undead. For himself, however, he wished living *kest* in the pattern, for he had no interest in arriving in the Vaitura as a wraith.

Happily, there were five sources of *kest* standing with him, and the pattern was very simple, indeed.

Chapter Twenty-Nine

"HOW MUCH FURTHER?" BECCA ASKED. THEY WERE resting in the center of a frizenbush following a dinner of morel, vinut, and bonberry. Meri was stretched out on his side, head pillowed on his arm, and it was only the fact that he looked every bit as weary and as grimy as she felt that allowed Becca to preserve any pride at all.

"If we sleep until moonrise, then run the night, we will raise Sea Hold at dawn," he said, drowsily.

Becca sighed. They had already run two nights— between the trees, not through them, which would, so Meri had told her, have been the quicker route.

"We cannot risk it," he'd said, as they sped through groves littered with ghost trees. "What if you or I leapt from a true tree into one of—those? We would be lost, like that poor sprout."

The lost sprout weighed on him, she knew, and the poor mad Wood Wise who had tried to chop the offending phantom down. What weighed on him more, as she had learned these last few days of travel and infrequent rest, was the violation of Vanglewood.

"You could not have stopped them, if you had been there," she'd said. "Indeed, you might have been among the first to be lost, when the Wood Wise called you to help them."

He had laughed then, somewhat. "I have—just a little!—more sense than that," he'd told her, and rose from that resting place, reaching down to help her rise. That time, they'd run on well into the night, surprising the dawn into a shout as they raced across a high windswept ridge.

Becca stretched out on her side, tucked her head into the crook of her arm, and considered his face, just a handspan from her own.

"Meri?"

"More questions?" Which had become a joke between them.

"Only one," she answered, soberly. "What will Sian do?"

For a moment, it seemed as if he had forgotten to breathe. Then, he sighed, and opened his eye to consider her.

"I don't know," he said. "It—if I am to speak of hope, then I hope that, somewhere at Sea Hold or at Xandurana there is a philosopher who has been studying these phenomena and will have crafted an answer. Sian is the Engenium of Sea Hold; her power is not that of Diathen, speaking as she so rarely may with the support of her Constant, the trees and the Vaitura, but—Sian's power, though lesser, is unfettered."

He fell silent.

"That is your hope." Becca said after a moment,

hearing her own voice fuzzy with sleep. "What is your expectation?"

"Is that two questions where one was promised? We only have till moonrise to rest."

"But—"

"Peace. My *expectation*, though perhaps *fear* is the better word, here—is that there is no such brilliant and foresighted philosopher among Sian's court, and so they will send those they have, who are not inconsiderable, for Sian does not tolerate fools. And they will work and strive and expend *kest* in great quantity, only to find that none of what they have wrought has been fruitful."

"And then what will happen?" Becca asked, fear making her shiver though the air was warm and the frizenbush protected them from the breeze.

Meri shook his head. "I don't know," he said. "But I fear for the Vaitura, and I very much fear for the world." He gave her a tired smile. "Sleep now, Questioner, or shall I say the word?"

"We share *kest*," she said pertly. "Will you not put yourself to sleep, as well?"

"It is," he told her, "an experiment I am more than willing to undertake."

"No," she answered, settling her cheek against her arm. "Dream well, Meri."

She was asleep before he gave answer, if, indeed, he had stayed awake so long.

"There! Did I not say she would come here!" Aflen's voice echoed triumphantly. He twisted his fingers in her hair and pulled her head back. Abused neck muscles screamed, and he smiled hatefully down into her face.

"See how *frightened* she is," he crooned.

He struck her across the face and threw her down on the cold stone floor. Ribbon went 'round her right wrist, shocking in its softness; and again, around her left. There was a moment—a lull—and then agony as both arms were yanked above her head, pulled hard and high. Her legs were pulled apart until she thought her hips might break, each ankle tied with another ribbon.

"Now..." he said, and held it up to show her. In form, it was not unlike a male member, but it glowed with inimical powers. He smiled, then thrust it into her, laughing while she screamed and screamed...

...and screamed herself awake, into a present where strong arms confined her, trapping her— She *pushed*, felt a flare of heat, a splash of rain—

"Becca, Becca, peace," the light voice panted in her ear, while in her head, his thought, so strong and certain—*Becca, a dream. Two dreams, yours and mine. Wake, wake, be calm...*

Sobbing, she collapsed against him, her face pressed into his shoulder, feeling the presence and the interest of trees, relaxing again as their murmured comfort soothed her.

"Why?" she gasped. "Why do we want to repair the world's ills? We are terrible—Fey and Newmen alike! Look, look at what we've both endured..." Her voice choked out, she lay there, strengthless, as a warmth began to build, and inside her head a picture formed, unhurriedly, like the unfolding of a flower.

An elitch leaf, as bright and as perfect as anything she had ever seen; looking at it made her feel good and whole, and then—a voice spoke, inside her thoughts, but different, so deep and wise, that she felt love rise with her infant *kest*, and she closed her eyes, the better to hear it said again.

Welcome, child. Vanglewood accepts you.

She sighed against his shoulder, feeling *kest* yet warming her blood.

"Is it all and only for the trees, that we go on, then?" she murmured.

Callused fingers slipped under her chin and raised her head until she was looking up into his face, so stern and lovely. His aura showed as lucent and pure as the light at the heartwood. She raised her hand and touched his cheek.

"No," he whispered, his voice unsteady. "Not only for the trees..."

Becca the Gardener... His arms trembled, and his inner voice failed.

She stirred, feeling the heat and the familiar, yet new, drawing of desire. *I should,* she thought, *end this.*

But she did not want to end it.

His face, his aura, his *kest*. She wanted to remember him, to wrap herself in the flowing green cloak of his aura, to hold him as part of her, to have him hold her as part of himself.

Show me, she said, speaking him mind-to-mind. *Meri, can you abide it?*

His laughter shook them both. *Oh, yes. I can abide it. But you...*

Us, she sent, and slid her fingers behind his head, pulling his lips down to hers.

His skin was smooth, a delight to her fingertips. She traced the white lines of scars, tenderly, thinking of easewerth and mint. Meri shivered under her touch and laughed, breathless, his hand molding her breast.

"Why not simply ask me to give you my virtue?" he asked, and gasped as her fingers brushed his hip.

Becca laughed then, soft. "But there is no harm in pleasure," she said, "save it harms none." She bent and kissed his chest, nuzzling his nipple, shivering as his *kest* washed through hers, enriching her... "Does that give pleasure, Meri?"

"Pleasure..." He ran his hands into her hair and lifted her face, looking into each of her eyes in turn. "More than pleasure," he whispered. "Becca..." His hands were trembling, the interplay of their auras striking desire.

It was she who trembled now, and she bent her head to kiss him, her blood aflame, sheets of gold-laced green enveloping them, piercing each.

"Root and branch, Becca..."

She molded her body to his, his hands stroking her as the fires heated; desire burned, and a need, an imperative, raised her up. Shivering, on fire, every fiber of body and soul yearning for completion, she straddled him. His hands came about her waist; his hips rose to meet her.

Light thundered, the skies poured glory; they rose, branches grazing the sky, roots delving deep, thoughts and memories, loves and hates, knowledge and desires, rising like sap, nourishing them, forging them in a conflagration of *kest*, melding them.

Changing them.

The pattern was complete, saving the positioning of the last branch. Altimere walked from Ranger to Ranger, drawing their *kest*, and allowing it to fall. Between them, they had little enough, though it would suffice, if he was not wasteful. He considered Xandurana as his proper destination, and trusted that his needful tools would come to his hand when called from within the Vaitura.

He checked his watch, delighted to see that it still functioned; and paused for a moment, head bent, reviewing his plan.

There were risks associated with an immediate return to Xandurana, certainly. Artifex was the seat of his power, and the prospect of reentering the Vaitura there, and recruiting himself somewhat before attempting Diathen, contained more than a grain of wisdom. It was, indeed, what anyone would expect him to do.

"It is decided, then," he murmured, and smiled down at the pretty painted face. "One does not wish to become . . . predictable."

Tucking the watch away, he picked up the final piece, transferred his smile to the bound, doomed Rangers, and walked toward the gap in the pattern.

❦⟨⟨⟨⟩⟩⟩❦

Meri opened his eye to a night soaked in emerald and azure, at once achingly familiar and wonderfully new. Becca woke with him, and sighed, her head moving against his shoulder.

We are forever altered, she sent, her thought as bracing as a long sup from a deep spring.

We are melded, he replied, reaching to stroke her warm hair. *We have grown.*

He felt her laughter ripple on two levels and smiled.

And I a Gardener. But, Meri, will we always be thus close? Those others with which I shared kest . . .

He recalled, as if it were something he had read,

once, and long ago, those others with whom she had shared *kest*, and how. Altimere, were he still in the Vaitura, had much to answer for—and not only from Diathen the Queen.

Those others—to share kest *is not a melding, as you know.*

"And yet," Becca murmured aloud, her voice languid, "even when we had—only—shared *kest* there was a connection, such as I did not experience with anyone else." She moved her head, kissing the side of his throat.

"Recall who was the mind behind the plot," Meri said, his own voice sounding absurdly relaxed. "Depend upon it, the artifact had some inhibitor woven into it, though no one else in the Vaitura may ever be able to puzzle out how it was done."

"I suppose..." Becca sighed, and raised her head, looking down at him with such tenderness that he felt his heart melt anew.

"I note, Ranger, that it is moonrise."

"Gardener, I note this as well." He smiled up at her and raised a hand to trace the angle of an eyebrow, the arc of her cheek. "We had best be about our business, then. Sea Hold, by dawn."

"By dawn," Becca echoed, and kissed him once more, sweetly, before turning to find her clothes.

Chapter Thirty

THEY CAME OUT OF THE TREES AT DAWN, THE SUN rising behind them, striking rose-colored sparks from the walls of Sea Hold, and gleams of pure malevolence from the rows of silver trees marching down to the sea.

"No!"

It scarcely mattered which of them shouted in protest. Both went to their knees beneath the hammer of shock.

"No," Meri repeated, staring down at the silver-covered hillside. If Sea Hold had fallen, then they did indeed stand at the ending of the world.

"Where..." Becca whispered, around his sense of doom and hers. "Why are there so many?"

"I'm a fool," Meri said at the same time. "Of *course* they are more numerous in the West. Sea Hold has a shortcut."

Becca shook her head. "Shortcuts are transient," she began, and then pressed her lips together, remembering—but she had never known! Had she?

And yet—it *seemed* a memory: Sea Hold maintained a shortcut, that drew its power off of one of the anchors of the *keleigh*.

"I didn't know that the *keleigh* had anchors," she whispered, and on the instant recalled that there were precisely three—at Sea Hold, at Rishlauf Forest, and at Donich Lake. "Meri, how do I know these things?"

"We melded," he answered, his voice just as soft. "I daresay I now recall your way of making a salve." He said the last word as if he had just learned it, then rose, warily, and held his hand down to her.

She slid her fingers around his and came to her feet. For a moment, they stood, looking down the slope as if the act of standing might have somehow altered what lay before them.

But no. The undead trees marched in disorderly clusters, down the hill, to the very edge of the sea. There were no birds, nor much of a breeze, the sea itself lay at the foot of the hill like a discarded mirror.

"Where are the ships?" Becca asked.

"Sian may have ordered them away, or they may have gone themselves. Sea Wise prefer to face danger from the back of the waves. No," he continued, his voice still soft, as if he did not wish to ruffle the unnatural silence; "the question we must ask is—where are the philosophers? Surely, Sian would have sent them out to deal with this..."

"Perhaps they're at the shortcut," Becca offered, and Meri nodded his head thoughtfully.

"Perhaps they are."

Who hears me? he asked, his thought bracing and clear.

There was no answer. It was as if the trees, too, were wary of disturbing the silence.

"Well, then." Meri sighed. "Let us to Sian. She will be able—"

"Gone," a familiar, growly voice said from the approximate vicinity of Becca's knee. She looked down into the Brethren's beast-yellow eyes, and wondered why she was so certain that this was, indeed, their late companion of the road.

"Gone where?" Meri asked. His voice was cool as if they were discussing the weather, but with a thrill of inner alarm that prompted her to squeeze his fingers in intended comfort.

"The High don't tell the Low their errands."

"That is regrettably so," Meri said. "However, there's very little need, when the ears of the Low are so sharp."

The Brethren gave a low cough that Becca would not have recognized as laughter two days ago. "The High Queen draws in her power."

"Sian's gone to Xandurana?" Meri frowned. "With Sea Hold in peril? Did she take her philosophers with her?"

The Brethren blinked its yellow eyes and scratched the underside of its chin meditatively. "I can," it said at last, "show you the way."

Becca felt a frisson run down her spine; she felt Meri's fingers hard around hers.

"There's a hole in the hedge."

"Yes, there is!" she cried, pulling her hand free and rounding on the creature. "And we have been through it and back again, with no help nor care from you!"

"Wait," Meri said softly. He looked down at the Brethren. "*Another* hole in the hedge?"

"Maybe so, maybe no. How many holes can there be?"

"That is an excellent question. Now, I have one for you. The last hole led us to land under the protection of Becca's kin. When we returned to the Vaitura, we stepped out into Vanglewood." He tipped his head. "Why was that?"

"Silly Gardener wanted to go home," the Brethren said with a yawn. "Longeye, too."

Becca looked to Meri. "It's saying that the holes go wherever we wish to go?"

"In which it is not dissimilar to the *keleigh*."

"When Altimere and I came through the *keleigh*, we still had half a day's ride through badlands until we came to Artifex," she protested.

"Fair enough. But you might have had a longer, if Altimere had wavered, and the *keleigh* let him out inside the mountains."

Becca closed her eyes—and opened them at Meri's soft laughter.

"Now," he said to the Brethren. "This new-or-old hole in the hedge. That would be Sea Hold's short-cut, surely?"

The Brethren tipped its head to a side and closed one sun-colored eye.

"I never did see the charm in these holes," Becca commented after it became clear that the creature was not soon going to produce a sensible answer. "Shall we go after Sian, to Xandurana? Oh!" She pressed her fingers to her lips and raised her eyes again to Meri's face.

He tipped his head, eyebrow well up.

"I only just recalled—to get to Xandurana, one must... traverse a shortcut."

"Which action, in the present climate, can only be seen as foolhardy," he agreed with a faint smile. "Well, then, are we to be less foolhardy than the Engenium of Sea Hold, and all the Queen's Constant?"

"Yes, but, Meri—" She shook her head, and showed him empty palms. "Why is the Queen calling the Constant in?"

"The heroes are busy, inside the mist," the Brethren growled. "There are more holes, even if it is all the same."

Meri nodded, his mouth grim now. "If I recall my philosophy correctly, the weight of the... rejected... trees is placing a burden on the fabric of the Vaitura which it cannot long support."

Becca frowned. "So there will be more... holes?" she ventured. "Until the Vaitura... tears?"

"I would think that among the more likely outcomes," Meri said. "In any case, Diathen must act, and in order to do so, she must convince the Constant to release the *kest* it holds in keeping for her."

"But, if Altimere and Zaldore are still missing?"

Meri shrugged. "If she has the majority of the Constant with her, so that she speaks fully with the will of the Vaitura, she will draw any *kest* withheld from her, like a sea spout draws water. If Altimere and Zaldore have returned to the elements which birthed them, then their *kest* will be one with the Vaitura."

"Because," Becca murmured, "*kest* is never lost."

"Aye."

"I can show you the way," the Brethren said, breaking its silence.

Becca sighed and shook her head. Meri bowed lightly.

"If you please, Younger Brother; show us the way."

~~~∞≫≪∞~~~

Altimere had theorized—indeed, he had ardently desired!—a . . . livelier effect in a transfer which utilized living *kest* as its energy source, rather than the vapid release achieved by using *keleigh*-stuff.

Neither theory nor on-the-fly calculations had led him to expect the explosion of power that hurled him headfirst into his workroom. Who would have thought, he wondered, as he lay with his cheek pressed against the living wooden floor, that the Rangers had had so much to give? Cai's exultant anger would have lent an added fillip—had he not observed that principle in action with Rebecca? Yet it was true, he had not expected such a release, in such garish and thundering quantity that he had almost—almost—lost his focus. Happily, he had meditated for a dozen heartbeats upon the image of his workroom at the house in Xandurana before he had taken his place in the pattern.

Carefully, now, and noting aches and pains incompatible with one of his station, he pushed himself, first, to his knees, and then, by a process that included clawing his way up the leg of his worktable, to his feet. He rested, then, with his palms flat on the table's cool surface, shivering.

After a time, he began to feel stronger, and the relief that accompanied this observation revived him still more. He had expected some decline in his *kest*;

the *keleigh* would have its tithe, after all. The sensation of weakness—of being without power—had been . . . distressing, but happily short-lived.

He straightened and looked about him. The workroom was orderly and well dusted, of course; his servants would scarcely neglect that duty, whether he had been absent a single night, or ten thousand.

And that, he thought, walking to the door, was a matter of not inconsiderable curiosity to him. How long, precisely, had he been captive within Zaldore's little whimsy? How long had he afterward spent wandering the mists of the larger *keleigh*? He felt a flutter of regret, that he would likely never know the precise number of days he had spent separated from the Vaitura. It would have been amusing to entertain Zaldore for the exact number of nights he had lain within her care. He would of course reveal his intention before the pleasantries began, and make sure to remind her occasionally of how long she had yet to suffer. Watching her vacillate between desire and dread of the coming hour would have lent an edge.

Well. Doubtless something else would recommend itself. There was, after all, no hurry—and tasks in queue before it.

The first of those being . . .

Simultaneously, he opened the door and extended his will.

There was a moment of—almost, he would have characterized it as *surprise*, save the Gossamers were incapable of such an emotion—or any other. He took note, and then forgot it as they manifested, tentacles weaving welcome, eager to receive his commands.

The welcoming scene before him smeared for a

moment, as tears rose to his eyes. He blinked them aside with a vague feeling of disgust that was all but entirely swept away by an uprushing of joy as intoxicating as new-drawn *kest*.

He was home.

They followed the march of undead trees up the slope, Meri in the lead and Becca coming after. The Brethren made its own way, now and then allowing a glimpse of a tufted tail, as if to reassure them that they had its company still.

Becca moved with a graceful silence that she had surely learned from Meri, and kept the best distance she could from the unnatural trees. Before her melding, they had seemed to her to be strange in the extreme. Her new sensibilities pronounced them perversions. Her nerves clamored, lest the undead do some mischief to a true living tree, and therefore she kept a close lookout, even as she dreaded the need to come among them.

She shivered, wondering how Meri could tolerate such feelings of desperate horror and maintain so cool a countenance. Years of practice, doubtless—and the education bestowed upon a prince.

A stick lay in her path, concealed by grass and fallen leaves. Once, she would not even have seen it, much less avoided it altogether, choosing not to risk a stumble, should it turn underfoot.

Truly, she thought, she had gained all manner of useful things from Meri. It did occur to her to wonder, with a feeling of guilt, what he could possibly have learnt from her, to balance the richness of his lore. Making salves and mixing elixirs seemed tame stuff in trade, and of limited use to one who might merely ask a plant for its grace to be healed. Such a person had no need for lists of symptoms and hopeful cures, nor even—

"Here," Meri said, softly.

She stood at his shoulder and looked with him at what had once been a grassy knoll, now bedamned with undead trees, encircling a burned spot on the grass.

"What," she asked, keeping her voice low as well, "am I looking at?"

"The place where the shortcut was," he said. "Sian must have realized—and either closed it, or had it closed." She felt a ripple of mirth that was certainly not hers; it seemed to be directed at the scorched spot.

"I'd say she closed it herself," Meri added, giving her the key to his amusement.

"Ah," Becca smiled, seeing Sian flinging turquoise fire toward a mist-filled gateway crowded by silvered trees—and then frowned.

"Closing the gate—didn't help."

"Recall that they have been pushing trees out of the *keleigh* using their own methods for some while," Meri said. "The shortcut may have made it easier for them, but they could get on very well, without."

"This way," the Brethren growled, abruptly at Becca's knee. "The hole in the hedge."

Becca eyed him. "You say yourself that one hole is much like another," she commented. "Or, indeed, may be the other."

"We may wish to observe this one, in either case," Meri said. "Unless you prefer to run to Xandurana?"

She looked at him, reading weariness in his face—and wariness, too.

"Must we still seek Sian?" she asked slowly. "If the Queen is preparing to act..."

"We have seen what has happened, across the *keleigh*," Meri said. "Diathen must be told."

She frowned. "Because the Fey must repair that ill?"

"Precisely," he said, and took her hand, looking earnestly into her face.

"We destroyed our enemy, and his lands," he said slowly. "Then, like children, we hid from what we had done, and threw up the *keleigh*, to keep us safe. We have sundered the world, in our arrogance. Now, it lies with us to mend it."

"But—the Queen. Surely, she will know this and—"

"The Queen must convince the Constant," Meri interrupted, turning away. "And that were the problem before."

"The Constant...withheld its support? Its *kest*?"

He shook his head. "The Constant—you understand that the Queen is the focus for the will of the Constant. Not only did they decree the *keleigh* against every argument and persuasion she could bring before them, but..." His voice died.

But Becca had remembered, now. "Not only did they agree to the *keleigh*'s construction, but they lent the builders their support. Through her."

Head still averted, he nodded.

"It is," he said, "no easy thing, to be Queen.

"Well." He shook himself and looked about, his eye lighting on the Brethren.

"Lead on, Little Brother. We are eager to behold this new wonder you have found for us."

Chapter Thirty-One

IN SHORT ORDER, ALTIMERE WAS BATHED AND DRESSED. Others, perhaps, might think there were tasks more pressing than mere grooming confronting him. Indeed, it was true that he stood upon the edge of a momentous event, one that would, upon its culmination, change him, the Vaitura, and the world.

To present oneself as challenger at the foot of the throne, sweat-stained, and reeking of the *keleigh*—no, it would not do. A bookkeeper from a house of book-keepers, Diathen surely was. She might be—indeed, she was!—his inferior in philosophy, and in artifice. Granting those things and a dozen deficiencies more, she was yet the Queen, and he would not make the error of believing her a weakling.

It was with these thoughts very much in his mind that he slipped his watch safely into his pocket and ambled into the dining room, where he partook of an excellent meal made up entirely of foodstuffs that had grown in the good soil of the Vaitura, rather than conjured from chaos-stuff. Afterward, he pleased to observe that he felt nearly much his old self, and that his *kest* was much improved.

"Excellent," he murmured and rose from the board, carrying his wineglass with him to the library.

The next step—ah, the next step... He paused before the shelf bearing the bound notes of his completed projects, running his fingers lightly down the battered bindings. Surely, the next step was to claim his power in fullness?

Curiously, now that the hour was upon him, he found himself... reluctant. Altimere sighed.

He did not consider himself a romantic, and he had learnt long ago that tools were but the means to an end. It was folly of the worst sort to consider even for a moment that he might preserve her inside the sleep, waking her for brief periods in order that he might partake of her pretty foolishness.

"No," he said firmly, turning from the shelves. "It will not do." Who knew better than he how very dangerous she was? While his Rebecca might regard him with the simple fondness of her kind, she *was* but a tool, vulnerable and unable to defend herself. Doubly unable to defend herself, now that the necklace had somehow been broken. Obviously, someone else had found her a tool fit to his hand, and worth considerable trouble. He, Altimere, dared not falter now. The tool was his, to retrieve, and to destroy.

And yet... Perhaps he might preserve some small portion of that unique and glorious power. Having perfected the technique, why should he not do so? A portion sufficient to animate an artifact—that was surely no danger to him. And it would give him, perhaps, some solace, or even pleasure.

He would think upon it, further. In the meanwhile...

He snapped his fingers, twice, and nodded at the Gossamers as they came to attend him.

"Bring me Rebecca Beauvelley," he said calmly, "and the artifact called Nancy." He paused, glancing around at his books, and added.

"I will see them in the garden."

"No," Becca said, staring at this newest manifestation of the Brethren's "hole." "I will *not* go into that."

Meri glanced up from his crouch far too close to the thing's perimeter, mouth grim and eyebrow quirked. "Pretend there is a unicorn chasing you," he suggested.

Becca pointed. "You do not fool me, sir! You are quite as terrified as I am."

"Am I? Perhaps that's true. And yet I see no other trail, if we are to gain Xandurana."

Becca sank to her knees on the rough ground, staring from him to the Brethren, and, reluctantly, back to the object of their study.

"It's a *rabbit-hole*," she protested.

"If it were, I would not be nearly so terrified," Meri said softly. "Nor would you. Well." He looked to the Brethren. "You had best come, Little Brother."

The Brethren made a rude noise. "The Queen will be pleased to see me."

"I don't doubt. Yet this matter lies close to you, does it not? The Brethren are the children of the *keleigh*. What will happen to you and your kin, if the *keleigh* is struck down?"

"The mists are hungry," the Brethren observed.

"Brethren taste as good as High Fey." He blinked his sun-yellow eyes at Becca. "Or Newmen."

"So it is decided," Meri said with feigned briskness. "I will lead and shape our path, because I know the court and the chamber. Little Brother, you will come after, and Becca at the last."

She stared at him, her heart suddenly tight. "But—what if I lose the Brethren in the mist?"

"You may," Meri admitted, and gave her a tight smile. "But you will not lose me. The sunshield will see to that, eh?"

Becca blinked. She had forgotten about the sunshield, and was not at all sure that she cared to be reminded of it—especially when it was offered as a source of comfort.

"Very well, then," she said, grudgingly. "I will follow the Brethren." She glanced at the tunnel and away again, her stomach profoundly unsettled. "And I will hope that this trip is not a long one."

<hr />

The garden had undergone a . . . change, Altimere noted. Somewhat alarmed, he looked about him, cataloging orderly groups of flowers and greenery, some beds lying fallow, while others bloomed with full enthusiasm, and yet others showed browning leaves, or tender stalks just beginning to put forth their first shy leafling.

And there! The so-called *wheel garden* his Rebecca had nattered on about in her artless way. Here, more than any other place in the garden, could be seen the progression from birth to decay—one quarter of the wheel in exuberant bloom; its opposite quarter lying brown. One quarter carpeted with pale sprouts; and the last quarter showing some browned edges and nodding blooms.

Altimere took a breath, somewhat...dismayed...by this display of order. The garden at Artifex, of course, grew to his specifications, and in accordance with his will. This—this had been designed and carried out by a will both focused and powerful. It seemed unlikely that the plants had banded themselves together to produce this effect, though one could never be entirely certain with regard to the whims of plants.

The trees, now...But the trees of Xandurana had previously been content to let their small-kin proliferate as they would.

It was, to be sure, a puzzle. Altimere bent his attention once more to the *wheel garden*, noticing in particular a pale pink flower peeking out from its glossy, overlarge leaves, like a coquette from behind her fan. Quite apart from its pleasing aspect, it seemed to glow, not with a plant's usual small aura, but with a knife's edge of pure white light. Bending, Altimere extended a hand—and pulled it back as he encountered heat.

"Well," he murmured. "And was it you who burned my pretty child's hands?"

The plant made no answer, and after a moment, Altimere walked on, to the bench near the elitch, where he seated himself.

It came to him then that the Gossamers had been an uncommon while in fetching Rebecca and the artifact. Well. It must be expected that whoever had broken the necklace would set powerful wards about his newly acquired treasure. But the artifact—surely there would be no need to protect *it*, even if it had been taken to placate and serve Rebecca.

Altimere closed his eyes. The breeze was light and pleasant against his face, scented agreeably by the abundant flowers. He would rather, he thought, know the location and estate of all of his pieces before he made challenge. However, he felt that he could not tarry long. It would soon, if it had not already, come to the attention of those who made it their business to know, that he had returned. And at that point—

A gong sounded, seeming to rise up from the Vaitura itself. It reverberated in his chest, became one with the beat of his heart.

Altimere, seated on the bench beneath the elitch in his garden at Xandurana, sighed lightly.

Time was short, indeed. Shorter by far than he had imagined.

Diathen the Bookkeeper Queen had summoned the Constant.

It *was* a rabbit-hole, Becca thought despairingly, feeling her way through the fog. She could see nothing, and it was as if the mist had gotten into her ears and stopped them up, for all the sound she could hear from ahead. Her shoulders rubbed the sides of the tunnel as she crawled on, praying that the mist hadn't gotten into Meri's head and fuddled his sense of their destination, willing with every fiber that the journey would end soon—preferably before she was reduced to wriggling on her belly like a worm.

As if in answer to her petitions, the tunnel widened somewhat, the moist dirt beneath her hands becoming drier. She thought that the mist was thinning, and surely—*surely* that was the Brethren ahead of her, tufted tail twitching from side to side?

A picture was growing inside of her head: a picture of a room she had never seen, and yet knew in intimate detail. A circular room it was, grown within the largest tree in Xandurana. There was nothing here of artifice, not so much as a rug, or a cushion; only the living wood. A chair grew at the center of the room. Around the edges tier on tier of benches grew. The room was illuminated with a deep green light, as if the tree had dedicated its aura to this purpose.

Becca crawled on, the room becoming clearer and more precise in her mind's eyes. She barely noticed that the mist had lifted entirely; scarcely heeded the moment that she came to her feet and walked out onto the living floor.

Meri was looking about him, the Brethren crouched at his feet, horns held at the defensive, though what it defended against, Becca hardly knew. The circular room was empty.

Or—not quite empty.

Out of the corner of her eye, she saw a pale flash, as if an errant curl of mist had followed them out of the rabbit-hole.

Then, they were around her—tentacles gripping arms and waist.

"No!" she cried to the Gossamers. "Release me at once!"

Chapter Thirty-Two

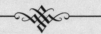

ALTIMERE SIPPED HIS WINE WITHOUT TASTING IT. It was senseless to pretend that the summons had not touched him, or, in doing so, left him unmoved. Yet, he assured himself, forcing himself to sip again, as if there might be a witness to his leisure—it had been but the first call. He had—

"No," he murmured, the summons ringing yet in his very marrow. "No, I am in error. That was the *second* call."

He closed his eyes, and bent his head, listening to the pleasant sound of the breeze among the leaves. How different from—and infinitely preferable to—the muffling of the vexed mists! He must make it a point to sit in the garden more often.

So, then. Another breath. He, a high-ranking member of the Constant, was in receipt of the Queen's second call. Very well. He needn't present himself until the third call had gone out. He might yet recover his missing game pieces. If he did not...

The wind whipped briefly. There was a *fwump* of displaced air, followed by a scream composed more, he judged, of frustration than fear.

Altimere raised his head, and considered the various parts of the apparition before him.

"You are tardy," he said to the Gossamers, "but successful. Leave us."

The alacrity with which they obeyed that order might have been amusing had he any attention to spare. As it was, his attention was wholly focused on the vision before him, twigs tangled in her hair, mud streaking her face, and dirt beneath her fingernails.

Art and artifice! he thought, keeping a firm grip on both his glass and his countenance. Was it possible that she had become even *more* desirable?

"You have no hold on me," she said sharply, and, ah, look! See the shimmers of anger and dismay punctuate the flow of blue-green and gold! Wholly enchanting. But, he was boorish. His Rebecca deserved better of him.

"In fact," he said gently, "we are bound by several threads. We have shared *kest* on numerous occasions, and while I do not hold your name, I know it." He raised his glass and sipped, watching her over the rim. She met his eyes—not without a flinch, but neither with that childlike naïveté to which he had been accustomed. Something had changed his Rebecca. How . . . interesting.

"The strongest thread that binds us, *zinchessa*, is that of teacher and student. For you must admit that I taught you . . . much."

"You taught me much," she agreed. "And all of it false. I reject you." She turned.

He raised a hand, murmuring a word—there came another explosion of displaced air, and—

"Meri, no!" Rebecca cried.

❧

Meri shaped his image of the Queen's Hall with deliberate care, being most especially certain not to people it with any of the folk he might have expected to find there during his unhappy youth. He crept along the thin, dank tunnel on his hands and knees, his attention—his *belief*—on that fearsome chamber. He gazed upon it until his head was full of nothing else, then pushed the reality of the room ahead of him, a single step ahead of him, until all at once the tunnel gave up its game. Meri stood, and walked onto the floor.

Who comes? The voice of the tree which encompassed this chamber rang in his head like a bell.

Meripen Vanglelauf, Ranger. Rebecca Beauvelley, Gardener. A Low Fey. We bear news of interest to the Queen.

Who else comes? the tree demanded, and Meri blinked, looking about him for perhaps the first of the arriving members of—

"No!" Becca shouted. "Release me at once!"

He spun, saw her attackers, and jumped forward, though what he meant to accomplish he could not have said.

As it happened, his intentions were of no matter. Tentacle-wrapt, Becca vanished, her voice chopped off in mid-complaint, her abductors leaving a spangle of *kest* on the wind of their departure.

"Where have they taken her?" he demanded, and

threw his thought wide, calling out to all the trees of the city: *The Gardener has been taken. Where?*

For a heartbeat—two—there was no answer. He held himself still, recruiting patience, aware of the Brethren growling at his knee.

She is here, an elitch said suddenly. *In my garden.*

Show me! Meri sent, feeling a tug, and hearing a sound, as if the surf were pounding out a storm against the land.

The Queen's Hall snapped out of existence; there was a moment of breathless tumbling, as if he had been caught in treacherous seas, then a boom.

He crashed to his knees among flowers, his sight confused, and Becca's voice crying out.

"Meri, no!"

He shook his head, and came to his feet, turning to face her.

"This is hardly my preferred method of travel," he told her, and then took in her pale face, and the thrill of her fear. "Becca?"

"Run!" she cried.

"But how rude in a guest," another voice commented in the ornate accents of an earlier time. Chilled, Meri turned to face the third occupant of the garden.

He sat at his ease on a stone bench beneath the elitch tree, a wineglass held negligently in one long, white hand. Hooded amber eyes considered him with a coolness belied by the bands of crimson that marred his mauve and cream aura. Excepting those telltale signs of passion, he looked much as he had when Meri had last seen him.

Altimere the artificer.

"Rebecca, have you brought me a Wood Wise to

replace Elyd?" he asked, languidly. "How very kind
in you." He sipped from his glass, then held it out.
A tentacled creature darted from somewhere to pluck
it out of his fingers and bore it away up the path to
the house.

"I have not *brought you* a Wood Wise," Becca very
nearly snarled. "Meri, please leave."

"I don't believe I can," he told her truthfully, and
saw her understand that with a horrified shake of her
head. "Perhaps if we both left together?" he suggested.

"I am afraid I cannot allow that," Altimere said,
sternly. He rose, and shook out his lace, giving Meri
another glance. "No, that I *certainly* cannot," he
murmured. "The child brings me not merely a Wood
Wise, but *a hero.*" He inclined his head, ironically.

"Be welcome, Longeye."

Ridiculous, Meri thought, that it was gentle words
of hospitality that finally woke his own fear, and
brought him to a sense of where he stood. He took
a breath, and did not allow dismay to stain his aura,
while hoping ardently that Becca's control continued.

Regally, he inclined his head. "Altimere, I thank
you for your welcome. Alas, I am wanted in the house
of my cousin, and Miss Beauvelley, as well. Let us
come to you again when we are all more at leisure."

"We are not so pressed as that," Altimere purred.
"The second call has only just gone out." He smiled,
his aura only a creamy swirl. "Indeed, we shall enter
the Queen's Hall together."

"No," Becca said, her voice shaking with the effort
of courtesy. "Altimere, we must make ready. Surely
you know..."

"Rebecca," the Elder interrupted, turning away from

Meri as if he had forgotten his existence—"Rebecca, you must allow me to compliment you on your growth! Not only a lovely aura, but as plump of *kest* as— But what is this?"

He paused, amber eyes narrowing, and looked to Meri frowningly.

"Hero Longeye, this were my property."

Meri felt a jolt of anger—his *and* Becca's, doubtless. He felt no surety that it had not stained his aura; certainly Becca displayed a brief, if searing, bolt of crimson. Carefully, he took a deep breath, feeling after the vocabulary of diplomacy.

"Elder Altimere, you are aware of the Queen's Rule. The powerful may no longer subvert the service of those lesser than themselves."

"The Queen's Rule," Altimere said, with a tender smile at Becca. "Do you think the Queen's Rule protects mongrel-Fey, as well? There having been no such creatures when she Spoke, the case might well require argument before the Constant."

"What are you talking about?" Becca asked.

He looked to her, to Meri's eye an amused and tolerant host.

"Surely, *zinchessa*, you recall the tale of the Fey lady who came to review your father's tenant records, when you were but a babe in arms?"

Becca frowned, and Altimere laughed fondly.

"Come, come! I had the whole mysterious tale from your brother one evening whilst we lingered over a friendly glass. The Fey lady was looking for news of kin—that was the tale she told your father, and the tale she herself undoubtedly believed. Alas, the *keleigh* has disturbed temporal factors as well as physical, and the lady did not know that the child she sought—the fruit, so I have come to believe, of a melding between a Wood Wise attached to her honor, and a wife of the House of Barimuir—was a generation dead." He tipped his head, clearly amused. "I gathered from your brother's story that the current babe in arms—yourself—was not shown to the lady, else she might have seen what was left to me to discover."

"I am a halfling?" Becca said, slowly.

"Quarter-Fey," Altimere told her. "Like your horse. Small wonder that you understand each other so well." He shook his head, suddenly stern.

"Rebecca, what became of your beautiful necklace? Did Hero Longeye reft it from you?"

"I took it off," Becca panted, as if she were withstanding some very great force. "I, myself."

"Really?" The Elder Fey raised thin eyebrows. "I own myself impressed by your will, and your willingness to risk . . . all. Well done, Rebecca. Now," he said briskly, "I have uses for both of you. The Longeye shall, in deference to his station, receive his orders first."

The air suddenly became heavy, almost too thick to breathe. Panicked on his own behalf, Meri recognized the feel of power being raised, and all of it—all of it, focused on him.

◦──≫≫≫≪≪──◦

Power infused the air, glittering; like ice crystals thickening a winter sky. Her feet rooted to the ground, Becca watched the seductive creams approach Meri, plucking at the edges of his blue and green silks. They rippled, like tide, and the cream swirled gracefully away, except, she saw with horror, the tiniest thread of mauve that had adhered among the ripples. Even as she watched, it began to weave itself into the fabric of Meri's aura.

Who hears me? Becca sent, desperately.

I hear you, Gardener, came the voice of the very first tree who had spoken to her, here in this garden. The tree who had helped her and given her shelter. Becca bit her lip, in an agony lest her sudden spike of hope be reflected in her aura, and Altimere see it.

Please, she sent carefully. *This Ranger is Meripen Vanglelauf. Please, do not allow Altimere to subject him.*

Of course the Sea Ranger is known and has our kindest thoughts, the tree answered.

You will help him?

The mauve and cream thread had spread now, into a blot, a mar, as if it were some inimical substance that was burning a hole through Meri's aura. Sickened, Becca recalled the golden blot of her misguided will deforming Jamie Moore's simple aura.

And the tree had not answered her.

She swallowed, watching the stain grow—almost as large as her palm now, and the thick air tasting of brine, and mint, and saltpeter.

The Ranger has the mark of a greater service upon him, the tree said at last, and as if it were an answer.

Send to the Alltree, then! Becca thought furiously. *And tell it that its service stands in danger of subversion!*

The tree did not reply; she hadn't really expected that it would. And she—she could not—she *would not*—stand and watch this happen. To see Meri melt into subservience, desiring only what Altimere allowed him. Or—infinitely worse!—aware of his captivity, as Elyd had been, and all too cognizant of his inability to break free.

Meri's face was set into the stern lines that she knew now meant he was afraid. He did not look at her, nor at Altimere, but gazed up into the elitch branches, as if in meditation. Their bond brought her an attitude of intensely focused will, tightly controlled eddies of fear, and one cold certainty: *The sea may not be bound.*

For Altimere, his attention was wholly focused upon Meri, his head tipped slightly to one side, as if they were old friends enjoying a slightly spirited argument over the merits of a horse they both fancied. As far as she could determine, he was not paying the slightest attention to her, so certain was he that she could neither interfere nor escape.

Very well, then. She had surprised him more than once. He had told her often enough that her ability to do so was one of the many reasons he held her as a treasure of his house. It would, therefore, not displease him, Becca thought grimly, if she surprised him once more.

She brought her attention to her feet. Now that she looked for them, she could see quite clearly the cream-colored wisps about her ankles. If she shifted, they tightened; when she relaxed, they did the same. Recalling the healing of her arm, she wondered if she might burn the wisps away, while Altimere's attention was elsewhere. It was a desperate plan, at best, and she had no illusions that the Elder Fey's attention would remain elsewhere, if he should perceive that he was under attack.

If she were to risk something so perilous, she thought, it was necessary to have a plan to follow on. Her knife was lost with her pack. Simply throwing herself against Altimere and shouting at Meri to run

seemed . . . ineffectual at best—even if she believed that
the sunshield would allow them at last to separate.

No, she needed a weapon—a distraction, perhaps,
or—

Pain, like a wash of acid along her nerves. Becca
ground her teeth to hold in the scream, her *kest* rising like the tide, cooling, if not healing. She swayed
where she stood, took a breath, and raised her head.

Fully one-quarter of Meri's defense had fallen, by
the measure of the blot upon his aura. And she—their
bond. The pain she felt was the action of Altimere's
kest on Meri.

Perhaps she did not need a weapon, she thought,
wildly. Perhaps she *was* a weapon.

She looked about her, taking no pleasure in the
flowers, or in the display of seasons. Something,
somewhere in this garden was a weapon that would
give her a chance, at least, of rendering Altimere
impotent. But if the trees would not—

The elder trees remembered, Gardener, the elitch
said. *Do you find the seasons represented properly?*

*As properly as they can be, without the true aid
of seasons,* she answered, and sent another plea. *Can
you not assist me?*

In what endeavor?

Becca swallowed an urge to scream, a white gleam,
sharp as a knife's edge, catching the side of her eye.
She turned her head . . .

The season wheel . . .

Altimere uttered a small sound, perhaps of surprise.
A quick glance showed sweat on his pale brow, the
edges of his aura stained, oh so faintly stained, sea-blue.

I would visit the season wheel, she sent to the tree,

her eyes on Meri's face. His eye was closed now, his hair lying across his shoulders in wet strips of brown, auburn, and black, like seaweed. The smell of brine was very strong, and though the air was still thick, there was a different quality to it—more like a storm a-boiling, than the heaviness of ice.

Scarcely daring to breathe, Becca reached to cool power coiled at the base of her spine, and began cautiously to draw—

Something touched her ankle.

She bit her lip hard enough to draw blood, staring downward, as a horny nail touched the pearly wisp binding her left foot. It dissipated like so much mist, and a moment later the right binding did likewise.

Becca stepped back, one cautious step. Neither combatant seemed to notice her. She took another step, turned, and ran.

The Brethren was in the garden; Meri had seen the flick of a tufted tail beneath the bench Altimere had lately quit, and the outline of a horn against the elitch trunk. The Low Fey were potent mischief-makers when they chose to be, as befit the offspring of chaos.

He did not wish for the Little Brother to place itself in harm's way. On the other hand, he surely required *some* assistance, with Altimere's *kest* already contaminating his, a sensation not unlike that of the Newman's poison metal corroding his flesh. It was well that the Elder High had been surprised by the strength of his defenses. What was *not* well was that he had immediately altered his own attack and was beginning to push Meri's will hard.

Truly, he thought, eye closed, he stood between the devil and the sea, and whichever won this contest, there would be at the last little remaining of Meripen Longeye.

He heard a crashing, and the rattle of stones told over by waves; then silence, unbroken even by the scream of a gull.

"Meripen Vanglelauf," Altimere's voice breathed into his ear, sweet as any lover. "Surrender your will to me. Why should we contend? Do we not hold as our goal to seek Diathen the Queen, and to testify before the Constant? Come! Ally yourself with me. Let us be of one will, and one desire..."

He was caught, bound, his flesh burning; the air tasted of dust and blood.

Who hears me? he sent, despairing, as he had done over and over from the Newmen's stone prison, his answer only and always silence...

I hear you, Ranger, the resident elitch answered, swiftly. *You are under leaf, and your roots are deep.*

I am lost...

"Come..." the sweet voice breathed. "There can be an end to agony, and a service like no other. Cede to me."

Not so. You will endure.

Meri's knees wobbled. He locked them, gathered the rags of his will, and rejected the intruding poison. Altimere laughed, as if amused by the bumbling of a sprout.

His *kest*—strange desires boiled in his blood, deceit wounded his honor, ambition soured his service. He—

His *kest*...rose. Potent and moist, rising from his deepest roots; the *kest* of the Vaitura itself, diluting the poison.

Meri pulled his will around him.

"Cede..." Altimere whispered, his *kest* rising even to meet this new level of power.

Cede? Meri thought, shaking his head. Cede the sunshield? Cede the trees?

Cede Becca?

"No," he whispered.

The duainfey flower burned like a star among its dark, plentiful leaves. Becca extended a hand, and snatched it back, knowing it would burn the flesh off the bone if she attempted to pluck it.

She looked quickly over her shoulder—and all but cried aloud.

Meri's aura was an incoherent smear of blues and greens, seen through a hard creamy glitter, as if he were encased in glass. He swayed, and caught himself, as Altimere stepped toward him, his posture triumphant.

Becca whirled back to the garden, and bent close, cupping her hand as close over that burning flower as she dared.

"Please," she begged, feeling her *kest* rise, as if she meant to meld with the plant. "Please, give me of your essence—the virtue only of two leaves."

The flower seemed to shimmer in its own heat. A point of bitter cold lanced Becca's outstretched hand. She snatched it back and looked down at what appeared to be a pearl, or a milky drop of ice on her palm. It melted into her flesh between one blink and the next, and her *kest* rose like a bonfire, blazing greens and blues, as she came to her feet and turned back to Altimere.

Chapter Thirty-Three

THE RANGER HAD BEEN STRONGER THAN HE HAD anticipated, Altimere acknowledged, and he himself more diminished from his late adventures than he had fully known. A simple subjugation should not have taken so much effort. The Low—even heroes—were not generally so robust. Still, the natural order would prevail. Meripen Vanglelauf wavered, wounded; his will in tatters. He had, surprisingly, endeavored to pull one last tithe of *kest* for protection—perhaps from the very tree they did battle beneath—and rallied his will behind it.

A noble effort, Altimere conceded, and one worthy of a prince, however mixed his heritage or Low his beginnings. Of course, it were a short-lived rally. The nature of Wood Wise service was to protect the trees at all and any cost. Meripen Vanglelauf would not endanger the tree that supported him, nor drain its *kest* to save himself. He *could not*.

And Altimere the Artificer was the equal of any tree.

"No," the Ranger said, his voice like dried leaves.

Altimere smiled, and thrust strongly, meaning to draw the tree's protection. He had other business, which was rapidly becoming more pressing. Let the Ranger cut his own lifeline, and accept the inevitable.

And what an ornament to his challenge, he thought, exultant with the triumph of his *kest*, was Meripen Vanglelauf! Kinsman to the Queen and to the ever-annoying Sian of Sea Hold! Yes, *this* binding would create a furor in the hall.

He thrust again, the tree's *kest* boiling away like steam, yet rising still, and—yes! The Ranger made a counterthrust, one desperate stroke that could not succeed, his *kest* falling alarmingly as Altimere parried.

Altimere stepped close to his reeling captive, the word ready on his tongue. He felt a shiver in the air, and paused, the word unspoken, wondering if there was yet another bolt to his Ranger—*his hero's*—string.

"Altimere." The voice was smoky, resonant with power.

Rebecca. How had she escaped her bindings? Truly, the child had learned much in her time away from him! Well, he would not underestimate her again. He leaned toward the Ranger . . .

"Altimere." Her aura intruded on his senses, eclipsing the hectic, swirling maelstrom that had once been Meripen Vanglelauf's aura. So beautiful. His *kest*, already risen in service of conquest, overboiled the limits he had placed upon it, and he turned toward her, feeling the edge of her aura press against him like a knife, and for a heartbeat the garden splintered into a myriad of glittering images, as if he beheld the *kest* of the Vaitura entire as discrete, bewildering particles.

A tug at his coat. Dazzled, he grabbed, felt a hairy arm slide through his fingers, and spun again, his vision clearing sufficiently to see a Child of Chaos vanish into the plentiful flowers, and in its horny hand—

"My watch!" Fury informed his *kest*. He raised a hand, lightning already forming at his fingertips—and thrown into the crushed, disordered flowers as Rebecca struck his arm aside.

The Brethren vanished, and Altimere spun, grabbing her and throwing the full force of his will against hers, beyond caring if he harmed her.

"Call Nancy," he snarled. "Now."

❦

The Brethren had vanished; up into the tree, Becca thought, or over the garden wall.

For herself, it was as if she were seeing the world for the first time. *Kest* glimmered everywhere, confusing her sight, which was so clear. She saw *every*thing, and knew it for good or ill.

Meri—Meri stood slumped, a wounded and willless thing, and yet she saw the vital green *kest* and the shimmer of blues, like waves. She saw—she saw the bonds that tied them—one by the heart; and the other to a vast uncertainty, a reservoir of power so deep that even the duainfey's gift could not clarify it for her.

Altimere snatched at her arm, his will slamming into hers. She staggered, blinking up at him, halfstunned. His aura, which had been so smooth and pale, was now a bonfire of yellow, orange, rust, and black, threaded through with a substance like fog. *His* kest, she thought, wondering. Altimere was old beyond

measuring; he had walked in the Old World before
the war; and in both worlds, after. Without doubt, he
had melded...countless times, and stolen *kest*, too.
Students—surely so gifted and great an artificer had
had students? And those he had dominated, for surely
Elyd had not been the only one...

All of that *kest*—so much power; gathered and
but rarely shared. And he had need of more? Sun
and scythe!

"Call Nancy!" He shook her so that her head snapped
on her neck, and the force of his will was a terrible
thing. "Will you have it three times, *zinchessa*?"

Faintly, she felt Meri's horror, and recalled as if
she had always known it that to be told three times
was to surrender yourself willingly.

She must not cede. Not yet.

"Nancy," she whispered, looking into hot amber eyes.
She could not look away. "Nancy, I am with Altimere."

The tree's *kest* continued to rise, pooling at the
base of his spine. Meri concentrated his will and the
feeble remainders of his skill on keeping his replen-
ishment hidden, though there had been a heartbeat
when he was certain that he had dissembled too late,
and Altimere with the word of binding on his lips...

Yet, the Elder had not spoken, and Becca— Root
and branch! He could scarcely look upon her. She
blazed, her aura showing a white edge like a knife
blade. The bond between them trembled under the
raw assault of power—trembled, and grew deeper,
accommodating this new aspect.

For himself, he kept as still as any rabbit in the

wood. Altimere appeared to have forgotten him, distracted by Becca's beauty and the Brethren's small theft.

That had been a bold moment, and a tale of mischief to be told among the Little People for many days to come. Very nearly he broke his charade when Altimere whirled to fling lightning at the Brethren—and very nearly cheered when Becca struck his arm aside.

Meri held himself still, very still now, as she lay half-stunned beneath the assault of Altimere's will; and dared not even send her a thought, lest he somehow detect it.

"Nancy," Becca whispered, staring up into his eyes as if her will were already subjected to the Elder's. "Nancy, I am with Altimere."

There was a flash of jewel tones; the air misted and the artifact appeared, wings busy, just beyond Altimere's grasp.

"Excellent," Altimere purred, and Meri felt the instant that he lifted his will from Becca and applied it to the tiny artifact.

Meri, Becca's thought was as sharp as her aura. *Can the sea be bound?*

The sea can be neither bound nor contained, he replied, as his mother had taught him so long ago.

Will you open yourself to me, entirely?

She did not need to ask, melded as they were, and he loved her the more because she did.

Everything I am is yours.

"What have you done to it?" Altimere's voice was harsh, the pressure of his will like being crushed beneath a boulder.

Becca moved her head, gasping for breath, desperate lest the punishment she endured reach Meri, her vision edged with black.

"She . . ." she panted, scarcely able to form the words. "She left your service, and—entered mine."

There was silence, though the terrible weight did not lift, and a sense of some manipulation made beyond the range of her senses.

Altimere sighed, softly, and Becca looked up, seeing Nancy standing frozen and apparently lifeless in the air.

"What have . . . *you* done?" she gasped.

"I am simply holding it," Altimere told her, his face softening into a tender smile. "I should never have let you name it, of course. Ill-done, but recoverable." His smile grew sad, as he extended a hand to brush her hair from her face. "Everything is recoverable, *zinchessa*."

Becca's *kest* trembled, shamefully, and she whimpered when he ran his thumb lightly over her bottom lip.

"There," he murmured, "it will be just like old times."

She did not remember moving, but she must have done, and stood now pressed against him, her forehead resting on his shoulder, feeling desire rise with her *kest*, even as she wanted to scream and fight . . . but she did *not* want to fight this, she reminded herself.

This was what she wanted.

His will moved her and she stretched high on her toes, laying her arms around his neck, and raising her face for his kiss.

His hands were firm at her waist, his lips cool and knowing. He drew her *kest* greedily, and so quickly

that she scarcely had time before she swooned to
reach out to Meri along their bond.

Altimere took Becca as if he had a right to her, drawing her *kest* so quickly that she guttered like a candle
flame, fading in an instant to a shadow of herself.

Meri felt her senses spin away—and in the heartbeat
before he lost her entirely, he felt her touch upon his
heart, and opened himself to her.

The child's *kest* had grown richer, so seductive that
he knew no restraint, no savoring. He drank, senses
reeling, not even the cut of the odd white edge of
her enough to make him break the kiss. She gave
unstintingly, without struggle or demur, as if she
wished him to drain her.

And so he would.

He drank, and still she gave, her *kest* seeming to
well from the very ground. And of course, he thought,
his thoughts barely coherent; she had melded with the
Ranger, *his* Ranger, who was—how had he forgotten
to bind the Ranger?

No matter. However it were done, both were caught
in his net. Best to drain both, and thus enrich his
holdings. He would deal with the artifact after, and
challenge Diathen the so-called Queen to overcome
an opponent worthy to rule the Vaitura.

Would the child never run dry? Was he consuming
the *kest* of entire forests, bound to Rebecca through
the Ranger? He felt himself a giant, who had only to
form a thought in order for it to become so.

Heat built, reminding him uncomfortably of the place of his captivity, and surely, he thought, terror clearing his mind, surely he had drunk enough? Was this some trick, or some fevered dream born out of the *keleigh*?

Altimere tried to move, to lift his head, to pull away from those arms that lay heavy as lektrim chains on his shoulders.

His efforts were futile.

And then he heard it.

A roaring, as of a wave rushing toward shore. His senses were filled with it; he saw it, towering, monstrous; filled with more power than even the Vaitura might encompass.

Trapped, Altimere threw up his will, his *kest* forming a seawall...

❧

Becca looked down from the high branches of the elitch, watching the events unfold in the garden below. Altimere was bound to the swooning doll in his arms by slender vines of tree *kest*, unable even to lift his head from the kiss that had become, if the flashes of panic in his swollen aura were a guide, most unwelcome.

Meri stood at some little distance, head up, and craned slightly backward, as if he would spy out her resting place among the leaves, which perhaps after all he could. Power flowed through him; green tree *kest* mixed among turbulent blues. Gradually, the blues became more dominant, and she heard something—a roaring, rolling thunder that shook the very treetop where she reposed, watching the drama below.

Altimere had become sensible of his danger. Caught though he was, yet he struggled and contrived. Becca shivered in her comfortable nest, and sent a small thought to the elitch.

This will be terrible, will it not?

The sea is pitiless, Gardener, and it cleanses as it must.

She saw it now, bearing down upon Meri: power inconceivable; a mountain of *kest*, boiling a little at the leading edge. No one could withstand so much—not Altimere, not—

"Meri!" she screamed.

The wave struck.

Becca tumbled from her branch.

A chime sounded, reverberating inside the chambers of her heart.

Chapter Thirty-Four

MERI KNEW IT WAS NOT THE FULL POWER OF THE SEA come hurtling toward him. He hoped never to behold or to encompass the full power of the sea. He closed his eye and relaxed his will, offering no resistance, and yet there was still a timeless and terrifying time when he felt stretched far too thin, diluted; the bits of himself mixed about indiscriminately—and then it was past, and he was whole.

Becca was lying among a litter of elitch leaves, still as a broken limb. For one heart-stopping moment, he did not see her aura, but by the time he had gathered her into his arms, it was manifest, flowing with all the blues of the sea and every conceivable color of leaf.

A chime struck, solemn as a heartbeat, and she stirred against him.

Meri? Her thought was bright and bracing, and he almost wept at its touch.

Yes?

What is that?

"The third call to the Constant," he said aloud, and looked about him, seeing nothing but littered leaves, and tousled flowers.

"Altimere?" She squirmed, and he helped her to sit up.

"I . . . don't . . . know. Surely, he wouldn't have sublimated—"

"Gone to dust," a growly voice said. The Brethren stepped out from behind the elitch, Nancy sitting at her ease on one hairy shoulder.

"Dust?" Becca repeated, and it shook its horns.

"Silly Gardener, asks for bright sight, and then doesn't look."

"Look at—" Her voice cut off in mid-question, and she stiffened in Meri's arms.

He followed her gaze, to the base of the bench beneath the elitch, and the modest pile of grey dust, wisping in the breeze like mist, already returning to the Vaitura.

She shuddered, and turned suddenly, pushing her face into his shoulder. He shivered as well, and put his cheek against her hair.

"Are you sorry?" he asked, though the sense he received through their bond was . . . deeper.

"No," she whispered fiercely. "I am not sorry. I just wish—that it hadn't needed to be done."

"Aye," he said softly. "We all wish that." He shivered again, his arms tightening around her. "He drained you so quickly, I thought you were gone before even I felt your touch." He laughed, shakily. "Two fools—and they will name us heroes."

"They will name you world-breakers, if we do not make haste!" the Brethren growled. "The call has come three times."

"Yes." Becca sighed, and he felt her will firm. "We should finish it."

"Must finish it," he corrected, and the two of them scrambled to their feet, muddy, and weary as they were.

"The Queen will be happy to see us!" the Brethren said, sounding pleased with itself as they moved toward the gate at the bottom of the garden.

"I am certain that she will be," Meri answered, feeling Becca's fingers 'round his.

Ahead, the gate opened.

"Well!" Sian put her hands on her hips and looked down her long nose at them.

"Diathen our gentle cousin dispatched me to gather up Altimere, who dances on the edge of being tardy to his place. Imagine my surprise, *dear* Cousin Meri, to arrive amidst such a raising of power as I would not have imagined to exist, outside of the old tales of the Elders at their height." She shook her head. "Hast seen Altimere?"

"Altimere is dead," Becca said baldly. "His power has returned to the Vaitura."

The Engenium inclined her head politely. "Then my task is completed," she said, turning away.

"Not quite," Meri said.

She sighed, proud shoulders dropping for so brief an instant one might have supposed it an illusion.

"Why, how may I serve you, Cousin Meri?"

"By acting as our escort to the Constant."

Sian looked at him over her shoulder, sea-colored

eyes bland. "Under what guise do you go to the Queen and the Constant, Meripen Vanglelauf?"

"As heroes," he said calmly, and moved his hand. "All four of us."

There was a pause, and then a sigh.

"Very well," Sian said. "You look the part, at least."

Chapter Thirty-Five

THE CHAMBER IN THE HEART OF THE TREE WAS crowded now, row upon row of Fey sitting quietly, their combined auras a blare and an insult to Becca's duainfey-enhanced vision. She clung to Meri's hand and to his sense of cool purpose as they followed Sian down the room to the living chair, and the Fey woman seated there.

Sian bowed, ornately, and Becca felt a ripple of humor from Meri.

Diathen, her subtle aura betraying neither humor nor temper, inclined her head. She wore a crown of woven starlight; artifice of the highest order. The crown, Becca recalled, though she had never known it, was as old as the Vaitura itself. Beneath it, the stones, feathers, leaves, and flowers woven into the Queen's hair seemed commonplace, embarrassing.

"Where," the Queen asked in a cold, high voice, "is Altimere the Artificer?"

"By report of Meripen Vanglelauf, he is returned

to the elements from which he was born," Sian answered.

Diathen closed her eyes. "Is that two of my counselors gone, then, not forgetting our previous losses? Has the news of Zaldore's return been verified?"

"Yes, my Queen," a grizzled Wood Wise spoke from behind the throne. "Zaldore and her estates have gone, all, to mist."

"And we with the greatest disaster of our age upon us," Diathen murmured. She opened her eyes and inclined her head to Sian. "What do you bring me in their stead, Engenium of Sea Hold?"

"Heroes, my Queen." Sian's voice was perfectly serious, her aura unruffled. "Meripen Vanglelauf. Rebecca Beauvelley. A representative of the Little Folk, and... Nancy, an artifact."

Becca stiffened, expecting Diathen to protest Nancy's presence—and relaxed as Meri squeezed her fingers.

The Queen inclined her head. "Thank you, Engenium," she said calmly, and lifted her chin. "Stand forward, Heroes."

Meri took one of his long fluid strides, bringing Becca with him. At his knee came the Brethren. Nancy, wings busy, was at Becca's shoulder. Meri bowed, and Becca did. The Brethren bowed. Nancy dropped to one knee on the overcharged air, and inclined her head, arms extended, palms turned up.

"Be welcome, Meripen Vanglelauf, Rebecca Beauvelley, Little Brother, Nancy. What news?"

"My Queen," Meri said gently, "you will perhaps have heard of the trees which the heroes have been excising from the *keleigh*."

"Indeed, I have heard of *and* seen these trees,"

Diathen answered with some asperity. "The Vaitura groans under their weight, nor is there any method known to my philosophers that will either return them or persuade the mist-bound to give over their mad project." She sighed. "Forgive me, Master Vanglelauf, but it is our considered opinion that the Vaitura could do with fewer heroes."

"My Queen, I agree," Meri said, a ripple of laughter in his voice. "To be a hero is an uncomfortable business at best. However," his voice grew serious once more. "We did not venture before you, heroes though we be, to bring you cold news. Guided by our Little Brother, Rebecca Beauvelley and I crossed to the other side, and there we found..." He glanced at Becca, who bowed and took up the tale.

"The land we crossed to, Queen Diathen," she said, wishing her voice was cool and calm, "has been under the care of my kin for...since the Charter was granted at New London. The Beauvelley family takes their responsibilities to the land and those who tend it very seriously. I—it is our service. When I left in company with Altimere, the land was green and lush, reflecting long seasons of care. When we returned..." She paused, seeing again that blasted field with its few sorry weeds drying even as they tried to set roots in the sand.

"When we returned," she said, "the land was...a ruin. There were no trees, the soil could not support plants—not even grass! We went to the house of—and spoke to a man who claimed to be my own brother's grandson. I—" She looked into Diathen's face, seeing only distant patience, and continued.

"It may be, Your Majesty, that he was...a little

mad, for when I left my family's holding my brother
had not yet wed, much less produced a son, and
that son produced his own. Yet, on the subject of
the disaster that had overtaken the land, I believe
he was sincere...

"A wind, he said, had blasted across the world, drying everything, everywhere. The trees fell, the plants
died, the crops failed. The folk fail now..."

"And so they would," Diathen interrupted. "Is
there more?"

Becca shook her head. "No, Your Majesty."

Diathen looked to the Brethren. "Little Brother,
what news do you bring us?"

"There is a hole in the hedge," the Brethren said
predictably. "The same hole or many, not even the
Longeye will venture. The wind blows up the hole,
and the wind blows down the hole, and the roots of
the Alltree stretch and break."

Diathen sighed. "Is there more?"

"No, High Queen."

"Yes," Meri said, frowning down at the Brethren
with a small shake of his head. "There are monsters
leaping into the Vaitura, from out of the *keleigh* or
from the far side, is not certain. Rebecca Beauvelley
was attacked by a portion of these creatures, and I
have myself seen a *unicorn* inside the Vaitura, which
I am assured is a creature known only to the tales
told on the other side."

"I see." Diathen looked to Nancy.

"She is mute," Becca said softly. "She can mime
somewhat, but—"

"Nancy." Diathen's high voice overrode Becca's
easily. "What news do you bring us?"

There was a pause, then Nancy rose on effortless wings and flew into the ranks of the counselors. At each empty seat, she alighted, and also upon the shoulders of Fey whom Becca had cause to remember well.

So many! she thought, and recalled that Altimere had always chosen his guests from among the High Fey, and most especially from among those who sat on the Queen's Constant.

"Forgive me," Diathen said, as Nancy returned to her place by Becca's shoulder, "if I do not perfectly comprehend your news. Is there someone here who might act as interpreter?"

Becca cleared her throat. "Your Majesty," she whispered, forcing herself to meet Diathen's cool eyes. "I believe Nancy wishes you to know that—that those whom she indicated are those who lost . . . greater or lesser amounts of *kest* to—to myself, who then, though the means . . . which you and I have previously discussed, gave it up to Altimere."

"Is that so?" The Queen raised her head and looked out across her Constant. "Small wonder that we show so weak upon this day, of all our days." She looked back to Nancy.

"Is there more?"

Nancy shook her head: No.

"Very well. Accept, O Heroes, our thanks. And stay! For you have a right to witness what your news has bought us."

She rose, the stars in her crown piercing the chamber with a cold, pale light.

"My lords and ladies, I can add nothing to what you have heard from these Heroes—nay! from what you have seen and confronted upon the very lands that lie under your protection! The Vaitura staggers and falls to her knees, and we are powerless to aid her."

She raised one white finger, rings glittering balefully.

"We are the spirits and the guardians of this land. Once, in our folly we allowed fear to rule us and in doing so damaged not only ourselves, and not only the Vaitura, but the world entire. There is now as there was then only one right action available to us. The single question we have before us is this: Will we accept the charge that is come to us, or will we cry craven once more?"

Silence rang in the Queen's Hall. It was Sian who rose next, to bow to Diathen with no hint of anything but respect, her voice unwontedly gentle.

"Though the act end the Fey, yet we must embrace it, for our ancient duty and our service is to the world. To assuage our horror and our regret, we had made ourselves forget. We must remember now. Remember, and make amends."

"The end of the Fey is no small matter, my Queen— Lady Engenium!"

Diathen raised her eyes. "It is to the world, my lord Mondair. We are the makers of the *keleigh*, the smiters of the world. It is we who broke faith; who huddled in our closet like frightened children and rejected our most holy duty."

She looked around the room. "Is there more?"

Silence.

Diathen swayed a bow, her crown too bright to look upon.

"My lords and ladies, I call the question. Who will stand with the world, and mend our greatest wrong?"

Again, it was Sian who spoke first.

"I join my power and my honor with the Queen. Let us mend what we have cast asunder."

Diathen's silver-green aura gained an edging of turquoise.

Becca expected argument, politicking, outright refusals. What came was a simple—surprisingly orderly—vote.

The Fey lord seated next to Sian rose, bowed, and joined his power to the Queen's, adding a filigree of tangerine to her aura.

The third lord did not join his power, nor did the fifth, nor the twelfth, nor the twenty-third.

Becca, with Meri's memories, began to worry in earnest. The Constant must be unanimous in its support. If they were not . . . the Vaitura would fall, the trees would fail, both sides of the world would falter and die . . .

"My lords and ladies," Diathen cried again, "I call the question a second time! Who stands with me?"

The fifth lord rose hesitantly, looking about him at the others who had not pledged—and threw his lot in with the Queen.

They are weak, Meri sent, worry tainting his thought. *Altimere's predations may have left them unable to act as they must, even if the Constant joins together*.

Becca stirred. Altimere's predations . . .

"Nancy," she murmured, extending her hand. The little creature landed lightly on her palm.

"Do you know," Becca whispered, as the twenty-third again refused to join herself with the Queen. "Do you know where Altimere stored the *kest* I stole for him?"

A vigorous nod, wings bouncing.

"Will you help me join that *kest* to the Queen's purpose?"

A pause, the tiny head tipped to one side, then another nod, less exuberant than the first, but firm.

"Can it be done when the Queen calls the question for the third time?"

Another nod, emphatic.

"Thank you," Becca whispered. Nancy bounced into the air with a flash of wings, swooped close, and kissed Becca's cheek with her cold lips.

"My lords and ladies!" Diathen cried. "I call the question for the third time! Do you die a coward or a hero, my lords? Look into your hearts. I am patient."

"Your Majesty." Becca stood forward and bowed, feeling Meri's shock.

The fiery figure of the Queen turned. "Rebecca Beauvelley. What would you?"

"I would," she said, firmly, "join the *kest* harvested by Altimere to your purpose."

"Would you, indeed?" the Queen said softly. "If you are able, O Hero, you may do so now."

"Yes," Becca said, looking around. A flash of jewel-tones warned her, and the shake of surly horns.

The Brethren walked up to the Queen's brilliant form and, coaxed by a series of pats and pushes from Nancy, knelt and held up a leathery hand.

Diathen bent and plucked something from its palm, holding it up for all the room to see.

Altimere's watch.

Nancy patted the Brethren's unkempt head approvingly. It backed away from Diathen and scurried over to hide behind Meri.

"Nancy," Becca said. "Is the stolen *kest* in the watch?"

The little creature pirouetted, shaking her saucy head.

Becca sighed. "Will you teach the Queen how to release it to her own use?"

A brisk nod. Nancy threw herself spread-eagled against the air. Slowly, she brought her arms up until they met above her head. She rested in that position for a moment, then turned a somersault and assumed a stance, hip-shot, stick-like arms folded over her silver breast.

Baffled, Becca shook her head.

"Well?" Diathen said. "Riddle me these instructions, Rebecca Beauvelley."

"Your Majesty, I don't myself under—" She stopped, replaying Nancy's odd mime, recalling Altimere's pride in this watch, made by Becca's own people, that ran through artifice, without *kest*, only needing to be wound . . .

"Set the hands," she said slowly at first, then more surely. "Your Majesty, there is a stem at the top of the watch. Pull it out and you may manipulate the hands. Set both the small hand and the large onto the twelve, and—" She looked to Nancy, standing on the air. The little creature gave her an encouraging nod.

"Yes," she whispered, tear-choked. She kept her eyes on Nancy's tiny form. "Set both the large hand and the small onto the twelve, and push the stem back in."

There was a pause while Diathen manipulated the unfamiliar object.

"I love you, Nancy," Becca whispered; "and I will never forget you."

She had expected—noise. An explosion.

A zephyr wafted through the Queen's Hall, bearing the scents of violets, pine, and culdoon blossoms.

Nancy faded softly into the air, like a snowflake melting against a windowpane.

Becca covered her eyes with her hands, not because she was ashamed of her tears, but because Diathen was far too bright to look upon.

"Rebecca Beauvelley, stand forward!"

Becca started, feeling Meri's arms tighten briefly around her, then let her go. Lost in mourning, she had paid no attention to the final round of voting, but Meri had done better, even as he comforted her.

The Constant entire had cast in its lot with the Queen.

Hesitant, Becca stepped forward, and did her best to look at the terrible beauty that had been Diathen the Queen.

"Rebecca Beauvelley, as the one here who has ties to both sides of the world, it is meet and proper that you shape the new world that is about to emerge from the crucible of our error. Think well, and when you have thought, join with me."

A fiery hand extended.

I'm to shape the world? Meri—

Who better? His thought was calm and pure as ever. *You needn't plan every grass stem. Choose what seems good, reject what you know is ill.*

Help me, then!

We are melded. How can I not help you, and you, me?

"Rebecca Beauvelley?"

"A . . . moment, Your Majesty."

Panicked, she closed her eyes. She tasted the distinctive tang of duainfey along her tongue. Clear sight. Reject what is ill.

Domination and subjection, she thought—*those I reject. Care for the land—and for the sea!—that we must keep, or the world might as well die as I stand here. Kest... let there be magic in small things, but let it not be subject to collection, or hoarding, or misuse. Let there be halflings and those to whom the land speaks. Let us each accept our service and find joy in it. Let there be an accord between the high and the low.*

"Art ready, child?"

"Lady," Becca said slowly. "I am."

She stepped forward and clasped that fiery hand.

Chapter Thirty-Six

THERE WAS SUN IN HER FACE. OVERHEAD, BIRDS were arguing; a blade of grass tickled her nose.

Becca sneezed and opened her eyes.

A young man lay stretched on his side in the grass before her, his head propped on his hand. His hair hung in a tail over one shoulder, brown-black streaked with auburn. That and his brown skin spoke of someone who had spent most of his years out-of-doors. The worn leathers suggested that he might be a woodsman.

"A fresh new day to you, Rebecca Beauvelley," he said, and his voice...

Becca sat up, staring down into a lean face made up of stern smooth lines. His eyes were mismatched—one blue and one green—and both focused upon her with some measure of irony.

"*Meri?*"

The corner of his mouth quirked in a way that she

knew all too well. "In this brave new world you have made for us—aye. Meri."

What happened? she sent, but her thought felt strangely flat, as if it had struck the inside of her skull and fallen. After a moment, she asked again.

"What happened?"

The smile this time was full, and only a little ironical. "Diathen threw down the *keleigh* and mended the world." He nodded beyond her. "Look, at what your vision has brought us!"

She looked up at an azure sky laced with the green branches of trees. The breeze was gentle, the sunlight warm. Beneath her hand, the grass was silken and agreeably damp. There was no mar upon the air, nor any glimmer of ominous forces.

Dropping her gaze, she found two horses grazing near at hand, a big grey stallion and a smaller chestnut mare, a white star on her forehead.

"Rosamunde!" she cried joyfully. "And—"

"Brume," Meri murmured. He paused, then said, hesitantly. "I have something here for you to see."

She turned back to him, blinking at the dry flower of bone in his palm.

"The sunshield," she said, remembering. "But I—" She looked up into his face.

"I do not see any threads binding it," she said slowly. "But, Meri—I cannot see your aura!"

"Nor I, yours," he said gently, and added, with an air of quoting: *"Let there be magic in small things, but let it not be subject to collection, or hoarding, or misuse . . ."*

"But . . ." Tears rose; she blinked them away.

"*Kest*," Meri reminded her, "is never lost."

She made shift to smile. "That is true." She nodded at the sunshield. "What will you do?"

"Eventually, I will go to the sea, and return the gift, with thanks."

"And we—we are no longer bound?"

He laughed, slipping the sunshield into his pouch. "That, like so much, may need to be tested," he said so softly that she was not entirely certain that he was speaking to her. He looked up, and spoke more briskly. "If you are rested, Elizabeth expects us at New Hope Village. Palin has a forest to plant, and there's the matter of who will stand tree-kin."

"The Fey?"

"It may be that the High are no more," he said slowly. "Insofar as I understood your thought, that was what you wished."

Becca bit her lip, thinking suddenly of Sian and Diathen, who had been brave and honorable. Surely, there had been others and she had—

"Hold—" Meri took her hand. "They fell, if they did, honoring their service. However, before we mourn them, let us be certain that they fell, and are not simply—" he laughed—"simply!—remade." He grinned. "It is a new world, and warrants exploring, you know."

She smiled back at him. "So you will be a Ranger again."

"So I will be a Ranger, as ever I have been," he corrected, and rose, holding a hand down to her.

She let him help her to her feet, and turned around, looking at the new day.

Who hears me? she sent.

I hear you, Gardener, came a deep and distant voice. *My roots are deep and my branches strong. Let the world endure forever.*

"What will you do?" Meri asked her as they turned toward the horses.

Becca threw him a grin and swung astride Rosamunde.

"Surely, a Gardener may be a Ranger, too?"